11/07

W9-CDC-765

WITHDRAWN

My Lady Judge

My Lady Judge

A MYSTERY OF MEDIEVAL IRELAND

CORA HARRISON

ST. MARTIN'S MINOTAUR

NEW YORK

www.minotaurbooks.com

Library of Congress Cataloging-in-Publication Data

Harrison, Cora.
    My lady judge : a mystery of medieval Ireland / Cora Harrison.—1st U.S. ed.
        p. cm.
    ISBN-13: 978-0-312-36836-4
    ISBN-10: 0-312-36836-4
    1. Women judges—Ireland—Burren—Fiction. 2. Burren (Ireland)—Fiction.
3. Ireland—History—16th century—Fiction. I. Title.

PR6058.A6883 M9 2007
823'.914—dc22

                                                                2007023529

First published in Great Britain by Macmillan, an imprint of Pan Macmillan Ltd

First U.S. Edition: September 2007

10 9 8 7 6 5 4 3 2 1

For my husband, Frank; son, William; daughter,
Ruth; son-in-law, Pete, and grandson, Shane,
with all my love and thanks for their help

ACKNOWLEDGEMENTS

It gives me great pleasure to acknowledge a debt of gratitude to my agent, Peter Buckman, of the Ampersand Agency, for his unfailing support and encouragement, and to my editor, Sarah Turner, for her commitment and enthusiasm for my book.

I would also like to express my thanks to all those, such as Fergus Kelly, Daniel Binchy and Kuno Meyer, among many others, whose research made the fascinating subject of Brehon law available to the general public.

In addition, I must express my gratitude to Domhnall O'Davoren and his scholars, who, in the mid-sixteenth century, laboured within the stone walls of Cahermacnaghten law school to record, and preserve for posterity, the ancient laws of his ancestors.

PROLOGUE

It was then, as it is now, a land of grey stone.

Then, as now, the Burren, on the western seaboard of Ireland, was a place that had been stripped of almost all soil. The fields were paved with stone: broad slabs, or clints, of it; the mountains were cones of rough rock, or spiralling terraces of gleaming limestone. But among those swirling mountain terraces were tiny, stunted bushes of juniper and of holly; and in the fields, between the clints, rich, sweet grass grew, winter and summer. Then, as now, the cattle were fat and their owners were prosperous.

Everywhere the stone had been used. Thousands of years earlier the people of the Burren had built themselves vast tombs: court tombs, cairns, wedge tombs and huge dolmens, silhouetted against the sky like the tables of some giant race. They built miles of stone walls to enclose their small stony fields, and they built great fortified dwelling places: *cathair*, *lios*, or *ráth*, and, later, monasteries, churches, tall, grey crenellated tower houses and small oblong stone cottages, some in the fields, and some within the encircling walls of a *cathair*.

Over 400 ruins of those ancient *cathairs*, or forts, still remain and in the year 1509, many were still occupied. On the west side of the kingdom was Cahermacnaghten whose great stone walls, ten foot wide and twenty foot high, enclosed a law school. The exquisitely written documents penned within its walls tell the story of a community, living by the ancient laws of their forebears in the stony kingdom of the Burren.

To the east of the kingdom stood the mountain of Mullagh-more. The great sheets of ice that swept across the west of Ireland almost a million years ago had gouged out terrace piled on terrace of gleaming bare limestone, and left Mullaghmore towering over the flat stone pavements in the south-eastern corner of the Burren. This high and lonely hill was, from time immemorial, an ancient place of pilgrimage. The Celts climbed it to celebrate their great festivals: *Lughnasa, Samhain, Imbolc* and *Bealtaine*; and the descendants of the Celts continued to climb it on the Christian festivals of Lammas, Halloween, St Brigid's Day and May Day.

On the eve of the first of May, in the year 1509, people from all over the Burren, young and old, climbed the mountain. The young men carried bundles of hazel rods for the bonfire and heavy leather bags filled with strong Spanish wine. The girls wore flowers in their hair and carried baskets of food. Many carried fiddles, horns or pipes and all sang on the slow climb up the stony terraces.

When the moon rose to its midnight height they lit a great bonfire and danced and sang until grey dawn came, and the singing of thousands of small birds joined the chorus of human voices. Then, young and old, they went back down the mountain and made their way home to *cathair, lios,* or *ráth,* to the tall grey tower houses, or to the small oblong stone cottages.

But one man did not come back down that steeply spiralling path. His body lay exposed to the ravens and to the wolves on the side of that bare mountain for one whole day and two nights and no one spoke of him, or told what they had seen.

And when Mara, Brehon of the Burren, a woman appointed by King Turlough Donn O'Brien to be judge and lawgiver to that stony kingdom, came to investigate she was met with a wall of silence.

ONE

British Library MS vellum leaves:
Egerton 88

Notes and fragments of early Irish law, or Brehon law,
transcribed by law scholars, in the mid-sixteenth century,
at Cahermacnaghten law school in the barony of Burren,
west of Ireland.

One older document, dating from the beginning of the
sixteenth century, consists of judgement texts and case notes
from the time when Burren was a kingdom under the rule of
King Turlough Donn O'Brien. These notes are signed by
Mara, a female judge, or Brehon, from this era.

EARLY SUMMER IN THE Burren has a glory about it: in
the valleys a glory of soft greens, creamy hawthorn blossom
and purple foxgloves; on the sparkling limestone of the uplands
tiny jewel-like flowers of purple, yellow and blue sprinkled in the
grykes between the flat, shining slabs of stone. Orange tip butterflies
swoop among the cuckoo flowers, vibrant blue-green dragonflies

haunt the crystal waters of the spring wells and larks soar high above the contented cattle.

The sky, on that morning of the eve of *Bealtaine*, 1509, was a clear bright blue with wisps of bog-cotton clouds drifting slowly across. There had been rain during the night, but the heat of the sun was already strong enough to draw a fine mist from the clints that paved the fields, turning the limestone from blue-black to silver-grey and warming the massive stone walls that enclosed the scholars' house, the farm manager's house, the guest house, the schoolhouse and the kitchen house of the law school of Caher-macnaghten. No one was awake there – no sound of scholars' voices, no clatter of breakfast pans, no clank of the water pump. All was silent except for the excited high vit, vit, veet call of the swallows and the distant lowing of cows, knee-deep in the golden dust of the buttercups.

A hundred yards away from the law school was the Brehon's house, a substantial two-storey building of well-cut stone with a wispy plume of aromatic peat smoke drifting from the central chimney. Around the house was a garden of about one acre. From the front door to the gate ran a path of stone flags lined with pots of lilies. A small woodland of hazel trees to the west protected the plants against the strong salt-laden winds from the Atlantic. To the north was a hedge of gleaming dark green holly, tall white flowers growing in its shelter. To the east and the south were low hedges of perfumed lavender and in the centre a gently curving bed crammed with tiny blue gentians twisted and coiled through the garden.

In the garden Mara, Brehon of the Burren, was kneeling on the path pulling out weeds from among her gentians. She was a tall woman, still slim despite her thirty-six years of hearty eating, and her raven-black hair, plaited and coiled at the back of her neck, showed no signs of grey. She wore the traditional linen *léine*, a creamy-white tunic which suited her dark hair and her olive skin. Over it she wore a green fitted gown, laced up at the front, its flowing sleeves caught in tightly at the wrist.

Mara was an immensely busy woman with responsibility for the law school as well as for maintaining law and order in the stony kingdom of the Burren, so these few moments that she spent every day in her garden in the early morning, or late evening, were very important to her. However, she was also a very sociable person who enjoyed a chat with her neighbours so when footsteps sounded on the stone road that ran between Cahermacnaghten and Baur North, she looked across the wall.

'You're out early, Brehon.' The voice was familiar and with a smile of pleasure Mara stood up, abandoning her weeding.

'It's a beautiful morning, Diarmuid,' she said.

'Yes, it's a beautiful morning, God bless it. The grass is beginning to grow fast now with the strength of the sun. It'll soon be haymaking time.'

'Would you like a cup of ale?'

'No, no,' Diarmuid said, shaking his head.

Mara said no more, just waited. Diarmuid O'Connor would not be walking along the road past Cahermacnaghten so soon after dawn just to discuss the weather with her. Something else was troubling him.

'I was hoping I might see you,' he said eventually, avoiding her eyes.

She surveyed him carefully. He was about her own age, a man of medium height and red-blond hair, his skin covered with freckles from daily exposure to the clear skies and the fierce winds of the Atlantic. She had known him since they were both children; she knew him to be trustworthy, a good neighbour, loyal to his clan, to his neighbours and a self-sufficient man. He lived alone on a farm in Baur North, about a mile from Cahermacnaghten.

'What's wrong?' she asked.

He fidgeted uneasily. She suspected that he would have preferred to go on talking about the weather.

'Well, you know there has been a bit of trouble between our kin-group and the MacNamaras?' he asked after a while.

'Yes,' she said encouragingly.

'Well, my brown cow was missing this morning,' he went on. 'I went to look at her first thing. I thought she might have dropped a calf last night, but she wasn't there.'

'Was she out in the field overnight, then?' asked Mara.

Diarmuid shook his head. 'No,' he said. 'I put her in the little cabin just next to the house last night. I knew I'd hear her there if she was distressed. It's just beside my window. She was shut in securely. There's a latch on the door and there's a bolt on the gate to the yard. This morning I found the door was wide open, and the cow was gone. She was stolen; there's no doubt about it. And I can guess who stole her.'

Mara frowned. This was bad news. At best, an uneasy peace existed between the O'Connors and the MacNamaras. Absent-mindedly she dusted the earth from her fingers.

'Walk down to the schoolhouse with me, Diarmuid,' she said. Smoke was beginning to drift up from the kitchen house within the law school enclosure and they could hear a few raucous boyish shouts from the scholars' house. The corners of her mouth relaxed; she always enjoyed her scholars; their high spirits and their energy kept her young.

'I've disturbed your peace,' said Diarmuid with his usual courtesy.

'No, no,' she said as she replaced her small fork in the willow basket beside her and walked towards the gate. Then she frowned again. The shouts were silenced by a scolding, slightly high-pitched, masculine voice. Colman was so stupid, she thought vehemently. Why couldn't he leave them alone? He would have more authority with the boys if he allowed them to indulge in a few high spirits when it didn't matter. Why did I ever take him on as junior master? she asked herself for the hundredth time.

'I'll send my assistant Colman to take notes,' she said quickly. 'We'll go and get him now and you can tell him everything. I'll hear the case at today's judgement day.'

This will be something for Colman to do this morning, she thought with relief as she walked down the road at Diarmuid's side. Once the young man had finished his studies and graduated from Cahermacnaghten she should have let him go off as a wandering *aigne*, or advocate lawyer. He was clever; he would have made his way. He would have earned far more than she gave him. It had been weak of her to agree to his suggestion that he do a year's teaching at the law school to broaden his experience before he left. She had been worried about him; that was why she thought another year under her influence would be good for him. Now it seemed that she was forever inventing ways to get him away from the boys for a while, and relieved whenever he absented himself to go to Galway.

'You'll come in and have a cup of ale while you're waiting for him, won't you?' she asked Diarmuid when they reached the law school.

'Just a *doiche an dorus*, then.' He followed her through the great iron gate of the law school and into the enclosure. The six law scholars were dashing out of the scholars' house and calling out greetings to her with broad smiles on their faces. They all looked unusually neat and tidy, she noticed, faces shining from soap and water, damp hair showing the ridges of the combs that had been ploughed through the tangles, leather boots shining with polish. The night before Brigid would have put out the clean *léinte*, tunics of bleached linen, for them. Today was an important day for the law school of Cahermacnaghten. Today was one of the four big judgement days on the Burren, the eve of *Bealtaine*.

Mara eyed them affectionately. From eighteen-year-old

Fachtnan to ten-year-old Shane they were like a family to her, closer in some ways than her two grandchildren in Galway. She noticed with concern that twelve-year-old Hugh looked a little tearful. There was a red mark across one of his cheeks and at that sight her lips tightened in exasperation. She had told Colman again and again that there was no need for him to hit those boys; they were all so motivated to learn and to succeed at the difficult profession of lawyer that a withdrawal of privileges was the only punishment ever necessary. Hugh's mother had died a few months earlier of the sweating sickness, picked up on a visit to the city of Galway, and Hugh had been nervous and anxious ever since. Colman should know that. She would speak to him later, she decided, but she would say nothing in front of the scholars. She could not undermine his authority.

'Colman,' she said coldly, 'will you take your breakfast quickly and go with Diarmuid. He has had a cow stolen. Make notes of the case and bring them back to me as quickly as possible so that I may study them before we go to Poulnabrone at noon. Hugh,' she added gently with a smile, 'will you bring our visitor a cup of ale and one of Brigid's oatcakes?'

'Just a *doiche an dorus*,' repeated Diarmuid, standing carefully by the heavy wooden door of the kitchen house to prove that, quite literally, this was just to be a drink at the doorway. He tossed down the cup of ale that Hugh brought to him and disposed of the oatcake in two rapid bites. Colman grabbed a couple of oatcakes for himself then went rapidly out of the kitchen house and crossed the stone-flagged enclosure.

Mara followed him into the schoolhouse. She found him packing some leaves of vellum, a quill and an inkhorn into his leather satchel.

'Take careful notes, Colman,' she said. 'Do a drawing of the house and the cabin where the cow was and the position of the gate. Look for any footmarks.' She walked towards the door and then added over her shoulder, 'Come on, Colman, Diarmuid is waiting for you at the gate.'

He fidgeted a little, obviously wasting time, filling the horn with fresh ink from the flask, rejecting the first quill and then selecting one more to his liking, leafing through some of the scrolls of judgement texts from the shelves. 'Would you ask him to go ahead, Brehon?' he said with his usual smooth politeness, but with a slight trace of panic in his light-toned voice. The tightened lips of his narrow mouth distorted his pale, small-featured face. Mara looked at him in surprise and then his cheeks flushed with blotches of red.

'That will give him time to lock up his dog,' he said, nervously running his fingers through his yellow hair.

Mara concealed a smile. So that was it! Of course, she had forgotten about the dog. Diarmuid's dog was famous for its ferocity and Colman, a sly, undersized, nervous child, had always been terrified of dogs; he had even been frightened of her big wolfhound, the mother of her present dog, Bran. He had been a strange child: a very hard worker, obsessional about making lists of tasks to be done, studying continually and shunning the play activities of the other lads. Even when he was older, he never petted or played with Bran, the gentlest wolfhound on the Burren, in the way that the other scholars did. She looked out at Diarmuid, still waiting patiently at the gate, and swiftly made up her mind. Colman would not do justice to this case if he were worried about Diarmuid's dog. He would just accept Diarmuid's explanation that the missing cow had been taken by a member of the rival clan and then get back to the law school as soon as possible.

'I'll come with you,' she said aloud. 'I think I should look into this case myself. You can take the notes.'

He bowed stiffly, looking angry and humiliated, but she ignored him and glanced across the cobbled yard of the enclosure. 'Fachtnan,' she called and the dark-haired boy ran out of the kitchen and across the enclosure, still stuffing an oatcake into his mouth. She looked at him with affection. He was the exact opposite to Colman, she thought: tall, broad-shouldered, kind, open and honest, with a thatch of rough, dark hair and a pair of gentle brown eyes. He had always been a great favourite of hers.

'Yes, Brehon,' he said indistinctly.

'Fachtnan, you organize a chess tournament for the lads,' said Mara. 'Tell them that there will be a prize for the winner – some silver to spend at the fair this evening.' I'll have to make sure that Hugh gets a prize, she thought, and little Shane also. These two had been with her since they were five years old and they had a special place in her heart. She would probably end up giving prizes to everyone, she thought wryly, but it would be worth it to keep them clean and tidy until noon.

Mara joined the farmer. 'I'll walk down with you, Diarmuid, I may as well take a walk. I'll be sitting for most of the afternoon and perhaps the early evening. There are quite a few cases already for judgement day and we may have yours to add to them also.'

He smiled with pleasure and she smiled back. She was fond of Diarmuid and at times she suspected that he was more than fond of her.

At that moment a huge white wolfhound came lolloping across the road to join them. 'No, go back, Bran. Stay at home, good dog.' Bran's tail drooped; he was a very sensitive and devoted dog, but he obediently turned back and went towards the kitchen house.

'Yes, better not take him,' said Diarmuid, 'my dog is a bit of a fighter. A lovely dog to me, but he doesn't like the rest of the world too much. Is King Turlough Donn himself coming today for the judgement day?'

'He is, indeed,' said Mara, smiling with satisfaction. She always enjoyed a visit from Turlough Donn O'Brien, king of three kingdoms: the large kingdom of Thomond and the two smaller kingdoms of Burren and Corcomroe. They would have supper together after the judgements were over – Brigid, her housekeeper, had orders to cook a couple of wild duck and they would have a fine flagon of French wine to go with it.

'You won't be going up Mullaghmore tonight, then?' said Diarmuid after they had climbed a few unstable stone walls and set off striding across the stone pavements of Baur North. The heat of the sun was bringing out the sharp bittersweet smell of the ground-hugging juniper growing in the grykes between the slabs of rock that paved the fields.

'No, I won't,' said Mara, neatly jumping the gryke and then bending down to pick a few needles of juniper. She pinched them between her thumb and forefinger nail and then held the little bundle to her nose. 'I'll have to entertain the king. Colman will look after the lads for me when they are on the mountain,' she said, trying to include her assistant in the conversation. Her consciousness that she disliked Colman, and that she had always disliked him, made her make more efforts with him than she did with Fachtnan. 'Are you going yourself, Diarmuid?' she asked.

'I thought I might,' he admitted. 'It's time that I gave the old fiddle an outing. The evening promises fine.'

'Of course I knew you would be going; they wouldn't be able to do without you. I'd dance myself if I heard a tune from your fiddle,' she said with a smile. Colman, she noticed to her annoyance, was staring into the middle distance with his usual air of slightly despising the company that he was in.

'Rory the bard has made up a new song – there's a bit about your garden in it; the garden from heaven tied with a ribbon of blue, he calls it in the song – and I've been practising a tune to go with it,' said Diarmuid. 'It's a great tune, as lively as yourself. Are you sure you won't come tonight? You do every year.'

'I've promised King Turlough a good dinner, otherwise I might, just to hear your tune,' she said. 'I can hear your dog bark,' she added. 'He knows there are strangers coming. I always hear him if I go along this road.' She half-glanced at Colman to see if he had picked up the clue, but no trace of interest showed on his narrow face. No doubt he wished he were back in the schoolhouse studying Latin or the wisdom texts, she thought. He would not make a good Brehon. Probably he would be better off staying in a law school as an assistant master. Not my law school, though, she thought with exasperation. She wondered whether she could get Fergus, the Brehon in the kingdom of Corcomroe, to take him on.

✻

Diarmuid's dog was huge: huge and ferocious. Mara surveyed him with interest, avoiding eye contact so as not to excite him too much. He lunged against the gate and his bark reverberated off the slopes of the Aillwee Hill. She turned away, but the dog still continued to deafen them with his barks. Mara nodded to herself. Yes, she was right. This was not a rival clan raid.

'Wait a minute,' said Diarmuid. 'I'll shut him up in the cabin.' He squeezed his bulky frame through the narrow gate, taking extreme care not to allow the frantic dog through, and then shut the gate carefully after him. It had a large bolt on the inside, just at the top of the gate, noticed Mara, easy enough for a man to open it from the outside, but then what man would dare to do this with such a ferocious guardian inside the gate? The dog, she noticed with interest, was not barking now but was jumping wildly around Diarmuid, licking the man's hands and wagging his tail as a puppy would. He was a beautiful dog, almost as tall as a wolfhound, black and tan in colour with an enormous ruff around his neck, pricked-up ears and a large domed head.

'Where did you get him from, Diarmuid?' she asked, speaking softly and keeping her eyes averted from the dog so as not to provoke another storm of barking.

'I got him from my cousin, Lorcan,' said Diarmuid.

Mara gave herself another congratulatory nod. Her memory had not failed her.

'Lorcan had him for a year,' continued Diarmuid, 'but he was getting too much for him. He was great with Lorcan himself; you can see what a loving fellow he is with his own family. But he's a difficult dog and Lorcan wasn't good at fencing him in. He did a lot of damage and people were scared of him. He's half-wolf, you know. Lorcan had a big sheepdog bitch that was in season so he staked her out by Mullaghmore, there where the lake is, at the bottom of the mountain. A wolf mated with her.'

'Took a bit of a risk with his dog, didn't he?' said Mara tartly, furious at the thought of the unfortunate dog left staked out there at the mercy of the wolves. But she knew from long experience that everything she said or did was of great interest to the people of the Burren, who were proud of their woman Brehon. Her slightest word was taken up, inflated and blown all over the Burren. So, as she had done so often, she bit back the angry words and watched Diarmuid fondle the wolf-dog.

'You could say that,' agreed Diarmuid. 'You see, the puppies were all too big for the poor bitch. They all died except for this fellow, and the bitch died after she had given birth.'

'What's his name?' asked Mara.

'I call him Wolf,' replied Diarmuid. 'He looks like a wolf, though he's finer than any wolf that I have ever seen.'

'And he didn't bark last night,' stated Mara.

'No, he didn't,' said Diarmuid with surprise. 'How did you guess that?'

Mara smiled. 'I think we'll take a walk down to Lorcan's farm, Diarmuid.'

'But . . . but what about the cow?' asked Diarmuid, staring at her in bewilderment. 'Don't you want to see the cabin? And what about Eoin MacNamara?'

Mara smiled sweetly at him. 'Come on, Diarmuid, you know what I'm like about dogs. I'd like to find out more about Wolf. Let's go down to Lorcan; it's not far. I'm not forgetting about your cow, I promise you that. You come, too, Colman.' There had been no need to add that, she thought. Colman would not have liked to stay there with that ferocious dog, called Wolf.

❉

Lorcan's farm was at Cregavockoge, a lush valley below the flat, high tableland that spanned the three miles between Cahermac-naghten and the dolmen at Poulnabrone. The grass in this valley, growing thickly in the well-drained rich soil that lay above the limestone, was a deep, soft green. There were several small farms there, but Lorcan's stood out from the rest by the dark brown muddy fields and the broken-backed walls. His cottage was small, as were most of the cottages on the Burren. Lorcan's cottage, however, was not snowy-white like the other cottages, but a dingy grey with moss growing on the badly thatched roof. It looked as though he had not repaired the thatch nor limewashed his walls for years. Mara looked at it with interest. Lorcan O'Connor was obviously a poor farmer. The fields were over-grazed and thistles and ragwort had seeded themselves everywhere into ugly clumps.

Lorcan himself was in his yard. Mara moved quickly, striding out ahead of Diarmuid and Colman. She passed the bemused Lorcan with a friendly smile and went confidently through the filthy yard to the small cabin beside the house. There was a cow there. It was a handsome, well-fed large brown cow, quite unlike the small dark cattle that she had seen in the fields. The cow was obviously in calf.

'Diarmuid,' she said over her shoulder. 'What do you think of this cow?'

Looking puzzled, Diarmuid came forward. He still suspected nothing, thought Mara. He was an honest man himself and he expected the world around him, especially one of his own kin-group, to be equally honest. The cow, however, had no doubts. She gave a robust 'moo', lumbered out of the cabin and put her head affectionately on Diarmuid's shoulder. Diarmuid patted her absent-mindedly and stared speechlessly at his cousin.

Mara looked at Lorcan. 'Can you explain what Diarmuid's cow is doing in your cabin, Lorcan?' she asked quietly.

Lorcan stared back at her but said nothing. There was a flare of panic in his widely opened eyes.

'Well,' said Diarmuid. Words seemed to have left him and it took him a few minutes before he said with dignity, 'I'm sorry that you did a thing like that, Lorcan. It wasn't very neighbourly and it wasn't very cousinly. I'll be taking the cow back to my place now and it will be a miracle if her calf is born safe after all of this.'

'I found her straying,' muttered Lorcan.

'No, you didn't,' said Diarmuid scornfully.

'And, Lorcan, I'll see you today at Poulnabrone,' said Mara firmly. 'I'll hear the case and I'll apportion a fine.'

'I'm a very poor man, Brehon,' said Lorcan piteously. 'The young master here knows that,' he added, looking at Colman.

'That's true,' said Colman unexpectedly. Mara shot him an irritated glance, but kept a firm grip on her rising temper. She marched back out of the dung-filled yard and waited at the roadway. Diarmuid followed, leading his precious cow carefully with a handful of hay to her nose. Colman, noticed Mara, had stopped for a quick word with Lorcan before picking his way carefully out to join them. She concealed a smile as she watched him. His rather sharp nose was twitching uneasily and his narrow shoulders were contracted as if he shunned his surroundings. It was easy to see that he had never been a country boy.

'Well,' said Diarmuid heartily when they were out of Lorcan's hearing, 'I don't know how you guessed that, Brehon. You're a great woman entirely. That was the last person that I would have thought of. My own cousin!'

'Ah, well, it was easy,' said Mara modestly. 'That's a good dog you have there, Diarmuid. Some day when I have a bit of time on my hands I'll come over and try to make friends with him. I'd say he would have been better if you had had him when he was a puppy. He needs to learn to trust people that you trust. He needs to get out and about a bit more.'

While she spoke, Mara's mind was busy with the problem of Colman. It was odd how he was only now beginning to show himself for what he was. It was as if, while he was a student, he had kept a close guard on himself and tried his best to fit in with her way of thinking. Otherwise, she would never have appointed him. Luckily it was only for a year and the year would end soon. I'm not going to have him behave like this, though, she thought with determination.

After they had parted from Diarmuid and his cow, going shoulder to shoulder down the road to Baur North, Mara said mildly, 'It was not a good idea to agree with Lorcan there, Colman. You can rely on me to apportion a just fine. Now he may think that he can twist and wheedle his way out of anything.'

'I was just following your instructions to be sympathetic and understanding to people, Brehon,' said Colman smugly.

Mara tightened her lips, but said no more. They walked in silence along the road and then turned into Cahermacnaghten.

Cumhal, Brigid's husband, was sweeping the flagged surface of the enclosure. Brigid herself was scrubbing out the kitchen and singing loudly and the schoolhouse rang with the shouts of the boys playing chess in their usual exuberant way.

'Thank you, Fachtnan,' said Mara as she entered. She could see that Fachtnan had worked out an intricate tournament on the whitewashed piece of board that she used for her lessons. Each boy was allocated points according to his age. Unfortunately

Fachtnan had managed to get some black specks from the charred stick, which he had been using to write on the board, on to his clean *léine*, but no doubt Brigid would manage to make the tunic presentable before the judgement session.

'You touched your castle; you must move it now,' yelled Shane.

'No, I didn't,' yelled Hugh. 'My hand just hovered; it didn't touch.'

And then, quite suddenly, Hugh caught sight of Colman emerging from behind Mara. His eyes locked on Colman's with the look of panic that comes into the eyes of a baby rabbit in a snare. What had Colman done to that boy? thought Mara. She scowled and then her lips relaxed into a slightly vindictive smile. Let Colman have a taste of his own medicine. It would do him good to know what it was like to be terrified. At least she would get rid of him for the rest of the morning. She turned to her assistant.

'Colman,' she said. 'I think we should probably have the dog at the judgement session, don't you? After all, he may be an important witness. Go back and tell Diarmuid to bring him to Poulnabrone. Wait with him. Stay at the farmyard all the morning and take note of the behaviour of the dog when strangers come near to him. Come with Diarmuid to Poulnabrone and you can give evidence, and of course you will be able to help Diarmuid to control the dog. It's an interesting case.'

This should amuse King Turlough Donn, she thought with a smile. This case may go down in the history of judgement texts. The case of the silent witness: the dog who did not bark.

Two

CASE NOTES AND JUDGEMENT TEXTS FROM MARA,
BREHON OF THE BURREN, 15 MAY 1509

Judgement day: last day of April 1509. On the eve of
Bealtaine I judged the case between taoiseach *Garrett*
MacNamara and his kinsman, young Feirdin MacNamara.
Garrett MacNamara swore that his kinsman's behaviour was
so wayward that he should be kept in the close custody of a
male cousin. Feirdin's mother, Gráinne, pleaded that her son
be allowed to live with her and that she be held responsible for
his behaviour . . .

❧

THIS WAS THE CASE that worried Mara the most. And so,
on that morning of the eve of *Bealtaine*, she left Fachtnan to
look after the younger scholars for a little while longer and went
across the fields to Caherconnell. She wanted to see Malachy, the
physician, a distant relative of hers, and she wanted to discuss this
boy, Feirdin, with him.

Malachy's house, at Caherconnell, was a handsome two-storey

building set within the rounded enclosure wall of an old *cathair*. Several other old forts lay around it, all in a ruinous state. In the near distance was an ancient circle of thirteen tall stones.

Nuala, Malachy's daughter, a pair of small sharp shears in one hand and a basket in the other, was working in the herb garden at Caherconnell when Mara arrived. Nuala was a tall girl for thirteen, her skin tanned to a deep brown and her glossy black hair neatly braided into two long plaits. Her face was intent and serious as she industriously sheared off the soft grey-green tops of the rosemary in her herb garden, but she lifted her head at the sound of footsteps and when she saw Mara she ran to open the gate, her brown eyes shining with welcome.

'Mara, I was hoping you would come,' she said with pleasure. 'I really need your help in talking sense into Father. You will talk to Father, won't you? He's got this idea in his head that he doesn't want me to be a physician. He's been talking about Mother all the morning, about how she had planned this marriage with Naoise O'Lochlainn as soon as I was born. He wants me to get married on my fourteenth birthday but I don't want to! It's all so stupid. Just because we are second cousins! Why can't I decide for myself?'

The words poured out of her and Mara smiled. Nuala was always like this, always bubbling over with excitement, anger or fun. Mara was very fond of her. However, she had to remind herself that this was Malachy's daughter and that this marriage would have to be his decision.

'Well, your mother's wishes would be very important to your father,' she said diplomatically. 'You know how much he misses her.'

'At least he's stopped drinking himself silly in alehouses now,' said Nuala sternly. 'And besides' – her clear strong voice wobbled slightly – 'I miss her too.'

'I know,' said Mara, putting her arm around the slim shoulders.

Mór O'Connor had died of a malady in her breast over a year ago. She had only been twenty-seven years old and her death, though a merciful release from intense suffering, had had a devastating effect on Malachy. Strong drink seemed to be his only way of enduring the unendurable. The people of the Burren, compassionate towards a man who had suffered such a great loss, had looked after him, taking him home night after night and making sure that no harm came to him. Even Colman, she had heard, had been seen taking him home one night.

The effect on Nuala must have been great, although the housekeeper had done her best to shield the child. Nuala herself had seemed to deal with her mother's death with a show of almost frightening maturity, but Mara had kept an anxious eye on her.

'Be a sensible girl, now,' she said, stroking the shining hair. 'Say nothing, and leave your father to me. He wants the best for you. Your happiness is the most important thing in the world to him at the moment.'

'Well, he must be pretty stupid if he thinks I will be happy married to that stupid Naoise,' said Nuala with her usual forthrightness. 'That stupid boy thinks of nothing but hunting. He's such a show-off, too, and he has nothing to show off about. He's just stupid.'

'That's three "stupids",' said Mara briskly. 'If you are going to be a good physician, Nuala, you must learn to judge people less harshly. Everyone has their own way of conducting their lives.'

'Oh, do you really think I might be able to be a physician?' Now Nuala glowed with excitement, ignoring the reproof. 'Oh, please do tell father that he must allow me.'

'I think you could be a good one,' admitted Mara cautiously, 'you certainly cleaned that nasty cut on Fachtnan's arm very well. It was beginning to go bad, Brigid said, when you put a green paste on it and then it healed up very well. Now, bring me in to your father, like a good girl. I have a few things to talk over with him before the judgements at Poulnabrone this afternoon.'

Nuala led the way indoors. 'It was a paste of goosegrass that I used on Fachtnan's arm,' she said seriously, 'I think that works very well. I read about it in one of father's old scrolls. I've read every one of them about six times now. Father is in here in his still room. I'll go in with you. I want to get some twine to tie up the woodbine.' She added in a whisper, 'You won't forget to talk to him about me, will you?'

'Take some of my tape,' said Mara, producing from her pouch a strip of pink linen tape that she used to bind her documents. It would be easier to tackle Malachy on her own.

Nuala slipped away with a quick smile, while Mara took a deep breath, prepared for battle, and opened the door of the still room. Malachy was a very tall, dark-haired man of almost forty, a strong-looking, handsome man, thought Mara, wondering whether he planned to remarry and have a son to carry on the long line of physicians at Caherconnell. Perhaps that was why he wanted Nuala off his hands. She felt irritated at the thought. He owes Nuala his full attention and affection now, and there is no reason why there should not be a female physician at Caherconnell, just as there is a female Brehon at Cahermacnaghten. She looked at him sternly. He smiled a welcome and then held up his hands in mock surrender.

'I know, don't tell me,' he said in his pleasant, deep voice. 'You've come to persuade me to allow Nuala to become a physician and to postpone her marriage to Naoise.'

'Actually, I came to talk about Feirdin MacNamara,' said Mara, sinking down on a stool and looking around her with interest. She had not been in this room for over a year. It was hung with fragrant drying herbs and the shelves that lined the walls were filled with flasks and jars, all labelled in Malachy's untidy scrawl. Tiny black seeds were drying in one shallow dish and fat white ones in another. An iron brazier, burning lumps of charcoal, stood in the middle of the floor and a pot bubbled with something that smelled sweet and pungent.

'Seaweed, honey and a few berries of juniper,' said Malachy, following her glance. 'Just a cough syrup for summer colds.'

Mara nodded. 'I'm worried about this boy, Feirdin,' she said, coming quickly to the point. 'Garrett MacNamara thinks that he might be dangerous. I can't find any evidence that he is, but he has frightened a few people. He seems prone to great fits of anger. Garrett, of course, is in the right. He is *taoiseach*, so he is responsible for the behaviour of his clan and if the boy is insane he has a perfect right to place him under the care of a cousin, Eoin MacNamara. The boy's mother would not be strong enough to restrain him. What do you think?'

Malachy hesitated, stirring his brown mixture around and around with a wooden spoon. Mara tried to control her impatience. She herself was quick at everything, could usually conduct a conversation and at the same time do some gardening or cooking, or keep an eye upon her scholars. Malachy, however, waited until his mixture boiled and thickened and then he moved the iron pot to the stone beside the heat before speaking. He put down the spoon carefully and turned to face her.

'I'm not sure,' he said reluctantly.

'You can tell me,' said Mara encouragingly. 'You know I will speak of it to no one else.'

'No, no,' he said quickly, 'it's not that. I know that I can always trust you. It's just that I don't know what to say. He's a strange boy, quite shy, and perhaps he is just a bit melancholic. I went to see him at Garrett's request. He never looked at me once while I was talking to him. I stayed quite a long time, chatting to his mother just to try to put him at ease, but he wouldn't speak to me at all.'

'I see,' said Mara thoughtfully. 'Mind you, a lot of boys are shy and tongue-tied at that age – what is he? Nineteen?'

'He did say something before I left,' said Malachy, knitting his black eyebrows in a puzzled frown and not answering her question. 'I was just going out the door when he said, quite suddenly: "You know what's wrong with me? I've got a little man in my head and he keeps spending all of my silver." '

Mara looked at him with startled attention and Malachy nodded.

'Mind you,' he added, 'Gráinne and I had been discussing the silversmith, Cian – you know Cian, the father of young Hugh at your school – and it may be that the lad tried to make a joke.'

'Sounds strange to me,' said Mara, brooding over all of the young boys that she had known. 'It sounds like a joke, but it sounds like a joke that a seven-year-old might make, not a nineteen-year-old. Perhaps the boy is just slow and the frustration of that makes him explode into tempers. What do you think? Should we leave him with his mother for the moment?'

'I'll keep an eye on him if that is what you decide,' said Malachy.

He'll leave the decision to me, though, thought Mara. Well, it has to be my decision, I suppose, although this is more a matter of medicine than of law. She looked at him carefully. He was not looking well. His dark skin was sallow and there were black wells of anxiety or melancholy under his brown eyes. He can be no more than forty, she thought, and yet he is beginning to look like a man nearing sixty. She thought about the third case on her schedule for the day and decided against discussing it. He had enough on his mind and his advice would probably not be too useful, either.

'So,' she said abruptly, 'what about Nuala?'

Malachy grimaced though he tried to force a smile. 'I knew she would get you on her side,' he said.

'She's very young for marriage,' observed Mara mildly. He must know how often these thirteen- and fourteen-year-old children died of bearing a child too big for their young bones.

'Her mother wanted it, this marriage with Naoise,' he said stubbornly.

'Wanted it, yes,' said Mara. 'But would she have forced it?'

'She was married herself at fourteen,' he replied. 'And so were you,' he added.

'So I was. And a mother at fifteen. And divorced at seventeen!' She smiled to herself, thinking back. 'I don't suppose that I was forced into it, though. He was quite a handsome young fellow, Dualta, the handsomest at the law school. I had my eye on him from the time that I was thirteen and I pestered my father to allow me to marry him. He wasn't too keen. He didn't care too much for Dualta even though he had been a scholar at Cahermacnaghten law school since he was seven.'

Malachy laughed but his face was slightly embarrassed. The people of the Burren had long memories and the story of Mara's divorce would never be forgotten. Divorce was quite common; the law was very clear on this subject, but normally it was just used for cases of adultery or impotence. Her divorce had shocked everyone.

'Well, it all ended well for me,' she said happily. 'I had my beautiful baby daughter. I got my divorce and I kept my *coibche*, bride price, as well,' she added with immense satisfaction. She returned to the subject. 'This is a different matter entirely. Nuala does not want this marriage and she dislikes Naoise. She's not a girl to change her mind easily. You know that.'

Malachy's eyes were anxious. 'The O'Lochlainn is in favour of this marriage,' he said. 'He has promised to give Naoise a good farm.'

Mara nodded. The O'Lochlainn, Ardal O'Lochlainn, *taoiseach* of the O'Lochlainn clan, had been Mór's brother. It was only natural that he would take an interest in the future of his niece and be happy to see her make a good match with another of the clan. Nevertheless, Mara doubted whether Ardal would spare much thought for Nuala's happiness.

'Won't you think about it?' she asked gently. 'At least allow her to finish her studies and qualify as a physician so that she has that to fall back on if this marriage does not work out. Naoise will want her to be a farmer's wife and that may not suit her.'

He did not reply. His brown eyes were full of pain. He looked at her appealingly. 'I just want someone to look after her. If anything happens to me she would be alone,' he said.

Mara considered this carefully. Perhaps he, also, was ill. Could those growths pass from one person to another? She didn't know. She prayed inwardly to God to give her the right words, but knew that it was for her own brains to say the right thing. The thought of all that burning intelligence and ambition within Nuala being confined to a mountain farm made her indignant, but she knew she had to handle the matter carefully. After all, Nuala was Malachy's daughter and he probably was sincere in his wish to do his best for her.

'If anything ever happened to you,' she said solemnly, laying her hand on his arm, 'I would look after Nuala. After all, I am a distant cousin of yours. Nuala would be a daughter to me. I swear to that, and I will draw up a legal document if you wish. Let her go on studying, Malachy, and then you can think again when she reaches fifteen or sixteen.'

His face cleared. 'Do you really mean that?'

'Of course I do. Did you ever know me to say something I didn't mean?'

'I'll do that, then,' he said. 'Do you want to tell her?'

'Tell her yourself,' she said gently. 'She'll prefer to hear it from you. I'll go now, Malachy. Don't bother coming with me.'

That was a waste of time, she thought as she made her way

out, with a quick wave to Nuala who was industriously tying up the straggling stems of the woodbine in a shady corner of the garden. I would have been better off to see Feirdin myself and now I don't have the time. Still, it wasn't a waste of time to have managed to persuade Malachy not to sacrifice his clever child to a disappointing marriage with that brainless Naoise O'Lochlainn.

She resolved to make up her mind when she saw Feirdin MacNamara at Poulnabrone that afternoon. Her experience was that boys are funny creatures at that age. They can be up and down. The chances were that Garrett MacNamara was making a fuss about nothing. He was a fussy individual. He reminded Mara of the pot that Brigid kept on the fire, full of wholesome soup for the scholars – perpetually bubbling and from time to time suddenly over-boiling. Feeling more cheerful at this mental picture of the pompous Garrett, she hitched up her calf-length *léine*, or tunic, and swung her leg over the stone wall that separated the townland of Caherconnell from Kilcorney.

Once across the wall, Mara stopped for a moment, running her hand over the rough slabs of sun-warmed stone set in a herringbone pattern, each huge slab dependent on its neighbour for stability. A few gentians, like tiny specks of dark blue jewels, were sprinkled on the south side of the wall. She bent down to touch them gently and then drew in a breath of triumph. Yes, there was a purple one among them. These were very rare. Mara looked all around to find some landmarks that would identify this site again to her. She would gather seed when the flower faded and then next year she would have purple pools in the blue river of gentians in her garden. Between the stone circle in the townland of Kilcorney and the thorn tree in the townland of Caherconnell, she thought, making a mental note, and then narrowed her eyes.

There was a small, thin, frail figure standing motionless inside the stone circle. She knew immediately who it was. It was Father Conglach, the parish priest of Kilcorney, and she knew that he had seen her. Reluctantly she raised her hand in greeting. She watched him with distaste as he came to the edge of the circle and beckoned to her. The sight of him reminded her of the fourth case on the schedule of this afternoon. A child of twelve in the parish of Kilcorney had possibly been raped and had undoubtedly produced a dead infant and Father Conglach had refused burial in the churchyard to the baby. Mara was suddenly filled with hatred for the man. How could he have refused the request of that unfortunate child? How could he have refused to bury her still-born baby? She herself was not a religious person; her prayers to God were perfunctory and mechanical – she usually worked out a few law problems during the weekly obligatory Mass – but she could never have done what he did. Nevertheless, he was an important part of the community of the small kingdom of Burren and she had decided a long time ago that peace within the community was one of her main aims in life. So, although she was tempted to give him a cheery wave and then ignore his summons, she turned aside from her path and joined him at the stone circle.

People called this place Athgreany, the Field of the Sun. It was a huge circle about forty yards across, made from thirteen tall stones plugged securely into the grykes, or crevices, of the limestone beneath. On the north side of the stone circle, even taller than the stones, was a cairn, its rounded sides covered with small white pebbles of quartz. In the centre of the circle was a flat slab of gleaming quartz, placed on top of two white limestone boulders, like a vast altar, and Father Conglach had moved across to stand beside this altar when she reached him.

'Look,' he said commandingly, and she saw what he was pointing at. There were some dark stains on the white stone and a few flies buzzed above them. Mara bent to look, but she knew immediately what it was.

'Blood,' she said calmly.

'Of course it is blood,' he said furiously. 'You know what's been happening here, don't you? Devil worship, that's what's been happening.'

More likely some silly youngsters bored and looking for excitement, thought Mara. She would have to defuse his anger or his unfortunate parishioners would be harangued for months to come. She continued to pretend to study the bloodstains and the area around them intently.

'It's just a fox, Father Conglach,' she said after a minute. 'Look,' she pointed at the ground near to his feet. 'That's fox fur.' She picked up the small piece of golden-brown fur and held it out to him. 'No human sacrifice,' she added, smiling.

He glared at it. 'The sin is just as great,' he said stiffly. 'The Lord God sayeth: "Do not place false gods before me." Who are these sons and daughters of iniquity who would do such a thing?'

'They probably meant no harm,' said Mara soothingly. 'It was probably a fox from a trap. He would have been dead already.'

'That doesn't concern me,' he replied loftily. 'Sin is my concern. Whoever has been here and taken part in these filthy revels has a sin on his soul and that sin must be cleansed through penance and suffering.'

And what about your soul? thought Mara. Have you no sin on your soul for the anguish that you caused to that poor young girl, Nessa? What does God think of you refusing to bury her dead baby in the churchyard, refusing a blessing, or even a prayer, for the poor little mite?

'I want you to bring this matter up today at Poulnabrone,' he continued. 'I want a full investigation and the people concerned brought to justice.'

'I can't do that, I'm afraid,' said Mara. 'My office is to investigate breaches of the law. There is no law regarding the killing of foxes.'

'There would have been dancing and singing and other matters going on,' he continued, ignoring her. 'I saw Rory the bard near here late last night. He had a girl with him. I couldn't see who she was as she had her head turned away – but I have my suspicions. And I distinctly saw Roderic the horn player with the young girl, Emer. What do you think that they were up to?'

'What indeed?' murmured Mara. She sighed theatrically. 'Young people!' She tried not to let a smile creep out. Had he ever been young? she wondered. But no, he would have been swept out from the world and immured in some monastic establishment before he knew what the world was about. He was of the Roman school of ecclesiastics; the Celtic church was milder and more forgiving, and, until fairly recently, priests had married. One of the Heptads, she remembered, stated that the wife of a priest must keep her head covered in church.

'I require you to investigate this matter, this morning if possible, and bring the culprits to justice,' he said angrily. 'There should be a heavy fine for all of them.'

Mara shook her head firmly and allowed a note of iron to creep into her voice. 'No, Father, I can't do that,' she said. 'I've studied the law since I was four years old and I've never come across a law that prevents the young from singing and dancing and enjoying themselves.'

'I'll report you to the bishop,' he snapped. 'Bishop Mauritius of Kilfenora will be most angered to hear about this.'

Mara shrugged. 'King Turlough Donn O'Brien will be here himself today at Poulnabrone. You can speak to him if you wish,' she said coldly. 'I am his officer and it is for him to tell me what to do. Bishop Mauritius is in the kingdom of Corcomroe. Now, I must say farewell to you and get back to the law school. I have my scholars to care for.'

'I hope none of them were involved in last night's devilry,' he said spitefully. 'There are things going on near your own law school, you know. I've heard sounds from that cave. I've watched them. You should take better care of your scholars; you should keep them harder at work, Brehon. The devil finds mischief for idle hands to do . . .' And then, when she said nothing, he called after her, 'I am going up Mullaghmore Mountain myself tonight. The bishop requires a report from me. He is thinking of banning these pagan festivals like *Bealtaine* and substituting a Christian service in the church in honour of Our Lady.'

Mara had turned away but now she faced him. 'I'm going up myself, also,' she said, making an immediate and swift decision. 'King Turlough will come too.' The king would probably not be too happy, she thought with an inward chuckle, but he would enjoy his dinner all the better after the exercise and it would do him good. After all, he was not yet fifty – not too old. No need to go right to the top and no need to stay until the bonfire at midnight. They could just climb the first few terraces, and then come back. The important thing was to be seen to do it. Even the bishop would be wary of interfering with a custom sanctioned by the king himself.

That gave Father Conglach a shock. He stood staring at her, his grey eyes as cold as those of a raven.

'The king!' he said, and then he rallied. 'I've heard that the king is a man of poor judgement.'

'He is a man of warmth and integrity,' said Mara evenly. 'And I am surprised to hear you criticize your king.'

The priest knew he had gone too far and he tried to retract. 'All of us can make mistakes,' he said loftily. 'If the king's chief advisers, his Brehons, do not give him the right counsel then he may be led into deeds unworthy of him.'

Mara was walking away, but then she stopped. She took a deep breath. Would she ignore this or retaliate? Retaliate, she decided immediately. She whirled around and walked back to him.

'By the way, Father Conglach,' she said stonily, 'one of the cases that I will be hearing today at Poulnabrone is about poor young Nessa. What can you tell me about her?'

'What do you mean?' he asked furiously. 'What have I to do with that girl who committed such a grievous sin?'

'One of your own flock, nevertheless,' said Mara. 'She, her father and her mother worship at your church every Sunday. I understand that her mother cleans the church, so I would have thought that Nessa's welfare would be of great concern to you.'

'Her spiritual welfare is of concern to me,' he replied gravely. 'And so is the spiritual welfare of everyone within the parish of Kilcorney. And this devilish work' – he stabbed a finger dramatically at the stone circle – 'this endangers the souls that are in my charge.'

With that, he swung around and stalked rapidly away across the stones towards the church of Kilcorney.

Well, that got rid of him, thought Mara, but her sense of satisfaction was soured by the thought of poor young Nessa. Her religious mother might have been better taking care of her than spending all her free time cleaning and polishing the church. Nessa was left on her own to get up to mischief and the mischief had resulted in a stillborn baby. Who really was the father of the baby? wondered Mara for the fiftieth time. Why had the girl obstinately refused to give his name for the whole of her pregnancy, and then suddenly changed her mind? And why had Nessa given such an unlikely name for the father of her child?

THREE

TRIAD 176

There are three destructive elements to the wisdom of the court:

1. *A harsh pleading*
2. *A talkative court*
3. *A judge without knowledge*

During the proceedings of the court, the Brehon may be addressed as 'Tighernae', my lord judge, or 'Ban Tighernae', my lady judge.

ԾՃ

THE DOLMEN OF POULNABRONE stood at the eastern edge of the four miles of flat tableland called the High Burren. Four huge upright slabs, each of them the height of a man, supported the soaring capstone of rough, lichen-spotted limestone. The field around it was paved with limestone clints, the grykes between them dotted with purple-spotted orchids, and the dolmen stood silhouetted against the sky, towering above the clints.

By the time King Turlough Donn and his bodyguards arrived

32

for judgement day Mara was seated at the foot of the dolmen with Colman by her side and her six scholars gathered around her. The field was full of people who had walked or ridden from all corners of the hundred-square-mile kingdom of the Burren. The only empty spot was immediately around Diarmuid who stood unhappily, holding a wildly barking dog by a stout iron chain. People backed away nervously and the space around man and dog grew larger by the minute.

Turlough Donn had become king of Thomond, Corcomroe and Burren in the year 1499. He was a heavily built man, about fifty years old, with the brown hair that had given him the nickname of 'Donn' just turning grey, light green eyes and a pleasant open face. A pair of huge moustaches curving down from either side of his mouth gave his face a warlike look, which was denied by the gentle amiable expression in his eyes.

'Mara!' He greeted his Brehon as always with a hearty kiss and Mara responded with a hug. She was fond of the king. His warmth and his generosity appealed to her.

'We're honoured by your presence, my lord,' she said formally as the four *taoiseach*s of the principal clans of the Burren – the O'Lochlainn, the O'Connor, the MacNamara and the O'Brien – came up to greet him.

'Ardal! Finn! Garrett! Teige!' With his usual lack of formality, the king saluted each of his chieftains with a quick slap on the back and then seated himself beside Mara.

'I'm looking forward to having dinner with you afterwards,' he said in a low voice. 'There's a favour I want to ask of you.'

She looked at him in surprise, wondering what it was.

'I have a favour to ask of you, also,' she said quickly. 'I want you to come up the mountain, up Mullaghmore, after we finish here. Father Conglach, the parish priest of Kilcorney, is trying to stir up the bishop of Kilfenora against the custom. I know that the bishop is in Corcomroe, not in the Burren, but his diocese spreads up here and it could make things very unpleasant if priests try to forbid their parishioners. It's an old custom and a harmless one. Will you come? If you show approval, then it will be hard for the bishop to stand against you.'

'Of course, I will,' he said with all the good humour that she had learned to expect from him. 'I will enjoy that. I'm sure it will be good exercise for me, too. Your lads are going too, I suppose. How many of them have you now at your school?'

'Just six,' said Mara. 'The four oldest scholars graduated last year – Cormac went back to Cork, his father is Brehon there, Aodh got a position in Ossary, Giolla went to Donegal, and Colman, you know Colman … well, I kept him as an assistant master. He'll move on when this term finishes.'

'Funny, you keeping him,' mused the king, his eyes on Colman who stood a few feet away, wearing the severe expression of one who bore the burden of the whole day's proceedings. 'I'd've thought that some of the others would be more your type. Cormac, now, he was a boy of great spirit.'

'Come to court all ye people of the kingdom of the Burren and hear the judgements of the Brehon,' called Colman in his shrill, reedy voice and everyone obediently drew nearer, all the while casting uneasy glances at Diarmuid and his dog.

Mara rose to her feet and picked up a scroll of parchment. 'The first case is between Diarmuid O'Connor and his cousin Lorcan O'Connor,' she said, raising her voice more than usual. Normally she could pitch it perfectly to the back of the crowd, but the barking of the dog made her doubt whether her normal tones could be heard. She unrolled the parchment, glanced over it and then rolled it up again. She had, in fact, not got round to writing up this case, but the scroll was like a wand of office to her by now, always held in her hand, but seldom referred to. Her memory was excellent, trained by years of study.

She wondered briefly whether it would be worthwhile telling

the dog to be quiet, but decided not to bother. After all, he would prove her case better if he kept barking.

'Diarmuid's cow was stolen from a latched cabin within the yard around his house,' she continued, her eyes scanning the back of the crowd to make sure that everyone caught her words. 'The door to the yard was bolted on the inside, but the bolt could be reached over the top of the door from the outside. This dog, named Wolf, was free in the yard.' Abruptly she pointed her scroll at the dog and it stopped barking and eyed her uncertainly. Mara took advantage of the quiet and proceeded. 'During the night someone entered the yard and stole the cow. But,' she paused dramatically, and heard the sigh of anticipation from the crowd, 'this dog did not bark. Why did the dog not bark? The dog did not bark because he knew the man that came in and stole the cow. Who was that man?' Again she paused and again the crowd sighed. Mara felt a familiar rush of pleasure. She loved these occasions.

'That man was the only man on the Burren, apart from Diarmuid, who could approach this dog. That man was the breeder of the dog.' Here Mara stopped and turned around and pointed at Lorcan, who was looking down at his feet. 'And the breeder of the dog was Lorcan O'Connor. What do you say, Lorcan? Do you plead guilty?'

'I found the cow straying,' muttered Lorcan. 'I was going to return her. Someone else must have stolen her.'

'And who, except yourself, could have gone into that yard and faced the dog?' said Mara, raising her voice. The dog had begun to bark again. 'Diarmuid's bedroom window was just above the yard. One bark would have woken him.'

'Other people knew the dog,' said Lorcan with desperation in his voice. 'He would not have barked for some people that he knew well.'

'Who?' demanded Mara. 'Is there anyone here today who can

approach this dog without making him bark?' She glanced all around the assembly, but no one shifted his position. Most people were looking amused. Lorcan was unpopular and they were enjoying this.

'Is there anyone here who will go up to the dog and test him?' asked Mara.

'I'll try,' offered the king after a long silence.

'Oh, no, my lord,' said Diarmuid. The sweat broke out on his forehead at the very idea of what might happen if his dog bit the king.

'I won't go too near,' said Turlough Donn. He got up from his seat and steadily strode towards the dog, eyeing him carefully. The dog leaped and strained at his chain and barked with rage. The crowd cheered and laughed.

'Well, I think that was convincing,' said the king, returning to his seat with a grin.

Mara waited until the echoes of the dog's frenzied barks died down. 'We'll do another test. Colman, my assistant, has been with this dog all the morning. The dog surely knows him by now. Colman, will you approach the dog, please?'

Shane, Mara noticed, was nudging Hugh and smirking, but Hugh was not smiling; just staring straight ahead, his eyes fixed on Colman. All of the other boys, even eighteen-year-old Fachtnan, were sniggering as Colman walked slowly and reluctantly towards Wolf. The crowd fell very quiet. There were none of the gleeful smiles and cheers that had greeted the king. Colman was not popular, thought Mara. She had noticed that before. The people of the Burren were uneasy with him.

There was no need for Colman to go too far. The dog immediately lunged at him and broke out into a passion of barking. Colman drew back hastily, licking his lips. There was a slight sheen of sweat on his high white forehead.

'Now we'll try a last test,' said Mara. 'Lorcan,' she ordered, 'approach the dog.'

Slowly and reluctantly, Lorcan began to move. The crowd parted to allow him through, a broad smile appearing on everyone's face. Even Finn O'Connor himself was laughing at his clansman's discomfiture. Lorcan, a ferocious scowl on his face, tried looking away from the dog but Wolf was not deceived. His barking was replaced by a soft puppy-like whine and he began to wag his bushy tail.

'Stroke him,' commanded Mara and Lorcan stretched out his hand and stroked the massive head. The dog's tail now wagged so hard that it wagged his whole body. A deep sigh of amusement came from the crowd. The case was proven.

'Have you anything to say, Lorcan?' enquired Mara.

Lorcan shook his head miserably.

'In that case, I pass sentence,' said Mara. 'Fine imposed is one *sét*, or half an ounce of silver, to be paid within five days. Case dismissed.'

'May I take the dog home now, Brehon?' asked Diarmuid.

'You may, indeed,' said the king with a chuckle. 'That dog has been an excellent witness. He did not fear to speak out and to convict the guilty.'

The ensuing roar of laughter made the dog bark again and King Turlough Donn smiled with satisfaction.

❖

'Next case,' called Colman, regaining his poise and indicating to Gráinne MacNamara to come forward with her son, Feirdin. Garrett MacNamara, *taoiseach* of the MacNamara clan, strode out and faced them both. He was a tall, aggressive-looking man with a high sloping forehead, a fleshy nose and a heavily swelling lower lip.

Garrett made his case as convincingly as he could. Mara listened carefully, although she did not look at him as he was speaking. Her eyes were fixed on Feirdin. She felt quite puzzled. There was something strange about him. After all the stories about his fits of rage, she expected him to protest, to get angry, but he said nothing. He did not seem even remotely interested in the proceedings. He was a good-looking boy, she thought, with large blue eyes and brown curly hair.

'I don't see much wrong with him,' said the king in an undertone. 'What does the physician say?'

Mara beckoned to Malachy and he came over and took his place beside Colman.

'Give your opinion,' commanded Mara.

Malachy held up a scroll and read the account of his medical examination of the boy in a monotonous voice. Mara did not listen very carefully this time. The report contained very little and did not mention that strange joke about the little man in the boy's head. She had already made up her mind what to do.

'Gráinne,' she said gently. 'The court feels that your son has certain problems. There have been times when he has frightened others on the Burren. Do you feel confident that you are able to keep your son from harming anyone?'

Gráinne lowered her eyes for a moment and then looked straight at Mara. 'Yes, Brehon,' she said defiantly.

'And yet, in the past, he has exploded with rage and your *taoiseach* is worried about him and about you.'

'It's the other lads, Brehon,' explained Gráinne, 'they will tease him and call him names. He likes to be on his own. He likes walking around and collecting bits of rocks. He has them all on shelves at home.'

'That sounds very interesting,' said Mara. 'You must show me your collection sometime, Feirdin.' She looked directly at him, but he avoided eye contact with her. There was definitely something wrong with him, but was it enough to condemn him to the harsh stewardship of his cousin who might well keep him tied up? This would not only frustrate him more, it would be likely to drive him into full madness. She paused for a moment, whispered to the king, and then rose to her feet.

'The court finds that Feirdin MacNamara is to be classified as *fer lethcuinn*, a half-sane man. This means that he has the protection of the court and the community. Anyone who incites him to commit a crime must himself pay the penalty, anyone who mocks him will be fined five *séts*, two and a half ounces of silver, or three milch cows. This is the law of the king.'

The crowd moved and sighed once more. Mara could hear the soft murmur of conversation swell as neighbour turned to neighbour. Heads nodded. It had been a popular judgement. The crowd approved. She only hoped that they, and she, were right. I'll go and see him tomorrow myself, she thought. I'll check on him at least once a week.

'Next case,' called Colman.

FOUR

*Judgement day: last day of April 1509. On the eve of
Bealtaine I judged the case between Declan O'Lochlainn and
Rory the bard. Declan O'Lochlainn declared that his daughter
Nessa, aged twelve, had been raped by the aforementioned
Rory at the festival of Samhain of the previous year . . .*

☙❧

'WHAT'S THIS ABOUT?' ASKED the king, leaning over
and speaking in Mara's ear as Colman announced the
case and called the witnesses.

'Well, the child, Nessa, looked pregnant in January, but she
kept denying it,' whispered back Mara. 'I sent Malachy, the
physician, at the request of the parents, but Nessa became hyster-
ical and he, rightly, in my opinion, refused to force her, so he
was unable to examine her. However, it was obvious that she was
pregnant. The baby was stillborn last week and Nessa's father,
Declan, sent for Colman to take down the statement. Apparently,

Nessa named Rory, the young bard, as the father of her baby and accused him of raping her.'

Mara got to her feet; Nessa, her parents and Rory were all standing in front of the dolmen with Colman and Malachy on either side.

'The accusation has been made,' she said, her clear voice carrying to the back of the crowd. 'How say you, Rory the bard? Are you guilty or not guilty?'

'Not guilty,' said Rory firmly. Mara looked at him with interest. Rape of a girl of Nessa's age was a very serious crime and carried a heavy fine of an *éraic*, or body fine, similar to that given for murder, and also a fine equivalent to the honour price of the victim's father. Nessa's father was an *ócaire*, a small farmer, so his honour price was only three *séts*, or one and a half ounces of silver or two milch cows, but when the *éraic* was added, this amounted to forty-five *séts*, or twenty-two and a half ounces of silver, or twenty-three cows. That would be a huge sum for this young bard to find. Mara suspected that Rory earned very little money. He had no patron; what silver he possessed would come from the selling of his poems or ballads at fairs. He had no land, no livestock, no kin here in the Burren. It would be impossible for him to pay a fine like that. Rory, however, did not look worried; only annoyed and slightly embarrassed.

'What evidence can you give in support of your innocence?' asked Mara. She had been surprised when Nessa's parents had accused Rory of this crime. Since he had come to the Burren a year ago all of the marriageable girls and a few of the married ones had sighed after him. He was an extraordinarily beautiful young man, his hair was a pale blond with a shade of red in it, his eyes were intensely blue and he was tall with broad shoulders and slim hips. Mara looked at poor little Nessa – small, fat, with the spotty skin of early adolescence. Would Rory really have raped her? she wondered cynically.

'My first witness is Aoife O'Heynes,' said Rory firmly. Mara tried to conceal a smile. Aoife was the only daughter of Muiris O'Heynes, a self-made prosperous farmer of obscure origins. Muiris and Áine O'Heynes had four hard-working sons and one spoiled daughter. Aoife was quite a beauty with long blond plaits and cornflower-blue eyes. Mara remembered now that she had seen Aoife and Rory together on that night of *Samhain*, the eve of All Hallows, on the last day of October. She had gone to the feast to keep an eye on her two young scholars, Hugh and Shane. They had both been desperate to go to the fair so she had promised them that they could stay until ten. Then she had taken them home, but before she left, she vividly remembered noticing Rory and Aoife kissing and cuddling in a dark corner of the field where the fair was held.

'Yes, Aoife?' she said. 'Was Rory with you all of that night of *Samhain*?'

Aoife blushed at the direct question, and the rosy colour enhanced her creamy skin and blue eyes.

'Yes, Brehon,' she said demurely. 'Emer and I were with Roderic and Rory for the whole evening. We all went home together.'

Hmm, thought Mara, my memory is that you split up, each couple going in different directions. But it didn't matter. Would Rory have left the delicious Aoife for that spotty, pasty-faced child? I don't think so. The memory of him disappearing into the bushes with Aoife was very clear in her mind. He had looked extraordinarily handsome. He had been wearing a saffron *léine*, she recalled, and a *brat*, a cloak, woven from purple and red strands of wool. She had wondered how he had got the silver to pay for them. She remembered thinking at the time that he had looked just like the picture of the hero king, Conor Mac Nessa, in her father's copy of *The Book of Ballymote*. The thought of that beautiful illustration gave her an idea.

'Nessa,' she said gently. 'What was Rory wearing that night?'

Nessa stared at her blankly. 'I don't know,' she said eventually.

'Aoife,' asked Mara. 'Can you remember what Rory was wearing that night?

Aoife's colour deepened even more. Her eyes were fixed on Rory. In the background, Mara noticed Muiris shifting uncomfortably. Muiris had worked very hard to build up his farm. He would not want his daughter to marry a penniless bard. On the other hand, he was an honest, straightforward man. His evidence would be worth listening to. But not yet, thought Mara. Let me be sure in my own mind. She turned to Aoife.

'Yes?' she queried.

'He was wearing a saffron *léine* and a red and purple striped *brat* and his hair was bound with a purple fillet and he had brown strapped sandals made from goatskin and he was carrying a satchel made from calf's skin,' said Aoife dreamily.

Mara smiled. 'That was my memory, also,' she said. Young love, she thought indulgently. The picture of the first beloved never fades. There was now no doubt in her mind, but she would ask a few more questions so as to satisfy her audience.

'Muiris and Áine,' she said. 'Can you confirm that Rory and Roderic brought your daughter home that night?'

Muiris stepped forward. 'Yes,' he said, shortly. 'They brought her home. They stayed until daybreak. They stayed with me after Aoife and her mother had gone to bed.'

All of them fairly merry after the amount of mead they had drunk, surmised Mara. The drink, made from fermented honey, was heavily alcoholic and, from what she had seen, there was plenty of it consumed that night.

'Brehon,' said Colman courteously. 'May I question?'

'Yes, certainly,' said Mara. She went back and sat next to King Turlough Donn.

43

'You trust your assistant to conduct the investigation?' asked the king in a low voice.

'Let him talk for a while,' she whispered. 'This will drag the case out and save the faces of poor little Nessa and her parents.'

'But you don't think that Rory the bard did it?'

'No,' Mara shook her head firmly. 'If Rory had seduced Nessa that night, he would have had to entice her away from her mother. She would have remembered what he was wearing. She didn't, but Aoife did. Girls always remember what a person is wearing if he is important to her. I don't think Rory was anywhere near Nessa that night.'

'Can you remember what I was wearing the first time that you saw me?' whispered Turlough Donn in her ear.

'My lord, I was blinded by your brilliance,' whispered back Mara. In fact, her only memory of that day, fifteen years ago, had been the thrill of being appointed Brehon of the Burren by Turlough's uncle, the then king of Thomond.

What was Colman doing? she thought with annoyance. Rory was almost losing his patience. The same questions were being asked over and over again. Now Colman had summoned Roderic and was trying to get him to admit that he had separated from Rory at one stage in the evening. Roderic, however, with an uneasy glance at Daniel, Emer's father, stood firm. No, he declared. The four young people had spent the evening of *Samhain* together. They had danced and sung; they had eaten supper, they had drunk some mead – a small amount, to be sure – and then he and Rory had taken the two girls home. First they had taken Emer to her home at Caheridoola, where, Mara gathered, Daniel had shut the door on them, and then they had taken Aoife home to Poulnabrucky where Muiris had proved more hospitable.

Mara rose to her feet again and smiled sweetly at Colman. He had done his best, she thought, trying hard to be fair to him. It was strange how such sharp intelligence could be married to a complete lack of common sense.

'We have heard all the evidence in this case,' she said evenly. 'I find this case as not proven against Rory the bard. Nessa, is there anything else that you would like to say? Is it possible that you made a mistake and that Rory the bard was not responsible, but that perhaps someone else was?'

Nessa shook her head silently.

'There is just one other witness, Brehon, if you will excuse me,' said Colman suavely. 'I call on Father Conglach.'

Mara's lips tightened and her eyes narrowed. She had not expected this. What was the priest going to say? She looked around. He had been standing on the far side of the dolmen but now he advanced towards her. The people drew back courteously and made a long clear passageway for him. He advanced without a glance or a nod of acknowledgement. Mara did not sit down, but stood facing the priest, her dark eyes fixed on him.

'Yes, Father?' she enquired, her voice as chilly and hard as she could make it. With her left hand she signalled to Colman to sit down. She would conduct this interrogation herself.

'I saw Nessa with Rory the bard, on the evening of *Samhain*,' stated the priest.

'Indeed,' said Mara. She let a few long moments of silence fill the air. He had been there; that was correct. She had seen him, like an ill-omened bird of prey, hovering around the merry youngsters. She waited, looking at him carefully. Why was he doing this? she wondered. He himself had not even had the common humanity to allow the poor child to bury her dead infant in the churchyard.

Nessa had had to take the tiny body to a *killeen*, one of the little lonely ancient burial places where the ancestors of the people of the Burren had laid their dead, and where now, unbaptized infants and suicides were sometimes placed. When Mara had heard from Brigid, her housekeeper, what was going to happen, she had hurried over, taking Fachtnan and a shovel with her. Neither Nessa's mother nor her father had come with Nessa. The poor child had carried the baby, wrapped in an old piece of sacking, and was digging in the earth with a rusty trowel when they arrived. Fachtnan had dug the grave, his face white and his eyes wet with tears. Mara had said a prayer over the little waxen body and Fachtnan had joined in with a steady voice. Nessa had said nothing.

She continued to say nothing; according to the general rumour she was still resolutely denying that she had done anything wrong. She had even accused her mother of believing the story of the Virgin Mary and not believing her own daughter. Mara had smiled at that. There had been no mention of Rory until Colman had come in with the news that Declan was going to bring the case to be heard at Poulnabrone.

So why was this priest now creating falsehoods before his king and his parishioners? Perhaps a belated sense of responsibility for the daughter of that religious woman who did so much for his church? Perhaps a hatred of all that Rory and his like represented? Whatever it was, there was no doubt in her mind that he was lying. She stared hard at him, but his eyes did not drop before hers. She allowed the silence to continue. Silence, she had discovered long ago, was as effective as words on many occasions.

In the distance a bull roared in Baur North and was answered by the high treble of the calves and the soft, deep mooing of the cows. The people stirred uneasily. This was a sad, unpleasant case. They wanted it finished and then the merriment would surface and the long climb up the mountain could begin. Mara let her eyes travel over the assembled crowd. She raised her voice slightly, projecting its fully trained power to the back of the assembly.

'Was there anyone else who saw Rory the bard with Nessa, daughter of Declan O'Lochlainn, on the night of *Samhain* last?'

There was a complete silence. Mara allowed her breath to escape from her lips. That had been a high-risk strategy, but it had paid off.

'Does anyone else wish to speak?' she asked mildly.

'I saw Nessa go home early with her mother,' said Murrough. 'Aoife and Rory were still dancing around the bonfire when they left.' Murrough was a breeder of wolfhounds, who lived at Cathair Chaisleáin, on the steep cliff behind Poulnabrone. He was a very reliable, kind man. Mara knew that she could trust his word. And the community would trust his word, she knew that also. It was time to put a finish to this.

'I find this case not proven,' she said firmly. 'Rory the bard has no case to answer. Case dismissed. Are there any other matters to be brought before the court?'

'Yes,' said a husky voice. Mara frowned and turned her eyes to Daniel O'Connor, father of Emer, popularly considered by many to be the most beautiful girl on the Burren. Everyone in the kingdom had a right to bring a case for consideration on judgement day, but after her long years as Brehon of the Burren, everyone knew that she liked to know all the details of cases beforehand.

'I bring a marriage contract for my daughter, Emer, to be ratified before the king and the people of the kingdom, Brehon,' said Daniel as he pushed his way through the crowd. Mara looked at him in puzzlement. It was no surprise that Emer was to be married. She was now sixteen and there was no shortage of suitors for her father to choose from. She was one of the prettiest girls that Mara had ever seen. Her hair had the glossy blue-black of a raven's wing and her eyes were extraordinary – the dark blue of an ocean on a sunny day. What surprised Mara was that she had not been asked to draw up the contract. And yet, there was a contract in Daniel's hand. It was even tied with the pink linen ribbon that she always used for her documents.

'Come forward, Emer,' she said encouragingly and Emer came forward. Mara smiled at her, but there was no response from Emer. The girl's face was white, the blue eyes were shadowed and she was clearly trembling. So, the bridegroom was not to be Roderic! Mara scanned the faces in the crowd and found the stocky figure and open, honest face of the young horn player. About ten minutes ago he had been smiling and joking with the young men around him and casting amorous glances in Emer's direction. Now he looked bewildered and apprehensive. He had not known of this contract, obviously. With a stony face, Mara held out her hand for the scroll. There was little that she could do; the disposal of a daughter in marriage was an affair for the father. If Daniel had come to her in private she could have talked to him, perhaps persuaded him to put his daughter's happiness into the scale, but now, if a contract had been drawn up and witnessed there would be no way out for Emer. Without a word, she took the contract and unrolled it. It was beautifully written in a flowing hand, the letters all exactly the same size, the lines evenly spaced and mathematically straight. Mara knew this hand; this was Colman's writing. How dare he draw up a contract without a word to her! She felt her cheeks flush with anger, but she suppressed it. In a clear, cold voice she began reading:

'A contract between Daniel O'Connor, *ócaire*, of Caheridoola, of the kingdom of Burren, in the first part and Colman Lynch, *aigne*, of Cahermacnaghten, also of the kingdom of Burren, in the second part.'

Mara stopped reading and turned around. She gave Colman a long, cool stare. There was no legal reason why he should consult her about his marriage. He was nineteen, a qualified lawyer, independent of his parents and of her. There was no legal reason, but every other reason. He must go, she thought grimly. I'm not having this behaviour, this lack of any common courtesy. She beckoned to him calmly and he came forward and stood beside Emer, his pale face looking as blank as it always did. Emer took three steps away from him, and away from her father, but that was all that she dared do.

Mara scrutinized the contract carefully. One word out of place and she could declare it as null and void, but Colman had been too well taught, was too clever, she admitted to herself, to make any mistakes. The contract was as perfect as it could possibly be.

Daniel had asked for a hefty *coibche*, or bride price, she noted with interest. Where had Colman managed to get the silver to pay that? She paid him very little. Presumably, he had been doing some legal work around the Burren, and perhaps outside the Burren. He had often asked for a few days' leave of absence and she granted it each time without searching enquiries – it was often good to get rid of him for a day or two. He may have been doing some work in Galway or in Thomond. Even so, it was a lot for a newly qualified young man to have acquired. He would not have got it from his parents; he had told her once that, in fairness to the rest of his many brothers and sisters, he would get no more from them once they had finished paying his law school fees.

Steadily and clearly she read the contract to the end. Daniel would provide some cows – not as many as he could have been asked to provide, given the difference in status between the parties, but the agreement was a fair one. The lawyer was very young and had no settled position and the girl was extraordinarily beautiful.

'Does anyone know of any reason why this contract should not be ratified?' she asked. No one spoke. It was odd, she thought, how silence could sometimes speak louder than words. There were none of the customary cheers, nor calling out of good wishes, nor good-natured jokes, just this cold silence. Was it a sense of sympathy with Roderic, a kind, good-natured young man, who was so popular with everyone, or was it pity for the young girl? And yet, there was nothing unusual about this situation.

Daniel had done well for his daughter. Colman would be a rich man within a few years and he was young and, she supposed, quite good-looking in a narrow, slightly effeminate way. Girls were not normally consulted about marriage plans and Roderic would not be the first landless young man to be disappointed. The silence must result from something else, a dislike for Colman, perhaps, and yet there was nothing to be done now; this contract of marriage would have to go ahead.

Mara glanced at Daniel's *taoiseach*, Finn O'Connor, and then at the king. Both nodded, and Turlough Donn got to his feet.

'This contract has been ratified,' he called out in his booming voice and he walked over to slap Colman on the back and bestow a warm kiss on the lovely flower-like face of the bride-to-be. This broke the tension, and the crowd stirred and relaxed. A few laughed and most turned their faces towards the east, contemplating the swirling heights of Mullaghmore, impatient for the evening's fun to begin.

'Judgement day has ended,' said Mara formally, and added, as she always did, 'Go in peace with your family and your neighbours.'

'And I will come up the mountain with you all,' announced the king.

There was a huge and genuine cheer at that. Turlough Donn was highly esteemed, not just within his own clan, the O'Briens, but also within the dominant clan, the O'Lochlainns. In the past, O'Lochlainns had been kings of the Burren, O'Connors had been kings of Corcomroe and the O'Briens kings of Thomond, but that was a long time ago and Turlough Donn, in his ten-year reign, had reconciled all differences so that the three kingdoms of

Burren, Corcomroe and their large neighbour, Thomond, were all happily united under his rule.

The people had begun to move. Some would go to nearby houses and collect the stacks of food and flagons of ale deposited there earlier, others would fetch musical instruments; most of the young men, led by Muiris, Aoife's father, were plunging into the hazel thickets in the square-shaped deep hollows near Poulnabrone. They would need to bring wood for the bonfire up to the top of the mountain. Muiris had a long, wickedly sharp thatching knife that glinted in the late afternoon sun and, despite his fifty years, he was the first to complete a bundle of hazel rods. There was a lot of good-natured laughing and joking as the others strove to be the one to cut the largest number of bundles in the shortest time. The six law scholars, suddenly released from good behaviour, followed the others into the thickets.

'That's a very fancy knife your young Hugh is holding,' said Malachy at her elbow. Mara looked across at her scholars. Twelve-year-old Hugh was brandishing an ornate knife with a gem-studded silver handle. The red and blue stones caught a few eyes and several young men had stopped to admire it.

'When did he get that?' asked Mara with a frown. 'I suppose his father gave it to him when he visited last week.'

Hugh's father was a prosperous silversmith, inclined, especially since the death of his wife, to spoil his clever youngest son with valuable gifts. It was immensely important to him that Hugh would qualify in the prestigious profession of lawyer and perhaps even become a Brehon in time. For a moment she almost called the boy back in order to confiscate that valuable knife, but then the memory of his tear-stained face earlier in the day softened her. Let him enjoy the admiration and the envy, she thought.

'Just a word, Colman,' she called coldly as her assistant prepared to follow the other young men. He turned courteously, his face as devoid of expression as always, and she moved towards him. Malachy was now deep in an argument with Nuala who was pleading to be allowed to climb the mountain. Malachy's house-keeper stood beside them with a look of amusement on her face. Mara half-smiled also, then remembered herself and looked sternly at Colman.

'I'm surprised that you did not think to consult me about your marriage plans, Colman,' she said. With satisfaction she noted that her voice betrayed no note of hurt; he would have enjoyed that too much. He was shrewd enough to know all of her weaknesses, shrewd enough to know that, despite her mock ferocity, she relished being a mother to her boys at the law school and that she enjoyed the feeling of being in their confidence.

'Oh, I apologize, Brehon,' he said with his usual charm. 'I thought it would be a nice surprise for you and I couldn't resist the temptation to draw up my own contract, though, of course, I knew that you would do it so much better. I hope that it was acceptable to your high standards,' he added with the false humility that he had used from early childhood in an effort to ingratiate himself.

Mara stared at him in disgust. Did he really think that he could get around her in this fashion?

'Do your parents know about this proposed marriage?' she asked abruptly. Colman's parents lived in the city of Galway, some miles away across the mountain pass.

'No, Brehon,' he said politely. 'I wanted you to be the first to know.'

She ignored this. 'I think you should go and tell them immediately,' she said decisively. 'Go there first thing tomorrow morning. Take a horse from the stable if you wish. And Colman ... do make sure that you look after the boys tonight, especially the younger ones. Make sure that they have a good evening, but don't let them get into any danger on the mountain. I'll hope to hear from them tomorrow that you have been kind and attentive to them.' She turned her back on him without waiting for a response. The king was beckoning to her and suddenly a marvellous idea came to her. She crossed over to him.

'Turlough,' she said, 'you know that you once said to me that you wished you understood the English better and that you wished you understood all the differences between their law and our law? Well, that young man there, Colman, is one of the cleverest scholars I have ever had. Why don't you employ him? Send him on a journey to Dublin, or even to England. Get him to gather information for you. Get him to find out about this Tudor king, Henry VII, and he can tell you all about his laws and policies. Colman is wasted here, to be honest; I can easily manage the law school and the business of the kingdom without an assistant. I've never had one before.'

Turlough Donn looked at her in amusement. 'You don't like him much, do you?' he said. 'Well, perhaps I might be able to make use of him.' He wheeled around and beckoned to Colman. 'Young man,' he said, looking at him keenly. 'I hear you are interested in English affairs. What can you tell me about the English king, the Tudor Henry VII?'

'He's dead, my lord,' said Colman, bowing with great respect. 'He died recently. His son, Henry VIII, is now king. Henry VIII's eldest brother, Prince Arthur, died seven years ago, so now he is the one to inherit the throne. The English do not have our system of electing a *tánaiste* from the kin-group; the eldest son is always the heir.'

'Good, good,' said the king. His light green eyes gleamed with amusement. He shot a quick glance at Mara, who shrugged. Henry VII or Henry VIII; it was all one and the same to her. She had no interest in the English. Let them stay in Dublin or Waterford; she only hoped they would never come as far as the west of Ireland. They hated the Brehon law and tried to suppress it wherever their rule ran. A barbarous law, they described it as. And yet, Brehon law seemed to her to be much more humane than their own laws. In England, she had heard, a man could be hanged for stealing, leaving his wife a widow and his children orphans; under Brehon law he would be asked to pay a fine and if a man was too poor to pay it, then his clan would help.

'Well, we must have a chat sometime,' the king said genially to Colman. 'Now for the fair and then this mountain.'

FÍVE

CRITH GABLACH (RANKS IN SOCIETY)

The honour price of a king is deemed to be forty-two séts,
or twenty-one milch cows, or twenty-one ounces of silver.
The king loses his honour price if he:
   Works as a commoner
   Goes unattended
   Flees his enemies

☙❧

THE SUN WAS SETTING over the Atlantic by the time the climb began. Long streaks of gold gilded the polished surfaces of the clints, and the grykes between them were filled with the sharply etched oval shadows of the glossy green hart's tongue ferns. The limestone terraces on the western side of the Mullaghmore were flushed with a pink glow though the sky was still darkly blue.

Mara and King Turlough Donn had made their way slowly – enjoying the rare opportunity to meet and talk – but the crowd, even the eager young, had waited politely for them on the far side of the lake at the foot of the mountain. It would be the king's privilege to be the first to set foot on the mountain.

Roderic was playing his horn. Mara had often heard him play, but she had never before heard such wonderful music from him. It seemed as if all his misery and his love for Emer went into the tune. Rory was singing the song very softly, but the crowd remained very still and the sound floated across the quiet water of the lake. Mara knew the song well; '*Eibhlín a Rúin*' had been composed in a bardic school on the Burren in the time of her grandfather, but on this quiet evening the story of frustrated love and longing seemed to have a special poignancy. When the music stopped, there was a short silence and it almost seemed as if a stir of emotion went through the crowd. And then all faces turned to welcome the king.

'That's a marvellous musician, that horn player . . . what's his name?' asked Turlough, nodding and smiling to everyone as he and Mara made their way through the people.

'He's Roderic, the son of the old horn player, Cormac,' replied Mara.

'I wonder would Roderic like to come to Thomond? I could do with a musician who plays as well as that. I get tired of the harp myself; there is something wonderfully uplifting about horn music.'

'Ask him,' said Mara. 'He has no position here. Ask him now. He needs cheering up. He loves Emer, that lovely dark-haired girl over there, the one whose father has betrothed her to Colman.'

'Young man,' boomed Turlough when he was only several yards away from Roderic. 'Would you think about coming to the court at Thomond and bringing that horn of yours with you?'

'Yes, my lord,' said Roderic, the blood rushing to his cheeks and his eyes shining. He took a step towards Emer and then turned back to the king. 'My lord, I would be very honoured,' he said respectfully.

'Well, that's it then,' said Turlough, smiling broadly. 'Now for this mountain.'

A great cheer went up as soon as he took a few steps up the slope and very soon he and Mara were passed by the strong and the energetic, everyone in that huge crowd going at a pace that suited him.

Most people from the Burren were there, all except for the very old and the very young. Not Nuala, Mara noticed; Malachy was on his own, climbing fast. Father Conglach was behind him, obviously trying to catch up, but it looked as if Malachy were trying to avoid the priest. Behind Father Conglach came Diarmuid and Lorcan, their heads close together, talking eagerly – Mara smiled at the sight.

'Lorcan will talk his way out of that fine that I imposed,' she said to the king. 'Diarmuid is his cousin, of course.'

'Well, that means a lot,' said the king heartily. 'Where would we be without our families! By the way, how is Sorcha?'

'She's well.' Mara always felt warmed when she thought of her pretty daughter. 'She has two children, would you believe it! The eldest, Domhnall, is four now. He's a clever little fellow. The little girl, Aisling, is two. Sorcha's husband, Oisín, is doing well, too. Galway is a great place for trade and he brings goods in from Spain and France. He brought me a fine barrel of wine from France on his last voyage. You'll be sampling some of it with your dinner.'

'I'm looking forward to that,' said Turlough with the beaming smile that made Mara think what an attractive, open face he had. 'How much further do you think we should go?' he asked with a glance up at the seven terraces, piled one on top of the other. The smallest top terrace was slightly shrouded in mist, its rounded summit barely visible.

'We'll just go to the first terrace,' said Mara reassuringly. 'Most people will stop for a rest there, and a few will go back down.' She shaded her eyes with her hand and scrutinized the mountain slopes. She wanted to make sure that Colman was looking after the boys. She could see Fachtnan's dark hair and a cluster of boys with him, but Colman's neat fair head was not with them. She counted heads – only five. Hugh's flaming red head was missing, also.

'Your young man is not with his bride-to-be,' said Turlough, looking further up the mountain. 'Isn't that she, with the other pretty girl, the one with the blond plaits, who gave evidence in the case against the bard?' He chuckled. 'They've got the two young men with them, Rory, and what's the name of the boy with the horn?'

'That's Roderic,' said Mara, just as the triumphant toot of the horn came floating down the mountain. She looked around. Daniel was even further down the mountain than themselves. There was nothing he could do. She smiled. 'Well, let them have their fun,' she said indulgently. 'I suppose Emer will have to marry Colman but it's a shame, especially now that Roderic's prospects have improved. I think she is very much in love with him.' Once again she counted the heads around Fachtnan's tall figure. 'I wonder where Hugh is.'

'That's your young man, your assistant, over there, isn't it?' said Turlough pointing. Mara looked and let out a sigh of relief.

'And that's Hugh with him.' She narrowed her eyes against the horizontal glare of the setting sun. 'Perhaps Hugh is tired and couldn't keep up with the others. Funny, though. Usually he is as energetic as a puppy. And Shane is with Fachtnan, how strange. They're always together, Shane and Hugh.'

'Stop fussing over them. You're like a mother duck with her brood out from the nest for the first time,' said Turlough affectionately. He struggled up the last few yards and announced breathlessly, 'There we are: the first terrace. Let's take a seat on this rock. I'm not as fit as you.'

'You should get a dog, and climb a hill with him every day,' said Mara, sitting beside him and stroking the brittle rust-coloured stain of the lichen. 'That would keep you fit. I should have brought Bran, but I didn't want him near Diarmuid's dog. Bran isn't a fighter, but Diarmuid's dog would fight with his own shadow.'

She stood and walked over to look at some creamy mountain avens that grew in a small crevice on the side of the mountain. She picked one of the small daisy-like flowers and brought it back and tucked it inside the king's brooch, resuming her seat beside him.

'That was good of you to give Roderic a position in court. You will like him. He's a very nice fellow.'

I wonder, would there be any chance of arranging a marriage between Emer and Roderic now, she thought. Perhaps I could get Turlough to talk to Daniel. After all, Colman is under twenty-one; he should not, perhaps, have entered into this contract without his parents' permission – though, of course, he does have his independence from them and they will always do, and say, as he wants. Her mind trawled through the steps that she could take to annul the marriage contract until it was interrupted by a series of excited barks.

'Look, Murrough has got some of his dogs with him. Murrough,' she called as the small round man struggled over the edge of the first terrace. He had three enormous wolfhounds with him, the leather leashes gathered loosely into one hand. 'Murrough, I was just saying a minute ago that I wished I had brought Bran; he would have enjoyed it, poor fellow.'

'I'm coming up here again on Saturday,' said Murrough, pausing and panting slightly. 'There have been a few wolves sighted on the north side of the mountain. My neighbour Fiachra lost a few sheep so we will have to clear the mountain of wolves. I wouldn't want to let dogs loose today with all the people around.'

'No, indeed,' said Mara, glancing up and down the mountain. A herd of black and white goats, accompanied by their kids, were thundering down, leaping from rock to rock, and there were shrieks of terror from many of the girls.

'Tonight and tomorrow the wolves will be very wary after the bonfire,' continued Murrough. 'You'll find that they'll stay off the mountain tomorrow and go down some cave or other. Wolves are funny creatures. They are very nervous, very wary. That's how they survive, I suppose. Saturday will be just right; it'll give them another day to settle down again and to come back up. Will you come, and bring Bran? We'll just go as far as the first terrace and then release the dogs.'

'I'd love to do that,' said Mara with pleasure, fondling the narrow hairy head of the nearest dog. Saturday was a holiday at the law school and she would enjoy a day's hunting. 'The lads might like to come as well, will that be all right?'

'The more the merrier,' said Murrough. 'I've got plenty of dogs. They can have one each. Young lads like that, they can have a bit of a competition to see whose dog gets a wolf.' He turned towards the king. 'It's a pity you won't still be here, my lord.'

Turlough Donn sighed. 'Do you know, I would really enjoy that. A day's hunting on the mountain, it's a long time since I've had a good day out like that.'

Mara hesitated. The note of appeal was unmistakable. She would enjoy his company; she always did. However, she was very busy; she could not neglect her scholars and Turlough would be a demanding guest.

Turlough sighed again and then patted one of the dogs. Mara looked at him and then melted. He was lonely; she knew that. His wife, Ragnailt MacNamara, had died a few years ago and his four sons and one daughter were all married with their own families.

'Why don't you stay until Sunday morning?' she asked. 'The guest house at the law school is always kept ready. There's plenty of room for your two bodyguards, as well. Brigid will be delighted. She will think it much more worthwhile to cook for you than just for me.'

The king's face brightened. 'I'll do that with the greatest of pleasure,' he said. 'That would be a wonderful break for me.'

'I'll have my best dog for you, my lord,' said Murrough. 'And now I'd better be getting on; these dogs will pull my arm from its socket if I don't get moving.'

'God bless you, Murrough, and have a good evening,' called out the king as Murrough was towed up the next slope by the three muscular giant dogs.

'You don't feel like changing your mind and going to the summit for the bonfire?' teased Mara.

'I don't,' said Turlough. 'When you spoke about Brigid's cooking I suddenly felt a great void within me. Do you think we might disappear now?'

Mara took one last look around. Yes, Fachtnan had Enda, Moylan, Aidan and Shane with him. Hugh was still with Colman. Why didn't Hugh go and join the other lads? she wondered. Why was he acting so strangely? Mara wished that she did not have the king with her. She wanted to climb up and see what was troubling Hugh.

'Yes, let's go down now,' said Mara. King or no king, she thought, as they began their descent, tomorrow I'll find out what's going on with Hugh and Colman.

❉

The Burren seemed very empty, deserted except for the figure of one man on horseback, and very quiet also, as they strolled companionably back across the limestone-paved fields, their feet automatically stepping across the grykes filled with the bright green rounded leaves of the maidenhair fern and speckled with tiny rock roses. Turlough, like any country farmer, wore nail-studded boots and his heavy tread brought out the sharp bittersweet smell of the juniper bushes which grew prostrate over the flat rocks wherever some soil lodged in the crevices. Behind them, at a discreet distance, came the king's two bodyguards, the soft murmur of their conversation blending with the high sweet voices of birds twittering overhead. They passed the ancient dolmen of Poulnabrone, now standing sentinel over empty flat fields, and then paused for a while to rest.

The king sat down heavily on the nearest rock and the two young bodyguards stopped at a distance, eyeing the empty landscape keenly. There had been trouble recently between the O'Kellys from north of Galway and the O'Briens of Thomond. The bodyguards would not relax until they were sure that their king was safe from attack. After a few minutes, they also sat down on a flat-topped rock.

'You enjoy being Brehon, don't you?'

'I do,' said Mara, surprised at the question, seating herself beside him. 'I suppose it is what I have wanted ever since I was three or four years old.' She smiled at the memory of her young self. 'I used to come to judgement days with my father and listen to everything – it gave me a great thrill, though I'm sure I could not have understood it all. When I went back home I would play a game that I was Brehon and make a little model of Poulnabrone with a few flat stones. I would collect lots of small sharp-pointed stones and wedge them into the grass and pretend that they were the people of the kingdom and then I would address them. I must say that they never interrupted me,' she finished with a laugh.

Turlough did not laugh, just looked at her gloomily. 'It's your life; that's what I supposed,' he said shortly and rose to his feet again, the bodyguards immediately rising also. Mara raised her eyebrows but decided not to enquire. If something were wrong he would tell her eventually.

'You must be hungry,' she said, setting a good brisk walking pace across the fields of Baur North. Her feet stepped instinctively over the rock roses and the gentians that littered the grass between the slabs of stone, but Turlough stumped along without looking where he was going. He *was* hungry, she thought. Men were invariably bad-tempered when hungry. It must be getting late.

In the distance the bell for evening compline came faintly through the air from the Cistercian abbey Sancta Maria Petris Fertilis, Saint Mary of the Fertile Rock, and automatically they both stopped and made the sign of the cross on forehead, breast and shoulders.

'The wind is in the north-east,' she said with satisfaction. 'You can hear the bell as if it were only a few fields away. That's a good wind for this time of year. We'll have a few fine days now. You'll have fine weather for your trip around the kingdom tomorrow and a good day's hunting on Saturday.'

'And that's Cahermacnaghten there in front of us,' he said a little more cheerfully.

Mara saw with satisfaction that smoke was rising from the Brehon's house a hundred yards away. King Turlough would have his dinner soon and then his ill humour would fade.

❈

The light was fading fast as they crossed the last field. The brilliant sunset colours of the western sky were beginning to merge into soft purples, pinks and misty yellows. The tiny white rock roses in the grykes glowed while the intensely blue gentians darkened in the fading light. By the time they went quietly through the gates of the Brehon's house the dim softness of a May night had fallen. A hundred yards away the ancient enclosure of Cahermacnaghten Law School, usually filled with exuberant young voices, was silent and empty. The Brehon's house was lit up, though, with candles glowing from each window. As Mara and Turlough walked up the path the rich heavy scent of the lilies on either side flooded over them.

'There'll be food for you two lads inside in the kitchen,' said the king genially over his shoulder and the two young bodyguards moved obediently towards the kitchen at the back of the house. Mara smiled. This was to be a tête-à-tête supper. She hoped that the food, the wine and the company would be up to his expectations. She herself would have preferred to linger a little longer in the garden. She looked around her wistfully. The white flowers flamed against the dark holly hedge and the nightjar called, his song a strange far-carrying purr on the still night air. Mara paused for a moment, and then walked on quietly after the king. He pushed open the door and then stood back to let her enter.

The room was illuminated with one tall candle, and its light was golden against the blue-white of the limewashed walls. Brigid had lit the fire with small rounded logs of apple wood and the scent filled the whole room. The table was spread with a snowy-white linen cloth and Mara's precious crystal glasses sparkled in the light. The wine had been poured into a tall flask that stood warming gently in the heat from the candle. Mara filled the two glasses and they glowed deep crimson in the firelight. She looked at them with pleasure. Her father, soon after the death of her mother, had gone on a pilgrimage to the Holy City of Rome and had brought back a case of Venetian glasses. They were among Mara's greatest treasures, only to be used on occasions like this. Fit for any king, she thought with satisfaction.

'Sit here by the fire and have a glass of wine while I go and see Brigid.' She placed an extra velvet cushion on the oaken bench by the fire and when he was safely ensconced, and could be trusted not to drop her precious glass, she handed him the wine.

The kitchen was full of fragrant smells when she went in. Brigid was bustling around; a small, sandy-haired woman in her fifties, she seemed to be always filled with boundless energy. The fire was burning brightly and the iron bars above it were covered with black pots of every size. Mara smiled a greeting at the two bodyguards seated at the table, each with a horn of ale in his hand, and then crossed the flagstoned floor over to the fire.

'That smells wonderful, Brigid.' The two ducks would be roasting in the large iron pot, she knew, but she did not worry about them. She took the lid off the small pot. Brigid was an excellent cook; if she had a weakness it was to under-flavour the sauce. Mara dipped the ladle into it and tasted, her eyes shut so that she could concentrate. The flavours were all there: juniper berries from the bushes that grew wild on the Burren, wine from France, a hint of spice from the East, a touch of mint fresh from the garden, all smoothly blended.

'Perfect,' she said, putting down the ladle. Brigid beamed with pleasure.

'Shall I serve now, Brehon?'

'Yes,' said Mara. 'We'll eat now. Enjoy your supper,' she said to the bodyguards.

'I wonder what's happening on Mullaghmore Mountain at this minute,' the king mused when she returned.

'They won't light the bonfire until midnight,' said Mara. 'They'll wait to hear the bell from the abbey first. It's always a great moment. We'll be able to see it from here. There should be a great blaze as the wood will be very dry after all this good weather. Come and sit at the table, Turlough. Brigid will be in with the food in a minute.'

Turlough obeyed and looked around him. 'Well, this is lovely, what a treat it is for me. Just you and me and no business to discuss, no treaties, no negotiations, just pure pleasure.'

'It's a treat for me, too,' said Mara softly. She had plenty of visitors; each *taoiseach* and his family were entertained in strict rotation, and then there were neighbours, friends, relations and the annual dinner for the priests of the kingdom; the conversation was enjoyable, but always careful, words counted and automatically weighed up, the consciousness of being Brehon always in her mind. Tonight was indeed going to be just pure pleasure.

'Here's the duck,' said Brigid, bustling in with two platters, each bearing half a duck. The skin was roasted to a glistening golden brown and the platters were heaped high with yellow fingers of roasted parsnips and dark green clusters of watercress.

'And here's Cumhal with the sauce,' she continued. Cumhal was Brigid's husband and the manager of Cahermacnaghten farm. He was always pressed into service on these state occasions and he always had the air of hating every minute of it. He bowed to the king awkwardly and Brigid impatiently took the small iron pot from him and ladled some sauce on to each platter. She waited expectantly while both Turlough and Mara cut a small piece of duck, speared it on the end of a knife and dipped it into the sauce.

'Delicious,' said Turlough with his mouth full.

'Quite perfect,' said Mara. She exchanged a warm glance with Brigid. Both of them loved cooking and both knew that a successful meal was the product not just of skill but also of luck. So many things could go wrong: the fire could falter at a crucial stage, the bird may not have been of the best, the vegetables might have had too much rain at an important stage in their growth. But tonight the food was superlative, Brigid knew it and so did Mara. The duck was mouth-wateringly good – crisp on the outside with that strange, astringent flavour of juniper berries on the skin, and then it was succulent and tender on the inside. The sauce was perfect – a combination of smooth, sharp, bittersweet flavours. And then there was the slight peppery bite of the watercress to freshen the mouth.

'Mara,' said Turlough solemnly after his plate had been cleared. He poured himself another glass of wine, tossed it back and then refilled her glass.

She swirled the wine, holding the glass up to the light of the fire, before taking a sip and savouring the first mouthful. The burgundy was as silkily smooth as velvet and smelled of black-berries in the hot sun.

'Yes,' she said gently.

'Here's the other duck,' said Brigid, entering after a perfunc-tory knock. 'I've been keeping it warm for you.'

This time the duck had been jointed, with the legs and wings on cushions of watercress forming a decorative border to the neat slices of breast meat. Mara took a slice of breast meat, more to please Brigid than because she was hungry, but Turlough piled his platter high again. He seemed to have forgotten what he was going to say and Mara did not remind him. The day had been long and she was content to sit quietly and savour her wine.

'Tell me about this new king of England, Henry VIII,' she said.

Turlough helped himself to a second leg from the duck and poured a generous allowance of the juniper sauce over it. 'He's eighteen years old. It's a great age – eighteen. I remember being eighteen. The world opens up in front of you.'

Mara nodded. She had passed her final examinations to be an *ollamh*, professor, of Brehon law when she was eighteen and yes, she did feel that the world was there, wide open in front of her, and that there was nothing she could not do.

'You see, his father, this Henry VIII's father, Henry VII, he had quite a struggle to establish himself because there had been a very long war, in England, between the clans of York and Lancaster.' He paused and poured himself some more wine. 'I don't rightly know all the ins and outs of it,' he confessed, 'but this Henry VII ended up as king of the whole of England and Wales and I think he built up the coffers of treasure in his city of London. He got taxes from all his people, and he spent little on wars. But now he's dead and this young man has inherited a kingdom and a coffer of treasure. So what do you think he will turn his mind to?'

'War?' suggested Mara. It was the sort of thing that young men of eighteen thought about, she supposed.

Turlough beamed. 'Yes, indeed,' he said. 'War and marriage! He will need a son to inherit and in England, as your young man Colman said, the eldest son inherits automatically even if he is only a baby. But I'm not worried about his possible marriage plans; I'm worrying about wars. You see, he won't want to start a war with France – England and France have had their war. It has been going on for a century or so. No one will want to start that up again. He will turn his thought to the west and he will be over here before we know where we are. Two hundred years ago the English had got as far west as Thomond; now they are mostly confined to an area around Dublin. Even the English lords who came and settled here a couple of hundred years ago are now more Irish than the Irish themselves. Look at Desmond! Look at Ormond!'

Mara thought about it. 'It would mean the end of our way of life if this happened, wouldn't it?' she said gravely. 'Still, perhaps it may not happen. Perhaps this young King Henry will get involved in his marriage plans and leave us alone.'

'Some cheese?' enquired Brigid, coming in with a platter of crusty brown rolls, each crowned with a slice of warm goat's cheese sprinkled with seeds of fennel. Turlough made a noise in the back of his throat that was like a greedy purr of anticipation. With a quick change of mood he poured himself another glass of wine and helped himself to some cheese.

'Well, it may not happen for a long time. I certainly hope I won't be around to see it. Have some cheese, will you?'

'Just that small one,' said Mara. She chewed thoughtfully, considering the problem of this young king and his possible designs on the rich grasslands and huge forests of her country.

Then she took a small bunch of watercress, fresh from the crystal-clear streams that ran down Slieve Elva, and dismissed the matter from her mind. She had long ago decided that she would never worry about matters far beyond her control.

'You're looking very lovely tonight, you know,' Turlough said after Brigid had disappeared again. He took a large bite of bread and washed it down with a gulp of wine.

'You will definitely have to climb to the top of Mullaghmore after all that,' said Mara, smiling indulgently at him. It was very pleasant to sit there and watch him enjoy the food. His eyes were full of admiration for her and she enjoyed that also.

'How long have we known each other?' the king asked thoughtfully.

'I suppose it must be about ten years now.' Mara thought back into the past. 'I attended your crowning at Magh Adhair under the great oak tree. That was after the death of your uncle. I suppose I had seen you before with him.' Turlough Donn had been *tánaiste*, heir, for a long time; she knew that. He had only been seven years old when his father died and first one of his uncles inherited and then another. He had been almost forty before his time had come.

Turlough continued to eat and said no more. The clatter of wooden sandals sounded outside the door.

'Would you like anything else, my lord?' asked Brigid, her face hopeful. This was always a great occasion for her. For weeks she would be in demand by her neighbours, relatives and friends, all anxious to know what the king ate, what he said, and whether he enjoyed his food. He did not fail her.

'Brigid,' he said solemnly. 'I haven't eaten such food since the last time that I was here. If your mistress would allow me, I would sit here and eat all night. One of these days I swear I will be stealing you and bringing you back to Thomond with me.'

Brigid beamed with delight as she picked up some of the

empty platters and took them out to the kitchen. She would treasure these words, and once again Mara thought what a wonderful man this King Turlough Donn was.

'Let's come and sit by the fire,' said Turlough, getting up and stretching. 'I don't believe I could eat another bite. Will you have some more wine?'

'Just a little,' said Mara. She rose and moved over to her cushioned bench by the fire. Turlough followed with the two glasses and sat beside her. It was not really a seat for two, but Mara found his bulk beside her strangely exciting. She relaxed slightly against him. Certainly the wine was extraordinarily good, she thought, as she took another sip.

'It's strong, this wine,' she warned and put her glass on the small table in front of them.

Turlough drained his glass, placed it beside hers, and then suddenly threw his two arms clumsily around her, drawing her tightly to his chest.

'Mara,' he whispered. 'I wonder, do you realize how much you mean to me?'

'Wait,' she said quickly, gently pushing him away. 'Brigid is coming.' She stood, moved away from him, and was quickly beginning to pile the remaining platters just as Brigid came in with the tray.

'I'll do that, Brehon,' she said. There was a note of suspicion in her voice as she looked at Mara and then at the king. Mara flushed and walked over to the window. Brigid and Cumhal had been in her father's service since she herself was a baby. Sometimes she felt that they could read her every thought.

'That was a wonderful meal, Brigid,' said Turlough hurriedly. He has forgotten that he has already said that, thought Mara with amusement. He just wants to get rid of her quickly. Brigid smiled modestly but her eyes continued to move rapidly between the king and her mistress, her sandy brows drawn together in a slight frown. How quick she is, thought Mara. She has already noticed something different.

'Another flagon of wine?' she asked, hospitably seating herself again beside the king. Brigid cleared the rest of the table and retired to the kitchen. No doubt she would, this moment, be whispering to Cumhal.

'I only need one thing to make me happy at the moment,' he said, putting his arms around her again. He's had too much wine, she thought, smiling with pleasure. Then a flash of light from outside made her stand up and go to the window again.

'Your two bodyguards can't have enjoyed their supper too much, they certainly didn't linger over it,' she said, watching the two bulky figures pacing up and down the dark road, swinging the pitch torches and sending arcs of light across the grey limestone.

'They're just worried about the O'Kellys,' said Turlough casually, his eyes following her gaze through the window.

'The O'Kellys?' she questioned. 'What . . .'

Then there was a knock on the door.

'Come in,' she called.

'My lord,' said Cumhal, hovering in the doorway. 'Your bodyguards want to know when you would like to be escorted back to the guest house. They have been out and they have checked the road and the fields.'

As her eyes grew accustomed to the dark, Mara could see them more clearly, one outside the window now, and the other out in the road, checking both ways. The interruption of the tête-à-tête may have been Brigid's idea, but this threat from the O'Kellys must be a very real one if the bodyguards were so concerned. She had not remembered this degree of security on the king's last visit. Obviously they would be uneasy until they got the king safely behind the huge walls and high locked gate of Cahermacnaghten. There would be no protection for him within her small house. Mara turned to face Turlough, who still sat there with a stubborn expression on his face.

'Sleep well, my lord,' she said formally. 'And may the blessed St Patrick guard you and keep you safe through the night.'

He kissed her, but without his usual exuberance and there was a shadow of something which she could not quite read or understand on his face. She felt oddly restless, oddly disturbed, when he left, closely followed by the bodyguards. She knew she should go into the kitchen and thank Brigid again for the meal, but instead she found herself going out into the garden and smelling the heavy scent of the sweet woodbine. It soothed her restlessness a little to walk there for half an hour among her flowers, pausing to pinch a clump of lavender or to slice through an aromatic needle of rosemary with her sharp nail. In the moonlight everything was peaceful and beautiful and yet still she felt agitated.

'We're off now, Brehon,' said Brigid, coming out of the house, Cumhal at her side, carrying her basket filled with pots and pans in one hand and a large key in the other. 'Is there anything else you need?'

'No, Brigid, I'll be going to bed soon, thank you for a delicious meal. Everything was perfect. Thanks to you, too, Cumhal. Good night to you both.'

Not yet midnight, thought Mara with a glance towards the great mountain of Mullaghmore. She could see some pinpricks of light from the terraces but these would only be from torches; once the bonfire was lit on the summit there would be no mistaking it. The noise of Cumhal and Brigid's footsteps ceased and everything seemed very still and very quiet. It was almost as if the whole stony land of the Burren had been emptied and she was left alone. She sat on the stone bench and thought about that strange look on Turlough's face. What had he been about to say?

In the distance, very faintly, she heard the bell from the abbey and then almost immediately there came the great flare of light

from the summit of Mullaghmore as the bonfire was lit. Once
again the people of the Burren, like their ancestors before them,
had celebrated the ancient festival of *Bealtaine*. She gazed at the
bonfire for a few minutes, wishing that she were there amid all the
fun and merriment.

And then there was a slam of a door. She sat up a little
straighter and turned her face towards the law school enclosure.
She knew that door. It was the door of the guest house. There
was the turning of a lock, a clang of the iron gate and the sound
of quick young footsteps coming down the road. She could see
the figure now; it was the younger of the two bodyguards. She
rose instantly and went down the path to the gate of her garden.

'The king has asked me to give you this, Brehon,' he said once
he reached her. He handed her a small roll of vellum.

'Thank you, Fergal,' she said calmly as she took it from him.
'Sleep well.'

Mara waited until the guard had gone back into the law school
enclosure before unrolling the vellum. The moonlight was strong
and the handwriting large and bold. She read the opening saluta-
tion and instantly she knew:

'*Mara a rúin*', Mara, my love.

She put down the scroll and stared for a moment across the
flat tableland towards the sacred mountain with its flaming summit. Then she took up the scroll again and read it through
carefully, but she didn't need to. Once she had read the opening
words, she had known what it would contain. He loved her; he
loved her and he wanted to marry her. She would be his queen.

SIX

The honour price of a Brehon is sixteen séts, or eight milch cows, or eight ounces of silver. A Brehon must be learned in seven main areas of legal knowledge:

1. Cáin mac ina téchta, *the law of sons*
2. Cáin manac, *the law of monks*
3. Cáin flatha, *the law of lordship*
4. Cáin lanamna, *the law of marriage*
5. Cáin cairdesa, *the law of kinship*
6. Cáin criche, *boundary law*
7. Cáin cairde, *the law of treaties between territories*

&

ARA LINGERED IN THE garden for some time, not touching the letter, but gazing at the leaping flames on the distant eastern skyline. Eventually she went to her bedroom. She undressed slowly and thoughtfully, but knew she would not sleep. Her mind was busy with the surprising proposal from the king.

She would consider it; he had asked her to promise him that. He had vowed to give her all the time she wanted to think about her answer and he had promised not to press her, not even to mention the subject until she brought it up. This marriage would have much to offer her; she knew that. She was fond of him, perhaps even loved him, and she was honest enough with herself to realize that she liked men of power. Her brief marriage of a few years had given her a distaste for being dominated by one whom she regarded as inferior to her, but she had enjoyed lovemaking and realized now that this had been missing from her hard-working life. If she became the wife of King Turlough Donn she would have love, mental stimulus, status in the eyes of the world, she would be one of his Brehons; he had promised that also. And he would listen to her views. What could she throw on to the other side of the scales? Autonomy, freedom, the easy companionship of the independently minded people of the Burren, and the care, the education of intelligent boys, entrusted to her by their parents. Mara smiled. The scales were unevenly weighted.

Pulling her cloak over her shift, she went over to the window. The small panes of glass, set into their strips of lead, were opaque in the dim light. She pulled up the iron latch, pushed open one window and leaned her head against the sun-warmed stone of the mullion between the two windows. It was now quite dark, but the moon was full and its light picked out the veins of silver in the moon-whitened rocks of the Aillwee hill to the north.

Over in the east, she could see the orange glow from the top of Mullaghmore. The bonfire was beginning to die down; there were no more leaping flames or showers of sparks. There were flashes of light from pitch torches all over the Burren. Many people would be on their way home now, although most would stay until dawn. She hoped that her scholars were among those coming home. A yellow gleam came from a small window in the cottage at Caheridoola; Daniel must be home, and his beautiful daughter, Emer, also. Emer had had her evening of escape with Roderic; soon must come her marriage with Colman. That was probably Rory now, she thought, crossing the clints on his way to Dooneybharden, the fort, or *dún*, of the bard. Bards had always lived there from the time that she was a child, and it seemed as if, when one bard died, another wandering bard came to fill the empty cottage. No law, no settlement deeds, no *tánaiste*, or heir, just a simple filling of an empty space like a badger finding an empty set.

Where are those boys? she wondered anxiously. Colman should know I would not allow them to stay late. There was a torch now crossing Baur North. It looked too steady, though, for the law scholars and there were none of the usual shouts and laughter. Colman could not have subdued them to that extent. He might have been able to frighten the little ones, but Fachtnan and Enda would be unlikely to let him silence them completely.

The footsteps were audible now, though, and, yes, there were many sets of boots tramping across the stone clints. She leaned a little further out of the window. Still no voices, but certainly many heavy footsteps. Mara went back into the room and struck a light from her tinderbox. The king had given her a present of the new sulphur sticks, but she preferred her tinderbox. She lit the candle by her bed and carried it over to the window. Its light would not help her to see; it could not possibly reach the fields, but Colman would see that she was awake and would come to report. She could see them now, their shadows black against the silver of the stone pavements. She could not count the heads but there seemed to be a large number. She leaned a little further out of the window. They were clambering over the wall – not vaulting, not pushing and shoving, but scaling it like middle-aged men. She could see the heads now, and rapidly she began to count. Only four tall figures, she thought, feeling puzzled, and then, with a sigh of relief, two small ones. At least Hugh and Shane were safe.

'Colman,' she called softly. One head detached itself and came towards the Brehon's house. The others stayed by the side of the road. Mara frowned. This was not Colman, but Fachtnan; there was no mistaking the rough, dark bushy curls. She waited until he had pushed the gate open and had come up the path towards her window.

'Colman did not come back with us, Brehon,' he said quietly before she could question him. 'He said that you had given him leave to visit his parents.'

'Yes, but...' Mara stopped. She had to keep to her own rule never to undermine Colman in front of the scholars. 'Are you all safe? And did you have a good time?' she added.

'Yes, thank you, Brehon,' he said. 'We had a good time and we are all here, and all safe.'

She frowned in puzzlement. Fachtnan would normally not have been able to resist the temptation to tease her with stories of how many wolves they had fought off and how Shane had been plucked at the very last moment from the bonfire and Hugh almost carried off by a golden eagle. He was a boy who loved fun, but now his voice was empty of all emotion.

'Make sure that no one makes a noise going in,' she said eventually. 'The king and his bodyguards are in the guest house. If Brigid and Cumhal have a light on in their house, just whisper at the window that you are all safe. Are you sure that all of you are all right?'

'Yes, thank you, Brehon.' Again Fachtnan's voice was toneless and heavy.

'Tell the lads that they can sleep in tomorrow morning – this morning, I mean,' she said. 'I'll tell Brigid to call everyone at about nine or half past nine.'

He murmured goodnight and went back to join the others, who were waiting patiently in a cluster by the gate to the law school. Mara waited by the window until she saw them all go through the gates and heard the sound of the latch of the scholars' house click closed. How dare Colman do that? How dare he abandon the scholars? Perhaps someone offered him a lift in a cart to Galway the following morning, and he went home with them. This gives me a great excuse to get rid of him, she thought gleefully. I can always say that I could never trust him again since he betrayed my trust that night of *Bealtaine*. She took off her night-robe and slipped into bed, shivering slightly at the coolness of the linen sheets. She did not give another thought to the king's surprising proposal.

❋

Despite the late night, Mara rose early as usual. She thought about writing up her notes about judgement day, but the morning was too beautiful to waste. She loved May, loved the way the days lengthened and grew warmer. The sun was already high above Mullaghmore and the great mountain seemed to glow in the morning light with a mysterious soft blue, the spiralling terraces making it seem like a fairy castle from one of the beautifully painted books that she had once seen at the abbey. Mara set to work with energy. She had a new plan for her riverbed of gentians. Most of the gentians she had in her garden were of that intense dark blue, but some were as pale as harebells. She went along the bed with a sharply pointed trowel and dug the pale-coloured flowers up, placing them in a willow basket filled with cool damp soil.

'Cumhal,' she called, seeing Brigid's husband come back from milking her cows. 'Cumhal, could you spare a moment? Could you just get your mallet and pulverize this rock for me, this big flat one at the end of the flowerbed. I just want to make a bit of a hollow in it so as I can put some of those pale blue gentians in here. That's if you are not too busy,' she ended politely. She always tried to keep in mind that probably Cumhal privately believed that a garden used for anything other than vegetables was a strange piece of eccentricity.

'I'll get it straight away,' he said obligingly and was back in a few minutes balancing the heavy iron mallet in one hand. 'Brigid said to tell you that the lads are up and having their breakfast,' he said.

'Really!' Mara was astonished. After a late night she would have thought they would have been happy to sleep in. 'Just there, Cumhal, right in the centre, just make it look natural.'

The limestone split easily and a few blows of the mallet made a good deep hollow. Mara looked at it with satisfaction.

'Perfect. Thanks, Cumhal,' she said. She cast a quick con-science-stricken glance at the law school, but there were very few sounds coming from it. Brigid could handle them for another five minutes. Quickly she scraped the soil from the basket into the hollow and then carefully planted the pale blue gentians in an irregular circle. Now it looked like a pool of pale blue, almost as if the river of deep blue had splashed some of its water on top of the grey rock. She gazed at it with satisfaction for a moment and then rose to her feet and dusted the earth from her fingers.

'Tell Brigid I will be over once I have washed my hands,' she said.

❉

The boys were very quiet, very quiet and very docile, sitting up straight on their benches in the schoolroom, and answering all the questions earnestly. They were all pale, she noticed. Hugh had heavy black shadows under his eyes and Shane was biting his nails nervously. She would give them a couple of hours' work, she decided, and then release them for the rest of the day. Perhaps it was just the late night. Perhaps they would all be back to normal after the weekend.

'Shane, what is the crime of *fingal*?'

'The crime of *fingal* is the worst crime of all, Brehon,' recited Shane, rising to his feet politely. 'The wisdom texts say that it strikes at the heart of society. The crime of *fingal* is the slaying of a member of your kin-group. The punishment for *fingal* is to be placed in a boat with no oars and to be cast out to sea. If God spares the life of the murderer, he or she can never come back to the kingdom again, but must live out their life as a *cu glas*, a grey dog, or outcast.'

'Well done,' said Mara heartily. 'Fachtnan, what are the twelve doors of the soul?'

'The twelve doors of the soul, Brehon,' said Fachtnan, rising slowly to his feet and tugging at his black thatch of hair, 'are twelve spots on the body where it is dangerous to hit a man. One of them is ...' He looked around for inspiration. Aidan was making gulping sounds and Fachtnan's face brightened in gratitude. 'One of them is the Adam's apple,' he said quickly, 'and the others are ... the navel ... and the ...' He looked around, but no further help seemed to be forthcoming. All faces were blank, blank and worried.

'Well, perhaps we'll get out *Bretha Déin Chécht* and go over that again on Monday,' said Mara, ignoring a groan from Enda. *Bretha Déin Chécht* was a weighty tome full of obscure medical facts; most law students dreaded it. She looked around at the tired faces and she resolved to end by giving each boy one more question and then let them have a break. A game of hurling might wake them up. She left Hugh until the last – the boy looked ill, she thought. If he weren't any better by Monday she would ask Malachy to have a look at him. In the meantime she would give him the easiest question that she could think of, something that he would be bound to know.

CORA HARRISON

'Hugh,' she said gently, 'what is the word for the fine that is paid for a killing?'

He stared at her and his face flooded crimson. What was the matter with him? He must know the word *éraic*; it was one of the first things that they all learned.

'Can you help him, Shane?'

Shane's face went white as he got to his feet. He looked at Hugh and then turned away quickly. The other boys stirred uncomfortably. Fachtnan stared out of the window, Enda shook his blond mop over his face and Aidan chewed a fingernail. Shane dropped his long black eyelashes over his blue eyes. His hands, noticed Mara, were clenched tightly behind his back. Nevertheless, he finally managed to answer steadily.

'The word is *éraic*, Brehon.'

'Very good,' said Mara encouragingly. There was no point in asking them what was wrong, she thought. Boys were funny creatures and they would all stick together. She would talk to Fachtnan afterwards, and perhaps to Shane. Shane would know what was wrong with Hugh, though he might not want to say. She looked out of the window. There was no sign of anyone stirring from the guest house – the king obviously still slept, but by now the sun was rising high in the sky.

'Why don't you all have a game of hurling before the weather gets too hot?' she suggested. 'Then, after you have had your dinner, you can have a few hours' rest. You can study your Latin in the cool of the evening.'

She had expected a cheer and was ready to hush them but they rose to their feet and filed out quietly. After a moment, Fachtnan returned.

'Brehon,' he said. 'Brigid said to tell you that Diarmuid from Baur North is here to see you. He said that if you are busy he will come back another day.'

Outside Diarmuid was striding up and down, looking like a

81

dog who is deciding whether to make a break for freedom. He was a nice man, a decent, hard-working man, but a silent, self-contained one. He clearly had something on his mind and this was causing him great distress. The atmosphere of the schoolhouse would inhibit him.

'Run and tell him that I am coming, Fachtnan,' she said. 'And then go into the kitchen and get two cups of ale and some oatcakes. I'll take him over to the garden in my house and then we won't be disturbed by you lads playing hurling.'

Let them wake up the king if they liked, she thought with a glance at the height of the sun as she hurried under the stone lintel that spanned the entrance to the law school. He has slept long enough. She was probably in bed later than he was and she had been up since seven!

'Diarmuid,' she greeted him. 'Have breakfast with me in my garden. I got immersed in my flowers this morning and forgot to feed myself. The lads are tired and not feeling like work so I gave them a little break. Thank you, Brigid, I'll take the tray.'

When they reached the garden, Diarmuid accepted the cup of ale and an oatcake thankfully. He seemed glad of a few moments' pause before he had to divulge what he had come for. She looked at him carefully. This was not just his normal diffidence. He looked like a man who had lain awake all night and then come to a difficult decision. She would not rush him, but she would not let him go until he had emptied his mind of the matters that troubled him so much. She took an extra oatcake herself so as to fill the silence with companionable munching. I shouldn't do that, she thought idly, I'm beginning to put on weight for the first time in my life. She held out the wooden platter to Diarmuid.

He hesitated, then shook his head and shrugged the loose sleeves of his *léine* into place. His face had the look of a man who had just resolved to dive into the icy depths of a lake.

'Brehon,' he said. 'I wanted to talk to you about young Colman, your assistant.'

She was startled but tried not to show it. 'Yes, Diarmuid, what about him?'

He looked all around the quiet garden. 'He's not here, is he?'

'No,' she said. 'I gave him permission to go to Galway to tell his family about his betrothal to Emer.' A rush of anger went through her again when she thought of how he had abandoned her scholars in the middle of the night. What had he done to Diarmuid? Some sneer, some piece of rudeness, no doubt.

'Well, you see,' said Diarmuid, 'I got talking to Lorcan last night. He was telling me that he might find it a bit difficult to pay me the fine.'

'Go on,' she said. A half-smile came to her lips – she had thought Lorcan would get around the soft-hearted Diarmuid. But what had Colman to do with this?

Diarmuid gulped in air hungrily and then went on, speaking quickly. 'You see, Lorcan has no money – no money at all. He gets some silver, like us all, from selling his butter at Kilfenora and Noughaval markets, but he has nothing left. As soon as he gets any silver he has to pay it to Colman.'

'But why? Why does he pay it to Colman?'

'Well, not to put too fine a point on the matter,' said Diarmuid bluntly, 'young Colman has been blackmailing him for the past few months.'

Mara stiffened and stared at him.

'Lorcan . . . I don't know if you noticed this, but Lorcan has a few fine white calves,' continued Diarmuid. 'He keeps them in the field behind his house, the one with the hawthorn hedge. He'll be able to sell them soon. They are the best cattle that he ever had.'

'Did he steal them?'

Diarmuid shook his head. 'He didn't steal them, but he

borrowed the O'Lochlainn's white bull when two of his cows were bulling. Well, Colman found out – I don't know how, but he is always sneaking about and listening and prying into people's affairs – well, he found out and he threatened that he would tell the O'Lochlainn unless Lorcan paid him some silver. Lorcan agreed. You know what the O'Lochlainn is like about going to law over everything, and, of course, Lorcan should not have done this; I told him that. He had no right to use another man's bull without paying him.'

Mara nodded absent-mindedly. It was true that very few judgement days went by when Ardal O'Lochlainn did not bring a case against a neighbour, and it was typical of Lorcan to try to get something without paying for it, but her mind was not on either of those men. She was filled with anger and disgust. She was responsible for Colman. He had been a scholar from early boyhood at her law school; he had access to all of her documents – now she remembered with horror that he was forever tidying the shelves full of judgement texts in the big oak press in the schoolhouse. What information might he have gleaned from these? Was he blackmailing anyone else?

Suddenly she remembered Lorcan's words. *I'm a very poor man, Brehon. The young master here knows that,* he had said with a meaningful glance at Colman. She should have guessed that something was going on.

'I'll hear this case at Poulnabrone,' she said rapidly. 'Colman shall pay back all of that silver to Lorcan.'

'Well,' said Diarmuid cautiously, 'I'm not sure that would suit Lorcan. He would not want the O'Lochlainn to know about the bull. I think the best thing would be for you to have a word with young Colman and put a stop to this.'

He looked at her furious face and said hesitantly, 'I wouldn't be surprised if he were blackmailing some other people, as well. No one would speak of it, but there may be others. I saw him talking to Muiris last night and I heard Muiris shout at him. I've never seen Muiris look so angry.'

'I'll speak to the king about this,' said Mara decisively. 'If necessary, I myself will bring a case against him! One thing is certain: I will not have the law broken in this kingdom. And broken by my own assistant!'

SEVEN

Urairecht Becc (small primer)

All physicians have an honour price of eight séts, four milch cows, or four ounces of silver.

Three things give nemed, professional status to a physician:

   1. A complete cure

   2. Leaving no blemish

   3. A painless examination

⁂⁂

THE FROST SPARKLED ON the grass when Mara looked out of her window as the abbey bell went for prime on Saturday morning. A young fox in the field, his ears enormous and bat-like, and his back still covered in the grey downy fur of a young cub, hesitated, attracted by the movement at her window, and then bounded merrily away, scattering frozen drops of dew. The swallows were already hard at work, swooping in and out of the barn, ceaselessly feeding the future lords of the air. The air was cool and clean and the north-easterly breeze blew the sharp woodsmoke scent of bluebells from the hazel wood. The mountain of Mullaghmore was sharply etched in pale blue on the skyline.

'It will be fine today, Bran,' said Mara happily as the great wolfhound rose from his wicker basket at the end of her bed and stretched and yawned. This day of hunting would be a special day for him. It would do the lads good, also, she thought, and it would give her time to think about how she would cope with the problem of Colman.

Yesterday, once the midday meal was over, Mara and King Turlough Donn had toured the farms on the Burren and stayed for supper with Ardal O'Lochlainn at Lissylisheen. It had been late when they arrived back at the law school. No more had been said about his surprising offer of marriage. The king would keep his word and give her time to make up her mind. Mara had thought of confiding her worries about Colman to him as they rode home but she had been unwilling to break the atmosphere of friendship and easy happiness that existed between the two of them. Tomorrow night, she told herself, tomorrow night I will talk to him about Colman. There was no easy solution; she could not simply transfer the young man to Corcomroe or to Thomond. He was too flawed, too corrupt for that. The problem that Colman posed needed to be addressed as soon as he returned on Sunday night.

'The lads are brighter this morning, Brehon,' said Brigid, meeting Mara at the door and raising her voice to be heard above the raucous shouts from within.

'They're certainly noisier,' said Mara dryly, but she felt a flood of relief. Perhaps she needn't have worried; boys of that age were often moody. The intense long-drawn-out studies at the law school put a great strain on them. Her thoughts drifted to young Feirdin. Her last sight of him had been of a solitary figure making his way up the mountainside, stooping from time to time to pick up a piece of rock, or to study a stone. Hopefully he had a good evening watching all that went on. Obviously there had been no trouble or she would have heard by now.

'Come on, Bran,' she said and went into the kitchen house. The boys had eaten a big meal – the porridge pot was empty, as was the platter for oatcakes and there was a well-scraped-out pot of honey on the table. They rose politely and wished her the blessing of God, but the voices still sounded constrained and as they filed out into the open air she noticed again how pale and hollow-eyed they looked. They were making an effort to appear normal, she thought, and this alarmed her even more than anything else. At this age they seldom worried about saving the feelings of others; if they were unhappy they let the world know about it.

'*Dia's muire agat, a thirgene,*' they all chorused as the door to the guest house opened, across the stone-flagged yard. Mara turned to greet King Turlough Donn. He was looking well, she thought affectionately. His sunburned face was glowing and his eyes were bright with excitement.

'Have you had a good breakfast?' she called as she went to meet him.

'I have, indeed,' he said, greeting her with his customary kiss. His hands held hers for a moment. He won't take no for an answer easily, she thought.

'Where are we meeting Murrough and the dogs?' he went on.

'By Poulnabrone. Murrough's place, Cathair Chaisleáin, is on the cliff behind the dolmen. We'll walk,' she added firmly. 'It's only a couple of miles and there is no sense in taking the horses and leaving them tied up all day. The howling of the wolves might upset them.'

The six boys went ahead of the four adults and they were already at the dolmen by the time Mara, the king and the two bodyguards reached the last field of Baur North. She could see Murrough coming down the steep narrow hillside path from

Cathair Chaisleáin, accompanied by a pack of wolfhounds. The quiet cool air of the early morning was filled with their excited barking. Bran barked back; he knew them all well.

'Here you are, my lord, there's a great hunting dog for you,' said Murrough breathlessly, handing over a large grey wolfhound to the king, 'and here's one each for your bodyguards, for Fergal and for Conall. I'm afraid that the scholars will have to share. I've only got three more to spare.'

'That's fine,' said Mara. 'Fachtnan, you take Hugh, Enda you take Shane, Moylan and Aidan you go together.' Normally she would have put Shane, as the youngest, into the care of Fachtnan, but she was worried about Hugh and Fachtnan was not only the eldest, but also the most gentle of the boys. She saw him look quickly at Hugh and there was a comforting reassurance in the way that he took Hugh's smaller hand into his own large one and then handed the leash of the wolfhound to him.

'I had a word with Fiachra at *Bealtaine* night and he took his sheep off the mountain first thing yesterday morning. He said that he didn't see a sight or a sound of a wolf while he was doing it,' said Murrough. 'They'll be back by today, though.'

'There's no fear of any other sheep being on the mountain?' asked Mara. 'I know your dogs don't chase sheep, but if there were some in lamb they might frighten them and make them drop their lambs.'

'No, all of the lambing sheep are down in the valleys or in barns by now,' said Murrough. 'Fiachra just had some hoggets on the mountain. No one would have the lambing ewes up there – not with the prices that you can get for wool these days. Most people will be shearing today or tomorrow if this weather keeps up.'

'Where shall we try first?' asked the king, warily eyeing the 1,800 feet of the mountain. 'They won't have gone up to the top yet, will they?'

'Well, I thought we might split up when we get to the first terrace,' said Murrough. 'Each try a different direction; the dogs will let us know when they get a scent and then we can release them.'

The great dogs climbed effortlessly and the humans clung on to the leashes and panted. The sun was rising and the limestone mountain glinted.

'Hot, isn't it?' said Turlough Donn, leaning back heavily to stop his dog while he fumbled in his pouch for a fine linen handkerchief to wipe his sweating forehead.

'My dog is better trained than yours so I am getting more exercise than you,' said Mara with mock concern. 'Would you like to swap? You'd get more exercise with Bran. He wouldn't pull as much as Murrough's dog so you would have to do more climbing.'

'No, thank you! Anyway, you are younger than I am and used to this sort of thing. You wouldn't believe the number of hours I have to spend sitting listening to all my Brehons, and my poets, and then there is all the entertaining of guests and the meals and wine and mead. I can do with this sort of exercise, I suppose.'

'Come any time, my lord,' said Murrough enthusiastically. 'There's nowhere like the Burren for good sport like this.'

'Hugh and I are going to try Wolf's Lair,' shouted back Fachtnan, who had just reached the first terrace.

'Take care,' called Mara but she was not really worried. Wolf's Lair was, in fact, just a hollow on the side of the mountain; it may once have been the lair of a wolf, but she had been up there hundreds of times and had never seen a sign of one there.

Now there was a great scramble for the other boys to reach the first terrace and to shout out their destinations. Mara smiled indulgently as they all went in different directions. She sensed a certain relief of tension in the young voices. They would enjoy their morning, after all.

'Slip the leash as soon as your dog picks up the scent,' yelled Murrough.

'Come on, my lord,' said Mara teasingly. 'You have the best dog. Don't hold him back.'

'I'll slip the leash as soon as I reach the terrace,' grunted the king. 'He'll do better on his own.'

'The first one to catch a wolf will have the fur for a cloak,' yelled Murrough.

'Murrough does a great trade in fur-lined cloaks,' said Mara to the king. 'Sorcha's husband, Oisín, sells them for him in Galway. He . . .' Then she stopped. Bran was jerking her forward; that was not like him. He was very well trained.

'What's the matter, Bran?' she asked. He was whining now and scenting the air, his quivering nose pointing in the direction of Wolf's Lair. Mara grasped a rough projecting point of rock and hauled herself on to the first terrace. She could see everyone except Fachtnan and Hugh who were hidden by an outcrop of rock, but Bran was whimpering and pulling in that direction. Mara held him for a minute, straining her ears for a cry, but there was none. She looked down at Bran. There was something very wrong with him, she knew. He looked at her and there was fear, or a sort of agony of apprehension, in his eyes. He was not hurt; his breathing had hardly quickened. This was something different.

Then, quite suddenly, Bran sat back on his haunches, threw back his head and howled. The howl reverberated through the air, bouncing back from the stone terraces. And then the other wolfhounds took up the sound and the air was soon filled with the noise.

'They've scented,' shouted the king.

'No,' said Murrough. 'Don't release them yet. That was just Bran set them off. That's not the noise they would make. They would bark. There's something wrong.'

'I'm releasing Bran,' said Mara with decision. 'Hold the other dogs until I see what's wrong.' She bent down and unfastened the leash. 'Off you go, boy,' she said, and he was gone almost before the words were out of her mouth.

Mara followed as quickly as she could but Bran was out of sight in a second. Then, to her relief, she heard Fachtnan's voice.

'Bran,' he shouted.

'Bran,' came Hugh's high voice.

Mara's heart slowed down. They were both safe, but the puzzling thing was that Bran seemed to have gone ahead of them. She could hear Fachtnan shouting to his dog. 'Lugha, wait,' he kept yelling. The dog was trying to follow Bran and Fachtnan was trying to hold him. Mara climbed as fast as she could and had just rounded the rock outcrop when she saw Fachtnan bend down and release his wolfhound. Bran was still howling – it sounded as if he had reached Wolf's Lair – and then a second howl joined his as the other dog joined him. The short hairs on the back of Mara's neck seemed to stiffen. The noise was like something from another world.

Fachtnan had stopped now. His face was white and his arm was around Hugh's shoulders. Hugh was crying, but Mara did not stop to comfort him. She had to see what it was that made Bran howl like that. Quickly she brushed past them and climbed, using toes and fingernails, and exerting every muscle in her body, heedless of pain and exhaustion.

Huge, gleaming chunks of sharp-edged limestone lay about Wolf's Lair, but goats had sheltered for thousands of years between the rocks, and their droppings had fertilized the broken stone and made a small garden filled with exquisite flowers: delicate butterfly orchids, tiny dark blue gentians, late violets, white rock roses and tall purple butterwort on the sunny south-facing side, and delicate spirals of round-leaved maidenhair ferns on the shady north side.

There were no goats there on that Saturday morning, 2 May

1509. There were no wolves either, but there was a man. The man lay curled up on the ground. He was slightly built, fair-haired, with delicate, hardly distorted features. He was wearing a saffron *léine* and his cloak was pinned with a heavy, ornate silver brooch. That was not the only piece of silver on him. For a moment Mara thought Colman was sleeping and then she noticed the silver jewel-studded handle of a knife protruding from the back of his neck.

❄

Mara took two steps forward and then sank to her knees. The crinkled edges of the water-worn limestone pierced the fine linen of her gown and jabbed into the soft flesh of her knees. She was glad of the discomfort; it distracted her from the sickness that welled up within her. For a moment she had been afraid that she might faint. She stayed very still for a moment, her eyes closed, and then she opened them. She allowed the tears to well up and to run down her cheeks.

Colman had been one of the first students to come to her law school after she had become Brehon of the Burren. She had known him as a five-year-old child, as an adolescent, and then as a man. And now he was dead. She reached out blindly and her hand found Bran's comforting bulk beside her.

'Hush,' she said softly, her hand automatically stroking Bran's head, smoothing down the hackles along his spine and trying to quieten the muted howl that still emerged from him. Resolutely she wiped the tears from her cheeks and stood up. Yes, the man was Colman; but the silver knife was Hugh's.

Mara's mind and heart seemed to split into two. She had to mourn Colman; she had to mourn him and to find his murderer, but first she had to care for Hugh. The dog, Lugha, had returned to Murrough so she slipped the leash on to Bran and turned away, her mind automatically checking through everything that she would have to do that day. It took her only a few minutes until she was back with Fachtnan and Hugh.

'You knew about Colman?' she said to Fachtnan, drawing Hugh to her side.

Fachtnan quailed under her look, but said nothing.

'I told him,' said Hugh. 'I told them all. I told them to say nothing.'

Mara shot Fachtnan a glance and he coloured up to the edge of his thatch of thick curly hair.

'You knew he was dead?' she asked. 'You all knew?'

'We thought that someone else would find him,' said Fachtnan quickly. 'We couldn't believe it when no news came yesterday. So we thought we should . . .' His voice trailed away.

Mara considered this; it was a likely story. They probably did think that someone else would find him; that they would not have to bear the responsibility of reporting this killing. And why didn't someone find him? Almost everyone would have passed Wolf's Lair on the way back down the mountain.

Mara sat herself on a rock and drew Hugh towards her. She had a sudden impulse to take him on her lap, but she resisted it. He was small for his age, but he was twelve and she had to consider his dignity. She patted the rock beside her and he sat down. He already looked a little better, as if a weight had been taken from him.

'Brehon,' came Murrough's voice. 'Is everything all right?'

'Hold all the dogs, Murrough,' she called back. 'Keep them there with you. I'll be down in a minute.'

'Now, Hugh,' she said urgently. 'Tell me the truth as quickly as you can. You know the law. You know that no child under fourteen can be punished for a crime. If you admit everything now, your father will pay the fine to Colman's family.'

'I didn't kill him, Brehon,' said Hugh hopelessly.

'Hugh,' said Mara earnestly, 'if you don't admit to the murder it is classified as a secret and unlawful killing and the fine is double what it would have been. You know that, Hugh, so tell the truth now.'

'He didn't kill him, Brehon,' said Fachtnan. 'He told me that he was nowhere near when it happened.'

'But your knife is in him, Hugh!'

'I know, but I didn't kill him. He took my knife. He took it as soon as we started to climb the mountain. He had it in his hand.'

Mara frowned. Perhaps this was the truth. Perhaps Colman had confiscated it.

'We met Hugh at the bottom of the mountain after everything was over, Brehon,' said Fachtnan. 'He was crying. He told me that Colman ordered him to wait for him while he talked with some people. Eventually, after the bonfire was lit and everything, Hugh went to look for him and he saw him, and he saw his own knife sticking out of the side of his neck and he guessed that he was dead. He touched him and then he knew for sure. He wasn't breathing. And then he panicked and started to run down the mountain. And he told us the whole story when we met him. He was upset,' finished Fachtnan. 'I thought we'd better get home as quickly as possible.'

'All right, now let's go down,' said Mara. Hugh's full story could wait. Now she had to get the body off the mountain as quickly as possible. The rites of the church and the law would have to be observed. She got to her feet with a quick last glance of enquiry at Hugh. He did not respond.

He was a tense boy, over-indulged by his wealthy father who, nevertheless, laid the burden of his great expectations on his child's shoulders. His mother's death had made Hugh very dependent on his father. Hugh would not want to do anything that would jeopardize his father's affection, so confession would be difficult for him. Boys younger than Hugh had killed. She had known of cases. This was a warlike society. If, for some reason, Colman had dropped the knife and then bent to pick it up, Hugh could have forestalled him, snatched the knife and slashed Colman across the back of the neck. She would try one last appeal.

'Hugh, will you swear to me on your father's honour, that you did not kill Colman?' she asked, looking at him intently.

He did not hesitate but said solemnly, 'I swear on the honour of my father's face that I had nothing to do with Colman's secret and unlawful killing, Brehon.'

'Let's go, then,' said Mara, grasping the edge of the rock and lowering herself down. Hugh and Fachtnan followed her.

When they reached the first terrace the king came striding over to Mara, reaching up a hand and bracing her for the last step down on to the flat, rocky surface.

'What's the matter?' he asked, clearly relieved to see her.

Mara turned and faced them, the king and his two bodyguards, the four law school scholars, Murrough and the eight narrow hairy faces of the wolfhounds.

'Colman, my assistant, is dead. He is lying up there in Wolf's Lair. I'd say that he has been dead since Thursday night.'

'Dead!' echoed Murrough. Turlough Donn said nothing, but his blue eyes narrowed and the smile disappeared from his genial face. He put out his hand and took hers. It was only when she felt his warmth that she realized how cold she had become on this hot morning. She left her hand within his for a moment and then withdrew it. She could not indulge in any weakness for the moment. There was too much for her to do. She looked around. Everyone was looking at her, waiting for her instructions. She went through her list of tasks.

'I think we'll have to postpone the wolf hunt,' she said firmly. 'Murrough, I think you had better take the wolfhounds home. Fachtnan, Hugh and Shane will go with you to help you with them, if that is all right by you?'

Murrough nodded mutely. He looked shocked.

'Fachtnan, take Shane and Hugh back to Cahermacnaghten when Murrough has no further use for you. Wait there until I come.'

'Moylan, you fetch Malachy the physician,' she continued. 'Enda, go to Glenslade Castle and ask Donogh O'Lochlainn to send some men and a leather litter to get the body down from the mountain. Ask him, also, if we could borrow a cart to take the body back to Colman's mother and father. Donogh knows the Lynch family.

'Aidan, go and fetch Father Conglach. He will want to give the last rites to the body.' She briefly remembered that Aidan had been in some sort of trouble with Father Conglach, so Father Conglach might decide to ignore his summons, but then dismissed that from her mind. Aidan was the least reliable of all the boys and she didn't care whether Father Conglach arrived or not – the other tasks were of more importance.

'Now, all of you,' she said emphatically, 'when you have finished your errands, return to Cahermacnaghten. Go now, make haste, but go carefully. We don't want any more accidents.' And if that left Murrough thinking that it was an accident, that would be all to the good, she thought. He was a nice man, but a terrible one for gossip. Her own lads, she knew, would say nothing. Their loyalty to each other was that of brothers. No one would want to implicate Hugh.

'My lord,' she said formally to the king. 'I regret the spoiling of your day of pleasure. You may wish to go straight back to Thomond.'

Turlough Donn shook his head. 'No, Mara, I'll stay here with you,' he said with the easy charm which was part of the man, but behind the words there was an iron core of support and Mara was grateful.

'Let's go up and have another look,' he suggested when they

and the two bodyguards were left alone on the terrace. 'We'll leave Fergal and Conall here. They'll let us know if anyone is coming.'

He reached out a hand to her again and she took it. She felt rather ashamed, but his hand was very welcome at that moment. His grasp was warm and firm and her legs had begun to tremble again. Without a word they scrambled up the steep cliff to Wolf's Lair. Bran followed behind, but now he was mute, inured to the fact that one of his pack was lying dead on the mountainside.

Mara immediately crossed the small space and knelt beside Colman's body. 'Poor child,' she said pityingly, reaching down to smooth the fair hair from the pallid forehead. 'You know, he was unfortunate. He was gifted – I don't think I have ever had a student who learned as well as he did – but he was never at ease, never happy with himself. Perhaps he never had enough; he valued money, valued goods, too much. He thought that they would make him happy, but they didn't; they only made him want something more.'

'Why was he killed, do you think?' asked Turlough Donn, watching her closely.

'I think he was killed because he got too greedy,' said Mara, staring down at the ornate hilt of Hugh's silver knife sticking out from the thin neck of the young man.

'Too greedy?' echoed the king.

'Blackmail, I think,' said Mara. Briefly she told him Diarmuid's story about Lorcan and the secret borrowing of the white bull.

'That's a very fine knife,' said the king, looking down at the body. 'It should be easy to trace the man who owned a knife like that.'

'I'm afraid,' said Mara bleakly after a few minutes' thought, 'that the knife was his own. I think that Colman owned it at the time of his death.' It was not a complete lie, she thought; Colman had perhaps owned it if Hugh had been forced to give it to him. She did not wish to mention Hugh's name even to someone she trusted as much as the king.

Turlough Donn frowned, looking closely into her face, but he did not question her further. He knows me well, she thought. He even knows when I am not telling the full truth; not many people have ever been able to read me as well as that. She resolutely turned her face away from Turlough Donn.

Hugh was of more importance to her now than any king, than any lover. She had to protect him until she knew the whole truth. During her fifteen years as Brehon of the Burren she had learned to keep her own counsel, to trust only herself and to politely exclude all others from her thought processes. She got to her feet decisively.

'If it *was* Colman's knife,' said Turlough after a minute's silence, 'someone must have wrestled it from him; we should find some traces of a struggle.'

'We should,' said Mara, but her mind was still occupied by thoughts of Hugh and it was the king who found the trampled violets, their intense blue-purple now just a stain on the rock.

'Two men wrestled here,' he said with certainty in his voice.

'Yes,' said Mara and suddenly courage flowed back into her. 'Yes, you are right.'

The damp, mossy hollow, facing north, still retained the heavy dew of the night. The earth was moist. Not only the violets bore testimony, but also the earth itself held the imprint of several large feet. Mara picked a twig and carefully measured Colman's feet. One of the imprints was definitely his, but another was larger and some more were still bigger.

'A few men have been here at the entrance,' she said. 'But it seems as if only two men were here where Colman's body is.' She paced the entire area, looking very carefully for something that she did not want to find. She did not want to find it, but all of her training, all of her courage, all of her respect for the law made her look for it. She looked for a pair of small footprints – Hugh was small for his age; only the other day Brigid had remarked on the size of his sandals, compared to ten-year-old Shane's.

Throughout the length and the breadth of Wolf's Lair hollow there were no signs of Hugh's feet. It was not proof positive – his feet were small and his weight was light – but if there had been a struggle they would have left some mark. It was enough for the moment. Mara took a deep breath and her legs stopped trembling.

'How much strength would it have taken to drive a knife in like that?' she asked, staring down at the silver hilt protruding from Colman's neck. Turlough Donn was not a physician – this was a question that she would also ask of Malachy – but from his youth he had been engaged in clan wars; he would have seen many a dead man, and would undoubtedly have inflicted death, also.

'Depends,' he said sombrely. 'Depends on whether a bone was struck and it depends on how much he struggled. It doesn't take much strength to slice through flesh – if you are lucky enough to find the right spot, I suppose a blow like that would kill instantly. Odd that there is no blood, isn't it? Will you bury him here on the Burren, or send the body back to Galway?'

'Send him back to Galway,' said Mara. 'His parents should have him back to their own church and their own burial ground.' She said no more. Years of practice of keeping her own counsel made her cautious even of the king. Her unvoiced thought was that the sooner the Burren was cleared of all memory of Colman, the sooner matters would settle down again. For a while there would be a period of speculation and suspicion; perhaps even accusations, perhaps hot-tempered quarrels flashing up between young men from rival clans, as often happened in the case of an unexplained killing, but once the murder was solved everything would settle down.

'There is no doubt that this will be a secret and unlawful

killing,' she said bleakly. 'More than twenty-four hours have gone by since the death occurred, so the time has passed for anyone to confess and to pay the *éraic*.' In the past she had occasionally bent that law a little where she was fairly certain of the culprit and could extract a confession, but this death puzzled her. There were only two names in her mind: Hugh and Lorcan. Hugh, and the hold that Colman seemed to have had over him, she had to puzzle about in private. She would not mention his name to the king unless she had to. Lorcan, however, she could speculate about.

Turlough Donn read her thoughts. 'What about that man Lorcan, the man that stole the cow, is he a possibility?'

'He could be,' admitted Mara, 'but somehow it doesn't seem like him. He doesn't have the courage or the strength of purpose. Colman was clever. I think he didn't ask for more than Lorcan could just about manage to give. The question is, was he black-mailing someone else and, if so, what hold did he have over him, or her? I suppose there are many people who might have a guilty secret,' she added. During her fifteen years as Brehon she had known many secrets, as had her father before her. Her mind went through the people of the Burren, weighing possibilities, moving them around like figures on a chessboard.

Eight

Cáin Íarraith and Cáin Machslechta

(the law of children)

A child under the age of fourteen has no legal responsibility for any misdeed.

Liability for a child's offence is borne by his father or by his foster-father if he is in fosterage.

A dependent child is classed as a táid aithgena, thief of restitution, from the age of twelve to seventeen. If he steals something it has to be restored and no penalty need be paid.

Halachy was the first to arrive. Mara and Turlough had climbed down two of the terraces to wait next to the bodyguards when Mara heard his deep voice, followed a minute later by Nuala's light, clear voice. They were arguing. Despite her anxieties Mara couldn't hold back a smile.

'But how can I ever learn if I am not allowed to help you?' Nuala was shouting passionately. 'What's the point of me staying at the bottom of the mountain while you dress wounds a hundred feet above my head? I'm coming, Father, no matter what you say. I am your pupil. I have a right to be with you.'

Turlough Donn went to the edge of the terrace and peered over. 'Nice to be so young and fit that you can climb and shout at the same time, isn't it?' he said with a grin.

'She's coming up, then?' asked Mara. For a moment she was sorry, but that was illogical. Nuala was almost a woman. If she were old enough for a marriage to be arranged, then she was old enough to examine a dead man. Malachy could not protect her against death. She had seen her own mother's dead body and had had the strength and maturity to realize that it was a merciful release from agony.

'Thank you for coming so quickly, Malachy,' Mara said, moving over to the edge of the terrace. She said no more until he had scaled the last steep ledge. Nuala was slightly ahead of him, her *léine* well hitched up to knee-length by the leather belt, her long legs tanned to a deep brown, showing that this was the way she wore it normally.

'There's been an accident, Moylan told me,' said Malachy.

'It's really Colman?' enquired Nuala. She didn't sound as if she cared too much, thought Mara.

'Yes,' she said. 'It is Colman. His body is lying in Wolf's Lair. I think he has probably been dead since *Bealtaine* Eve, Malachy, but you will be able to confirm that.'

She felt a faint repugnance at the idea of going up there again – she had been glad to move further down the mountain on the pretence of guiding everyone to the right spot – but now she put her feelings aside. She had a last duty to Colman. She had failed him in all the years that he had been at her law school. She had failed to teach him a respect for the law and a respect for the community that he served. She would not fail to ensure that his remains were treated with as much dignity and respect as possible. Quickly she led the way up. Nuala moved up ahead of her, but

Malachy stayed behind. He said no more to Nuala; knew it was useless, thought Mara. Behind them came King Turlough, breathing heavily. This time the two bodyguards came also, their iron-nailed boots ringing on the rough limestone.

Malachy's examination was quick and thorough. He turned the body on its front, chest down, with one cheek resting on the rock. Nuala knelt behind him, her face slightly pale, but her demeanour calm and composed. She opened the medical satchel that Malachy always took with him, handed her father his knife and Malachy slit the back of the *léine*, baring the narrow neck. The king and the bodyguards stood with stern, reserved faces and a pair of grey crows flapped languidly above. Mara sat on a rock and wished with an aching intensity that she could close the staring eyes.

'Was it his own knife?' asked Malachy.

'I think so,' said Mara briefly, trying not to meet King Turlough's penetrating gaze.

Malachy picked up the right hand and examined it, moving it towards the knife handle in the neck.

'I'm just testing whether the victim's own hand could have dealt the fatal blow,' he said.

'Strange that you can move the body so easily,' said Nuala. 'I would have thought that rigor mortis would be present.'

'Not after twenty-four hours,' said Malachy. 'Rigor mortis disappears after that time. This means that he has been dead at least twenty-four hours,' he said, looking over at Mara.

'There are bruises on his arms,' pointed out Nuala. 'And an abrasion here on his hand,' she added, bringing out the word 'abrasion' with professional pride. 'Look how the skin of the right hand has been torn as the knife was wrestled from his grasp. He couldn't have done that to himself.'

'You're probably right,' said Malachy grimly. 'Let's see the wound.'

Nuala leaned over and peered, but carefully avoided touching anything. Mara got up and walked over. Nuala was right; there were bruises and abrasions. She drew in a long breath of the cool morning air and then let it escape in a sigh of relief. Even if it were possible for Hugh to have knifed Colman, he could never have wrestled the knife from his grasp. Colman was nineteen and Hugh only twelve. No, she was certain now; someone else committed this murder.

'I'm going to take the knife out,' said Malachy calmly. 'I'll be able to tell then if it severed the spinal cord. If it did, this explains the absence of blood, as death is instantaneous once that happens. The knife can be cleaned up then and given to Colman's parents. That looks like a very valuable knife.'

He compressed his lips, leaned backwards a little and pulled the knife out in one smooth motion. The wound did not bleed – despite Malachy's words, Mara had almost expected that it would gush – but the blade was sticky with a white fluid. Flies started to buzz around it, and Malachy plunged it into a thick sod of grass between two rocks and dipped it in and out for a few minutes. Nuala handed him a bundle of bog cotton and he took it without a word, wiped the knife clean and held it out to Mara. The king stepped forward, took it and gave it to one of the bodyguards. His face was impassive, but Mara knew that he had done it to save her having to touch the knife and she was grateful. Her belief in herself was shaken by this untimely death and the crimes that had preceded it.

'He would have died immediately,' said Malachy in a brisk, professional voice. 'The knife found the spinal cord instantly. It was a lucky blow. See, it sliced through here at the back of the neck. There would have been little or no blood.'

'Would he have died on *Bealtaine* night? That would have been about thirty hours ago,' said Nuala. Her voice was level and composed, an imitation of Malachy's professional detachment.

'I would say he died on *Bealtaine* night, all right,' continued Malachy. 'The absence of rigor mortis, given the frosty weather last night, probably fits time of death on that night.' He was half-talking to himself, but Nuala bent over eagerly and followed his pointing finger, nodding her head wisely. There was no doubt that the profession of a physician would suit her. She had brains, courage and integrity. She would be an asset to the community in a few years.

'What about that boy?' asked Malachy, wiping his hands on the grass, drying them on some cotton and then looking directly at Mara.

Mara started. 'Boy?' she said, faltering slightly. Did he know something? Turlough looked at her sharply and then looked back towards Malachy.

'Yes, the boy, Feirdin MacNamara, the strange boy, he was there on *Bealtaine* Eve. I saw him.'

'Yes,' said Mara with relief. 'I saw him, too. I wondered at his mother allowing him to come among that huge crowd, but he did not seem in any way aggressive; he was just climbing up by himself, picking up small pieces of rock and putting them in his pouch.'

'I told Gráinne, his mother, that I thought he would be all right,' confessed Malachy. 'I reckoned that your warning at Poulnabrone, where you threatened a penalty of five *séts*, would stop anyone from teasing him. As far as I know, these fits of rage always emanated from an episode of teasing and name-calling.'

'He's a big, strong boy, I noticed that,' observed the king.

Nuala opened her mouth, but then shut it again. She seemed determined to be on her best behaviour. Her black brows, though, were knitted in an angry frown. Her father noticed and smiled slightly.

'Nuala is fond of Feirdin,' he said. 'Feirdin finds herbs for her.

Nuala has taught him all about herbs, haven't you, Nuala? He has a great memory. He remembers all of the names.'

'I don't think he would murder anyone,' said Nuala decisively. 'He's so gentle and kind compared to the other boys.'

'I wouldn't have thought so either,' said Malachy doubtfully, 'but you never know ... Colman might have threatened him in some way. He could have made him feel unsafe. That might have been enough to trigger a fit of rage.'

'It's possible,' admitted Mara, but her mind moved from Feirdin to Lorcan. Colman had threatened him, had made him feel unsafe. Ardal O'Lochlainn would undoubtedly have started a lawsuit against the man if he heard of the unauthorized borrowing of his bull. In a fit of combined rage and terror, Lorcan might have murdered Colman in order to keep his secret.

'The men with the litter are coming now, my lord,' said one of the bodyguards. Mara went to the edge of the terrace and looked down. Donogh had not come himself but he had sent two sturdy men with a leather litter. They were obviously experienced climbers and they came up the mountainside with long, easy strides.

'The *taoiseach*, the O'Lochlainn himself, was there when your message came, Brehon,' one said to Mara when they eventually pulled themselves up on to the terrace. 'He had just come to see if the master wanted anything in Galway. He said to tell you that he would accompany the body to Galway. They are getting a cart ready and they will bring it over to the foot of the mountain.'

Mara drew in a deep breath of relief. Ardal O'Lochlainn, brother to Donogh, was a man of both courtesy and charm. He would be a great help as he was a close friend to the Lynch family in Galway. All of his trading, imports and exports, was done through them. In fact, it was he who had recommended Colman to her law school.

'We'll take the body down now,' she said, making a quick decision. 'Father Conglach will be able to give it the last rites before the cart goes.' He would not be too happy about the body being moved, she thought sourly, but he could have been here by now if he had wanted to. Kilcorney was nearer than Glenslade. Perhaps it might be just as well if Aidan had failed to deliver the message. She bent down and supported Colman's head while one of Donogh's men put his arms around the body and the other lifted the inert legs. Mara helped to straighten the legs and crossed the heavy arms over the breast. She took a piece of linen from around her shoulders and placed it over the face, hiding those accusing eyes. It seemed to her as if everyone breathed more easily once she had done this. She looked at Nuala and, seeing her own tears mirrored in the child's eyes, she put a comforting arm around the thin shoulders.

Even with the two bodyguards helping, getting the litter down to the foot of the mountain was a painfully slow business with a few heart-stopping moments when it looked as if both the living and the dead would slide down the loose scree to a certain death below. A light shower of soft summer rain fell when they were halfway down, and it cooled them, but added to the difficulties as the smooth sheets of limestone became treacherously slippery. Once again, Turlough Donn held out his hand and once again Mara took it gratefully. She would need all of her strength before this day was over. Malachy, she noticed with pleasure, was holding Nuala's hand, and for once Nuala did not proclaim her independence by rejecting his aid.

They could hear the rumble of the cart when they reached the foot of the mountain, and stood catching their breath while their sweat dried in the heat of the sun. A rainbow spanned the sky and Mara turned her face towards it, seeing it as some sort of symbol of the renewal of life, as the Bible promised.

The lake at the foot of the mountain was very still, its surface like a silver mirror reflecting the blues and pinks of the rainbow, broken only by a great splash of white where a score of sleeping swans rocked on its smooth surface. In front of the lake was a patch of sandy beach, golden in the midday sun. It was a bare spot, there: miles of flat rock, the lake, and the terraced slopes of Mullaghmore beyond. There was one tree: a strange tree, moulded by the western storm winds into a stiff, awkward asymmetrical shape, and beneath that tree, one hand on its bare trunk, was a small, thin figure. It was Father Conglach. No doubt he had heard them struggling down the mountainside and had decided to wait under the shade of the tree. And yet, thought Mara, how odd that he continued to stand there, very straight, very rigid, almost braced, making no move to approach them.

The cart rumbled into view. Three men accompanied it on horseback, each leading a couple of spare horses, and suddenly the peace was broken. The clatter of the iron cartwheels disturbed the swans and they reared up, their great wings spreading out as they rushed across the lake, their feet churning the water into waves. Then they were airborne, flying overhead in a great arc, the beating of their wings sounding through the quiet air like some strange music from distant pipes. The priest moved, as if suddenly released, and came forward to stand beside them as they waited for the O'Lochlainns. Father Conglach did not greet them and he did not look at the leather litter. Why not? thought Mara. Surely he could see the body there, surely that was why he had come over? Now she could see that he had a pony tied to the tree. If he came on horseback it should not have taken him so long to arrive – he must have been waiting for them to come down. King Turlough ignored him and began to stride forward to greet the O'Lochlainns, his two bodyguards marching after him. Donogh's men placed the litter on the ground, stretched their cramped limbs and waited silently for the cart.

'This is a sad business, Father,' said Mara, watching his face intently. He turned his head and looked at her as if seeing her for the first time. She was shocked to see that his face was heavy with sorrow and his eyes were pitted with black circles.

'It's Satan's business,' he said in a deep, harsh croak.

'You were there on *Bealtaine* Eve, Father,' said Mara. 'Did you see anything of this matter? You must have passed Wolf's Lair on your way down.' And so must everyone else, she thought once again. That was the easiest way to come down. Most people normally climbed the mountain on the eastern side and came down the western side. She had not properly thought about this yet. Only her antagonism towards the priest had brought it to the front of her mind. 'Did you see anything?' she repeated.

'I saw too much,' he said forbiddingly. 'I saw unmarried men and young women with them and their behaviour was the behaviour that only the devil inspires.'

'And Colman?' she asked.

He did not even glance towards the figure on the leather litter. 'He, too, was evil,' he said bitterly.

Mara considered this. From what she had seen on that evening, Colman had been with Hugh and then had gone to talk with Muiris. She had not seen him with any girl. 'Why do you say that, Father?' she asked. Suddenly she was devoured with curiosity. Why didn't anyone report Colman's death? Someone must have seen him lying there in Wolf's Lair. There was one guilty person; it made sense perhaps that the guilty would say nothing – though the mercy of Brehon law, unlike English law, meant that most people owned up to a murder and set about making reparation to the family. However, even if the guilty did say nothing, what about the many innocent? Why was there silence about this death? What had happened in that midnight hour?

'Did you see Colman, Father?' she asked. 'Did you see him before the bonfire was lit at midnight, or afterwards?'

He muttered something inaudible and suddenly seemed to

awaken to a sense of his duties. He pulled out the alb from his satchel and then the holy oils and the scrap of bog cotton. He took the linen cloth from Colman's head and then averted his eyes hurriedly. With a grim face, Father Conglach went through the motions of muttering the Latin prayers and touching the ears, eyes, mouth and the four limbs of the dead man. Mara prayed wordlessly, and yet with a depth of sincerity that she seldom felt during Sunday Mass at Noughaval parish church. She prayed for Colman, prayed that his sins be forgiven him and that he rest in peace now – perhaps for the first time in his driven, anxiety-filled, short life, and she prayed for his killer that God's grace would bring the courage to acknowledge the crime, to seek forgiveness and to make reparation. Lastly, she prayed for herself that her sins of omission in the schooling of Colman would be forgiven and that she would be given the strength to bring to maturity and confidence the six young lives entrusted to her.

'Go forth, Christian soul . . .' prayed the priest and Mara bent over and sketched the sign of the cross on the dead forehead and then, feeling comforted and strengthened by her prayer, went forward to greet the O'Lochlainns.

They had stopped at a little distance away from the body, keeping heads bowed until the priest had finished. There was Ardal O'Lochlainn himself, mounted on an iron-grey stallion, and behind him were Donogh's three sons, each leading a pair of horses. The cart was a good sturdy one and they had even taken the trouble to lay some green branches and a few early roses on it. Mara smiled up at Ardal. It would have been his thought, she knew. He was a man of great sensitivity. It would be good to have him at her side when she broke the news to Colman's parents.

'Brehon,' he said gently. 'This is a terrible thing. What happened? Was it an accident?'

'Were you there for the festivities, Ardal?' she asked.

He shook his head. 'No,' he said. 'I never bother about it

these days. I let my household stay all night. The men enjoy it more than I do.'

Pity, thought Mara. This is one man whose word I would trust as I trust my own. This is one man who would never hide the truth, or turn his back on wrongdoing. She looked at his tall, athletic frame, his eyes as blue as the lake water at their feet and his red-gold crown of hair and she wondered why he had never remarried. The death rate among young women was very high – perhaps many of them were too young for childbirth – but most men married again quite quickly. Every father in the kingdom of the Burren, or in Corcomroe, would be delighted to make a match between his daughter and the *taoiseach* of the powerful O'Lochlainn clan. Rumour had it that Ardal had a wife of the fourth degree, a fisherman's daughter, in Galway, but that would not stop him contracting another more suitable alliance.

'I've brought horses for you all, my lord,' he said, addressing the king. 'The young scholar told me that you were all on foot. I thought you would prefer to ride back to Cahermacnaghten.'

'Good man, yourself,' said Turlough Donn enthusiastically. He would not have enjoyed the long walk back across the Burren, thought Mara.

'I'll go with you to Galway, Ardal,' she said aloud. 'I'll want to see Colman's parents myself.'

He looked a little flustered. 'Oh,' he said. 'I thought you would go back with the king. I didn't realize that you were coming. Perhaps Donogh's wife would . . .' His voice trailed off. Mara did her best to hide a smile. Dear Ardal, she thought affectionately. He was the soul of honour and he would think it wrong that a woman should ride unescorted with a troop of men. But she certainly did not want Donogh's wife, Sadhbh, dragged away from her busy life as wife of one of the most important farmers in the kingdom.

'Perhaps Nuala would be allowed to come with me?' she asked Malachy. 'Would you like to ride to Galway, Nuala?'

'Yes, please!' said Nuala, giving her father no time to reply. Quickly she went across to where a pair of spirited bay horses was being held with difficulty by one of Donogh's men.

'I thought one of these for King Turlough and one for the Brehon,' called Ardal mildly but firmly. He went over and took one of the bays already provided with a side saddle and brought it over next to a large stone, holding it there while Mara mounted. King Turlough was beside her in a moment, holding her hand firmly while she arranged the loose folds of her *léine*.

'Go safe and return soon,' he said, using the words of an old prayer.

'Are you sure you would not want to go back to Thomond today?' she asked. 'You must have business to do.' Ardal had withdrawn and was helping his niece on to a demure-looking Connemara pony. Turlough Donn held the bridle in one hand and placed his other large warm hand on hers.

'I'll wait until you come home,' he said softly. 'I would not miss the opportunity of another evening with you for all the business in the world.'

Mara turned her eyes towards the priest but he had gone back to collect his own horse from under the hawthorn tree. What would Father Conglach think of this hand-holding and whispering?

'Tell Brigid to have supper ready at about seven,' she said aloud and quickly she returned the pressure of his hand before gathering up the reins.

'I'll have the pot boiling,' said King Turlough Donn with a cheerful wave.

'And take Bran back with you, will you? I can't take him to Galway. He'll run behind your horse. He'll go with you, don't worry.'

'Of course he will go with me,' said Turlough. 'Aren't I one of the family?'

NINE

There are three categories of mac béo-athar, *living son:*

1. Mac té, *a son of the fireside, dependent on his father and subject to his control*

2. Mac áuar, *a cold son, who has failed in his duty to his father*

3. Mac ailte, *a reared son who has been allowed independence to devote himself to a profession or to husbandry*

GALWAY WAS AN IMPRESSIVE sight with its hundreds of stone buildings rising up against the western sea. It had been named Gaillimh, the place of the foreigners, because it was an Anglo-Norman settlement, established soon after the Normans came to Ireland. It was the only remaining settlement controlled by England in the west of Ireland. A great wall had been built around it; the houses inside were large, handsome and, after the disastrous fire of 1472, all made from stone.

'I love the town of Galway,' breathed Nuala as they arrived. Her dark eyes were dancing with excitement and her cheeks flushed as she looked around at the crowds.

'City,' corrected Ardal. 'It's a city-state. It was given a charter in 1485 by the English king, Richard III.'

'I remember that. I was twelve years old, then,' said Mara. 'My father took all the scholars at the law school to Galway to see the celebrations.' She and Dualta, her future husband, had escaped, she remembered. They had gone down to the quays and Dualta had bought a flagon of wine. The memory brought a quick spurt of amusement to Mara. They had thought themselves so grown-up, she and Dualta!

'A merchant told me that it's the third most important port, after Bristol and London,' Ardal told his niece. 'They trade in wine, spices, salt, animal products and fish,' he added. Mara concealed a smile. They had kept pace with the cart the whole way so the journey had been slow and tedious and Ardal had seized the opportunity to improve the mind of his niece with various lectures, especially on the virtues expected of a wife and a mother. Undoubtedly he would be a moving force in the proposed match between Naoise and Nuala.

'When you are a physician you will be able to buy powders and remedies from overseas here in Galway, Nuala,' Mara said innocently and a slight frown appeared on Ardal's handsome face.

'Here is the city gate,' he said abruptly. 'Would you wait here for a moment, Brehon, while I speak to the man on guard.'

Mara reined in her horse and looked around with interest. Theirs was not the only cart; others were in front of them and behind, laden with leather, meat, mantles made from wolf fur, wooden barrels filled with butter. Large herds of cows were being driven along – they would be shipped over to Wales and to France. There were fourteen gates into the city of Galway, she knew, and if every gate was as busy as this one, then the city must be enormously wealthy.

'I've told the man at the gate to let the mayor know,' said Ardal, returning to them. 'He is a cousin of Seán Lynch, Colman's father. You knew he was related to the mayor of Galway?'

Mara nodded. There was no chance that she could not have known; Colman had brought it into conversation at every opportunity. The mayor was obviously of great importance here, as all the carts and the herds of animals ahead of them were being hastily moved out of their way, and they were waved through the gate with great speed.

'We turn here and go up Shop Street,' said Ardal. 'Shall I lead the way?'

He set off, Mara and Nuala followed, and behind them the cart trundled on with its shrouded body lying amid the green branches and the wilted roses. People in the crowded streets drew back respectfully and many made the sign of the cross as they passed. The news was spreading fast.

'Here is Lynch's castle,' said Ardal over his shoulder. He stopped beside a tall, oblong tower house. A man came running out to take their horses. His face was white and frightened. Mara hoped that the parents had not yet been told.

❖

Mara had not seen Colman's parents, Seán and Fidelma Lynch, for over a year – not since Colman's graduation – and as they stood at the window looking down at them she was struck by how old they looked. Colman had been a late son – and their pride and joy. She hoped that she would not have to destroy that pride. She stood at the heavy oaken door of the grey stone tower house and hesitated. In a moment, Ardal was at her side. He would tell the sad story for her, if she requested it; she knew that, but the story was hers and she had to be the one that broke the news.

'Mara, Brehon of the Burren,' she said briefly to the serving-man who opened the door. He knew Ardal; he was obviously a frequent and welcome visitor to the house, but he bowed with respect to Mara and, taking a silver candlestick, he escorted them up the steep spiral staircase to the Great Hall above. Why had Colman found a need to extract money from the people of the Burren? thought Mara. Even if his parents did not want to spend more money on him, they were wealthy and would probably have helped if he had needed money for any particular reason. Why did he have to blackmail a poor farmer like Lorcan?

'I bring sad news,' she said as soon as she had greeted the elderly pair. 'There has been a death . . .' She paused for a moment. Colman's father looked bewildered, but Fidelma knew.

'Colman . . .' she gasped and Mara nodded, reaching out and taking one of the old woman's gnarled hands between her own.

'He was killed on *Bealtaine* Eve, on the mountain,' she said gently. 'We have brought his body back to you. I do not yet know his killer, but I will let you know as soon as there is any news.'

She waited for tears, but none came. Neither of them sat down: both just stood and stared. They seemed uncertain of what to do, almost as if some living spring within them had suddenly dried up. Nuala slipped out of the room, closing the door gently behind her.

'He did not suffer, he died instantly,' Mara continued. It was the only consolation that she could give to the stricken parents. She could not think of anything else to say. Even Ardal seemed to have lost his usually fluent tongue. 'Come and sit down,' she continued gently, guiding Fidelma towards the tall chair by the fireplace.

'Sit down, Seán,' said Ardal, copying her actions. 'You will need all your strength for the time to come.'

They both sat, eyes full of bewilderment and shock. Eventually Seán Lynch spoke. 'On the mountainside?'

Mara nodded. 'Yes, it was the *Bealtaine* festival. He died on the side of Mullaghmore Mountain.'

There was another moment's silence before the frozen pall of sorrow was broken by Colman's mother.

'It was a hard, cold place for him to die, on the side of that mountain.' Her voice was barely audible. Her husband rose and came to her side. He put his arms around her but she ignored him; just stared ahead, looking at nothing. Outside in the street there was the noise of a wandering musician singing a song and then a harsh voice cutting through the music and then just the sound of cart wheels trundling. Inside the room there was no sound at all, except for the buzzing of a fly in the coloured glass of the window.

The door opened and in came Nuala, followed by a white-faced maidservant bearing a tray of pewter goblets filled with wine.

'Good girl,' said Mara softly to Nuala. She took a goblet and held it to the ashen lips of Colman's mother. Seán Lynch took a goblet and drank mechanically, first one and then another. He did not look at his wife. 'Tell Father Murphy to come,' he said to the maidservant as she hesitated at the doorway and then rapidly shouted after her, 'No, no, I'll go myself.'

'I'll go with you, Seán,' said Ardal. And in a moment Mara and Nuala were left with the woman. She seemed to be listening. There was a long silence. She asked no questions, just sat and listened. After about five minutes there were heavy tramping noises from downstairs, a door creaked open and then there was the sound of trestles being dragged noisily across the flagged floor. Nuala's eyes met Mara's: the body was being brought in.

'I must get something to cover him,' said Colman's mother,

jumping up feverishly. 'Come to his room with me and we'll find something.'

Colman's room was up on the second floor, luxuriously carpeted and curtained. There was an ornately carved chest at the end of the bed and his mother threw it open and delved inside it. She pulled out a magnificent bedcovering made from the finest silk and velvet and embroidered with gold threads. For a moment she buried her face in it, then she handed it to Nuala. Suddenly a muffled sob broke from the woman. She had pulled out roll after roll of vellum from one end of the chest. Frantically she tore them open and thrust them, one by one, in front of Mara. 'See what a scholar he was,' she sobbed. 'Look at all his lessons.'

Mara looked, tears filling her own eyes. There were all the early lessons, the penmanship large and round, though neat and careful, and then the later scrolls, filled with meticulous tiny writing. 'Even last week, when he came here, he was still working for you,' sobbed the mother. 'Look, I found this on the floor after he had left. He must have dropped it from his pouch. Some tasks that he had to do for you.' On the top of the chest there was a snowy-white *léine* and placed carefully in the middle of it was a scrap of vellum. Mara took and read it. It was a list of case numbers from the judgement texts and yearbooks that were stored in the oak press at the law school. One of them caught her eye: the year was MCCCXC and the number of the judgement text was XIX. It was the number of her own divorce case. She recognized it instantly. There were others, also, whose numbers were not familiar to her; two of them dated from the time of her father. Mara crumpled the piece of vellum in her hand and then thrust it into her pouch.

'He was an incomparable student,' she said with sincerity to the grieving mother. 'I have never had any student like him in all of my years at the law school.' She rose to her feet and gently took the rich bedcovering from Nuala, leading the way back downstairs. Nuala followed, a solicitous hand under Fidelma's elbow.

By the time they reached the bottom of the steep spiral staircase Colman's body had been carried into the house and placed on some boards across a pair of trestles in the bare, empty guards' chamber next to the front door. Mara handed over the richly embroidered cloth and stood back while Fidelma covered her son's corpse. Then a small round priest came in the door, with an acolyte swinging the censer containing the incense. Mara and Nuala sank to their knees behind the two parents and joined in the prayer for the dead. Behind them stood Ardal O'Lochlainn, his pleasant mellifluous voice murmuring the Latin words.

A stream of people – servants, neighbours, relations and friends – came silently through the open door and knelt on the hard flagstones. The room and the hallway beyond were thronged with people. It was amazing how quickly everyone could gather, thought Mara, and then remembered how closely everyone lived and how short the distances were in this crowded walled city. There would be a great wake tonight and tomorrow Colman would be buried in St Nicholas's Church. Galway had reclaimed him; there was no further part to be played by the law school in the kingdom of the Burren. When the prayer was over, Mara touched Nuala's shoulder, rose to her feet and silently crept out. Ardal O'Lochlainn followed.

'We'll go back now, Ardal,' whispered Mara. 'I'll send your horses back over to Lissylisheen tomorrow. You'll want to stay longer.'

'Oh, no!' Ardal was shocked. 'I can't allow you to ride back on your own. I'll escort you.'

Mara sighed. Ardal could be tiresome. He was stubborn and used to getting his own way.

'No,' she said firmly. 'You stay here. You have business to do. Nuala and I will be perfectly all right.'

He continued to look worried; he would not yield, she knew. He would prefer to lose a day's business, and perhaps an evening's pleasure, than show her any discourtesy.

'I'll tell you what,' she said cheerfully. 'We'll ride back behind your two men in the cart. Then we'll come to no harm.'

His brow cleared. 'You're sure? It won't be too slow for you?'

'No, no,' she said, lying without a qualm. 'It won't be too slow for us. Make our farewells to the Lynch family when it seems right to you. They won't miss us. Look at all those people still coming. Shop Street is full of them.'

'It will be slow and boring riding behind this cart again,' said Nuala in a low voice as they moved off down the street at walking pace.

'No, it won't,' said Mara calmly. 'As soon as we get on to the south road, outside the city, we'll say goodbye to the cart. Just ride quietly now while Ardal is still looking.'

❈

'Why was Colman killed, Mara?' asked Nuala as they followed sedately behind the cart and edged their way through the crowded gate.

'I don't know, but I'll have to find out,' said Mara. It was true, she thought. She would have to find out; cost what it might, the truth was important. 'Just move to the side here,' she said, looking down the road at a herd of cows thundering down towards them. Two skinny boys armed with sticks were doing their best to slow them but the lead cow was determined to make a bid for freedom and her sisters were doing their best to keep with her. Ardal's cart stopped and so did all of the other carts.

'Now, this is where we accidentally lose Ardal's men,' said

Mara, continuing to walk her horse on the grass verge until they were safely past the galloping herd.

'And this is where we gallop,' giggled Nuala, clapping her heels against the sides of the Connemara pony. 'Let's just go as fast as we can. I don't really want to talk about Colman.'

'Neither do I,' said Mara, enjoying the feeling of speed. She didn't even want to think about Colman. She would keep her mind clear and then she would be fresh tomorrow when she started the investigation.

'Look, we're already at the turn-off for the mountain pass,' said Nuala after half an hour of hard riding. She slowed down. 'I think I'd better get off at the hill,' she said. 'This pony is blown. Why did Ardal give me such a fat, slow pony?' she grumbled.

'I'll get off, too,' said Mara. She noticed that Nuala never called Ardal 'uncle'. A very independent young lady, she thought. She swung herself down from the horse and walked up the hill beside Nuala. 'We're back in the kingdom of the Burren now,' she said with satisfaction, but then said no more; the hill was so steep that it was almost perpendicular so she saved her breath until they reached Clerics' Pass at the top.

'Shall we ride now?' Nuala had just asked when Mara heard the shouts.

'Ssh!' she said, listening intently.

It's a large party of men riding, thought Mara, but that was not what worried her. The loud voices came to her ears very clearly. They were speaking Gaelic, but not the familiar Gaelic of the mid-west. This was Connaught Gaelic; she had learned it at the law school many years ago. It had an unfamiliar sound, but she could still understand it. What were Connaught men doing riding through the kingdom of the Burren? Suddenly she remembered the anxiety of Turlough's bodyguards when the king was having dinner in her house on *Bealtaine* night. They had been worried about the O'Kellys from Connaught. These men must be the O'Kellys.

Mara's first thought was for Turlough's danger, but her second was for the danger that she and Nuala now faced. If the marauding clansmen captured them, then, as Brehon of the Burren, she could be a valuable bargaining tool in the O'Kelly and O'Brien clan warfare. She had no fear for her own safety; there was a great respect for her office in Gaelic Ireland; her greatest fear at the moment was the prospect of explaining to a respectfully worried Ardal how exactly it had occurred that she had separated herself and his niece from the cart and continued along the lonely roads with no male protection.

'Quick,' she whispered in Nuala's ear. 'Lead your pony. Follow me. I know where we can hide.'

The Cistercian monks from the abbey of Sancta Maria Petris Fertilis had constructed Clerics' Pass and it was a magnificent monument to their skill and industry. They had built it several hundreds of years ago, but it still needed constant attention. Mara had often noticed the narrow, well-trampled path that led through the large heaps of broken stone at the side of the road to the abbey in the valley below and now she quickly guided Nuala along this way, praying that they would be out of sight before the men passed. Her heart beat a little faster as they pushed their way through the thorny hedge beyond the rocks; the passageway had been made for men, not for horses, but they were safely on the other side by the time the noise of the horse hoofs drew near. She could hear the men so plainly now that it seemed amazing that she and Nuala could remain unheard.

'Why didn't he come?' came one voice. The speaker's accent was not as strong as many of the others so the words were quite clear.

'Lost his courage,' said another. 'Afraid of what the O'Briens might do to him.'

Mara wished that she could stop and listen, but her first duty was to get Nuala out of the way as quickly as possible so she continued to move rapidly down the path. The tall hedge would hide them until the men had passed.

The next words were not so clear, but she thought she heard the word 'reward' and then their word for 'lawyer' among them. She frowned. Were they talking of her? But no, the word they used was not 'Brehon' and the pronoun definitely was 'he'. Who was this 'he'? Had Colman been involved with these O'Kellys? she wondered. It would certainly fit with what she was rapidly learning about his character. Perhaps they had promised to reward him for information about the king. This was something she would have to puzzle out afterwards, but first she had to get Nuala home safely and then warn the king of this danger.

'We'll walk on down to the abbey,' she whispered. 'Lead your pony. It should be safe now; they seem to have gone down the hill towards Galway, but we'll be less easy to see if we walk. They just might look back when they reach the flat road.'

The O'Kellys would skirt the city of Galway and go up past Maam if they were going home, she thought. On the other hand, they might not be going home. They could be camped somewhere on the flat empty salt marsh that formed the boundary between the sea and the north-eastern side of the Burren.

❄

The abbot himself was waiting for them as they came out from the lane. He had obviously seen them as they crossed the field leading downhill from the roadside hedge.

'Brehon, the blessings of God and of His Holy Mother be upon you,' he said gravely, and looked with suspicion at Nuala.

'And on you, too,' said Mara automatically, her mind busy with her plans.

'You are well?' he enquired.

She suppressed a grin. Why didn't the man ask straight out, 'What were you doing creeping along that path?'

'I am very well, Father Abbot,' she said with dignity, brushing some dead blackthorn twigs from her hair and noticing that her gown had acquired a long rent across the skirt. 'And you? And all the brothers?'

'We are all well,' he said after he had given her question a moment's solemn consideration. He looked again directly at Nuala, who had hitched her *léine* up to her knees as soon as they were clear of Galway. She stared back at him with interest.

'This is Nuala, daughter of Malachy the physician,' said Mara. 'We have a favour to ask of you, Father Abbot. We were alarmed by some men on Clerics' Pass; I think they were the O'Kellys. I would be grateful if you could send a message to Caisleán Seán-Muicinis to ask for an escort of ten men to accompany us back to Cahermacnaghten where King Turlough Donn awaits us. Ask him could we keep the men for a few days to guard the king.'

'Certainly,' said the abbot, looking quite alarmed. He rushed off towards a lay brother working in the field across the lane. King Turlough Donn was a patron of the abbey; one of his ancestors had built it for the Cistercians a few hundred years ago. The mention of his name would be enough to galvanize the whole abbey into action.

'Will you and your young companion take some refreshment?' he enquired when he returned. Mara's eyes followed the lay brother and saw with satisfaction that he had already jumped on a horse and was riding rapidly out of the gate.

'No, thank you,' she said gravely, unable to bear the thought of polite conversation for another half-hour. 'We will sit in the chapel and give thanks for our deliverance. Pull down your *léine*,' she hissed to Nuala, as they followed the abbot through the cloisters. 'Do you want to distract all the young brothers from their vocations?'

TEN

CRITH GABLACH (RANKS IN SOCIETY)

HONOUR PRICES

A person's place in society is measured by his honour price
(lóg n-enech – the price of his face).

A woman takes the honour price of her father and later of
her husband, unless she is a member of the nemed,
professional, class: a poet, a Brehon, a physician or a female
wright. In these cases, she has her own honour price.

The honour price of a Brehon, whether male or female,
is fifteen séts.

☙❧

KING TURLOUGH DONN WAS waiting at the gate of the
law school when Mara arrived back. She had asked the men
to wait at the Kilcorney crossroads so that she could explain their
presence to the king and not alarm the bodyguards. As she rode
up towards him her mind was busy with arranging the details of
her encounter so as to cause the least anxiety. However, at the

126

sight of him her heartbeat quickened slightly and she felt the muscles of her face relax into a broad smile. It had been a hard day and now she could enjoy a relaxed evening.

'You didn't bring the girl back with you,' he said as he held out his arms and swung her down to the ground. Not many kings would be so unconscious of their own dignity, she thought. This was the strength of the man. He needed no outward trappings of royalty; he was royalty itself, bred right back to seed of the High King, Brian Boru, five hundred years ago.

'No,' she said, 'I dropped her off at Caherconnell. Her father would be anxious about her.' Nuala and she had agreed to make no mention of the near encounter with the O'Kellys on the lonely mountain pass to anyone other than the king. If at all possible, Ardal O'Lochlainn was to hear nothing.

'We wouldn't like to cause him any worry,' Nuala had said, her virtuous tone spoiled by a quick giggle.

'You should have brought her back. She would have had a better time here with your lively lads,' said the king, gesturing towards the noisy crowd playing hurling in the field behind the law school. 'That father of hers is a sullen, dull sort of man. I don't know why Ardal O'Lochlainn's sister married him. She can't have much fun, that child, Nuala. She's too serious for her age.'

'We've had a bit of an adventure on the way back,' said Mara. 'We almost ran into the O'Kellys on Clerics' Pass.'

King Turlough raised his eyebrows. 'Really,' he said with amusement. 'And what did you do? Take them all prisoner?' His words were light, but his eyes were anxious.

'No, we didn't,' said Mara. 'We went down to the abbey and I got the abbot to send for ten men from Mahon O'Lochlainn. I brought them back with me. I think you should keep them with you until you get back to Thomond. Mahon knows you will be keeping them for a few days. Will you send your two bodyguards down to the crossroads to collect them?'

'My lord, there are a pack of *gallóglaich* down there at the crossroads,' said Cumhal, coming panting up at that moment.

'I hate those *gallóglaich*,' grumbled Turlough. 'Our own clansmen were good enough for us until recently. It was the O'Donnells of the north who brought in this idea of using mercenaries. They brought the Scots over.'

Mara did not answer. She was busy looking over at the field behind the law school and counting heads like any cattle farmer. Yes, they were all there and all looked to be having a good time. The two bodyguards were playing hurling also. Fergal, the heftier of the two, was standing in goal and Hugh was vainly trying to get past his bulk, shouting vigorously.

'Fergal, Conall,' shouted the king and Hugh scored a goal quickly as the bodyguard looked across at his master. Hugh seemed to be himself again, thought Mara, as a yell of triumph split the air. She sighed with relief. It was amazing how children shrugged off unpleasant events that would keep their elders awake at night.

❀

'Has Brigid fed you yet?' she asked Turlough Donn after the bodyguards had been sent down the road to fetch the *gallóglaich*.

'She fed me a great dinner six hours ago and now I'm ready for a great supper,' he said happily. 'The pot is boiling and there is a flagon of good wine on the table. I've been down to your cellar and I must say that you have good taste in wine. Some wonderful barrels down there, all beautifully labelled in your lovely handwriting. What are we going to do with those fellows now?' he asked plaintively as the *gallóglaich* trotted into view.

'They've got leather tents,' said Mara calmly. 'They can camp around the walls of the enclosure and then we'll all sleep more soundly.'

'Your supper will be ready in half an hour,' said Brigid,

emerging from the kitchen house. 'I'll feed the lads first, if that's all right, and then I'll come over to your house, Brehon. Glory be to God,' she said, staring open-mouthed at the *gallóglaich*. 'It's just as well I made a huge pot of soup and a new batch of loaves today. I'd better feed that lot first as well.'

'You do that, Brigid,' said Mara. 'I'll just go and get myself tidy enough to have supper with a king.'

'I could do with a change myself,' said Turlough Donn. 'I must confess, I've been enjoying a game of hurling, also.'

'At your age!' mocked Mara.

'I'm only forty-eight,' he said with dignity and strode off towards the guest house, holding himself very upright and keeping his stomach well tucked in.

❀

Back at her own house, Mara was tempted, as always, to linger a while in the garden; it was looking particularly beautiful with the setting sun slanting its rays across the blue gentians and drawing the scent from the purple lavender by the gate. However, she resisted and went upstairs to take an armful of clothing from the chest at the foot of her bed. Then she ran down the stairs again and into the small room at the back of the house. There was a big pump there and she rapidly filled the wooden bath tub with icy water from the hundred-foot-deep well. It was her father who had the well dug and she blessed his memory every time she used it. It had never gone dry – in some way that she did not quite understand, the streams that flowed down from the mountains seemed to fill a vast underground lake beneath the limestone of the Burren. In the wintertime she would light the charcoal in the iron brazier and add a large pot of boiling water to the cold water, but now she felt warm and stimulated by the thoughts of the evening ahead and the icy shock of the water on her bare skin was a tingling pleasure to her. Slowly she washed all of her body, using the lavender-scented soap that Brigid made from soap plant and distilled lavender water. She sat for a while and soaked and then climbed out and stood dripping on the flagstones. Slowly and meditatively, she dried herself on the white linen towel and then dressed in a fresh clean *léine*, adding a loose gown of rose-coloured wool over it and fastening the flowing sleeves to the shoulders with two small gold brooches. Her feet she left bare of stockings, but she discarded the heavy boots that she normally wore and slipped on a pair of light leather shoes. Her long hair was still soaking wet so she draped a towel around her shoulders and went out to comb it in the warmth of the sun.

'No grey hairs yet,' she said as she ran the ivory comb through the long strands and then smiled mockingly to herself. Quickly she plaited her hair and coiled the long braids behind her head. Everything was quiet at the law school – presumably Brigid was feeding the hungry scholars and the *gallóglaich* together – but there had been a sudden abrupt slam of the heavy guest-house door. The king was coming. She bent down and selected a perfect pale pink rosebud, held it for a moment, wondered whether to give it to him, then tucked it inside one of her own gold brooches and went to meet him at the gate. He had changed also, she noticed, and she looked admiringly at him. The royal saffron *léine* suited him, the yellow colour making his tanned skin glow, and over it he wore a fashionable padded doublet of purple velvet. His hair and his long curved moustaches were still damp and showed the grooves of the comb.

'Very fine!' she said with affectionate mockery and he grinned.

'A merchant from Limerick gave me this,' he said, looking down at himself appreciatively. 'He gave me this gold-embroidered pouch, also. One of my ships saved him from being robbed by the O'Malley from Clew Bay.' He stood for a moment surveying her and she smiled at him, enjoying the admiration in his eyes. 'You're looking very beautiful,' he said in a lower voice.

'Sit here and I'll bring you a cup of wine,' said Mara, directing him to her chamomile bench. She walked indoors, deep in thought. At that moment when the king spoke of his pouch she remembered the knife that had been drawn out from Colman's neck. The king had handed it to one of his bodyguards; she remembered that. The bodyguard had placed it in his own pouch. She had deliberately not taken it with her to Galway to give to the Lynch family, as Malachy had suggested. It was, of course, Hugh's knife. But should she give it back to the child? Perhaps she would suggest that it be given to the monks at the abbey to sell for charity.

She poured the two cups of wine, tasted one, rolling it appreciatively on her tongue and around the back of her throat. Yes, it was perfect. She had kept it for five years in the dark damp cellar below the Brehon's house and now it was ready for drinking. She topped up her own cup and carried them both outside, joining him on the bench.

'I made this bench last summer,' she said, passing her hand over the fragrant foliage and releasing an intense sweet perfume. 'The chamomile will be in flower soon, but the perfume is in the leaves. Your weight is just right for it,' she teased. 'It applies just the correct pressure to bring out all the sweetness.'

He didn't reply to that, just smiled with amusement.

'You're a popular woman, you know,' he said quietly after a while. 'When you were in Galway this afternoon there were all sorts of people came looking for you, hundreds of them.'

She considered this for a moment, sipping her wine and appreciating its full rounded fruity flavour.

'Hundreds?' she queried, raising an eyebrow at him.

'Well, dozens,' he amended. 'For one, there was the man with the fierce dog . . .'

'Diarmuid?' she asked.

'That was him, yes,' he said, taking a swallow of the wine.

He drinks too fast, she thought absent-mindedly; he should savour it more.

'What did Diarmuid say?' she asked.

'Nothing, nothing – not to me, nor to Brigid, nor to Cumhal. He wondered where you were, and then came to the right conclusion himself, nodded his head a few times, muttered a few words about Galway and ambled away. He looked as though he wanted to say something, though.'

'And who else came?'

'Well, that shifty individual, Lorcan, and also the father of the pretty girl.'

'Which pretty girl, Emer or Aoife?'

'At my age,' said King Turlough, draining his cup and rising to his feet, 'the name doesn't matter. The face is all that counts. Would you like another cup of wine?'

'I'll wait for the food,' said Mara. 'Wine always means more to me with food.' Was it Daniel or Muiris who had come to see her? she wondered. Had Colman been blackmailing Muiris as well as Lorcan? Or was Daniel worried about Emer's marriage prospects? And what about the other cases on that list she had picked up from Colman's clothes chest? Were these possible prospects for blackmail? After all, her own divorce case was there. She laughed suddenly. It was just like Colman to think he might blackmail her about this. Respect for her position would have meant that no one on the Burren would have mentioned her past to him, even if they still whispered about it among themselves. Suddenly her mind became very alert. She had a task ahead of her that would demand all of her energies. She would enjoy this evening with Turlough and then, next morning, she would begin work.

'Let's eat out here,' she said. 'It's a glorious evening and it may be raining in a few days. I'll go and get Cumhal to bring out the trestle table.'

There would be no talk of love and marriage tonight; she needed to keep her mind clear, she decided, as she went off to find Cumhal. Time enough to make a decision after she had solved this murder. They would have supper out there in the garden, with the lads in the field next to them playing hurling or throwing sticks for Bran. They would talk about the affairs of the kingdom, the affairs of the country of Ireland, and of its near neighbour, England.

'I'll tell the bodyguards,' said Cumhal when she found him digging in the bed of leeks, but there was a note of hesitancy in his voice and there was a small worried frown between his brows. 'The bodyguards were probably hoping that he would eat in the guest house,' he said quickly as he saw her look at him with surprise. 'They are worried about the threat from the O'Kellys. It would be easy for them to land at Fanore and come through the pass or over Slieve Elva. The *gallóglaich* have been talking about it in the kitchen house. They reckon that the O'Kellys might be over here when darkness comes.'

'We won't be late,' she said soothingly. She was not deceived, however, by his voiced concern for the king. There had been only about ten or fifteen of the O'Kelly clan there on the mountain pass, and these *gallóglaich* were trained soldiers. They would be more than able to handle any O'Kellys that arrived. No, there were other matters on Cumhal's mind. He had been her father's servant and then hers. There was little she did not know about him and she guessed that there was little he did not know about her. Cumhal and Brigid had noticed something about the king's attentions to her, and had probably even seen the bodyguard slip out with the letter. They would have talked it over in whispers last night. This would be what was worrying Cumhal, not any threat to the king. Cumhal and Brigid did not want any romantic tête-à-tête suppers. They would not want any change. They would not want their mistress to leave her school and go to Thomond, even to be queen.

'Set up another trestle table for the bodyguards over there by the wall so that they can be near to the king and can keep checking the road,' she said after a moment's thought. 'The *gallóglaich* could put up their tents around the law school first and then check the road while the bodyguards eat.' The bodyguards would be just out of earshot over there next to the wall, but their presence would inhibit any lovemaking and would reassure Cumhal and Brigid.

'So what's the trouble with the O'Kellys, then?' she asked when she returned to the king. She sat down beside him on the bench and did not draw back when he moved a little closer. There was no point in pretending that she did not take pleasure from his affection for her. She did not stir, either, when Cumhal arrived a few minutes later with a small stool as well as the trestle table. When he came back with the stiff bleached linen cloth and the flagon of wine he removed the unused stool without comment. She allowed the corners of her mouth to twitch slightly.

'Tell Brigid we are ready when she is,' she said, calmly pouring some more wine into her cup and pushing the flagon towards the king.

'These are nice,' said the king, holding up the slender goblet.

'Cumhal carved them from the apple tree that used to stand over there by the gable end of the house,' she said. 'I used to eat apples from that tree when I was a child and it's nice to have these cups as a memory of it. We should be using my Venetian wine glasses in your honour, but I am terrified of dropping one or having the breeze tip one over out here in the garden.'

'I prefer these,' said Turlough. 'Good, honest Irish-made wine cups – we are having too much contact with the foreign places now, especially England. Look at Galway – all English dress, English laws! Do you know that they even have a law there that says if your name begins with an "O" or a "Mac" you may not strut or swagger in the streets of Galway.'

'I know,' said Mara. It always amused her to picture these clansmen, with 'O' or 'Mac' in their names, with their huge moustaches and their fringes hanging down to their eyes, dressed in their long, shaggy Irish mantles, strutting and swaggering through the crowds of scented, curled citizens of Galway with their padded doublets, hip-length cloaks, their tight hose and their neat, pointed beards. 'You haven't explained to me about the O'Kellys,' she added as he gave her hand a quick squeeze.

'Well, it all started about five years ago with that battle at Knockdoe, do you remember that?'

Mara nodded – Knockdoe was about eight miles north-east of Galway city. The place had been called something different before that battle, but afterwards it was always known as Knockdoe, the hill of the battleaxes.

'Well, myself and MacWilliam were against the army gathered by the Earl of Kildare, and Red Hugh, the O'Donnell; and the other northern chiefs and the O'Kellys from Ui Maine. The O'Kellys lost a lot of men,' he boasted, taking a gulp of wine, 'and they've never forgotten it and they keep swiping away at me.'

'Why just you?' asked Mara. 'I would have thought Mac-William would have been nearer to him. He's up there in Connaught, just beside him.'

Turlough looked all around him carefully and moved his head closer to her cheek. 'To be honest,' he said in a low voice, 'I wouldn't be surprised if young Garrett MacNamara had something to do with it. We took quite a bit of territory from the MacNamaras around Caisin, to the east of here. It's now part of Thomond, of course, but the MacNamaras would like it back, I suppose. Could be the O'Connor of Doolin, as well, perhaps. You never know. The earl, Gearóid Mór, is in the pocket of the English, of course. His second wife is related to the Tudors. You should have seen Gearóid when he came back from young Prince

Arthur's funeral. He was all decked out in silks and velvets like
any popinjay. Anyway, let's not worry about him; here comes
Brigid with my supper.'

'Here's a lovely loin of venison, my lord,' said Brigid, coming
out from the house bearing two small iron pots and accompanied
by Cumhal, carrying the large iron pot that held the venison.

'Put it on the stone there, Cumhal,' she said with a quick
peremptory gesture of her head. 'I hope you like the venison, my
lord. I cooked it with plenty of butter and a few sprigs of rosemary, Brehon.' She turned to Mara.

'It smells unbelievably good,' said Turlough, leaning over like
a greedy boy as Cumhal took the lid off the pot. 'And two sauces!
What are they?'

'This one is a wine and cream sauce; I think myself that is the
best flavour with venison, but the Brehon likes that other one
best. That's made from bearberries. I got the lads to pick me a
basketful in the bog last year and I dried them and kept them for
sauces.' Lovingly, Brigid placed the two pots next to the large one
on the stone beside the table, and then she bustled back into the
house again, coming back with two wooden platters piled high
with watercress and tiny crisp spears of celery.

'Carve some slices of the venison, Cumhal,' she ordered and
stood with her ladle poised while Cumhal filled each platter with
neat slices.

'I'll try both sauces,' said Turlough. 'A man of peace like
myself never likes to take sides between two women.'

'I'll have them both, also,' said Mara. After her long and
difficult day she felt that she could do with the soothing silkiness
of the cream sauce as well as the piquant bite of the bearberries.

'Wonderful,' said Turlough, shutting his eyes to savour first
one, and then the other sauce.

'You're not too worried about the O'Kellys, are you?' asked
Mara after Brigid and Cumhal had returned to the kitchen. She

cut a piece of venison with her knife and then speared the cube and popped it into her mouth. It tasted delicious: crusty with burned juices on the outside and succulent and tender on the inside.

'Not in the least,' said Turlough, crunching the celery noisily. 'If they want trouble they can come looking for it, of course. I'll give them something to think about.'

'As a man of peace, of course!' inserted Mara.

'Well,' said Turlough with a grin, 'it's like this venison, there is an art in never overdoing anything.'

'How's Conor?' enquired Mara. Conor was Turlough's eldest son.

'Good,' said Turlough. 'Have you been to his fine new tower house at Inchiquin? He's pleased to be the *tánaiste* since my brother died. It will be good to have my own son to take over when I am gone.'

'Pity he's not called Turlough,' said Mara. 'Then you could be like those Richards and Henrys over in England – you could have Turlough I and Turlough II and so on.' Let's keep talking about the kingdom, she thought. I don't want to think about the murder and I don't want any pressure about marriage tonight, either.

'He'll make a good king, Conor,' said Turlough, 'but of course it will be one of his brothers or his cousins who will follow him. It might be my second boy, and I wouldn't be too pleased about that. He has too much interest in English ways. He won't make a good king of Thomond. I don't trust him at the moment, at any rate. Anyway, let's not talk about anything troubling tonight. We'll just sit here like two old friends and enjoy our burgundy and our venison and let the tomorrows come when they are due.'

He placed his hand over hers. 'Mara,' he said quietly. 'I meant what I said in the letter. I won't bother you for a decision. Take your time; think it over, and perhaps when you come to see me with your reports at the end of the month you might want to discuss it then. There's only one thing more to say and that is that I know if you decide to be my wife I will be the happiest man in Christendom. I think we would get on well together,' he added in a lighter tone.

'I know that,' said Mara earnestly. 'It's just that I do need time to think and it is very generous of you to give me that time . . . Oh, thank you, Cumhal. I don't think we need another flagon of wine at the moment, but leave it there just in case.'

This is worse than when Dualta and I were thirteen and my father kept hovering around, she thought, watching Brigid ceremoniously bringing an unnecessary second dish of parsnips over to the table.

'So what about Kildare?' she asked.

'You heard the story about him going over to London and asking Henry VII for extra troops to deal with me?' asked Turlough. He paused to chew on a piece of venison and then added with huge enjoyment, 'Do you know what he said about me? These were his very words: "He is a mortal enemy to all Englishmen and the most maliciously disposed of any that I heard speak of." He wanted the Tudor king to give him 6,000 men to deal with me, but Henry was too mean a man for that. He had too many other things to occupy him at the time. He was in the middle of the Burgundian negotiations and that was of much more importance to him than Ireland. Too much had been spent on us, over the past few hundred years, for too little of a return. These were his views. Tomás MacEgan told me that and he is a very learned Brehon. You know Tomás, don't you?'

Mara nodded. She knew Tomás; he was a man who never opened his mouth until he had carefully considered his words, a man of immense learning, skilled in English, as well as Brehon, law. Briefly she thought about Colman and his interest in England. She herself had never bothered, but perhaps she should. Knowledge is power, her father often told her, and power was important to her.

'Tell me about English law,' she said.

'I don't know too much about it myself,' said Turlough, dipping a finger of yellow parsnip into the bearberry sauce and munching it. 'You'd want to talk to Tomás. All I know is that it is supposed to be based on Roman law. They hold their courts indoors, in big buildings – not like us where we have our courts out in the open, on top of hills, or beside ancient places like you do here on the Burren. They have many lawyers in these courts, as well as judges. They say that they have very savage punishments. Men can be hanged for theft there.'

'I've heard that,' said Mara. 'Is it any kind of theft or just something very serious like stealing from a great lord?'

Turlough shrugged. 'Almost any kind of theft,' he said. 'Anything from a loaf of bread to the theft of a horse.'

'So no matter what the crime, everything is punished in the same way?'

'Oh, they have worse punishments than hanging,' said Turlough. 'They can also hang a man, cut him down before he is dead, then draw out his guts before his eyes and then cut him up into quarters. Then they stick his head up on Tower Bridge so that everyone in London has to pass under it and be reminded that they must not break the law.'

'It's barbaric,' said Mara with conviction. 'What good do punishments like that do to anyone? I wonder that the English don't devise a more civilized set of laws.'

'By the way, one of my Brehons got a copy of English laws when he was in Galway. You might like to look at it. My Latin is too rusty to make too much of it.'

'I was thinking,' said Mara, 'that we should make a record of all of our laws. There are books of them in every law school, but these books need to be put together. It might be a good idea to have a Brehons' Conference some time. We could start this off in Thomond, with Brehons from your three kingdoms, and perhaps invite other Brehons from different kingdoms. If we are in danger from England, as you think, we will need to have this up-to-date record of our laws so that they don't get lost or forgotten.'

'That's a great idea,' said Turlough, slapping the trestle table with such force that the platters jumped and the flagon of wine tilted alarmingly. His face was illuminated with enthusiasm. 'When you come to see me we'll discuss our plans for this. It will be another thing for me to look forward to,' he added with a meaning-ful glance.

'I should make a start at this here at Cahermacnaghten,' said Mara thoughtfully. 'I should find all those old law texts, wisdom texts and judgement texts that my father collected, and things that he taught me, that his father taught him, and his grandfather before him, judgements and laws that have never been written down, but have been passed from generation to generation by word of mouth. I should write all these down and then put them together. It will be a lifetime's work; we will need to search through the whole of Ireland. Perhaps my grandson, little Domhnall, will carry on the work after I am gone. It should be done, though, no matter how long it takes.'

'There may come a time,' said Turlough sombrely, 'that no matter what we do, the law of England may prevail in Ireland and our Gaelic way of life and our Brehon laws, with all their humanity and their mercy, will be lost for ever.'

ELEVEN

HEPTAD 6

There are seven bloodlettings which carry no penalty:
1. *Bloodshed inflicted by an insane person*
2. *Bloodshed inflicted by a chief wife in jealousy of a concubine who comes in spite of her*
3. *Bloodshed by a physician authorized by the family to care for a sick person*
4. *Bloodshed inflicted in battle*
5. *Bloodshed by a man who enforces suretyship*
6. *Bloodshed by a man who takes part in a duel*
7. *Bloodshed by a boy in playing a sport*

☙❧

THE KING LEFT THE Burren early the following morning to go to the bishop's Mass at Kilfenora and afterwards on his formal tour around the kingdom of Corcomroe. As soon as he departed Mara called all of the scholars into the schoolhouse.

'I know it's Sunday,' she said to them. 'I don't want to break into your holiday, but I just want to get a few things straight in my mind before your memory of them fades. You can all be of great assistance to me, as you were all there on that night before *Bealtaine*.' She paused and looked around at them. All seemed at ease, alert, with bright eyes and eager faces.

'Hugh,' she said quickly. 'That was your knife – the knife that killed Colman. Is that right?'

'Yes, Brehon,' replied Hugh with the promptness of a well-trained hound.

'And you gave it to Colman? Why?'

He stared at her. A look of panic had returned to his small, freckled face.

'He asked me for it,' he said eventually.

'And you just handed it over to him?'

'Yes,' he said, looking a little relieved.

'Why?' she asked calmly.

'Because he . . .' Hugh's voice tailed away.

From the corner of her eye Mara could see Shane making signs to Hugh. She could interpret them easily. *Tell her*, the sign said, but Hugh was silent. She looked at him thoughtfully; he had clearly told Shane, possibly Fachtnan, too. She would not pursue the question now, she thought. He would tell her soon.

She turned away from Hugh. 'Now, you'll all have to help me. You are my scholars and you have always helped with my law cases. This is one case where you know more than I do. That night, I turned back after the first terrace, but you all went on. Even if none of you saw the killing, you were present and will have seen who was there. So when did you first see Colman's body, Hugh?'

He opened and shut his mouth once or twice and then, strangely, closed his eyes, almost as if the picture in front of them was too painful to bear. 'Just after the bonfire was lit,' he said in a low voice and half-opened his eyes again.

142

Mara beamed at him. 'That's wonderful evidence,' she said enthusiastically. 'And who put the torch to the bonfire?'

'Ardal O'Lochlainn,' said Hugh, his blue eyes now wide and candid.

Mara looked at the others. They were all nodding. 'You were all with Fachtnan, all the rest of you?' she asked and waited until the heads nodded. 'Now, what I want you all to do is to think back to the time before the bonfire was lit by Ardal O'Lochlainn . . .' She stopped suddenly, remembering that ride into Galway. Hadn't Ardal said that he had not been there? She tried to remember his words . . . something about allowing the men to go . . . but perhaps she had misunderstood him.

'Yes,' said Moylan and Aidan, speaking together as they often did. These two had come to the law school on the same day eight years ago. They were both six years then and had bonded together like a pair of puppies from the same litter. 'We were up on Eagle's Rock.'

'A great place for seeing the whole mountain,' said Mara. Their attention would have been mainly on the bonfire, she thought. Nevertheless, they were at an age where memory and eyesight are at their best. She turned back to Hugh.

'But you weren't on Eagle's Rock, were you?' she said gently.

The unhappy look was back in Hugh's eyes. 'No,' he said shortly.

'Colman told him to wait for him,' explained Shane.

'Wait a minute,' said Mara. She seized the long stick of charred pine that always stood at the side of the fireplace and drew a large oval on the whitewashed board that stretched the length and the height of the wall. 'Now, this is the first terrace on the mountain,' she said, indicating the outer oval and quickly sketching in another, slightly smaller oval inside of it. 'The king and I got as far as here, but most people were going on to the second or third terrace by the time we left. Now let me put in the other terraces.' With a steady hand she drew six more irregular oval shapes inside the first.

'Here is Wolf's Lair, on the fourth terrace,' she said, drawing a large 'X'. 'Where were you waiting, Hugh?'

'Over there,' he muttered.

'On the fourth terrace?'

He nodded silently. His face had gone pale. 'I couldn't see inside Wolf's Lair,' he said suddenly.

'Well, Wolf's Lair is on the western side of the mountain, so were you over there on the eastern side, the way that people come up?'

Shane was nodding encouragingly, so Mara moved on. Hugh had been very badly frightened; it would take him a time to trust her and to come out with the full story.

'And you other boys were up here on Eagle's Rock,' she continued, letting her voice take on a note of excitement. 'That's wonderful – just the place to see everything!' They would love the idea of a mystery and a chase, she knew. 'Quickly, now, don't even talk about it. Just think of a name and then come out and show me where they were just when the bonfire was lit.'

Colman was probably killed before the lighting of the bonfire, she thought, but it would have been quite dark by then. Little could have been seen on the mountain, just shadowy figures moving with pitch torches in their hands. Still, the sudden flare of a torch would illuminate a face for a minute. Once the bonfire flared up the light would give clarity to the figures, of course.

'Emer and Rory were over here,' said Enda, coming out and seizing the charred stick. He drew two stick-like figures, one with very large breasts outlined, and then stood back with a smirk, shrugging his blond hair out of his eyes. It's interesting how the art of adolescent boys seemed to reproduce the fertility symbols of ancient pagan times, she thought idly, as she said aloud, 'Good, so they were on the top terrace at the north side.'

'And Rory and Aoife were over here on the west side,' said Moylan, coming out and copying Enda's daring drawing. Even Hugh was sniggering now, Mara was glad to see.

'So they were also on the top terrace,' she said tolerantly.

'Father Conglach was on the fifth terrace over on the west side,' said Aidan, getting to his feet.

'No, he wasn't, he was on the fourth terrace,' contradicted Fachtnan.

'Yes, Fachtnan's right,' said Shane. 'I heard him shout at Nessa and she was on the fourth terrace.'

'No, he didn't shout at Nessa,' said Hugh quietly. 'He shouted at Colman; I heard him.'

Mara looked at him with interest, remembering the priest's condemnation of Colman. Hugh flushed under her gaze.

'Well, he shouted at Nessa, too,' insisted Shane.

'He might have yelled at Colman; I heard him yell, but I didn't take too much notice,' said Aidan. 'He is always shouting about something or other. He was shouting at me the other day for having pimples. He said that they were the mark of the devil,' he added in aggrieved tones.

Mara concealed a smile. 'Well, it looks as if Father Conglach was on the fourth terrace near to Wolf's Lair. Do you agree with that, Aidan?'

'I suppose so.' He thought for a moment and then said graciously, 'Yes, that's right.' He came out and drew a stick figure for Father Conglach on the fourth terrace.

'And Feirdin was going down,' said Fachtnan suddenly. 'I remember looking and wondering why someone was going down before the singing and the dancing started. And then I saw that it was Feirdin and I thought he might be frightened. He's a bit strange about some things. He was with someone. I don't know who it was. It wasn't anyone that I know.'

'Which terrace was he on?' asked Mara, her heart sinking.

This, of course, would be the conclusion that most people of the Burren would jump at and only Feirdin's mother would be upset. Even the MacNamara clan would not mind too much if it turned out that Feirdin MacNamara was the man who killed the young lawyer. After all, their own *taoiseach*, Garrett MacNamara, had taken his case for judgement and had wanted to have him kept under restraint. The responsibility to leave him at liberty would be borne by the Brehon.

'He was probably between the third and the fourth terrace when I saw him, or perhaps it was the second and the third,' said Fachtnan. 'I heard Malachy the physician call down to him, but Feirdin didn't stop. He was going down quite fast.'

'I'll ask Malachy, then,' said Mara. 'Put the two of them in, Fachtnan.'

After that the suggestions came thick and fast. The top terrace was filled with figures – most of the young people were up there: Donogh O'Lochlainn's young sons, represented by Moylan with a series of crosses. The older ones, the mothers and fathers, were content with the lower terraces – most of them were marked in on the sixth terrace; Daniel, probably deciding that this was to be Emer's last evening of fun before settling down to married life, had certainly been on the sixth terrace.

'Murrough and his wolfhounds were over there on the eastern side on the fifth terrace,' said Hugh unexpectedly. He walked forward, did a neat little sketch of a wolfhound head and then went over and sat on the floor with his arm around Bran who had come in to sit at his usual place under the lintel of the open door. If Murrough was on the eastern side there, he might have seen Hugh on the terrace below him, thought Mara. I'll have to ask him. At least one part of the boy's story could be confirmed.

'Oh, and Diarmuid was over there near Wolf's Lair,' said Shane. 'I remember seeing him, because I remember wondering if his dog, Wolf, would make a good hunting dog.'

'He's half-wolf himself,' said Mara. 'He may not want to hunt his relations.' But one half of her mind suddenly focused on Diarmuid, rather than his dog. Turlough had said Diarmuid was looking for her when she was in Galway. What had he to tell? He was a shy, reserved man. He would not have been up there with the boisterous crowd around the bonfire. He would have stood below and waited for someone to call on him for his fiddle music. Perhaps he wanted to talk about Lorcan, or perhaps he had seen something in the shadowy depths of the Wolf's Lair hollow. I'll see him after Mass, she thought quickly. He'd prefer an informal approach like that.

'Well, that was very worthwhile,' she said to the boys, 'thank you all for giving up your free time to me. Now I want an announcement to be made after Mass in each of the parishes of the Burren. I want all the people to come to the dolmen at Poulnabrone when the abbey bell rings for vespers. I will make a formal announcement of the killing of Colman and ask for the killer to come forward.' She paused and looked around. All heads were nodding. This secret and unlawful killing would have to be announced to the people of the kingdom. They all knew that.

'If we could divide ourselves among the parish churches of the Burren,' continued Mara, 'that would be the quickest and easiest. Fachtnan, will you go to Oughtmama, Enda you go to Drumaheily, Aidan to Rathborney, Moylan, you go to Noughaval as usual, and Shane, Hugh and I will go to Kilcorney.' She didn't go to Kilcorney normally; Noughaval was her parish church, the place where her father and mother and all of her other relations were buried, but Father Conglach was the most difficult of the priests in the kingdom of the Burren and she would be able to lean the whole weight of her office on him and make sure that her instructions were carried out. A request from one of the boys might be ignored by him. 'Go now, and get ready for Mass. I'll ask Cumhal to get the ponies ready. Hugh, Shane and I will walk, but the rest of you can have the ponies as you will have more of a journey.'

Shane looked disappointed, but a long, slow walk across the fields and back again might just trigger confidence in Hugh. She could arrange a little treat for them afterwards. Shane, though the younger of the two, had the stronger personality and Hugh was more likely to take notice of his advice than of his elders. She would work on him, she thought. Even if Hugh said nothing now, eventually he would tell all that he knew. She was beginning to guess the outline of his story and now she knew why Colman had met his death. She knew why, but she didn't know whose hand had plunged the knife into Colman's neck.

❈

'Cumhal,' she called as she went outside, 'will you get four ponies ready for the older lads? Make sure that you give the strongest one to Fachtnan. He has to go to Mass at Oughtmama and you know how difficult that climb up the mountain is.'

'He'll have to get off and walk for the last bit – he's a hefty lad,' said Cumhal. 'I'll tell him. You'll be getting the priests to make an announcement,' he stated. There was little that he did not know about the Brehon's procedures. Often she wondered what she would do without him and Brigid. She felt a sudden rush of affection for Cumhal, feeling sorry that she had teased him the night before. She noticed that he did not speed off in his usual quick, efficient way to do her bidding, but paused to straighten a stone on top of the wall. His face looked troubled.

'This is a bad business, isn't it?' she said, inviting a confidence.

Cumhal nodded. 'There's a lot of talk,' he said, carefully not meeting her eyes but apparently concentrating on straightening the stones to an unaccustomed degree of precision.

'Yes, there would be,' said Mara, bending down and pulling up a weed from among the gentians.

'People are saying things,' said Cumhal, taking one stone from its place and then replacing it in the same slot.

She nodded, without looking at him, and pulled out another couple of weeds. 'They'd talk to you when they wouldn't talk to me,' she said.

'There's talk that something was seen that night up on Mullaghmore.'

She considered this gravely. 'The killing?' she asked, straightening her back and looking at him.

'No,' he said quickly. 'But they're saying that plenty knew that he was dead before the night was over.'

Mara sank down on the wall, feeling one of the rearranged stones roll beneath her. Stones are perhaps better left undisturbed, she thought idly: move one, and the stability of a wall is lost.

'Would more than one have killed him?' she asked. It was possible, she thought.

Cumhal shook his head. 'I'm not saying that,' he said carefully. 'What I'm saying is that plenty knew that he was dead and they think they know why. There are no tears being shed over him on the Burren. He wasn't liked. No one trusted him. Some hated him; I know that for a fact. There was talk . . .' He hesitated for a moment; she could see the struggle going on in his face. He was one of the O'Connor clan himself. He would not want to betray any secrets, even to his mistress. Then he straightened. 'I'd better be getting those ponies ready now,' he finished firmly and she knew that he would say no more.

Why had no one said something to her before about the blackmail? she wondered. And yet, as soon as she considered the matter, she knew the reason. Families were all-important in this stony kingdom. Colman would have been regarded as one of her family and, because of the high respect in which she was held, no one would have wanted to complain of him. The people of the Burren had undoubtedly known what he was. Colman had been a blackmailer, she was sure of that – and now she faced the word, and acknowledged the evil intrinsic to that word. But whom had he blackmailed? And which one of his victims had eventually tired of his demands and taken that final step to silence the blackmailer for ever? Mara sighed and went indoors to select a suitable gown for Mass.

❋

Black, she thought, as she lifted the gowns from the chest at the end of her bed. Black was right for the occasion. It would mourn Colman, show her authority and in any case, black suited her very well. She pulled on a freshly laundered creamy-white *léine* and then laced the long sleeves to the shoulders of the gown and slipped it over her head. She studied her reflection in the long silver-plated mirror by the window, opening the one small casement to allow the sunlight to flood into the room. Yes, she thought, from the shining braids of black hair to the pointed toes of her leather shoes, she looked good. A pity that Turlough had gone to the bishop's Mass at Kilfenora in the nearby kingdom of Corcomroe. Still, he would be back this afternoon and they would have a meal together. She smiled wryly at her shadowy mirror image. Brigid had a great saying that she continually used to the lads: '*You can't have your cake and eat it*,' she would scold.

I'm trying to do that, Mara thought. I enjoy his company, I enjoy the compliments, the feeling of being admired, I would like him to make love to me, but I don't want to give up my position – I am probably the only woman Brehon in Ireland at the moment, I run a successful law school, I turn out good lawyers, on the whole; there are *aignes* and Brehons all over the country that have been trained by me here at Cahermacnaghten. If I married Turlough, I would have to give all that up.

A large white butterfly with a bright orange spot on each wing swooped in through the open casement and for a moment she stood and watched it as it fluttered around the room and then landed on a purple velvet cushion. It would not stay there long, she thought. It would prefer the liberty of the wide open spaces outside to the luxury of the inside; the clean, cool petals of the purple cuckoo flower to the softness of the velvet cushion. With a sigh, she turned and went down the stairs. The day was going to continue fine, she would leave the window open so that the butterfly could go free, and when she came back her chamber would be full of the scent of early summer.

❧

'Ride carefully,' she said to her scholars as she came out of the gate to her house. The ponies were all tossing their heads and whinnying with excitement. Cumhal had tied them to a long bar outside the gate piers and the four older boys were climbing up on to their backs. They looked relatively tidy now, but that wouldn't last after they had galloped across the Burren. Still, what did it matter? The two younger ones were shining with cleanliness and neat in their white *léinte*. Shane wore a brooch at his shoulder, but Hugh had none and suddenly Mara remembered the ornate jewel-studded brooch that Colman had been wearing. Was that belonging to Hugh? Very likely! Cian, the silversmith, had visited Hugh only a week ago. He had probably taken away Hugh's small silver brooch and given him the new one, as well as the knife, as reward for passing his examination. Hugh had got very high marks and Cian had been delighted.

'Let's go,' she said. 'Come on, Bran, you can come too.'

'But you have to wait outside the church,' said Shane gaily, resting his hand on the wolfhound's neck.

'Bran knows that,' said Mara as the ponies disappeared in a cloud of dust.

She waited until they were halfway across the fields to Kilcorney before she spoke again. Hugh was looking quite relaxed and happy, joining Shane in throwing sticks for Bran to retrieve and lay at their feet. She hated to break into their fun but she had to get this affair between Colman and Hugh clear in her mind before she started to disentangle some of the other threads of this complicated matter.

'Hugh, do you know what I mean by blackmail?' she asked, beckoning Bran to walk to heel by her side. Hugh nodded silently and dropped the stick that he had been carrying.

'Tell me what it is,' she said gently.

'Blackmail is the extraction of goods or silver by means of threats to reveal a hidden secret,' he said dully.

'And Colman was blackmailing you,' she stated.

He stopped and looked at her. There was a terrified look in his eyes.

'Does Shane know why he was blackmailing you?' she asked.

He nodded again and put his hand on Bran's neck.

'Do you mind if he tells me?'

He hesitated, slowly stroking the dog's muscular back.

'She probably won't be too cross,' observed Shane. 'A bit,' he added, 'but not too bad. You shouldn't have done it, you would probably have pa—' He stopped and bit his lip.

'You would probably have passed, anyway,' finished Mara. 'That was it, wasn't it, Hugh? You cheated at the examination and Colman found out. Come on, tell me . . . Was that it?'

He nodded reluctantly.

'He took in the Heptad about the seven types of women whose behaviour deprives them of their honour price,' said Shane eagerly. 'He kept just remembering the bit about the prostitute in the bushes and forgetting about the chantress of lying tales and . . .'

'I see,' interrupted Mara. 'And Colman caught you, did he?'

Hugh nodded.

'He had it stuffed into the sleeve of his *léine*,' said Shane. 'Colman saw him peeping at it.'

'And he said that he would tell you and I would fail my examination and I would be sent away from the law school for cheating,' said Hugh. His eyes filled with tears. 'He said I had to give him some very good presents, so when my father brought a new brooch and knife for me, I kept the knife a secret, but I gave him the brooch. I thought that would be enough for him, but I took the knife when we were going up the mountain. I thought Fachtnan would stop him, he stopped him bullying me before, but then Colman kept me with him and the others got ahead. Then he took the knife away from me and he said I had to get some more silver for him next month when my father visited me.'

'I guessed that was what it was.' Mara kept her tone calm and unruffled. 'Well, you shouldn't have tried to cheat, Hugh. For your punishment you will write out that Heptad five times in your very best handwriting. Give it to me before Monday morning and that will be the end of the matter. As Shane says, you would probably have passed your examination even if you did forget one or two categories so it was a foolish thing to do. Now, tell me, who did Colman talk to that night – when he told you to go away – was it Lorcan?'

'No,' said Hugh. He was looking much better, thought Mara with satisfaction.

'No? You're sure?'

'I'm not absolutely sure,' said Hugh doubtfully. 'But I didn't see Lorcan with him. It was Muiris that he was talking to . . . you know, Aoife's father. They were in Wolf's Lair together. But he may have talked with someone else afterwards. I wasn't near. He told me to go away. I . . . I was too scared to go over for a long time. And I missed the lighting of the bonfire, and the singing and the dancing. And I was just standing there in the dark. And Colman didn't come.'

'And when he got too fed up with waiting, he went over to Wolf's Lair,' said Shane.

'And you saw Colman,' said Mara. They had been walking fast and were coming near to Kilcorney now. The people in the Burren, wearing their best clothes, were thronging the small lanes, walking, riding or sitting in carts pulled by patient donkeys or stubborn mules. 'You found the body?' she asked quickly, conscious of the need to get the whole story before they arrived at the church.

Hugh shuddered. 'He was lying there with my knife sticking out of his neck.'

'And you saw no one else?'

Hugh shook his head. 'No, I was scared. I didn't know what to do. I thought everyone would think I had done it. It was my knife.'

'Why didn't you just pull the knife out and hide it?' asked Shane. Mara frowned at him, and Hugh shuddered again.

'I couldn't,' he said. 'I couldn't touch him . . . so I just climbed up and joined the others on Eagle's Rock.'

'And you told the others?'

'Later on,' said Hugh, 'when we were going home, Shane kept pestering me and asking what was wrong and asking where Colman was.'

Why didn't Fachtnan tell me? thought Mara.

Shane looked at her earnestly, seeming to read her mind. 'We didn't tell you, Brehon, because Hugh made us all swear on our fathers' honour that we wouldn't say anything. Fachtnan said that, anyway, someone else would be bound to have seen Colman's body on the way down, so it wouldn't matter that Hugh didn't tell. We couldn't believe it when nobody did see him. We kept waiting to hear the news. We didn't know what to do.'

'Well, never mind,' said Mara, dismissing this. There was no point in scolding at this stage. 'Hugh, are you sure you saw no one else? Up there near to Wolf's Lair?'

Hugh shook his head.

'Yes, you did,' said Shane. 'You saw Father Conglach talking to Nessa. You remember – you said she was crying. You thought he was scolding her about having a baby.'

'Oh, yes, I remember,' said Hugh, embarrassed.

The bells of the church had started to toll and Mara asked no more. The boys found the subject of Nessa's baby awkward. She was too young, too unattractive, for them to find it at all interesting.

'You go ahead and find a seat while I have a word with Father Conglach,' she said as they went down the path to the church. 'I shall ask him to make the announcement.'

❋

Father Conglach was looking unwell, she thought as she made her way back from the sacristy into the little church. He had agreed without protest to make the announcement and that was not like him. This latest evidence of evil and wrongdoing in the community seemed to have hit him badly. He swept out into the chancel in his usual way, but as he muttered the Latin prayer at the foot of the steps she thought his back looked more bowed than usual. His voice rose and fell as Mara considered the problem of Colman's death.

Why was Colman talking to Muiris? He would not have sent Hugh away if it had been just a normal conversation. It was undoubtedly a blackmail attempt. But what had Colman found to blackmail Muiris about? He was considered a good, upright farmer, a clever, astute man, a very successful man and a good family man. His son was courting the daughter of a *taoiseach* in Corcomroe. That would be a great match for him. No doubt he would want his daughter to make a good match, also. Mara tried to turn her head discreetly to see who was in Kilcorney church today. She dared not look openly around. Every eye would be on her – even more so than usual. Everyone would know about that secret killing and everyone would wonder what the Brehon was going to do. Diarmuid was there, she noticed, but she couldn't see Muiris. That was surprising; this was definitely the parish church for Poulnabrucky. She wondered whether Muiris had seen her crossing the high paved fields and had hastily decided to go to Mass at Carron, or Oughtmama instead.

❀

'Diarmuid,' Mara said after Mass was over and everyone was standing outside in the warm noontime sun, 'Diarmuid, you were looking for me yesterday. Brigid told me that you called.'

'Oh,' he said. He looked uneasy. 'Well, the truth is that I think I said a bit too much to you the day before. I had no right to say it. It was Lorcan's own business and I got it all wrong. It was just a bit of an argument that he had with Colman.'

'You're talking about that silver that Lorcan paid as blackmail to Colman,' said Mara briskly.

Diarmuid winced at her plain speaking. 'Well, it seems that I got it wrong,' he said unhappily. 'It wasn't that at all. Just a little wager between them, and Lorcan lost. That's all there was to it.'

'I see,' she said carefully. 'I understand what you are telling me, Diarmuid.'

They are all involved, she thought. The O'Connors will be worried about Lorcan being implicated, the MacNamaras will not really want Feirdin to be the one that killed Colman, the O'Lochlainns are involved with Muiris – was he not a foster-son to the old *taoiseach*? she wondered, trying to remember the past. And then there were the O'Briens. This was a clan that was much more numerous in Corcomroe and in Thomond, but there were still many minor members here on the Burren. Hugh's father, Cian, was a younger brother of an O'Brien *taoiseach* at Lemeanah Castle on the southern boundary between the kingdoms of Corcomroe and the Burren. The O'Briens would bring pressure on the king himself, if there were danger to one of their members.

Once she began her enquiries, the whole community would band together like a herd of threatened goats. They would present a solid front of prickly horns and it would be difficult to get behind the defences and establish the truth. She would have to do it, though. Without the truth the community would crumble away.

＋ᏌᎬᏞᏙᎬ

BRETHA CRÓLIGE

(JUDGEMENTS OF BLOODLETTINGS)

There are two fines to be paid by a person who murders
another. The first is called the éraic, or body fine, and this is
paid to the nearest kin of a murdered person. It is forty-two
séts, or twenty-one milch cows, or twenty-one ounces of silver.
Added to this is the second fine, which is based on the victim's
honour price.

In the case of duinetháide, *a secret killing, the éraic is*
doubled.

ᎧᎧ

THE BELL FOR VESPERS rang out clear and loud from the
abbey in the still evening air. Almost immediately all of the
parish churches took up its deep-toned note and the Burren was
filled with their clamour – not a joyful sound; these bells clanged
with a menace of past sins uncovered and present sins to be atoned.
There was no sense of merriment, no talking, no laughter nor
joking, when once again, only three days after the eve of *Bealtaine*,

the people of the Burren congregated at the ancient dolmen of Poulnabrone. They came slowly and they came reluctantly, but they came because for over 1,500 years they and their ancestors had lived by this system of justice that relied on the goodwill and the cooperation of the clans to keep the peace within its community.

Mara, Brehon of the Burren, the only woman in the country to hold this post of high honour, stood before them. Her face was grave and the black gown that she wore over the customary white *léine* gave extra weight to the solemnity of the occasion. Grouped around her were the six scholars of her law school, their faces as grave as hers. Brigid had quickly restored all the *léinte* to a state of early-morning cleanliness and the white stood out against their tanned faces, arms and legs. One face, however, was as white as the *léine*; Hugh stood there, silently suffering, his blue eyes wide with apprehension. Mara had spoken with him earlier; the boy knew what he had to do. He had only asked that his father, who was away in Galway, should not be summoned. Nevertheless, Mara's warm heart was sore for him. Her eyes met Brigid's and Brigid moved a little closer to the boy and stood beside him. Brigid had known Hugh for seven years. He was like a foster-child to her. It had been Brigid who had comforted him at night when he wept for his dead mother and Brigid who had coaxed him to eat with special tasty treats during the days that followed that sudden death.

Other eyes were on Hugh, also, Mara noticed. Suddenly she realized that most of the people present today knew as much about the events of that *Bealtaine* Eve as she did. Mara was sensitive to atmosphere and she could now feel waves of sympathy and protectiveness coming towards the boy. What had everyone seen that night? Did they know that Colman was killed on the mountainside? Did they know whose dagger lay buried in his neck? Did they suspect that Hugh had been driven by intolerable pressure to do the deed?

'Hugh!' Emer detached herself from the crowd and rushed forward, her beautiful, delicately tinted face blushing slightly. Mara noticed with amusement that all of the older boys had flushed a dark red as she approached. 'Hugh,' repeated Emer, bending over the boy and stroking the red curls with a maternal air. 'We've got a litter of new puppy dogs. Would you like to come over and see them afterwards, later on this evening? You can help me to name them. Would you like that?' she cooed.

'Can I come, too?' asked Shane.

'Of course,' she said warmly, but her eyes were still on Hugh, her small brown hand stroking his hair and patting him on the shoulder. 'You'll come, then?' and without waiting for an answer she bent down and dropped a light kiss on the top of his head. I wonder, does she think that Hugh has done her the service of getting rid of her unwanted suitor? thought Mara cynically.

Her eyes moved to the cluster of young men at the side of the dolmen. Roderic was smiling, his square young face illuminated with inner happiness, though his eyes were compassionate when they looked at Hugh. Hugh's knife had been seen in Colman's neck; that was for sure, thought Mara. Possibly many guessed that he was blackmailing the boy. Yes, this was the general view at the moment; the people of the Burren suspected that Hugh had killed Colman and that was the reason for the silence on *Bealtaine* night. Hugh was the only scholar at her law school who came from the Burren and the people of the Burren were fiercely protective of their own. She had to sort this matter out, at least. This crime must not hang over Hugh. Mara moved forward and held up one hand. Silence fell instantly.

'*Dia's muire agat*,' she said in the traditional greeting and back came the answer, 'God and Mary and Patrick be with you.'

'I, Mara, Brehon of the Burren, announce to you that a killing of the *aigne*, Colman Lynch, took place on Mullaghmore Mountain on the eve or the early morning of May the first, the feast of *Bealtaine*.' She paused and a little ripple ran around the crowd, with those nearest repeating her words so that those on the outside of the crowd could hear.

'I now call on the person who killed the *aigne*, Colman, to acknowledge the crime and to pay the fine. Colman's honour price as an *aigne* is the sum of six *séts* or three ounces of silver or three milch cows. The *éraic*, or body fine, for an unlawful killing is forty-two *séts*, or twenty-one ounces of silver or twenty-one milch cows. The whole fine, then, is forty-eight *séts*.' Mara paused and looked all around. There was no murmur, no sound from anyone. The people of the Burren stood as if they were carved from the rock beneath their feet and every eye seemed to be directed towards Hugh.

'For the second time, I call on the person who killed the *aigne*, Colman, to acknowledge the crime and to pay the fine of forty-eight *séts*,' said Mara calmly and without emotion. This time no one repeated her words. She heard them herself, ringing off the limestone cliffs behind the dolmen. She waited, surveying the crowd, but still no one stirred.

'For the third time, I call on the person who killed the *aigne*, Colman, to acknowledge the crime and to pay the fine of forty-eight *séts*,' said Mara, but she knew by now that no one would reply.

'More than forty-eight hours have now passed since this killing took place, so I now declare it to be a case of *duinetháide*, a secret and unlawful killing. The *éraic* is now eighty-four *séts*. Add to that the victim's honour price, and the fine is now ninety *séts*.' She waited for a moment. Now she could hear a low murmur of conversation. Heads were turned, one to the other. She held up her hand again, and again silence fell.

'Is there anyone who can bear witness to the events on that night?' she asked.

Again a murmur rose from the crowd and then, surprisingly loud, a light treble voice said: 'I can.'

A wave of pride came over Mara. She turned towards Hugh and beckoned. He came over and stood beside her, looking very small and pale, dwarfed by the immense dolmen that reared up beside them. She longed to put her arm around him, but she would not injure his dignity. Diarmuid came forward from the edge of the crowd and, with a quick swing of his muscular arms, lifted Hugh on to the dolmen itself and then sat beside him.

'Tell what you know,' said Mara formally.

'I was with Colman that night,' he said, his voice now unnaturally loud and strained. 'He was blackmailing me; he knew that I had cheated in an examination. First he made me give him my silver brooch and then he made me give him my knife. He sent me to wait while he talked with people. When I went to find him, I found he was lying dead in Wolf's Lair with my knife stuck in his neck.'

Mara waited for a moment. The buzz of conversation was too loud for her voice to be heard clearly. But there was a rumble of anger, deep anger, beneath the noise – was it anger against Colman, or against his killer? Against Colman, she was sure. She held up her hand and waited for the sound to die down before saying loudly and emphatically, 'Hugh O'Brien, I ask you now, did you kill Colman, the *aigne*?'

Hugh stood very straight. This time he did not address the crowd. He turned towards her and spoke out in a clear strong voice. 'No, Brehon,' he said. 'I did not kill Colman, the *aigne*. He was already dead when I found him.'

A deep swell of sound, almost like a breeze blowing through an ash wood, came from the crowd. It was wordless, but in it there was sympathy, understanding and indignation. Several women, standing nearby, dabbed at their eyes with pieces of linen. The colour returned to Hugh's face, and Emer rushed out to him, followed by Aoife. Diarmuid swung Hugh down from his perch and the two girls hugged him, Fachtnan slapped him on the back and then the other scholars did the same. Mara's eyes met Brigid's and she saw Brigid smile with a mother's pride, before slipping away to get supper ready for their return.

'That was very brave of Hugh,' came Nuala's clear voice. She was very maternal towards Hugh who was only a year younger than she, thought Mara. Nuala had come to terms with the loss of her mother and had tried to help Hugh but she had a stronger character than he did. Her suffering was locked within her and only showed in an occasional impatience with her father.

Mara's eyes were now scanning the crowd, trying to read the faces. She felt warmed by the support for the child, but she knew this was not the end of the matter. Someone had killed Colman; this could not be forgotten; could not remain hidden. She had to find out who it was. She held up her hand.

'Has anyone else any evidence to give?' she asked, her tone bland and neutral.

Now there was silence. From the corner of her eye Mara could see Diarmuid glance at his cousin Lorcan and then look away again. Other people were looking across at Gráinne Mac-Namara; her son, Feirdin, was not there. Gráinne must have left him at home, perhaps worried in case someone said something to him. The silence continued; nothing more was going to be said.

'By the authority vested in me by King Turlough Donn, King of Thomond, Corcomroe and Burren,' said Mara, 'I declare that the fine for this crime will be reduced to forty-eight *séts* if acknowledgement is made here at Poulnabrone within the next seventy-two hours. The victim may bear some responsibility for this crime, and I will take this into account.'

She waited for a few minutes, but she did not expect any open announcement. Not yet . . . That was not the way that they did things here. There would first be a tentative approach, possibly from a friend or relation, and then perhaps a long talk, with the matter slowly and cautiously touched on, and, eventually, a confession. That was the way things went. She had given a powerful incentive, though, for the guilty to confess. The fine was manageable now with help from the clan. What if a man had no clan, though? she thought and her mind went quickly to Muiris. Muiris was an O'Heynes. She remembered hearing that he had come to the Burren as a boy and had lived with the O'Lochlainn at Lissylisheen, either as a foster-son, or a servant. She had never heard any further details. Either the people of the Burren did not know, or else no one spoke of it. She looked around the crowds, narrowing her eyes against the western sun.

Where was Muiris? Aoife was there and so was Áine, Muiris's wife, and so were the two elder sons. Why was Muiris not there? She sighed as she thought back to that old case. Why had Colman gone through these old judgement texts? This was going to be a difficult and distasteful matter, but there was no more to be gained by keeping the crowd there any longer.

'Go now,' she said formally. 'Go in peace with your family and your neighbours.'

I have laid the bait, she thought; now to hook the fish. She walked over towards the crowd of youngsters. Without surprise she saw that Rory and Roderic had joined Aoife and Emer in the crowd around her scholars. Hugh had escaped from Emer's cooing attentions to chat with Nuala, so Emer was now free to devote her attention to dimpling and blushing prettily at Roderic's whispered remarks. Aoife had with her two of her four brothers: Felim, who was betrothed to the daughter of the *taoiseach* in Corcomroe, and Aengus who was just a year older than she. A handsome pair of young men, thought Mara, looking at them both with interest, for a work-worn, plain-looking woman like Áine and a low-stature man like Muiris to produce. Felim, especially, with his blond hair and large brown eyes was extremely good-looking. Aoife, though without the startling beauty of dark-haired Emer, was a very pretty girl with her thick blond plait and her cornflower eyes. By all accounts, she was her father's favourite. Muiris was a man who had a lot to lose, thought Mara. Felim had made a great match and now he would want the same for Aengus and for Aoife. He would certainly not be content to see his only daughter married to a wandering bard.

'Rory!' said Mara. Surrounded by all the young people, he had swung himself on top of one of those huge boulders that littered the tableland of the high Burren and stood there, outlined against the sky. He looked magnificent, she thought, rather like a god from one of the ancient stories, with his eyes as blue as the sky and his hair as golden as the sun. He had just begun to sing the first line of *'Cailín Ó Chois tSiúre Mé'*, but Mara's severe glance made him stop and clear his throat apologetically. After a moment he slid down again. Aoife giggled, and then turned red at the sight of Mara's serious face; the law school scholars shuffled their feet; Roderic hastily took his horn from his lips and concealed it behind his back.

Inwardly Mara's heart, always warm towards the young, sympathized with them, but this was no time to sing. Let them enjoy themselves out of sight of their elders. A man was dead, and someone on the Burren was guilty of *duinetháide*, one of the worst crimes. In England prison and the hangman's noose could enforce justice; here its success relied on the consensus and the cooperation of the community. The occasion had to remain solemn.

Thirteen

Din Techtugad

(THE LAW OF TAKING POSSESSION)

Sencha judged his first case wrongly. He judged that a female should take possession of an inheritance in the same fashion as a male would do so. Blisters came upon his cheeks. The wise female judge, Brig, showed him that he was wrong. He reversed his judgement and the blisters disappeared from his cheeks.

ᛝᚷ

MONDAY WAS A DIFFICULT day at the law school. The boys seemed restless and unable to concentrate. It had rained very heavily all night; several times Mara had woken to hear it thundering on the stone roof of her house and when she had finished her breakfast it was still lashing the stone clints in the fields with a ferocity that would have seemed impossible during the fine, balmy days that preceded it. She stood at the door for a moment, pulling the hood of her cloak over her head and listening to the hiss of the rain on the burnished stone. The slanting grey lines of the downpour were so dense that she could barely see the ten-foot circular wall of stone, which surrounded the law school buildings. It would be difficult conducting her investigations on a day like this, she decided as she set off to run down the road. Today would have to be a normal day of study at the law school.

The morning had started off well. The map of the seven terraces on Mullaghmore was still on the wall and Shane had suddenly remarked, 'I remember someone else, Brehon. He was near to Wolf's Lair a while before the bonfire was lit. I'd say he was one of the first to go down the mountain and he disappeared quite quickly.'

'Well, go on,' said Enda aggressively. 'Spit it out. Who was it?'

Mara frowned. Enda was a nuisance. He was just at the awkward age of adolescence when his behaviour and his control of himself seemed to be almost that of a two-year-old, but his vision of himself was that of a man of surpassing ability and charm, and he was resentful of any authority. Unfortunately he had a great influence over Moylan; and Aidan, also; the three of them tried her patience on occasion. This morning she decided to say nothing, but gave him a long, cold look and turned to Shane.

'Put a cross in the place where you saw him, Shane. Do you know who it was?'

She waited for a name; the lads knew most people within the four clans on the Burren, but Shane was shaking his head. 'No, I don't think I ever saw him before. He was very tall, even taller than Fachtnan.'

'Oh,' said Mara thoughtfully. 'I think I might have seen him, also. I saw someone on a horse when I was walking across with King Turlough. Yes, he would have been tall. And he had very black hair. Did you notice that, Shane?'

Shane turned to look at her, the stick of charcoal in his hand, and then shook his head again. 'No, I don't remember that,' he said. 'I only noticed him because he was so big. I think he was standing somewhere near Diarmuid. I saw him in the flare of Diarmuid's torch, but I didn't notice anything much about him.'

Mara nodded. 'No one else noticed him, did they?' she asked with a quick look at Hugh. He would have been the nearest, but he was shaking his head just as the others were.

'I could run down to Diarmuid and ask him does he remember,' offered Enda with an obliging air.

'We could go with him,' suggested Moylan.

'We'd like to help,' said Aidan, trying to put on a saintly expression which didn't quite work on his very pimpled face and heavy adolescent features.

Mara looked out of the window. Cumhal, his hood pulled well over his head, was trudging past with a bucket in either hand. He would be going to milk the black cow in the far meadow.

'Cumhal,' she called. 'Would it be a nuisance for you to call in at Diarmuid's house on your way? Shane saw a stranger on Mullaghmore on *Bealtaine* Eve. He was very tall: I think that I saw him myself, riding along the road near the lake. If it's the same man, he had very black hair. Diarmuid may have noticed him and may know who he is. Would you be able to do that, Cumhal?'

'No trouble at all, Brehon,' said Cumhal obligingly. 'I'll be passing Diarmuid's house on the way down to the Moher field.'

Enda blew out his lips with an expression of disgust; Moylan and Aidan copied him instantly and Shane giggled. Mara sighed. 'Let's do our Latin now,' she said cheerfully. 'Fachtnan, King Turlough gave me a document from a London court and you and I will see if we can translate it, Shane and Hugh, will you study your verbs, and you three,' she addressed Aidan, Moylan and Enda, 'I've written down some judgements here in Latin and I want you turn them back into Gaelic.'

'Boring,' muttered Enda rebelliously. Once again Mara ignored it. Later on she would wonder whether if she had tackled his behaviour then she might have been saved a lot of trouble afterwards, but at the time she felt a certain sympathy. He was an active boy, clever, quick-thinking, and easily bored. They had missed much of their usual fun on Saturday and Sunday, which they usually spent riding, hunting, swimming or playing hurling from dawn to dusk, and now he was in no mood for work. She would have to arrange something once the weather cleared. She took a quick glance out of the window. The sky still had a heavy leaden look, but over towards the west there was a faint lightening, a somewhat paler shade of grey, somewhere in the region of the Aran Islands.

❋

Cumhal was back within a half-hour. The boys heard the sound of his footsteps clumping over the wet flagstones outside the schoolhouse. They all sat up and their eyes brightened. Shane had jumped up to open the door almost at the same moment as the knock sounded and Bran, dozing by the fire, sat up eagerly with his tail wagging.

'Come in, Cumhal,' said Mara.

'I won't, Brehon,' said Cumhal, still standing in the doorway. 'I'm all wet. I'll only bring the damp in with me. I just wanted to tell you that Diarmuid saw the man Shane was talking about, all right. His name is O'Connor. He's from Corcomroe. He is one of the O'Connors from Doolin ... from the stone quarry in Doolin. He's the son of that man who was killed about a month ago.'

'Murdered?' enquired Moylan hopefully.

'No, it was an accident,' explained Cumhal. 'He was cutting out flagstones from the cliff side – they had a big order on and he was working late at it. I suppose he was tired, like. Anyway, he chipped away a bit too fast and a stone further up the slope came away and crushed him to death. The son has the business now.

His name is Oscar, Brehon. A fine big young fellow, Diarmuid says.'

'Thank you, Cumhal,' said Mara. Corcomroe, she thought, that's not in my jurisdiction. I'll have to see Fergus. Fergus MacClancy was the Brehon at Corcomroe, a kind, fatherly man who had uncomplainingly taken on the duties of the Burren as well as of Corcomroe after the death of Mara's father in 1489 and had encouraged her to apply for the post as soon as she became twenty-one, five years later.

'I'll have to go over to Corcomroe after school today,' she said aloud. 'Fachtnan, you can come with me. You'll be a help to me in this investigation. Now settle down to work, all of you, and if you work well I'll ask Brehon MacClancy to arrange a hurling match between the Cahermacnaghten and the MacClancy law schools.'

'Can we do some investigating too?' asked Moylan.

'It's not fair if Fachtnan gets a chance and we don't,' said Enda.

'Fachtnan is three years older than you are,' said Mara coldly. 'Now, Enda, that's enough. And,' she added looking over his shoulder, 'if you can't produce a better script than that you can stay behind after school and rewrite it.'

Then she turned her back on him and sat down beside Fachtnan. His Latin was still a little weak, but he was such a hard-working, pleasant boy with a very mature understanding of people that she was willing to put a lot of effort into helping him to pass his final examinations next year. He would make a good Brehon, she thought.

'It's interesting, isn't it?' he said thoughtfully after he had struggled through the first translation. 'It's interesting how very different their laws are to ours. This case here of the woman who was sentenced to be burned to death, tied to a stake...' He stopped and took a deep breath. 'That's absolutely terrible,' he said. 'She was to be burned because her husband sued the court for that sentence to be passed . . . and all she had done was take a lover secretly. It counts as treason – petty treason – in England if a woman deceives her husband! Why didn't he just divorce her if he was that worried about it?'

'They don't have divorce in England,' said Mara. 'I suppose because the eldest son always inherits the land and property that it is important for a man to be certain of who is his son. This man is an earl and he would have great lands and possessions.'

'Whereas here in Ireland,' said Fachtnan, 'any son that is recognized by his father gets a share whether it is a son of a formal marriage, or not. I don't think that I would like England very much,' he added. 'See this case of the homeless boy who was sentenced to death because he stole a hen. Here he would be called "a fox of a cooking pot" and it would be no offence for him to steal food to keep himself alive. In fact, it would be an offence not to give a boy like that hospitality if he asked for it. And look at this,' he said, pointing a grubby fingernail at another paragraph in the document. 'You can be sentenced to death for any theft of goods worth more than a . . . What's that word?'

'That would be a shilling in English,' said Mara. 'Have you heard of a groat?' she asked, guessing that he would not have heard of a shilling. 'A shilling would be worth three groats.'

Fachtnan was shaking his head. 'No, I've never heard of a groat, but I've seen a penny once,' he said. He would have little knowledge of coinage, thought Mara. Although the law texts spoke glibly about ounces of silver, most fines were paid with cows, calves or heifers – more trivial ones were paid with chickens, eggs, or even pots of honey. Gaelic Ireland was very different to Tudor England. This was a society based on small communities who all knew each other and who bartered goods to supply their needs.

'And look at that case,' continued Fachtnan. 'A woman was branded on the cheek, just like an animal . . .'

'Enda,' said Mara wearily, seeing from the corner of her eye a blob of soot-black ink being flicked from the end of a quill, 'this is your last warning. If I have to speak to you again you will stay in after school. And that goes for you, Moylan, as well,' she added, seeing Moylan slide his penknife back into his pouch. There was a new cut on the desk in front of him, but she decided to ignore it. It was a time-honoured custom for the scholars to cut names and complaints into the desks. Everyone did it sooner or later. She decided to devote another few minutes to Latin and then to discuss the case. After all, the scholars were there not just to learn the laws and to study Latin, but also to learn from her handling of cases. She left Fachtnan to struggle on by himself and went to sit in front of the schoolroom. She would have to ensure that there was no more bad behaviour, or else she had to keep her word about the threatened detention. She didn't want to do that. The sky was clearing and a few hours running around after school would do them all good.

'Put away your work now and let's discuss the case,' she said after a silence had ensued for at least ten minutes and sufficient work had been done by all of the scholars. She waited until they had all resumed their seats and then continued. 'We have two questions to solve here: first, who had the opportunity to murder, and, secondly, who had a motive to murder Colman?'

'Everyone wanted to murder him,' muttered Enda and then looked ashamed. She understood his embarrassment. It still did not seem real that Colman, who had lived here at the law school for fourteen years, was the victim that they were discussing.

'What are the usual motives for murder?' she asked.

'Revenge, a wish for gain, anger, fear,' said Shane promptly. 'That's in one of the wisdom texts,' he added.

'The murderer could be Fachtnan,' suggested Aidan hopefully. 'After all, he might become a master at the law school here now that Colman is gone. That would be a wish for gain.'

'Yes, but I had no opportunity,' said Fachtnan tolerantly. 'I was with you four all the time.'

'What about Roderic?' suggested Enda, his eyes bright and alert. 'He wants to marry Emer; everyone knows that. If Colman is dead, then Daniel might allow them to get married.'

'Yes, that's who it was,' said Aidan enthusiastically. 'She would definitely want to marry Roderic. Everyone knows that she has . . .' He stopped, obviously trying to put Emer's feelings for Roderic into words that Mara would accept, but that would not sound too sentimental.

'Did he have opportunity?' asked Mara, looking at the board for the horn symbol.

'Yes,' said Enda, coming out and pointing. 'He was there with Emer. They could both have done it. And I heard him say that King Turlough had offered him a position at court, so, if Colman were out of the way, he would be able to pay the bride price soon.'

'Any other suspects?' asked Mara. He was right, of course, Roderic had motive and opportunity; yet, somehow, she didn't think he was the type. And, of course, he had been with Emer all the evening. Would she have condoned a murder?

'Well, there's Hugh,' said Shane thoughtfully. 'He had a motive because Colman was blackmailing him, so fear would be his motive. And he had opportunity. And it was his knife.'

'It wasn't Hugh,' said Mara swiftly. 'Colman had bruises and scrapes on his hands where someone had wrestled the knife out of his grasp. Hugh is not strong enough to do that. And, also, the footprints seemed to show that two men wrestled there at the spot where Colman was killed. Both sets of footmarks were too big for Hugh's feet.'

'That's all right, then,' said Shane agreeably. 'Anyway, he told me that he didn't do it. He swore to me on his father's honour.'

'Stop talking about me as if I'm not here,' said Hugh resentfully.

'Well, I was just putting the case,' said Shane equably. 'A good lawyer has to put aside all emotion. That's right, isn't it, Brehon?'

Mara nodded slightly. Shane had the mind of a lawyer, she thought. With his good brain and his wonderful memory he would make a good one. She wasn't so sure about Hugh.

'Was Colman blackmailing anyone else, other than Hugh, Brehon?' asked Fachtnan. She looked at him with interest. Yes, he would make a good Brehon. She would discuss the matter with him afterwards in confidence, she thought. Enda was too immature and the others too young.

'That certainly should be one line of enquiry,' she said approvingly. 'I think, though, we should first concentrate on who had opportunity and this is where you can all help me. Perhaps if the weather is fine tomorrow then I'll make out a list for you and you can take your pens and tablets and go around the Burren making enquiries. Now, get out your sets of wisdom texts and see if you can learn at least ten new texts off by heart.'

FOURTEEN

URAIRECHT BECC (SMALL PRIMER)

A stone-cutter has an honour price of three séts. This is less than half the price of a stonemason.

If a stone-cutter accidentally injures another during the course of his lawful work, he does not have to pay any fine or compensation.

⊙⊙

AS SOON AS THE BELL for vespers sounded Mara and Fachtnan set off on their horses, going towards Corcomroe through the fields in the mountain gap. The rain had stopped, but there was a fresh wind from the Atlantic blowing strongly in their faces and the ground was soft. This was land where shale and heavy mud had formed a layer over the limestone: the wet fields were bright green with new rushes and sprinkled with marsh marigolds and cuckoo flowers, but the mud was near to the surface and the horses' feet sank at every step. Mara felt irritated by their slow pace; she had a lot to do. The sooner that this murder was solved, the sooner life could go back to normal. She was relieved when they came out on to the stony lane which led to the sea.

'The MacClancys are only just coming out of the school-house,' said Fachtnan. 'They must work an hour later than us. Unlucky!'

'Lucky!' said Mara with satisfaction. Fergus would be still there and she might get this business of young Oscar O'Connor over with quickly. She jerked the reins and quickened her pace.

'Fergus,' she called as they clattered up the path to the law school which, like her own, was housed within an ancient ring fort.

Fergus came out instantly. He was a thin, slightly built man with the stooping shoulders of a scholar. He had been a friend of her father and he was now in his sixties. His father, grandfather and great-grandfather had been Brehon of Corcomroe before him, but Fergus himself was childless. It would be a good position for Fachtnan, perhaps, when he qualified. Fergus could do with some help. He was beginning to look an old man. Mara had thought the same about Colman, but she was glad that she had never suggested it. Fergus was too kind, too diffident, to have someone like Colman with him. The master would soon have become the servant. Fachtnan would suit Fergus better. She looked at him with affection as he came towards the gate. His short-sighted eyes peered anxiously for a moment and then his face lit up.

'Mara,' he said, hastening out to meet her and offering a hand to help her dismount. 'We were just talking about you yesterday, King Turlough and myself.'

'He got off safely for the Aran Islands?' asked Mara with a glance at the turbulent sea heaving and erupting with enormous clouds of white spume.

'Yes, he would've got there before the storm broke,' said Fergus, smoothing his wind-blown grey hair out of his eyes and pulling his gown more tightly around his thin frame. 'He was going to come back tonight, but he'll probably leave it until the sea is a bit calmer tomorrow morning. That was a terrible business about your young assistant,' he added in a low voice.

'Yes, indeed,' said Mara gravely. 'A terrible affair. That is why I am here. I am gathering evidence from everyone about who was near to the spot where he was killed. My neighbour, Diarmuid O'Connor, thinks he saw a young man from Corcomroe there – an Oscar O'Connor, from the stone quarry. Do you know him?'

'Oh yes, of course I know him. Would you like to speak to him? I'll send one of the scholars to fetch him. You can come inside and have a cup of ale with Siobhan and myself. We were just saying last night that it was a long time since we had seen you.'

'No, no,' said Mara hastily. Fergus was a nice man, but his wife, Siobhan, was a woman of surpassing dullness whose conversation seldom rose above a monotone recounting of the boring discussions that she had with her servant girls.

'As Fíthail says, it is always best to see a witness in his workplace,' she said, improvising swiftly. Fíthail, she knew, had said many things: there were books and books of his sayings and, who knows, he may well have said that as well.

'You're right,' said Fergus, trying to look as if the saying was familiar to him. She smothered a grin. Dear old Fergus, he had a great respect for her memory and her learning. He would not question her any further.

'Could you lend us one of your lads to show us the way?' she asked.

'I'll come with you myself. I'll just send one of them over to the Brehon's house to tell Siobhan. You'll come in on the way back?'

'Oh yes,' said Mara, resolving that she would do no such thing. It would be easy to find an excuse after she had seen this Oscar O'Connor.

'We'll have to go back the way you came and then turn a little to the south,' said Fergus when he returned leading a bony old horse. 'It'll only take us about ten minutes.'

❋

'So the father died a month ago,' she said as they went along. 'Had he just the one son?'

'Just the one,' confirmed Fergus. 'There were others, two older boys, but one lad drowned in a boat going to the Áran Islands and another was killed on the cliff face in the same way as his father.'

'How old is Oscar?'

'I think he is about twenty-five,' said Fergus. 'I don't know him very well, to be honest with you. He's not been living around here for quite some time. He established a business in Galway. He used to come occasionally to order new supplies of stone from his father.'

'He was trading flagstones there, then?' asked Mara, trying to quicken the pace a little. Why didn't Fergus get himself a decent horse? she wondered. He must be quite rich; he had all the rentals on the Tuaith Ghlae property as well as his fees from the legal work as Brehon of Corcomroe and his fees from the law school.

'Yes, a very good trade,' said Fergus. 'He had boatloads shipped over to London a while ago, his father was telling me that the last time we met.'

'Why Galway?' asked Mara. 'Why didn't Oscar send them from the harbour down there at Doolin?'

'Well, he has an aunt in Galway who is married to a merchant called Seán Lynch and I suppose he started him off with contacts,' said Fergus, gently urging his horse away from tearing mouthfuls of grass from the side of the lane.

'Seán Lynch!' exclaimed Mara.

'That must be Colman's mother,' called back Fachtnan over

his shoulder. 'Yes, it is. I seem to remember him saying something about having cousins somewhere in Corcomroe.'

'He never visited them,' said Mara. 'I would remember if he had ever visited them when he was a boy at the law school.' She wasn't surprised, though. Colman was very prone to boasting about the Lynch family and their connections: a humble stone-cutter would not be anything to be proud of. His honour price would have been only three *séts*. Colman's mother had married well; she may have been the one to sever connections. Neither Colman, nor his parents, had ever mentioned cousins in Corcomroe to her.

'So that's why he went over to the bonfire at Mullaghmore,' said Fergus. 'I was wondering about that. We have our own bonfire here. I suppose he went to meet his cousin.'

'I suppose so,' said Mara grimly. 'Is that the quarry ahead?'

'That's it,' said Fergus.

There were men working everywhere, some on the cliff face and others on the ground. Fergus spoke to one and he went running towards a house set back a little from the quarry, a fine house, well built, with a fine stone roof of thin, evenly cut stone tiles.

'That's Oscar,' said Fergus in a low voice as a tall, black-haired young man came out from the house and followed his man to the quarry. Fergus handed the reins of his horse to Fachtnan and went down the dusty path to meet him. Mara looked after him with annoyance. This was Fergus's territory, but she would have preferred to deal with the questioning of Oscar herself. Quickly she swung herself down from her horse, handed her reins to Fachtnan and went after Fergus, neatly sidestepping the rocks that lay strewn on the path. They arrived at the same moment so all Fergus had time to say was: 'The Brehon of the Burren would like to speak to you, Oscar.'

Mara could see a flash of shock, even fear, in the young man's eyes. He clearly hadn't known who she was. Of course, he had just arrived at Mullaghmore Mountain when she was leaving; he may not even have noticed her that *Bealtaine* evening. But why should he be so alarmed?

'About your cousin's death,' she said rapidly before Fergus said any more.

That was not such a shock. He just nodded. 'You knew about Colman Lynch's death, then?' she asked. Fachtnan had handed the reins of the three horses to one of the quarry men and he came up to them quietly. He seated himself on a rock and took out his quill, his inkhorn and his writing tablets from his pouch.

'We might be more comfortable inside your house,' said Mara to the young man. She had seen him glance furtively around. The tapping of mallets had stopped and everyone seemed to be listening.

'Yes,' he said in a deep, husky voice. 'Come inside.'

'You knew of your cousin's death?' she repeated. As the four of them moved along the narrow path she deliberately stepped in front of Fergus and walked by Oscar's side. This was her investigation and she was going to conduct it in her own way.

'Yes,' he said again. 'I went to the burial. I was in Galway on Sunday. Just by chance.'

'So no one sent to tell you of the death?'

'No,' he said as he pushed open the door and stood back to let her enter. 'It was by chance that I was there,' he repeated and there was a note of slight bitterness in his voice. Understandable that he should feel bitter, thought Mara as she went in. She was not surprised, though. The Lynch family was one of the most powerful families in Galway. There would be plenty of people to invite to the burial without worrying about the poor relations in Corcomroe.

'And Colman Lynch was your first cousin; your father's sister married Seán Lynch,' she stated, sitting down on a stool. Fergus went and stood by the window while Fachtnan seated himself on another stool at the dusty table and took the top off his inkhorn. Oscar nodded wordlessly.

Mara waited until Fachtnan wrote a few lines and then she asked calmly, 'Why did you come to Mullaghmore on *Bealtaine* Eve?'

The window was covered in powdery flour-like dust from the limestone quarry and little light came through it, but Mara could not miss the convulsive start that Oscar gave. Obviously he had hoped that he had not been recognized on that night. He did not reply and she repeated the question, hoping that Fergus would not intervene to prompt the young man.

'I came to see Colman,' he said eventually.

Mara waited for Fachtnan to write this down and then proceeded. 'And did you see him?'

There was another long silence. Mara could almost read his mind while he struggled with various explanations and then rejected them. She waited patiently, looking around the room. It was a poor place, inside here, she thought, though the house was well built on the outside. The air smelled damp through the layer of dust. The wooden settle by the empty fireplace had no cushions. The table was roughly made, the legs slightly uneven with a piece of stone wedged under one leg, and its surface unplaned, splintered and spotted with rings of ale cups and stains of long-past meals. She looked back at Oscar and raised an eyebrow.

'I did see him, just for a minute or two,' he blurted out.

'And what did you talk about?'

There was another long silence and then Mara said encouragingly: 'Just tell the truth. Sooner or later I will find out what was said. There were plenty of people there that night and someone will have been bound to overhear you.' Was Colman blackmailing this cousin of his? she wondered.

'Did he ask you for silver?' she continued.

That startled him. She could see he gave a slight jump. His large hand balled itself into a fist.

'No,' he said bitterly. 'I asked him for silver. I thought he owed me something. He had taken away my trade. All I can do now is to crawl on the cliffs like my father and brother, and probably die like them, too.'

'Tell me about it,' said Mara softly, but suddenly she understood. It had only been a few days since she and King Turlough had discussed the laws of Galway and the excluding of the Gaelic clans.

Oscar O'Connor seemed glad of an audience, glad to pour out his grievances. 'I had built up a good trade in Galway,' he said rapidly. 'I was down at the docks every day when a ship came in. I would have a couple of our flagstones with me and I would show them to the merchants from foreign countries. Everyone liked them. These stones of ours are something they don't have in many other places. They don't ever become slippery in damp weather. You know what they're like.' He scuffed the dirty floor with the toe of his boot. Mara understood what he meant. The surface of the limestone flags from this area was ridged with an intricate pattern, rather like worm casts on the sand. She had them herself on the floors of her house; Brigid complained of how hard they were to scrub and polish but, it was true, no one could ever slip on them.

'Of course, the law is that if your name begins with an "O" or a "Mac" you can't trade in Galway,' he continued, 'but a lot of people don't take too much notice of that.'

This was true, thought Mara. Her own son-in-law, Oisín O'Davoren, had traded in Galway for many years and no one had caused trouble for him.

'How many years were you there?' she asked.

'About six,' he replied. Suddenly he was talking fluently, his black eyes burning with passion. 'Seán Lynch rented the premises to me originally, but then he wanted me to buy it and I did. I was making plenty of silver by then,' he said proudly. 'The ships from Spain and from France that had unloaded barrels of wine were only too keen to take back the same weight as ballast. Leather goods, which was what most of them wanted, don't weigh much, so the flagstones made up the weight.'

'And then . . .' prompted Mara.

His balled-up fist struck the table with a force that made a splash of ink shoot out from the horn. Fachtnan gave him a quick glance and steadied the inkhorn with one hand while continuing to write with the other.

'And then Colman came along and laid information against me with the Mayor of Galway and I was told to get out of the city and Colman claimed his reward,' he said rapidly. 'My shop, the place that I had bought, and paid for, and furnished, and kept in repair, that was all given to Colman as his reward for informing on me.'

'And what happened when you spoke to Colman on *Bealtaine* evening?'

She heard him draw in a breath. Outside the window the steady stroke of the iron mallet on the hard stone continued to ring, but inside, the damp, cold room seemed suddenly very quiet.

'I told him how angry I was and then I left,' he said tonelessly. Now the dark eyes were veiled by jet-black eyelashes. Fergus peered at him curiously, half opened his mouth but then closed it again.

Mara waited, but no more came. 'Colman said nothing?' she asked, allowing her voice to sound incredulous.

Oscar shrugged. 'He sneered a bit,' he said after a minute. 'He told me that he planned to set himself up as a lawyer in that shop. He was tired of the law school and he wasn't going to stay another year. He had plans to make a fortune, I suppose. There are always people buying and selling in Galway and Colman had been studying English law as well as Brehon law.'

Mara nodded. So that was what Colman had been doing during his frequent absences from the law school. He had been building up a client base in Galway and studying English law. Now she no longer wondered why he had stooped to blackmail instead of asking his parents for money. Colman's ambitions had been boundless. No doubt he had seen himself as a merchant prince of Galway and perhaps Lord Mayor as well. The legal business would be just a start.

'And what did you say?' she enquired.

'I thought it was no good talking to him so I just came away.'

'And he was alive when you left?'

'Of course he was,' said Oscar bitterly. 'He was alive and smirking.'

'It was still bright, then. You could see his face?'

'I could see his face, all right,' said Oscar. There was a brooding look on his own face.

'And did you see anyone nearby as you left?'

'There were plenty of people around,' said Oscar. 'But I didn't know any of them. I cursed myself for a fool for coming. I hadn't planned it: I was on my way back from Galway and I saw all the people going up. I knew he'd be there. The last time that I saw him, in Seán Lynch's place, he had been boasting about judgement day and how important he was.'

'You say that you didn't know any of the people, but you know Diarmuid O'Connor, don't you?' asked Mara sharply. 'He saw you.'

Oscar shrugged. 'I don't know. I don't remember the name. Who is he?'

Mara didn't answer. She was busy thinking. His story was fairly plausible; if he went away while it was still bright he was definitely not the one who killed Colman. However, she would need evidence of this before she took him off her list of possible murderers. He was very strong; he could definitely overpower Colman who had been slender and lightly built. Surely, if his story were true, someone would have seen him go down while it was still bright? This was a matter that the boys could investigate. Enda would love that, she thought indulgently. She would give him the task of looking for evidence of Oscar's arrival and departure. He could be in charge of organizing Moylan and Aidan to help him get evidence. At nearly sixteen he was yearning for some responsibility.

Mara rose to her feet. 'I may need to speak to you again,' she said. 'You will be here?'

He accompanied them to the door, opened it and stood looking over the dusty scene of back-breaking toil.

'I'll be here,' he said with a depth of bitterness in his voice that saddened her. 'I'll be here unless I'm at the bottom of the sea. At the moment I feel that's the best prospect facing me.'

'You'll find a way to combine your father's business and your own, Oscar,' said Fergus encouragingly. 'Galway should not be allowed to take all the trade. When I was young, Liscannor was almost as busy a port. Perhaps it will be again.'

Oscar did not look convinced, Mara thought, and she suspected that he saw the position more clearly than did Fergus. Perhaps Gaelic Ireland was at risk. Perhaps the gloomy thoughts of Turlough were prophetic. Perhaps this new king, Henry VIII, would turn his thoughts towards Ireland and would sweep away the Gaelic customs and the Gaelic laws. Still, she thought cheerfully, while I'm here I will do my best for the people of the Burren, and what I need to do now is to solve this secret and unlawful killing and allow everything to get back to normal.

'I don't think that I can spare the time to come back with you, Fergus,' she said when they came to the crossroads. She noted with pleasure how her voice held the correct note of regret. 'There is so much to do, so much evidence to gather, so many people to see and then, of course, there are my scholars . . .'

'Of course,' said Fergus solemnly. 'I do understand. Siobhan will be disappointed; she would have loved a good gossip with you, but she will understand, also. Another day . . . another day in happier times.'

'Another day,' echoed Mara, carefully arranging her face to look preoccupied and worried. She waved to him and hastily quickened her pace to catch Fachtnan up with the air of a woman who has many tasks on her mind. He is such a nice man, she thought with some compunction. Others in his position would have cross-questioned her, tried to impose their advice and opinions on her. Without his help, she might never have attained the position of Brehon of the Burren. Despite all the careful provision in the law texts for female poets, female physicians, female wood-wrights and female blacksmiths, it was generally held in Ireland that women were inferior to men.

'Better than in England, though,' she said aloud and Fachtnan turned to look at her. She laughed. 'I was just thinking that the position of women is probably better here than anywhere else,' she said.

'Was it difficult for you to become a Brehon?' asked Fachtnan curiously.

'Fergus spoke up for me,' said Mara, feeling a twinge of guilt. It would not have hurt, she thought, to have gone and spent ten minutes with him and Siobhan. 'We had to go to the court at Thomond; King Turlough's uncle was king then. Fergus brought along all the law texts and wisdom texts which showed that women had been Brehons in the past. He spoke for so long that the old king almost fell asleep. He even trotted out the old story about the judge Sencha being put right by the wise elderly female judge, Brig.'

'Well, I think you are a very good Brehon,' said Fachtnan awkwardly.

'Thank you, Fachtnan, I do my best,' said Mara. 'I only hope I can solve this case speedily,' she added, half to Fachtnan and half to herself. She hated to think of the slow poison of fear, suspicion and apprehension seeping into the daily life of the people that she served.

FIFTEEN

CÁIN LÁNAMNA (THE LAW OF MARRIAGE)

Imscarad, divorce, is permitted for many reasons. In the following cases the woman may retain her coibche, bride price:

1. *If the man leaves her for another woman*
2. *If the man is impotent or homosexual*
3. *If he is so fat as to be incapable of intercourse*
4. *If the man relates secrets of the marriage bed in the alehouse*

⚭

THE RAIN STARTED TO fall again around sunset and it rained all night. However, soon after sunrise it stopped and when Mara went down to her bathhouse on Tuesday morning thick white clouds were scudding across a sky as blue as the sea. As she washed and dressed her mind was busy with the tasks ahead of her. For once she did not stop in her garden when she came out of the house, but walked quickly down the road and into the empty schoolhouse. Brigid was in the kitchen and Cumhal was milking the goats in the yard behind, but there was no sign of life from the scholars' house. That was good; she would have a few minutes' peace.

She took the piece of vellum that Colman's mother had found and held it to the light of the window. His handwriting was clear, but it was tiny and the west-facing room was dim at this hour of the morning. She had already gone through the list and had a quick look at the first of the numbers: MCDLXX. The year had intrigued her. Her father was Brehon then; he had taken over from his father five years earlier in 1465. The case number was XXXV. She found it again instantly and settled down on her own chair to read it.

There were several shouts from the scholars' house by the time that she finished undoing the pink linen tape that bound the scroll. The lads seemed to have fully regained their spirits, she thought absent-mindedly. She put down the scroll and cast a quick glance out of the window. They were pouring out of the door of the house, their hair tousled, their faces unwashed. Brigid might send them back now, or she might have pity on them and give them their porridge and honey first. Either way, Brigid would ensure that they would be tidy and well groomed by the time that they came into the schoolroom, so Mara had a few more minutes to herself before they came tumbling in.

She took up the scroll again. It was not a public judgement at Poulnabrone dolmen; she had seen that when she had looked at it before. This was a private affair. There were two names at the head of the scroll. One was the O'Lochlainn, Ardal and Donogh's father, and the other was Muiris O'Heynes. Mara frowned. It was a strange document, not a formal document of fosterage, or of bondage, though it did hold a declaration from the O'Lochlainn that he would care for this fourteen-year-old boy cast up on the sands at Fanore until the boy reached the age of eighteen. She read it through and then rolled it up rapidly, tying it with the pink linen tape and pushing it back on to the shelf. She spent some time gazing through the window, seeing nothing, her mind busy. That indeed could have been a motive for murder. Muiris was not a man to take blackmail lightly, and this was a secret that he would not have been willing to share with anyone.

I must get the blacksmith to put a lock on this cupboard, she thought, eventually, turning away from the window. How could Colman have done this? How could he have betrayed her trust? How could he have forgotten the oath that all scholars swore every year at Michaelmas, the beginning of the law year, that they would never betray any secret that came to their ears during their time at the law school? She looked back at the strip of vellum and the case numbers written on it. She would look at these other cases afterwards, she thought, as she sat down at her desk. First she had to prepare a schedule for her scholars' day.

❆

'*Dia's muire agat, a bhean uasil.*' They were all jostling and pushing in through the door, their faces shining, their hair ridged from wet combs.

'It's a lovely day, Brehon,' said Fachtnan politely as he took his place on the front bench.

'It'll be just perfect for riding around the Burren gathering evidence,' said Enda enthusiastically.

'Have you made your list, Brehon?' asked Moylan, coming straight to the point instantly.

'Brehon, can we help too, me and Hugh?' asked Shane. 'Oh, and Cumhal says that the wind is going around to the east and we are going to have a few good days now. He is going to Fanore tomorrow to get some seaweed to put on the vegetable garden. He said that I could ask you if we could go as well?'

It was a tradition that the scholars had a day off to help with the gathering of seaweed, and at least it would give Mara a day of peace, a day to think quietly. 'Yes,' she said. 'Yes, I think you can all go. But now we will have to think about today and your task.'

'We'll work really well all of today if we can go seaweed-gathering tomorrow,' said Moylan earnestly.

'We might even solve your investigation for you,' chipped in Enda. 'We might come back this evening with the murder solved. That would be very useful for you, wouldn't it?'

'You might even give us an extra day's holiday,' said Moylan hopefully.

'Brigid said that she would pack some of her pork pies and a flagon of light ale into satchels for us all so that we don't need to waste time coming home to be fed,' said Aidan.

She smiled at them, warmed by their excitement and by the word 'home' that Aidan had used.

'You will remember the oath that you all swore at Michaelmas?' she said looking around.

'Of course,' said Shane promptly. 'We swore with our hand on the Bible.'

'Cross our hearts and hope to die,' said Moylan, sketching a rapid cross on his breast with his thumb.

'*Discretion and silence in all dealings with the people of the kingdom*,' said Enda, quoting from a wisdom text.

Mara gave a satisfied nod. 'Your task, Enda, is to trace the movements of Oscar O'Connor, stone-cutter of the kingdom of Corcomroe. Find out everything about him on that night of *Bealtaine*. Moylan and Aidan will aid you in this. Interview as many people as you can. The main reason for these enquiries, of course, is to find out what time Oscar left the mountain, but if he spoke to anyone, take careful note of his words. Do be thorough about this, because it may be possible that he left and then returned later on. Listen for the vespers bell from the abbey and return as soon as you hear it.'

'And what about me?' asked Fachtnan.

'See as many people as you can and ask them the memories they have of who was near to Wolf's Lair shortly before, and just after, the bonfire was lit. Make sure that you listen carefully and make accurate notes immediately after someone has spoken. Don't rely on your memory, Fachtnan. Write everything down.'

'And what about us?' asked Shane.

'Please can we have our enquiry?' pleaded Hugh. 'Just the two of us?'

Mara had been about to tell them to go with Fachtnan, but then she hesitated. They would much prefer to go on their own and Fachtnan would probably do better without them, also. He would have the judgement to know when to press a question or when to just leave it alone; the two young boys might spoil things for him by inserting their own questions.

'Yes,' she said solemnly, 'I want you two to interview Diarmuid O'Connor. You can take turns with asking the questions and writing down the answers. Don't rush; take plenty of time.' Diarmuid, she knew, would be tactful and patient with them. He was fond of children. She racked her brains for someone else for them to interview. She didn't want them riding all over the Burren with no supervision. She had a great sense of responsibility towards these two youngest scholars.

'Oh, and you could interview Roderic,' she added quickly. Roderic's house was quite close to the law school. He would probably delay them by playing some new tunes to them on his horn. No doubt he would be in a happy, if slightly nervous, mood, after the wonderful excitement of the king's offer to make him one of his household musicians.

'See Roderic first this morning, you can also ask him if he would like to go to Fanore with you all tomorrow. He'd enjoy that. Then, when you have finished with Roderic, go on to Diarmuid. Come back here as soon as you are finished. Tell Diarmuid that I expect you back at vespers.' With a bit of luck,

Diarmuid would detain them for a while, she thought. He usually had a few orphaned or rejected lambs to feed, or a few calves to be driven to fresh pasture.

After they had gone, Mara settled back to work in the schoolhouse. There was no doubt in her mind now that Colman had been a blackmailer, but did one of his blackmail victims murder him? Or was this a murder that was in some way involved with the complicated political situation of the times? Again she recalled the words that she had overheard on the mountain pass. Something about a young lawyer . . . and about someone who did not turn up. Or was it a revenge killing by Oscar O'Connor, triggered by Colman's monstrous act of informing upon his cousin?

She stared at the scroll marked MCDLXX/XXXV with the name of Muiris O'Heynes on the top, but she did not draw it out again. She would have to talk to Muiris; she knew that, but she wasn't sure how to approach the subject. Her own feeling was that these law texts in front of her held secrets that should be as inviolate at those told to the priest in the confession box. To give herself time to think she drew out her own divorce judgement text.

Yes, she was right about the number, she thought, picking up and unrolling the vellum. MCDXC/XIX. It amused and calmed her to read it. The facts were all so clearly stated by the *aigne*, Mara O'Davoren. All the names of the many witnesses to Dualta's ribald, drunken boasting in the alehouse, their places of residence and their occupations were stated, the references to the law texts, names and numbers, cross-references to other cases, everything was there. It had been a model pleading, she thought proudly. Fergus and a judge from Thomond had heard the case and the judgement given was divorce with the return of the bride price to the bride herself, since her father was no longer alive.

Was Colman planning to blackmail her? she wondered. What

did he think that would achieve? Everyone on the Burren knew the story of the divorce. There had been a lot of talk and disapproval at the time. Or was it perhaps Dualta? Had Colman discovered him? Perhaps Dualta was in Galway? Had Colman found some reason to blackmail him? She had never known or cared where her husband went. It had been a great mistake, that early and rushed marriage when she was only fourteen, and her husband was only seventeen. He had been a stonemason's son who had been sent to law school. He had been intelligent enough, but lightminded and too fond of drink and carousing. He would never pass his final examinations unless he took his studies more seriously, her father had often warned him. And year after year he had failed. She had been very much in love with him when she was fourteen and her father had given in to her, as he usually did. By the time that Sorcha was born, a year later, she had known it was a mistake. And then came the death of her father the year after that and then the emergence of the bully in the inadequate Dualta.

I could have waited a little longer, she thought. He would have undoubtedly strayed. Already he was eyeing other women; she knew that. That would have been a more usual and more acceptable reason for divorce. But she knew also that he had no hope of passing his law examinations: he spent little time in studying and long hours in alehouses, relying on the fact that he would be rich from the proceeds of his wife's property and law school. She needed to get rid of him and to be the one in charge of the law school. She was a qualified *aigne* at sixteen and an *ollamh*, professor, before her eighteenth birthday.

When, on that day in April 1490, Diarmuid came to her, distressed and embarrassed, after overhearing Dualta's boasting in the alehouse the night before, she knew immediately that she had a weapon in her hand to get rid of her husband. She smiled now at the memory of Diarmuid's freckled face flushing hot with blushes, and her own cool, calm probing until she managed to get from him the exact words that Dualta had used. He had been horrified at the idea of telling it again in public, but she had always been able to make Diarmuid do as she wanted since the time that they had played together when they were young children.

Judgement day, *Bealtaine* MCDXC. Yes, Diarmuid's evidence was there. Fergus had written that and he had heavily censored it, she had been amused to see that, after the case was over. Dualta's words, though, as quoted by Diarmuid, would have lingered in the minds of the community for a long time – probably still did, nineteen years later. She shrugged. She didn't care. She had been a passionate girl and she saw nothing to be ashamed of in that. The important thing was that she had kept her law school, kept her farm, had become Brehon of the Burren, and now all of these things would be for Sorcha's son, four-year-old Domhnall, or daughter, two-year-old Aisling.

MCDLXXXII/IX – yet another case before her time. This she read through quickly, lips parted, eyebrows raised. Yes, undoubtedly this could have led to blackmail, but had Colman just held this in reserve? Or had he already spoken to the man and blackmailed him? If so, there had been little sign of it. There were other cases, also, on his list – even a yearbook, marked MDVII, which held a record of all of the births, marriages and deaths in that year on the Burren. Some of the cases puzzled her; what had Colman found of interest in them? But she did not underestimate the depth of his intelligence and his greed and she knew that she would have to study each one of these cases carefully. First, though, she would go to see Muiris O'Heynes at his farm at Poulnabrucky.

※

The walk was pleasant; there had been one of those rapid changes that made the weather the most frequent topic of conversation in the west of Ireland. Cumhal was right; they would have a few fine days now. The west wind had veered around once more to the east and already the day seemed warm. The damp grass between the clints was steaming gently as the heat of the sun drew its moisture from it and the sky was as blue as the tiny gentians at her feet. There was no sign of sheep-shearing, she was glad to note as she neared Muiris's farm. If he had been shearing then there would have been no possibility of a casual, but private, conversation with him.

There was no sign of Muiris, but Aoife was sitting on the wall, combing her long wet hair – probably keeping a lookout for Rory, thought Mara. 'I wonder if your father is at home, Aoife,' she said, looking around.

'Yes, he is, Brehon,' said Aoife helpfully. 'I'll run and get him.' She was gone instantly. Mara bit her lip with annoyance. She would have preferred to go and find Muiris in some quiet corner of a field or barn. Now she would have to speak to him with Aoife there, scanning the horizon for Rory, but lending an ear to the conversation. She turned around and looked back towards the west. Yes, a young slim figure was lightly vaulting a wall in the distance. Hopefully, she would not have long to wait before Aoife left them.

With keener interest than in the past, she studied the farm and its farmhouse. It was a good house, with a neat, well-swept flagstone yard in front of it. The house itself had been sturdily and carefully built. Through the layers of whitewash the square-cut edges to the blocks of stone could easily be seen; most houses on the Burren were just built of random stones piled one on top of the other. Muiris's roof was thatched with pale gold reeds, much more durable than the thatch of soft oat stems or rushes used by most of his neighbours. The cow cabins in the yard were whitewashed inside and out and looked as clean as the yard. The fields around the house were emerald green, grazed by fat, contented cows and enclosed by well-built walls. A man who did everything well, thought Mara; a man who had risen high by dint of hard labour and determination; a man who had much to lose. She turned to look at him thoughtfully as he followed his pretty daughter from the barn.

'Ah, Brehon,' said Muiris coming to the gate. 'Will you come in and have a cup of ale?' The tone was courteous but his eyes were wary. Quickly she sought for a reason for her visit.

'No, I won't, Muiris, I just wanted to ask you about fishing,' she said blandly.

'Fishing?' He was taken aback.

'Yes,' said Mara. 'Brigid has been complaining that our stocks of salted fish are almost finished,' she improvised hastily. 'Do you think that the mackerel will be in at Fanore?'

'Should be,' said Muiris and now his voice began to lose its tension. 'After these few days of good weather, and then the rain, you should get a shoal of them in. They'll be there for the picking out of the water.'

'I was thinking of sending my lads over to Fanore tomorrow,' explained Mara. 'Cumhal needs seaweed and I thought the lads could do some fishing too if the mackerel would be in.'

'Could we go too, Father?' asked Aoife, with a warm smile at Rory who was now rapidly approaching the farmhouse. 'Felim,' she shouted to her brother, who had just appeared with a bucket in his hand. 'Would you and Aengus like to go fishing at Fanore tomorrow? We can all go, can't we, Father? We'll bring you back some shellfish for your supper. You know you love shellfish! Would that be all right, Brehon, if me and my brothers went, too?' she added.

Mara looked at Muiris. He was smiling indulgently and nodding. He could deny his pretty daughter nothing.

'That's fine, then,' said Mara. 'Shane and Hugh are going to ask Roderic if he would like to join in and I'll send a note to

Nuala's father to ask permission for her to come as well. It promises fine tomorrow, Cumhal says, so it might be best if everyone left early in the morning – perhaps meet about a quarter of an hour after the abbey bell goes for prime. It should be sunrise by then. They'll ride down the Spiral Hill and go through the mountain pass between Slieve Elva and Cappanawalla. Everyone should have a good day.'

'And what about me?' said Rory with a casual air. 'If Roderic is going I'd love to go too. What about the O'Lochlainn lads from Glenslade? They're all great fishermen. They'd love to come.'

'And I'll ask Emer if she'll come with me,' added Aoife demurely.

'The more, the merrier, as the old saying goes,' said Mara heartily. Muiris didn't look too pleased at the thought of Rory going, but the fewer interruptions there were tomorrow the better. Rory had a habit of dropping in to the law school when he had nothing better to do. Mara moved a little aside from the young people and Muiris followed her politely. She lowered her voice.

'I will be on my own tomorrow,' she said quietly. 'I have a lot of work to do. It seems as if Colman was investigating some old cases and it could be that one of them may hold the clue to his murder, that this murder was the result of blackmail. I'd like to be sure, though, to talk to the people involved in these old cases before making up my mind.'

His face paled, and his eyes hardened, but he had himself well in command and he just nodded and looked away. Her bait had been taken, though; she was sure of that. He would come to see her tomorrow morning. He was not a man to postpone an unpleasant task. But was he a man who would kill to rid himself of a threat to the happy world that he had built around him?

❄

198

Would he have killed a man? she asked herself again as she walked back. Looking around the well-tended fields, filled with happy, well-cared-for cows and sheep, she had her answer. Of course he would kill. He was a man used to killing. He butchered his own animals, and sold the meat at markets. After all, she thought with a sigh, a man is an animal. If this man, if this young lawyer, threatened his security, threatened the happiness of his beloved family, then Muiris might decide to kill and then hope to raise the money for the fine if he were found out. Perhaps, after all, the Bible was right when it said: 'Thou shalt give life for life, eye for eye, tooth for tooth.' For a moment the thought depressed her, but then she shook it from her mind and quickened her pace across the clints.

Like the flowers of the field, individual men withered and died, but principles remained constant. The Brehon law was founded on confession, forgiveness and compensation and so long as she lived that law would prevail here in the kingdom of the Burren.

sixteen

CRÍTH GABLACH (RANKS IN SOCIETY)

There are two kinds of outsiders within the kingdom.

One is an aurrad, *a person of legal standing such as a*
Brehon, *bard, a harpist or a* file, *a poet.*

The other is a dorad, *who has no legal standing.*

If a killer is an outsider, or dorad, *from another*
kingdom, a party of avengers may pursue a blood feud into that
kingdom one month after the fine is due.

❧

Hugh and Shane came noisily into the yard outside
the schoolhouse just as the last stroke of the bell for vespers
sounded from the abbey. Mara went out to greet them just as
Fachtnan's horse clattered over the stone flags.

'I've got all the notes here, Brehon,' said Fachtnan, swinging
his leg over the horse's back and digging into the leather satchel.
·He fished out a few scrolls and stared with dismay at the large
greasy stain making a blob in the middle of his roll of parchment.

'I must have put one of the pork pies in the wrong compart-
ment of my satchel,' he said apologetically.

'Never mind,' said Mara soothingly. 'You can always make a fair copy afterwards if anything is needed for evidence at Poulnabrone. This is just for me; I'll read through it while Brigid gives you your supper. Hugh and Shane,' she called as they sidled away in through the door of the scholars' house, 'have you got your notes?'

Shane had done most of the writing, she noticed. Most of the questions, too, she thought. She read through these carefully while they stood there. They seemed in a very silly mood, stealing glances at each other as she read through the script.

'You went to Roderic first?'

'Yes, we ate our pork pies there while Roderic played us a few tunes and got us to sing some of his new songs,' said Shane promptly. 'And then we went over to Diarmuid. He gave us another meal and lots of honey cakes.'

'And have any of you seen Enda, Moylan and Aidan?' asked Mara.

'No,' said Fachtnan.

She turned to look at Shane and Hugh.

'No,' said Hugh quickly.

'Noooo,' echoed Shane slowly after a pause. A smile plucked at the corners of Shane's mouth and Hugh's light blue eyes were dancing with amusement.

'There's King Turlough coming down the road,' said Fachtnan.

Mara turned away from Shane and Hugh and shaded her eyes against the strong south-westerly sun. There certainly was a troop of horsemen coming down the road.

'It's the king coming back *again*, Brehon,' called Cumhal from the field opposite. He had a slightly sour note in his voice and Mara's lips twitched with amusement. There was no doubt in her mind now that Cumhal and Brigid were very against any special relationship between the king and their mistress. She understood their feelings. This law school had been owned and worked by an O'Davoren for many years and if Mara married the king now, that would be the end of the O'Davorens at Cahermacnaghten and the end of the law school, perhaps. This would matter immensely to Brigid and Cumhal who were both so very proud of the status of their position at Cahermacnaghten.

'Go and have your supper, boys,' she said. 'Tell Brigid that the king may be going to pass the night here.' It was a good idea for him to break his journey between the Aran Islands and Thomond – he would have crossed over this morning, she guessed – but fond as she was of him, she wished that he had decided to spend the night with Fergus and Siobhan at Doolin rather than at Cahermacnaghten. She hastened down the road to meet him.

'My lord, it is good to see you,' she said formally. She was pleased to see that the group of *gallóglaich* from Mahon O'Lochlainn were still with him. She still shuddered to think of her close encounter with the O'Kellys. Was Colman involved with the O'Kelly clan? she wondered again. Was there, perhaps, a political facet to the murder of the young lawyer? Anyway, whether or not Colman was involved, the danger to Turlough was very real and he could not ride around virtually unprotected. Brigid wouldn't be too pleased to have to feed all of these *gallóglaich* again, but it couldn't be helped.

'Mara!' Turlough Donn's arms went around in a tight hug and the now familiar feeling of pleasure surged through her. I wonder how he would like to have me as a wife of the fourth degree, she thought. He could come to visit from time to time just as Ardal O'Lochlainn visits his fisherman's daughter in Galway. We could both carry on with our own lives in the meantime. I wonder what he would say if I proposed that.

'You'll stay the night?' she asked, disentangling herself with a quick, amused glance at Cumhal's disgruntled face. The news of this would soon be carried to Brigid. Hopefully it wouldn't affect the supper she served up.

'I'll stay the night and have breakfast with you in the morning, with pleasure,' replied Turlough, 'but I promised to have supper with Finn O'Connor – he crossed back with me on the boat from Aran. He's gone down to Ballyganner now to get ready, but I just turned off to greet you.'

'Ah, Brigid,' he called as she came out. 'I won't be having one of your beautiful suppers, but I will be coming back later this evening to sleep in your guest house so I will have breakfast here. Don't worry about those lads' – he indicated the *gallóglaich* – 'they've all got their tents and they'll put them up there in front of the gate and around the enclosure, if that's all right.'

'You'll have a something to eat when you come back, my lord?' asked Brigid. She might not be in favour of a marriage, but she could not resist the charm of the man.

'Just a glass of wine and something very light, then,' said Turlough, his face lighting up. 'Your mistress and I will have a few things to talk over.'

'We'll have something good for you,' promised Mara. Despite the slight awkwardness of knowing that he was still waiting for an answer to his letter, her heart felt warm at the prospect of seeing him again and having the pleasure of his company over a glass of wine.

'See you later in the evening, then,' he said, mounting his horse. 'Oh, I saw three of your lads over in Corcomroe this morning. Enda, isn't it, the tall blond boy, and the other two ... the boy with the pimples ... What are their names?'

'Enda, Moylan and Aidan,' said Mara with a frown. 'What on earth were they doing over in Corcomroe?'

'They seemed to be going towards the sea, near Doolin,' said Turlough, moving off down the road after his bodyguards. The *gallóglaich* formed into pairs, some riding behind him and others in front, all of them scanning the distant horizon for any sign of the O'Kellys. 'See you this night,' his voice floated back towards her.

'It's a wonder that he doesn't stay the night at Ballyganner,' said Brigid with pursed lips. 'Surely the O'Connor and his wife would be able to put him up. It would be more suitable.'

'He'll get a better bed and better food here,' said Mara calmly, ignoring the word 'suitable'. The tower house at Ballyganner was damp, draughty and comfortless. Turlough had probably been putting off taking his formal *cuide* from the O'Connor for as long as possible. Every *taoiseach* had to offer the king an evening's entertainment and supper for himself and his retinue in the winter months. Turlough, she knew, had already paid his formal visits to the O'Brien, the O'Lochlainn and the MacNamara.

'Perhaps some little baked salmon pies and some sorrel to go with them,' mused Brigid. 'Giolla from Ballyporty has been fishing.' Her face had softened. She did love to cook and she did love appreciation. 'You'll get out the wine yourself, will you, Brehon?'

'I will,' promised Mara. Yes, a marriage of fourth degree would suit her fine. That would give the people of the three kingdoms something to think about, she thought merrily, it would give them something to discuss in front of the slowly burning turf fires during the long winter evenings. In the meantime, she had work to do. She followed Brigid back into the law school enclosure, her mind running over the tasks that lay ahead of her.

❋

The schoolhouse was warm and comfortable and blessedly silent. The sun had moved around to the west, warming the stone building and lighting up the whitewashed wall opposite the window from floor to roof-rafters. Mara peered at Fachtnan's untidy scrawl. He had done a great day's work, but the information was all higgledy-piggledy and she needed to tabulate it and copy it all out in her clear, bold hand before she could reduce the possible murderers to something manageable. Now all I need is Enda's information about Oscar O'Connor, she thought. He might be another possibility for my murder list. But would Oscar climb all the way up a mountain and murder a man just as an act of revenge, or was it a murder done on the spur of the moment? Perhaps it's a pity that I didn't get Fachtnan to enquire about Oscar O'Connor as well and then I would have all the facts in front of me now instead of having to wait for Enda, Moylan and Aidan to make their appearance.

There's the parish bell for the angelus, she thought after a while; those boys should be here by now. She got to her feet to go to see Brigid and then stopped. There was something of significance in Fachtnan's evidence. She went to the shelf, took a small piece of vellum and made a note of her question, and then returned to her work.

Some time later she realized that the light was dimming. It's getting late, she thought. Where are those boys? She got to her feet. The broad band of sunlight on the wall had shrunk to a narrow orange strip high up near to the rafters. When she looked out of the window the high wall of the enclosure shadowed the flagstones in the yard. The sun had sunk down near to the horizon over the sea. Suddenly Mara remembered the king's words. Enda, Moylan and Aidan must have gone over to Corcomroe to see Oscar. They had no business doing that, of course. Their instructions were to interview the people on the list Mara had written out for them, but they had probably got bored with this. She wondered uneasily whether they had tried to force a confession from him. Enda had spoken of solving the murder. If they had done that, and if Oscar were the murderer, what might have happened? He was a very powerful young man; he could easily have overpowered three skinny adolescents. She pictured the huge iron mallets that pulverized the stone and felt an icy prickling at the back of her neck as she went hurriedly out of the door.

'Brigid, have Enda, Moylan and Aidan come back yet?' she asked, opening the door of the kitchen house.

'No, Brehon,' said Brigid, scrubbing a handful of wet sand energetically over the surface of the large alder-wood kitchen table. 'I was just going to come over to see you about them, but Shane and Hugh seemed to think that they might be quite late so I didn't worry too much.'

'But, how do . . .' began Mara and then she remembered the two mischievous faces. Something was going on.

'Where are the others?' she asked, looking around. Everything was suspiciously quiet.

'Fachtnan's gone for a walk and I think Hugh and Shane are playing chess in the scholars' house,' said Brigid, returning to her scrubbing.

Shane and Hugh were not playing chess, she guessed as she opened the door of the scholars' house. The house was too silent. They never played chess without shouting at each other. There were three rooms: one in the middle for study, reading and games, one bedroom for the older boys at one end and one for the younger boys at the other end of the small house. The doors to the middle room and to the older boys' bedroom stood ajar, but the door to Shane and Hugh's room was closed and from behind it Mara could hear urgent whispering. She opened the door swiftly and stood on the threshold. They were sitting side by side on Shane's bed and the two faces, illuminated by the last rays of the setting sun, no longer bore the mischievous, amused expressions of earlier, but now seemed worried and apprehensive.

'Where are Enda, Moylan and Aidan?' she asked abruptly.

They looked at each other. Hugh opened his mouth and then shut it and looked down on the bed.

'We don't know, Brehon,' said Shane. There was an uneasy note in his voice and she pounced on him instantly.

'Tell the truth,' she said fiercely.

'I am telling the truth, Brehon,' he said defensively.

She gave him a long look.

'When did you last see them?'

'We saw them here this morning, Brehon,' said Hugh.

'That was not what I asked you,' she said swiftly. 'I'll ask the question again and I want a truthful answer: when did you *last* see Enda, Moylan and Aidan?'

'This afternoon, Brehon,' said Shane with a despairing glance at Hugh. 'A while before the bell went for vespers.'

She sank down on Hugh's bed. 'Tell me what they said to you.'

'They asked us to give a message to Roderic, Brehon,' said Shane.

'To Roderic?'

There was a long silence. Mara felt bewildered, though relieved. Whatever prank Enda, Moylan and Aidan were involved in she would not have expected it to include Roderic, who was a sensible, balanced young man – far too old to have anything to do with these silly adolescents. At least they were safely back from Corcomroe; the king had seen them over there in the morning.

'What was the message?' she asked.

Shane hesitated. The corners of his mouth were twitching. He looked at Hugh for help.

'They wanted us to give a message to Roderic and to pretend that Emer sent it,' said Hugh.

'Really, how silly! And what was the message?' asked Mara.

'We were to tell him that Emer wanted to meet him down in Poll an Cheoil,' said Shane.

'Poll an Cheoil!' exclaimed Mara. Poll an Cheoil, hole of the music, was the entrance to a cave that ran underground quite near to the law school.

'You see,' said Hugh earnestly, 'Enda thinks that either Oscar O'Connor or else Roderic did the murder; he wants to find the truth before the end of the day. That's what he said. He wants to be the one who will solve this murder investigation.'

'So he had this plan,' said Shane. 'He left a note for Oscar telling him to come to the cave and he put on it: *We know the truth of what happened on the mountain. Come to Poll an Cheoil Cave in Ballyconnor North.*' He stopped and said rather uncertainly, 'Well, I think that was what it said.'

'You know the place, down in the cave, the place called the Cauldron? Well, they were going to use that for an interrogation chamber,' said Hugh.

I told them all never to go down there, thought Mara. She knew exactly where they meant. It was a small, round space only accessible by a sheer drop of about ten feet. She had been down it many times when she was a girl, although her father had forbidden it. She and Dualta used to go there.

'They were going to entice him down – tell him to go first, and then pull up the ladder and interrogate him and not let him out until he confessed.'

Mara sighed. 'Were Roderic and Oscar supposed to come at the same time?' she asked mildly.

'No,' said Shane. 'They were going to do Oscar first. They waited for ages, but Oscar didn't turn up so they came out and sent us with the message for Roderic.'

'Aidan was practising Emer's voice – you know the way that he can get his voice all squeaky sometimes – he was going to lure Roderic down.'

'And then Aidan was going to escape by moving a stone away from a hole on the other end, and then he was going to tip the stone back to block it and keep Roderic imprisoned while Enda interrogated him.'

'And did Roderic go?'

'Yes, he did,' said Hugh, giggling openly now. 'He went red in the face and said nothing, but we hid behind a rock and we saw him go out a few minutes later. He waited until Father Conglach passed by and then he went down the road.'

'And then we heard the bell for vespers so we raced back,' finished Shane.

But that was four hours ago, thought Mara. Roderic would have soon realized that it was a boys' prank and would have gone home once he had been sure that Emer was not there. She thought it unlikely that he would have been deceived, no matter how much Aidan tried to make his rapidly breaking voice sound like Emer's dulcet tones. So what had kept the boys? Could Oscar have come later on, after all? There had been a terrible note of desperation in that young man's voice. Could he allow his temper to take over? And could there possibly be some connection between Oscar O'Connor and the O'Kellys? The O'Kellys had caused trouble in Galway; Mara knew that.

The two young boys were staring at her, made uneasy by her long silence, and she tried to make her voice sound reassuring. 'I'll just go and fetch them back,' she said. 'You stay here. You can have a game of chess or do some study and make sure that you go to bed when Brigid tells you.'

She quickly left the room and crossed over to the kitchen house. 'Brigid,' she said. 'Hugh and Shane told me that Enda, Moylan and Aidan have gone down the cave at the back over there, at Ballyconnor North. They were planning some joke on Roderic to entice him down the Cauldron. I'm just going to fetch them back.'

Brigid made an exasperated sound with her tongue. 'Those

three are more trouble than a houseful of small children,' she said. 'And Cumhal has gone up the mountain to help Eoin MacNamara fetch down some cattle. Do you want to wait until he comes home and he'll go for them? Or do you want me to go, Brehon? Or we can send one of the men from the farm.'

'No, no, I'll go,' said Mara. 'A walk will do me good; I've been straining my eyes over old documents. I'll just change my shoes and then I'll be off. Don't worry about supper for Enda, Moylan and Aidan; they don't deserve it. I'll take the covered lantern in case I need to go down, but they are probably larking around near the entrance. I'll probably just need to call them.'

There were plenty of footmarks on the damp clay when she arrived. Certainly more than three sets, she thought. Several hobnailed boots, such as the boys wore, but also a smooth leather print. She went down the short, steeply sloping passageway; it was an easy cave to enter, though dangerous further down. All these caves under the Burren were dangerous, her father used to say. It had been a long time since she had gone down there and somehow the small steep-sided hole seemed further from the entrance than she remembered. She stopped for a moment. Everything was very quiet; she had expected to hear boyish shouts and horseplay but perhaps the strange booming noise in the distance masked all other sounds. Funny, she thought, I don't remember hearing that booming sound before. It's almost as if this cave leads to the sea. It couldn't, though. She had lived all of her life within a quarter of a mile of Poll an Cheoil and had never heard that there was a way through it to the sea. On the other hand, its name, hole of the music, probably meant that sounds did come from it from time to time.

Then she stumbled across something on the ground. She raised her lantern, opening one of the small horn windows in order to see better. It was a *sugán* ladder made from rough slats of wood and twisted rope. She recognized it. Moylan and Aidan had made it last summer. But what was it doing lying on the floor? Surely this was the place where the hole had led down into the Cauldron? She swung the lantern around but the hole did not seem to be there. She was just about to move on when she noticed a long scrape on the wet clay of the passage. Something had been dragged along there, and she could now see what it was. There was a heavy flagstone lying there at the side of the passage. She pushed it with her foot and it moved. She bent down and heaved it aside. A rush of air came up to her. She lifted her lantern and shone it down. Yes, this was the Cauldron. She looked down, but there was no trace of the boys.

Once again, though, there were patterns of footmarks, hobnailed-boot footprints, all over the wet, yellow mud on the floor. She stared at them for a moment. She couldn't decide whether any men's footmarks were there. Probably Enda, at least, had feet the size of a man's. He was a tall boy and Aidan was shooting up fast. There seemed to be no sign of the smooth-soled boot print here. She held up her lantern and shone it down the rest of the passageway, but there were no footmarks further on. The boys had come as far as here, had used the ladder to go down; the damp, smooth mud told that story, but what had happened next?

'Enda,' she shouted, and listened to her own voice returning to her, cutting through the continuous booming in the distance.

'Enda,' she called again, and then, with increasing desperation: 'Moylan, Aidan.' There was no answer. Where could they be? Perhaps they had already left the cave, she thought hopefully, but the memory of that rope ladder lying on the floor and the heavy flagstone sealing the opening chilled her. If they had climbed out surely they would have gone back to the law school, and surely they would have taken the rope ladder with them?

Then Hugh's words came back to her memory: once Roderic was enticed into the Cauldron, he had said, then Aidan was going to escape out the other end, block the hole, and join the others on top. There must be another exit. Someone had trapped the boys, whether by malice or for a joke, and her three young scholars were now somewhere deep in the confusing labyrinth of passages that honeycombed these caves. She had no memory of another exit, but it was over twenty years since she had been down here and this soft limestone of the Burren was always decaying and crumbling.

Mara hesitated for a moment; perhaps she should go back and wait for Cumhal. He and some of the other men from the farm could go down with torches and ropes and search for the boys. On the other hand, Cumhal might not come for a while and who knows, the boys could have got tired of the cave and gone elsewhere, planning to retrieve their ladder on the way back. Time meant little to boys of that age; she had learned that through experience.

I'll just go down and have a look to see if there is another exit first, she thought. If there isn't, then they must be elsewhere. If there is an exit then I'll go back and send some men down.

✳

The iron spar that Dualta had driven into the stone of the passageway twenty-four years ago was still there. They had used a rope, not a ladder, she remembered. She remembered also how he had filled the chamber with great armfuls of ferns so that no mud showed on their clothes when they went back to the law school and, despite her worries about Enda, Moylan and Aidan, a grin touched her lips. She hooked the ladder over the iron spar and scrambled down.

The chamber was about the size of a small room and perfectly round in shape as if it had been hollowed out by some giant hand. The roof, thirty feet above her head, was hung with spear-like stalks of petrified limestone. Except for one change, everything was as she had remembered it; the walls had been smooth and unbroken twenty years ago, but since then there had been a rockfall, and behind a pile of broken stone was a small passage-way.

SEVENTEEN

CÁIN ÍARRAITH (THE LAW OF CHILDREN)

*The relationship between a felmacc, pupil, and his master
is similar to that of a foster-father, dátan, and his dalta,
foster-son. The felmacc must be taught board games, such as
fidchell, chess, and must be instructed in all aspects of the
profession of his master. The master is responsible for
the safety of the felmacc.*

ᚖ

'ᏟNDA,' CALLED MARA. THERE was no doubt in her mind
that the boys had come through this exit from the Cauldron.
Smears of wet clay were here and there, and more footmarks from
hobnailed boots. The roaring sound was even louder now and her
anxiety sharpened. What could it be? Though there were very few
rivers on the Burren, there were several in Corcomroe and in
Thomond and this sound was the sound of a river in full flood.
Perhaps the caves were flooded further down. The caves at
Kilcorney flooded on a regular basis after heavy rain.

Mara knew that it would be sensible to go back, but her
anxiety for the boys made her press onwards. Just a little further,

she told herself, shutting her mind to the realization that she was being impetuous and unwise.

Further along, the passageway was more difficult. The rocks on either side were water-worn, their straight sides scalloped into gentle curves, but the stream that had carved its way through them thousands of years ago had been feeble and intermittent, leaving a narrow and twisted channel. She reached the end of it and came to a more open space. This passage forked and her common sense told her that she should go no further without help.

'Enda!' she called again, using all the power of her well-trained voice. She did not expect an answer and had turned to go back when suddenly she realized that there had been another sound deep within the booming noise that had been her constant companion. Could it have been a voice?

'Moylan!' she screamed. Her father had often told her that the letters 'm', 'p' and 'b' come out with the most force. She should have remembered this and shouted 'Moylan' before. It was a far better name to yell than 'Enda'.

'Help!' The word was faint, but it was unmistakable. It came from the left and Mara hesitated no longer. She could not turn back now or wait for Cumhal. The boys might be in danger. However, she could mark her way back. She had enough experience of these caves to know how passageways twisted and turned, and how easy it was to get lost. Like all lawyers, in her pouch she always kept a spool of pink linen tape and a small lump of sealing wax. There was not too much of the tape left; she had given some to Nuala to tie up her woodbine plant and she had used a lot the week before when she had visited Ardal O'Lochlainn and had helped him to sort a chest full of old leases. The documents had all been in an untidy jumble and she had gone through them methodically, rolling, labelling and tying them into neat bundles. However, there was enough tape left for her purpose.

With steady hands she opened the horn window of the

covered lantern, took the sealing wax from her pouch and held it carefully to the flame of the candle. Once it was soft, she squashed it against the rough edge of a protruding rock and dug the edge of the tape into the soft wax with a fingernail. The tape only stretched a couple of feet down the passageway but it would be enough to show her the correct way back. Brigid would instantly despatch Cumhal to Poll an Cheoil Cave as soon as he returned and this tape would show him the way that she had gone.

'Moylan,' she shouted again as she went rapidly down the passageway and this time she distinctly heard the word 'Help'.

There was no doubt in her mind now that the caves had flooded. The roaring, thundering sound was getting louder every second. It seemed to be coming from beneath her now, although this passageway was extremely wet and small pieces of glistening grass clung to its rough sides. The river from Slieve Elva must have swept along here recently, she thought, with an apprehensive glance over her shoulder. She held her lantern high and then stopped abruptly.

Just a little further from where she was standing, the wall on the right-hand side of the passageway had suddenly disappeared and jagged, broken lumps of rock showed how the river had burst its way through the decayed stone and found another level forty feet lower down. She moved a few feet further on. It was like standing on the side of a mountain and looking down a precipice to the roaring torrent below. For a moment she felt almost dizzy and the noise was so great that it took her another moment to realize that the word 'Here!' was coming to her ears.

Mara lifted her lantern and shone it on the craggy wall of the opposite side of the precipice. The three of them were there, only about the width of a room away from her. She could see them quite clearly by the light of her little lantern. They were huddled together on a small ledge and all three were soaking wet, but they were there and they were alive and there was no possibility that the river could reach them as long as they did not try any heroics.

There was no possibility of calling any instruction; the noise was far too great, so she just held up her left hand, palm facing them in the way that she trained dogs to stay. She hesitated to leave the boys, but she could not be sure when Cumhal would return. Getting animals down from the mountainside to their summer grazing land in the valleys was always a tricky task; it might take an hour, but it could take three. Once she got back to Cahermacnaghten, she could summon help. All the people of the Burren would turn out to rescue the boys; she knew that she only had to ask. She looked across at them to make sure that they were looking at her, pointed her finger back along the passageway to tell them that she was going back for help and once again held up her hand. Three heads nodded and she felt a little comforted as she turned, going as quickly as she could, back towards the Cauldron.

Then Mara heard a bark. It seemed at first as if it was one of the sounds of the fast-flowing water below, but then it came again; she knew what it was and a rush of gratitude towards Cumhal warmed her. She should have done that. How intelligent of him. He had taken Bran, and Bran would scent his mistress. She need not have bothered with the pink linen tape. Mara moved quickly up the passage. She rounded the corner and then stopped and waited, a smile broadening on her face.

Yes, it was Bran, but it wasn't Cumhal. Bran was being held by Turlough Donn, King of Thomond, Corcomroe and Burren, and descendant of Brian Boru. And behind him were the two bodyguards, and then Fachtnan, Roderic, and then the company of ten *gallóglaich*, some holding lanterns and some, coils of rope.

'My lord,' said Mara demurely as she patted the ecstatic Bran. 'This is no place for you.'

'I can't allow you out of my sight for a minute,' grumbled the king. His arms went around her tightly and from over his shoulder Mara could see the *gallóglaich* glance at one another and then look away. There were a few wide grins, but she didn't care. Suddenly she felt her legs tremble and she had never been so glad to see anyone.

'Three of my boys are down here,' she said in his ear. 'They're on a ledge above the river.'

He nodded. 'These lads will get them out; give them something to do. They're getting bored; there's not a sight or a sound of an O'Kelly anywhere. I suspect you killed them all off up there on Clerics' Pass and you're not telling me. Someone will find the bodies one day and then we'll have to have a big investigation. Now, let's see where those boys of yours are. Here' – he handed her the leash – 'you'd better take Bran. He has nearly pulled my arm out of its socket. I thought you said he was well trained.'

Mara grinned. They were back to their old good-natured, teasing relationship. For a moment, there in his arms, she had sensed that she wanted something different, but her legs had steadied and she felt in control once more.

'We'd better talk here as it's far too noisy to hear anything back there,' she said, moving away from him and addressing the *gallóglaich*. They straightened up at her cool tone of command and looked at her with immense solemnity. She kept her eyes averted from Turlough, knowing that he would be grinning.

'The heavy rain during the past few nights has caused the caves to become flooded,' she continued. 'I think the river came down here, probably when the three boys were in this passageway, then burst through some thin rock further on and fell to a level of about forty feet below here. I think that it probably swept the three boys along with it and, by the grace of God, they managed to scramble up on to a ledge. If some of you hold the ropes and a couple of volunteers would drop down into the river you could probably reach them. There'll be a flagon of mead to be shared when we are all safely back at Cahermacnaghten.' She started to lead the way back.

'Can the boys swim, Brehon?' asked one of the *gallóglaich*.

She turned back and nodded. 'Yes, they are all good swimmers,' she said. That was something that she always insisted of her scholars, that they all learn to swim, to ride and to climb rocks in safety. Cumhal taught each of them and let her know when they were safe to be allowed out on their own. She was realistic enough to know that young boys would always be adventurous and would always get into various dangerous situations but, rather than lock them up, she gave them the skills to extricate themselves.

There was a buzz of enthusiastic comments and suggestions from the *gallóglaich*, but she pressed on rapidly down the passageway. She would not be easy until she saw that the boys were safe.

They were still there, however, and now she could see them more clearly by the light of the many lanterns, each of them larger than her own. She drew in a breath of relief. None of the three appeared to have been injured. They would only be wet and very cold.

All the time that the *gallóglaich* were tying the ropes, swimming across the river, clambering on each other's backs, lowering Enda, Moylan and Aidan down, Mara's mind was busy. She looked speculatively at Roderic. He didn't seem as shocked and worried as did Fachtnan, but he looked concerned – normal, she thought. She would have to speak to him and she would do so tonight, but she thought it was fairly unlikely that his were the hands that pulled up the rope from the Cauldron and placed the heavy flagstone over the entrance to the hole. He was a well-balanced, good-natured young man; she had known him since he was two years old. If he had taken the rope away to give them a fright, he would have been back fairly soon to release them.

Once the boys had all been safely hoisted up she resisted an impulse to hug them all, though Bran made up for it, wagging his tail and licking bare, wet legs. She turned and led the way back down the passageway. No one spoke, even when they had reached a spot where the river's thunder was muted. The whole procession followed her in respectful silence.

When they came to the Cauldron, she stood back.

'Go straight to school,' she said severely to the wet trio. 'Boil yourself some water, have a hot wash and go straight to bed. I will see you in the morning. Fachtnan, will you go with them and make sure they do this? Oh, and Fachtnan, ask Brigid to prepare some hot water and some dry *léinte* so that these men can change. Ask her to get out the flagon of mead, also. Roderic,' she turned to the young horn player, 'could you wait for me at Cahermac-naghten? I would like to have a word with you.' Roderic looked a little bewildered at that, she thought, regarding him keenly. He certainly did not look like a man with a guilty secret.

The boys and the *gallóglaich*, one of them carrying Bran across his shoulders, filed up the ladder in silence, and she waited until they were all gone before turning to find Turlough with an amused smile on his face.

'What will you do to them tomorrow?' he asked. 'Hang, draw and quarter them?'

'No,' she said lightly. 'Brehon law does not exact punishment, just confession, repentance and compensation. They will confess; I'm sure that they have already repented; and the only ones hurt by this escapade were themselves. It was just a prank that went wrong.' Then she told him all about Enda's idea of extracting a confession.

'You're too soft with them,' said Turlough. 'They should be at my old school at Emly Abbey. The monks would have flayed them.'

'Well, the church has never really accepted Brehon laws,' said

Mara tolerantly. 'St Patrick did his best to change them to his own liking and Rome has been trying to impose her own laws ever since, especially the laws about "an eye for an eye", "a death for a death".'

Turlough laughed. 'I suppose Enda and his friends were pretty enterprising to try to solve the murder on their own. So which of them did they hope to get to confess, the horn player or the stone-cutter?'

Mara shrugged. 'Knowing Enda, possibly both,' she said. 'He is a boy of great ambition and belief in himself.'

'And why are you going to cross-question young Roderic, then?'

'Just to see what happened,' said Mara, seizing the ropes with both hands and climbing swiftly up the ladder. For the moment, she would keep to herself the mystery about the missing ladder and the flagstone, she decided.

※

Roderic was waiting for her, sitting on the wall of her garden, when she arrived. The king looked good-humouredly from him to Mara and then strode off to the law school courtyard where Cumhal had lit a large bonfire to dry and warm the men. Fachtnan was filling goblets and Brigid held a basket of newly baked rolls. The *gallóglaich* were enjoying their mead, she noticed, hoping that it would not distract them too much from their duties of guarding the king.

'Well, what happened?' she asked and then, as Roderic hesitated, she said quickly, 'Shane and Hugh told me about the silly message. Did you go down the cave?'

'I was going to,' he confessed. 'But I heard them giggling and I guessed it was a joke. Then, just to make sure, I went across to Caheridoola to see if Emer was there.'

'And she was?'

'Yes,' said Roderic. 'She was helping her mother with the washing so I came away.'

'And decided to play a trick on the boys in the caves?'

'No!' said Roderic, bewildered. 'No, I didn't know that Enda, Moylan and Aidan were actually in the caves. I saw Hugh and Shane running back towards the law school then. I met Fachtnan later on and went back with him. That was when I found that the boys were missing.'

'And you didn't see anyone else?'

Roderic shook his head. 'No,' he said. 'I can't remember seeing anyone.'

'Thank you, Roderic,' said Mara, rising to her feet. 'Well, you'd better get off home if you are all going to start off early in the morning. I'll walk down the road with you. I want to see Fachtnan.' Her eyes were on the tall, blond-haired figure that had just come out from the gate of the law school and was walking slowly down the road towards them.

'Yes, Enda?' she asked coldly. Roderic quickened his step and went on through the gates to make his farewells.

Enda hesitated. 'I know you said to go straight to bed and that you would see us in the morning, Brehon,' he said nervously, 'but I just wanted you to know that it was all my fault and that Aidan and Moylan didn't really want to do it. It was all my fault,' he repeated, 'and it was stupid and childish and I know I could have got them killed. I hope that I will be the only one to be punished, Brehon, and that you won't punish them. They're very upset.'

Mara considered this for a moment. It was a confession and if he took it to heart it might be a turning point for this impulsive boy. 'We'll talk about it all tomorrow evening after you come back from Fanore,' she said, ignoring his incredulous gasp. Obviously he had expected that treat to be cancelled for them. 'Or else the following morning, as you will be tired after a day at the sea. Just one thing, Enda. Did either Roderic or Oscar O'Connor turn up at the caves?'

'No, Brehon,' said Enda respectfully. 'We didn't see either of them.'

'So who do you think pulled up the ladder and closed off the hole with the flagstone?'

'I don't know, Brehon,' said Enda. 'Aidan was fooling around and he was . . . pretending . . . well, he was making a lot of noise and then Moylan whispered in my ear, "He's coming!" and we heard a sort of panting sound and the ladder was pulled up and a stone was slammed down over the hole. We couldn't reach the hole without the ladder so we thought we'd find another way out . . .'

Mara nodded. 'Yes, I know the rest of it. Go to bed now, Enda.'

'We did do the task that you set us, Brehon,' said Enda. He had turned away, but now he looked back at Mara. 'We questioned everyone that we could find. Not many people knew Oscar O'Connor – he's a stranger here. No one could remember seeing him go down the mountain.'

❊

After Enda had left, she stayed for a while in the garden, turning things over in her mind. Was it Oscar O'Connor, or was it someone else who had trapped the boys in the cave? She walked thoughtfully down the road to the law school. Fachtnan came to the gate to meet her.

'Brehon,' he said, 'Aidan and Moylan told me that Enda saved them. He stayed standing in the water and made them climb on his shoulders. By the time that Moylan got up on the ledge Enda was up to his neck in water; Moylan said it was a miracle that he managed to get on to the ledge. And then the water level fell so

Enda told them to stay because the waters would go down completely in an hour or so. He did behave well, Brehon,' finished Fachtnan earnestly.

'Thank you,' said Mara. He had told her what she wanted to know. She had made the right decision. Enda would turn out well. He was straight, honest and courageous. He would make a good Brehon once he had learned to control the impetuosity of youth.

'Good night, Fachtnan,' she said, thinking how he had never given her any anxiety. 'What would I do without you?' she added affectionately, but her eyes were on the tall, burly figure of the king coming to join them.

'My lord,' she said, 'you will need your supper. Will you be safe in my house, or should we eat in the guest house?'

'We have a whole army standing around with nothing to do,' he said impatiently. 'Let's go into your house. I can smell the salmon roasting.'

'I've not thanked you for coming to my aid,' said Mara.

'You can thank Finn O'Connor for that,' said Turlough in an undertone as they walked side by side. 'If his place hadn't been so uncomfortable I'd be still there, but even with my boots on the hob I was cold, and the food ... Anyway, I must make the most of your company. I have to leave at dawn tomorrow. I've been away from Thomond for too long. I get uneasy wondering what that lad of mine is up to when I'm not around to keep an eye on him. He'll turn everything English if I'm not careful.'

'Everyone will be up early,' said Mara. 'The scholars are all going to Fanore with Cumhal to gather seaweed and it looks as if most of the young people of the Burren are going to join them.'

'So you'll have a peaceful day,' said Turlough.

'I'll have a busy day,' said Mara resolutely.

EIGHTEEN

CRITH GABLACH (RANKS IN SOCIETY)

A bóaire *has an honour price of five séts. He has land*
sufficient to graze twelve cows. He has a house of twenty-seven
feet and an outhouse of fifteen feet, a kiln for limestone,
a barn, a pigsty, a calf-pen and a sheep-pen. He has a half
share in a plough team and a share in a mill.

The bóaire *must pay the rent of one milch cow per year to*
his lord. At the death of his lord he must take part in the
digging of the lord's gravemound, pay a death levy and attend
the commemorative feast.

ॐ

THE PARTY FOR FANORE had left over an hour before
Muiris arrived at Cahermacnaghten. Mara had decided that a
man like Muiris would be more likely to tell his story in relaxed
surroundings so she planned to interview him in her garden. She
was serenely pruning a rose when she saw his low-statured, squat
figure cross the fields and stand hesitating at the gate to the law
school.

'I'm over here, Muiris,' she called. 'I'm giving myself a little holiday for an hour or so. I've lots of judgements to write up, but the day is so beautifully hot that I couldn't resist a little gardening in the cool of the morning. Come over and have a cup of ale with me.'

Without waiting for a reply she went into the kitchen of her house and came back with a wooden platter of oatcakes and two foaming cups of light ale.

'I just thought I would have a walk since it's such a great morning,' he said, coming in the garden gate. 'The young people got off all right.'

'They did indeed.' She smiled inwardly. With the whole farm to look after, Muiris goes for a walk, she thought cynically, but aloud she said, 'What a handsome boy your Felim is! I suppose the marriage will be soon. I'm sorry that I couldn't get a better contract for you. That bride price of thirty cows must be quite a worry.'

'Well, you explained the position, Brehon, and I understand. Since the bride's father is a *taoiseach* and has an honour price of ten *séts*, and I am a *bóaire* so I have an honour price of only five *séts*, then we have to supply most of the cattle.'

There was an immense degree of satisfaction and pride in his voice. He had been a servant boy, then an *ócaire*, and now he was a *bóaire*, a highly respected member of the community; his son was about to marry the daughter of a *taoiseach* and he, Muiris O'Heynes, was in a position to supply the young couple with their means of livelihood.

'I suppose we will soon be drawing up a contract for Aoife's marriage,' said Mara genially. She took a sip of her ale and then went back to cutting the dead blossoms from her rose. It was just perfect this year, growing in pink clusters around the entrance to the little hazel wood at the side of the house. Within the wood the flowers of the lily of the valley and the lacy-leaved sweet cicely glowed white on the green mossy ground beneath the small trees, and the hazels framed a glimpse of blue sky beyond.

'You have a great flower garden here, Brehon,' he said, taking his cup of ale and looking all around at the roses, the orchids, gentians and the sweet-scented herbs. He sat on the stone seat and sipped the drink meditatively.

'It's beautiful on a morning like this, isn't it,' said Mara. 'Sometimes it's my despair, but mostly I get great pleasure out of it.'

'I'd like to make a garden for Áine like that,' said Muiris, biting into a piece of oatcake. 'Once I get Felim off my hands, and perhaps young Aengus too, we'll be able to draw breath. She's had to work too hard, there's no doubt about it.' He swallowed a mouthful of ale and stared over the garden.

'You've built up a great farm, though,' said Mara softly, willing the conversation to go on and the man to relax and tell what he had come to tell.

'It's not as good as I would want it to be, but of course I started from nothing,' continued Muiris, 'or at least, I had one cow and her calf. Finn, Ardal and Donogh's father, gave them to me. I was only sixteen years old at the time and Finn's cattleman had given up with this cow. He just could not pull the calf and the cow was dying anyway, so he left her. I went in and worked on her for two hours by myself and the calf was born alive. I stayed with the cow, propping her up and feeding her every few minutes; I stayed there all night and all the following day. The next day the cow got to her feet and began to suckle her calf. Finn gave the two of them to me. He said that without me they would both be dead. He was a very fair man, Finn, very generous. I owe everything to him.'

Mara looked at him with friendly interest. She poured out some more ale from the jug and this time Muiris took a long drink.

'That's good ale,' he said.

'Brigid makes it, Cumhal's wife, you know. She makes it for the lads and I drink some. I prefer wine myself, but not for breakfast.' She waited, anxious and tense, but trying to appear relaxed and receptive. Muiris was obviously finding it hard to come to the point of his visit, but Mara feared that saying the wrong word at this moment might silence the man.

'How old were you when you came to Finn?' she asked. 'Were you fostered by him?'

'No,' said Muiris bitterly. 'I was not fostered. Nobody ever cared enough about me to have me fostered or anything else. I was just a slave and a drudge in the house; something for my father to kick when the dog ran away; the only one of his family to live beyond a few months. It would probably have been better for my mother if I had died too because it added to her torment to watch me being ill-treated.'

They sat in silence for a few minutes. In the distance the cuckoo called, and from the woodland garden another answered, his stammered notes like an echo of the first. The sun was getting higher in the sky now and its heat was drawing a fragrance from the flowers. As Muiris continued, Mara was all the time conscious of the terrible incongruity of this gracious perfumed setting for his ugly story of harsh brutality.

'My father was a small farmer, an *ócaire*,' said Muiris, 'but he had ambitions to better himself.' He gave a wry smile. 'I am a bit like him, I suppose. He worked from morning to night. I worked and my mother worked. She was never allowed a minute to rest, to look after herself. She was kicked out of her bed a day after giving birth to yet another dead child, so that she could carry on with the work. He wanted more sons in the way a man would want more asses, in order to share the burden of the work, but my mother had no strength left in her. We had no proper feeding; he was a big man and he liked his food so whatever was available

228

he took. My mother and I were half starved most of the time.' Muiris stopped and looked down at his stunted body. 'You see the size I am and yet I had the best of food from the time I came to Finn at fourteen years old, but you never make up what is missing during the early growing time.'

'No, you don't,' agreed Mara, sensing that the man needed to feel her sympathy. 'What fine sons you have, though. They will all be big men,' she added.

Muiris's face lit up. 'Well,' he said, 'they've had to work hard, poor lads, but it has all been for them. I would never see them go short. My father wasn't like that; it was all for him. My mother and I were like slaves and it was like that from the day that I could walk until I was about thirteen.'

He stopped, gazing with unseeing eyes at a pair of goldfinches that twisted and spiralled their way around the garden. His right fist was clenched and his mouth tight. Mara said nothing, just waited.

'Oddly enough, it was a hot day like this,' said Muiris, drawing a deep breath and staring over the fields. 'I can never hear the cuckoo call without thinking about it. I was picking the stones out the field above the house and building a wall, when I heard my mother scream. I stopped and then I heard her scream again and it was worse than the first time. I went to go down to her, but then I stopped myself. I always made it worse and she always asked me not to. It would only end in the two of us getting beaten and he was worse to her when I was around, just as if he wanted to show me that he could do what he liked. So I did nothing; that is something that I will remember for the rest of my life. I did nothing and he killed her.

'When I came back at noon, my mother was lying on the floor and she was dying. Just when I reached her she opened her eyes and tried to say something, and then ... then she died. On the ground beside her was an iron bar and it had blood on it. I picked it up and went looking for him. He was drawing water from the well. He was bending down, pulling up the bucket, and I came up behind and I hit him as hard as I could. I was very strong. Even though I was so small, I was very strong. I hit him so hard that I killed him.'

The skylark began to sing now, its voice high and sweet. The swallows swooped in and out of the open stable door and a blackbird rooted among the dead leaves under the holly hedge. Mara moved her hand across the small thyme leaves that grew next to the stone seat and released the sharp, spicy fragrance into the air. Muiris turned to look at her.

'Well, you can imagine that I didn't know what to do with myself then.' His voice was flat now, all emotion burned out by the constant recalling of events over a period of nearly forty years. 'I didn't know what to do with myself and I just sat there on the ground. Then one of my father's brothers came. I told him what had happened. He was a man like my father; a brutal, angry man and he would not believe me. He said that my mother probably died by striking her head on the floor and that the only blood on that iron bar was my father's. He chained me up, like a dog, and gathered all of the kin-group. It was a cold night when they came. They lit a fire outside the yard where I was chained; there were too many of them to fit in the house and they wanted me to listen. There was no Brehon there, nobody but the kin-group. They decided that I was guilty of *fingal* because I had slain my own kin.'

Muiris picked up his ale and once again took a long drink. 'I often wonder why they did not put me to death that time,' he said. 'You would think that they would. It was the only revenge that they could take. I could not pay any blood price. I had nothing.'

'They could not do that,' said Mara quietly. 'If they had done so, they also would have been guilty of *fingal*. The killing of a blood relation, of a member of the kin-group, is classed as *fingal*, no matter what crime needs to be avenged.'

'Well, that explains it then,' said Muiris in a matter-of-fact voice. 'They didn't kill me, but they did condemn me to death. God Himself saved me.

'They dragged me down to the beach and put me in a small boat with no oars, and they launched me out to sea. There was a strong south-east wind blowing. I was out of sight of the land in a few minutes. I didn't care much, I think, though it's hard to remember exactly what I was like before the fever came over me. I can just remember the terrible thirst and drinking the sea water and then drinking it again until I spewed up my guts and lay on the floor of the boat and hoped I would die.'

Mara stared at him, appalled. This was a punishment that was frequently used in the old days for the crime of *fingal* – not so often these days, though not unknown – but certainly never for a thirteen-year-old boy. She reached over, took his hand but then released it. He was a self-contained, proud and reserved man; he might not welcome her sympathy.

'I don't know how long I was in that boat,' continued Muiris, hardly seeming to notice her gesture, 'but I do remember how I was rescued. The wind changed, you see – it must have been after a few days – the wind changed to the west and it started to rain and the rain cooled my fever. I lay there with my mouth open and drop by drop the rain went into my mouth and down my throat, and, of course, the wind was no longer blowing me out to sea, but in towards the shore and I was washed up on a sandy beach. It was the beach at Fanore, but of course I didn't know that then.

'It was still very windy, but the rain stopped and the sun came out and I lay there on the sand and I looked up and there was a man bending over me. I had never seen a man as big as that before; they are all small men where I came from, though not as small as me, and this man's hair was like the sun itself – well, I don't know whether you remember Finn, before his hair went grey, but you know Ardal. Finn was like him to look at, anyway, although he was a kinder, softer sort of man, I think. He took me home with him. He put me in his own bed, he fed and tended me as if he was my mother. When I was well again, I lived in his house like one of his sons. Everything I did around the farm, I did because I wanted to do it. He never asked anything of me. He was a prince among men.'

Muiris stopped. That scene from all those years ago was as fresh in his mind as if it had been yesterday. He got up from his seat and walked down the garden, stopping to stare intently at the velvet blue of the tiny gentians. He stayed there for a long time. When he returned Mara could see the glint of unshed tears in his eyes. The horror of his father's brutality, of his mother's death and of his own ill-treatment had not drawn from him this emotion, only the memory of Finn's simple kindness. It was a few long minutes before he spoke, but by then his voice was dry and under control.

'But you know this story, Brehon?'

'No,' said Mara. She was conscious that her eyes, also, were wet. She wiped them on a soft linen handkerchief from her pouch. It was true that she had not known the story. The bald details were there in her father's notes; the boy's crime and the decision of the O'Lochlainn to care for him, that had all been there; but not the true and terrible story.

Muiris turned to look at her. 'Well, perhaps your father knew,' he said. 'Someone must have known. I told no one, except Áine, and Finn told me that he would tell no one. Not even Ardal or Donogh know. They were young at the time.'

'Why do you say that someone knew?' asked Mara, though she knew what was coming next.

'Because Colman knew,' said Muiris. 'He told me that he had found out about it at the law school.'

'Yes,' said Mara. 'The O'Lochlainn would have had to tell the Brehon, as the king's representative, about the new arrival on the Burren. My father would have written it down. I hadn't read it myself, but Colman must have. And he blackmailed you?'

'Yes,' said Muiris.

'He broke his oath,' said Mara bitterly. 'Every law student swears an oath every year at the beginning of the Michaelmas term never to reveal anything learned within these walls.'

'He came to me just after the marriage contract for Felim was signed. He said that he knew the whole story. He said that if I did not pay him six ounces of silver then he would tell everyone, including Felim's bride and her father. I would be disgraced and the marriage would not take place. No one would want his daughter to marry the son of a man who had killed his own father,' he ended simply, and Mara knew that he was right. This was the sin of sins in Gaelic society. As young Shane had recited only so recently: *The wisdom texts say that it strikes at the heart of society.* Muiris would have been ostracized and his family would have suffered with him.

'So you paid?'

'Yes, I paid. I sold a few cows and paid him and I thought that would be the end of the matter.'

'But it wasn't,' said Mara softly. She was beginning to understand Colman now. If this had gone on, he would have become immensely rich – richer, by far, than his father, the merchant, who worked hard and took many risks. There would always be guilty secrets in a community and as a lawyer he would have had the means to find these secrets out.

'No, it wasn't. He asked for more.'

'At *Bealtaine*?'

'Yes,' said Muiris. He gulped in a few breaths of air with the appearance of a man who has decided to tell the whole truth. 'Yes, up on the mountain that night.'

'And what did you say?'

'I told him that I had no more to give,' said Muiris. He gave an angry laugh. 'But I suppose I would have found the silver some way or another. I couldn't risk him talking and that was the truth of the matter. I would have paid.'

'When did you know that he was dead?'

His pale grey eyes avoided hers, and when he turned back they were as hard as granite and his lips were set firmly.

'Yesterday,' he said.

'So you didn't know he had been killed that night?' persisted Mara.

'No, I didn't know.'

'But you had threatened to kill him,' said Mara gently. Not a very inspired guess, she thought wryly. A man of Muiris's well-known toughness would have undoubtedly threatened Colman. The willowy, effete young lawyer would have been an easy target for his strength and determination.

Suddenly Muiris became very still. He stiffened and sat up a little straighter. 'So you heard that,' he said softly. 'The priest, I suppose; he would have told you.'

'I usually hear things, sooner or later,' agreed Mara. Now she was alert, on her guard; her sympathy for Muiris was almost overwhelming, but she must know the truth. The community could not survive if a secret and unlawful killing were blanketed over and forgotten. If Muiris were guilty then he had to acknowledge his guilt before everyone on judgement day. Then they could think about the fine. If necessary she would pay it herself. After all, some of the guilt was hers; she should have trusted her instinctive dislike of Colman. He should never have been set loose to prey on the people of the Burren.

'So you threatened him,' she continued.

'I frightened him,' acknowledged Muiris. 'He took his knife out. I thought it was his own knife. It was only later that I found

234

out that it was young Hugh's knife. I walked away then. I could not trust myself with him.'

'Did you go to the top of the mountain?'

'No,' said Muiris heavily. 'I had no heart for it. I climbed back down and went home once the bonfire was lit.'

'So, was Colman still alive when the bonfire was lit?' asked Mara.

He shrugged. 'I couldn't tell you,' he said indifferently. 'I had plenty to think about. How was I going to get the money to pay him off, and get the money for the bride price for Felim? And then there is Aengus coming up. I would want him to do as well as Felim. And Aoife. I want the best for them all. I don't mind working all the hours that I can stay awake, but I didn't want to be bled dry by that whey-faced fellow that never did an honest day's work.'

'Muiris,' said Mara. 'I want you to think very carefully about this. You were not at Poulnabrone yesterday but I'll tell you what I said. I said that the fine for this crime would be reduced to forty-eight *séts* if acknowledgement were made at Poulnabrone within the next seventy-two hours. I said that the victim might bear some responsibility for this crime, and I would take this into account. I ask you now, Muiris, to tell me if you were the one who killed Colman that night in Wolf's Lair.'

Muiris met her friendly eyes, but his own were blank and hard. 'No, Brehon,' he said emphatically. 'I did not kill him, and nothing, and nobody, will make me say that I did. I only came to tell you this because Aoife was telling me about young Hugh and how he got up and told how he was being blackmailed. I came to you this morning to tell you what I know about Colman. A man that will blackmail a child will blackmail anyone. There are plenty of people here in the Burren that are glad that he is dead. I'm glad that he is dead, but I didn't kill him. I have control over my temper, Brehon, I know – I knew that night – what would be the consequences if I did kill him. I walked away, but another might not have.'

'I appreciate what you have told me, Muiris,' said Mara. 'I am more sorry than I can tell you that such a thing should have happened and that a man who was trained by me and employed by me should do such a thing. I feel that I bear a heavy responsibility.'

'No one blames you, Brehon,' said Muiris, getting to his feet. 'No one would blame you, either, if this murder remains unsolved. The man is dead and buried. Let him lie. Don't let him do any more harm and tear the kingdom apart.'

He stood by the wall, a low, solid shape silhouetted against the morning sun, a menacing shape, thought Mara, a man who had killed once and who would certainly kill again without hesitation if he thought it was the right thing to do. But lie? Would he lie? Muiris's family was all-important to him: his wife, his four handsome sons and his pretty daughter. Would he let anything, or anyone, get in the way of giving them everything that he himself had lacked?

She rose from the stone bench and watched him until he had disappeared across the fields. Then she walked down the road and in through the gates of the law school. The hastily drawn map of the terraces on Mullaghmore was still on the wall of the school-house and she stood in front of it for a long time, studying the neatly printed names beside the little scrawled figures. Something was nagging at the back of her mind. A name had been mentioned; it had been mentioned before, but there was no marker for that person on the map. She would add that name to the list of people she needed to see.

nineteen

CRITH GABLACH (RANKS IN SOCIETY)

An ócaire has an honour price of three séts.

He has land sufficient to graze seven cows.

He has a dwelling house of nineteen feet and an outhouse of thirteen feet.

He has a quarter share in a plough team and a share in a kiln, a mill and a barn.

An ócaire must pay food-rent and services to his lord.

☙

THERE COULD BE NO greater contrast between the farm of Muiris, a man who had risen from a servant boy to being an *ócaire* and then a *bóaire*, and the farm of Lorcan, a man who had inherited some of the clan land farmed by his father and who was still an *ócaire* and would never be anything better. Nevertheless, this was good land here in the small valley between the high tableland of Baur North and Baur South. Over thousands of years the winter rains had washed the limy earth down from the rocky places so the soil was thick and fertile and the grass was sweet and lush. A good land for cattle; calves would grow fat and strong there. 'Great land,' Cumhal had said on many occasions. 'That's the sort of land where a good farmer could double his stock in a few years.'

Lorcan would be lucky to even keep the land, thought Mara, looking around at the neglected farm. It was fortunate for him that the O'Connor was so easy-going. Many a *taoiseach* would have taken the land from him and given it to a promising youngster. Not only was Lorcan a hopeless farmer, but he would also leave the land in a poor state for anyone else to inherit. These patches of nettles and thistles would take a long time to eradicate; the broken walls and fences would need months, if not years, of work. She stood and watched him as he came out of the filthy cow cabin. He stopped abruptly when he saw who it was and then came reluctantly across the yard towards her. She waited by the gate. The hem of her gown would get filthy in his yard and, in any case, it wouldn't do any harm to give him time to feel a little apprehensive. She could see by his slow pace that he was wondering what to say, so as soon as he arrived at the gate, she decided to attack before he gathered his wits.

'Lorcan, I have several questions for you and I want you to tell me the truth,' said Mara severely. 'There is only one person who needs to lie to me . . .' She paused and eyed the man carefully. He was sweating heavily. '. . . and that is the person who killed him. So I'll ask you my first question and I want a truthful answer. Did Colman ask for silver from you?'

Lorcan's pale blue eyes were heavily dilated, the pupils black and glittering. 'I had nothing to do with what happened at *Bealtaine*,' he said hoarsely.

'That was not the question that I asked,' said Mara. 'Did he demand silver from you?' She wondered whether Lorcan had asked Diarmuid to talk to her, or whether Diarmuid had decided himself to try to get his cousin out of the trap. The latter seemed the most likely, she thought. 'I must know all the facts about Colman before I can solve the mystery of his death,' she added.

'There's plenty could tell you about him, Brehon,' he said, his voice low. Mara nodded. There was an air of sincerity about this last sentence.

'I know that.'

He picked up a rusty rake and placed it against the wall. It slid forward and toppled to the ground.

'Anything you tell me, stays with me,' said Mara. 'I'll be talking to others as well as to you, I have the day ahead of me.'

He opened his mouth once or twice and then looked at her imploringly. 'Could you come back later?' he asked, with a note of desperation in his voice. 'I should be doing the milking now.'

Mara glanced at the nearest field. The cows were quietly tugging at the sparse grass. No animal seemed to be in distress. Lorcan probably wanted to talk to Diarmuid before he committed himself.

'Talk to me now,' she said. 'Best to do these things without too much thinking about them; it's a simple question.' It was interesting, she thought, her eyes on the neglected land, how so many gorgeous bright yellow cowslips grew in the muddy hollows left by the heavy feet of the cows as they ploughed their way through those over-grazed fields. Mother Nature coped good-humouredly with the mistakes and sins of humans; so should she.

'Tell me, Lorcan,' she said coaxingly. She would get more from him by soft methods rather than hard, she thought.

He nodded then; slowly and reluctantly, but he did nod. 'He was blackmailing me,' he said. His voice was low and husky and she had to strain forward to hear the words.

'About the use of Ardal O'Lochlainn's bull? Was that what it was about?'

He gave a swift, hunted look around the empty lane and fields as if he imagined that the tall figure of Ardal might be concealed behind one of the scrawny, neglected hedges, and then he nodded. Now there was a look of terror in his eyes. 'You won't tell the O'Lochlainn, Brehon, will you? He would utterly destroy me if he knew! I'm in a bad enough way as it is. I might not be able to hold on to the land if things get any worse. My father and my grandfather were *bóaires* on this land at Cregavockoge before me. I'd hate to be the one who lost it. My sister's youngest son is hoping for it after my time. If I lose this land, then I will just be a servant to the O'Connor. I will lose my honour price.'

There was a terrible panic in the man's voice. Mara was touched by it, but she forced herself to go on. She could not ignore any possibility.

'So you killed him because you could not afford the blackmail,' she said quietly.

'No, I didn't kill him!' he protested. 'I suppose I could have easily paid the silver,' he added hastily, contradicting his earlier statement. 'It would have been no bother to me.'

'I see,' said Mara, looking around the dilapidated farmyard. She didn't believe that he could afford it, but would he have murdered? More likely that he would have borrowed it from Diarmuid, or any other of his O'Connor relatives, she thought reluctantly. 'And what part of the mountain were you on when the bonfire was lit on *Bealtaine*?'

'Right at the top,' said Lorcan firmly. 'Well away from Wolf's Lair.'

That's a lie, anyway, thought Mara, the picture of the mapped terraces of Mullaghmore firmly in her mind. It's a lie, but does it mean anything? Lorcan is scared, and when people are scared they tell lies. Aloud, she said, 'Well, I'll leave you to think about the matter, Lorcan. Come and see me tomorrow at Cahermacnaghten if you want to tell me any more.' She nodded to him and strode off. She had reached the rusty gate at the end of the potholed land and was fumbling with the broken latch when he called after her.

'Brehon,' he said. 'Diarmuid tells me that there was a stranger there. A fellow from Corcomroe, he said. Is that true?'

Mara eyed him coldly as he sidled up to her. 'Do you want to tell me something, Lorcan?'

'No,' he said hastily, bending down and picking up a broken woven willow basket from the ground. He gazed at it and then, rather uncertainly, placed it on the wall. It toppled off and fell into the lane, but Lorcan made no move to retrieve it. It would stay there until the winter winds blew it across the field to stick in some hedge, surmised Mara. Aloud she said briskly, 'Well, I have a busy day ahead of me, and many people to see. Have you any more to say, Lorcan?'

'No,' he repeated, and then he rallied and said sulkily, 'the word is going around that this stranger was the one that killed the young lawyer.'

'Why?' asked Mara.

'It stands to reason,' he muttered. 'After all, he was a stranger. What was he doing outside his own *túath*, if it wasn't for some purpose?'

It was interesting how this view still prevailed, thought Mara, watching him carefully. Unless of the *nemed* class, such as Brehons, poets and harp players, people were expected to live and die within the narrow confines of their own kingdom; indeed, some of the older law texts suggested that a man had no legal rights beyond its borders unless he was attending a fair.

'So what purpose could this stranger have in coming into the Burren?' she asked mildly.

'He came to kill the lawyer, of course,' said Lorcan bluntly. 'He's one of the O'Connors of Corcomroe,' he added helpfully.

'One of your own name,' smiled Mara.

'Not of my *fine*, nor of my clan, either,' he snapped.

Oscar O'Connor and Lorcan O'Connor had probably a common ancestor, the king of Corcomroe, going back hundreds of years, but now the kin-group and the clan, rather than the name, would be where the loyalty would lie. Diarmuid O'Connor would feel the same. In fact, the whole community of the Burren, whether O'Connors, O'Lochlainns, O'Briens or MacNamaras, would fasten with a sigh of relief on the solution that Oscar O'Connor, from Corcomroe, had murdered the young lawyer from Cahermacnaghten.

'Why would this man from Corcomroe murder Colman?' she asked with a feigned air of surprise.

He shrugged. 'Probably been blackmailing him, too,' he said, but he sounded unconvinced. Obviously he did not know the story about Colman's betrayal of Oscar to the Mayor of Galway. The people of the Burren had little interest in Galway. The farmers had their own markets in Noughaval and in Kilfenora; the merchants had their own fairs at Eantymore and at Coad. Very few of them would even have been to Galway. Their life was based on the kingdom, the family, the *fine*, the clan and their neighbours. Oscar O'Connor would be a convenient scapegoat. She would have to try to scotch that rumour quickly. If the murder were not solved soon, some hot-headed youths might try to organize a blood feud into Corcomroe.

'I don't think that is true,' she said, trying to sound positive and authoritative.

'You don't know about that fight then, do you?' he asked nastily.

'What fight?' she asked. She didn't want to give him the satisfaction of asking, but she had to find out the truth, no matter how flawed and dirty the vessel was.

He feigned surprise. 'You didn't know about that fight he had at Corcomroe?' he asked.

'Which fight?' she asked.

'He had a fight with a sailor in an alehouse at Doolin,' he said readily. 'Diarmuid told me about it. Oscar laid the man low with a blow from his fist. He died a day later.'

Why didn't Fergus tell me about that? thought Mara furiously. She knew the truth, though. Fergus, like herself, was protective towards his people. He probably thought that Oscar had been provoked. He would not have liked to expose him to suspicion in this case on the Burren.

'That has nothing to do with this case,' she said firmly.

He shot her a quick glance and with a dirty fingernail broke off flakes of rust from the gate, watching them intently as they drifted to the ground. She could see that his mind was working hard. If he could not divert her by some means, then he would try another.

'Brehon,' he said eventually. 'I saw all of your young people going off this morning.'

'Yes,' she said patiently.

'They had lots of others with them.'

'Yes,' she said again.

'I saw Emer, Daniel's daughter, with young Roderic, the horn player. They were with them.' He hesitated for a moment, but she was silent so he was forced to continue. 'I often go for a walk across the valley in the evening. I've seen them: Aoife, Muiris's daughter; the blonde girl, I've seen her too, with Rory. I've seen them all larking around in the stone circle. There's some courting going on there, I can tell you! Daniel wanted that match between Emer and Colman, but Emer didn't want it. I heard them the other night when I went over to borrow a hay rake from Daniel. Emer was screaming at him. She was saying: "I'll kill him, or I'll kill you, before I'll marry that fellow. I hate him."'

'And what did Daniel say?'

'He knocked her to the ground; and quite right, too! A girl shouldn't shout at her father,' said Lorcan piously. 'She had a fine old bruise on her cheek the following day.'

'And what has this to do with Colman's death?' asked Mara stonily. There was no Brehon law against mistreating a daughter; though a wife could claim a divorce if her husband's blow left a mark on her. Nevertheless, Mara's trained mind ran through various possibilities for getting Daniel before her at Poulnabrone and teaching him a lesson.

'I'm saying that there were a lot of people who wanted Colman dead,' said Lorcan firmly. He smirked slightly. 'That surprises you, Brehon, but there's no reason why Emer and her lover couldn't have done it. I saw them myself sneaking away just before the bonfire was lit. Ha, ha, I was thinking to myself, they're up to a bit of lovemaking in the dark; there'll be a fine old fuss if Daniel sees them. And what about if Colman sees them! Then there'll be murder. That's what I was thinking that night, Brehon, and that's the God's honest truth, so it is.'

'And they passed you?'

'They did, indeed; going down to the fourth terrace, they were, just beside Wolf's Lair. They passed me just as the bonfire was lit.'

'So you were on the fifth terrace. One of my scholars saw you there.'

Lorcan hesitated and then smote himself on the forehead. 'What a mind I have,' he said with false humility. 'I'll forget my own name next. Yes, I was on the fourth terrace and then I climbed up to the fifth when the light came from the bonfire. Well, I hope I have been some help to you, Brehon, and now, if you'll excuse me, I'll be getting the cows in for milking.'

The cows didn't look as if they had much milk to give, thought Mara as he vaulted the wall, knocking down a few loose stones as he did so, and went across the muddy field calling

244

loudly. Had he given her something to think about? she wondered. Could Emer and Roderic have murdered Colman? Unlikely, but certainly possible. Would Daniel really allow Emer to marry Roderic, even with Colman murdered? Emer was his cash crop. He would have got a large amount of silver from Colman as a bride price. Colman was dead now, but there were other men around – Ardal O'Lochlainn was a possibility. A *taoiseach* would be a wonderful prize for a beautiful girl like Emer, or for Daniel, rather, who would not care that the bridegroom was thirty years older than the bride. Emer, with her perfect figure, her cloud of black hair and her delicate wild-rose complexion, would grace the tower house of Lissylisheen and would provide Ardal with the sons that he needed. Despite the king's offer, Roderic was still landless. Would Emer really have hoped that Daniel would settle for Roderic if Colman were off the scene?

Mara remembered their cheerful faces this morning and shook her head. This crime, she thought with a sigh, was committed by a man who had sunk into the depths of despair, who had no resilience, no self-belief left within him.

❁

'Brigid, have you got any sausages?' Mara asked, coming into the kitchen house where Brigid was busy making cowslip wine.

Brigid turned around, her hands full of the fragrant yellow pips. 'Sausages?' she said, her sandy brows raised in surprise. 'Yes, I have plenty, Brehon. I was going to cook some for tonight. Are you hungry? Would you like me to cook you some now?'

'No, no,' said Mara. 'They're for a friend – at least, I hope he might become a friend and I think, to be honest, he would probably prefer them raw.'

Brigid stared at her bemused and Mara smiled sweetly. She always enjoyed keeping Brigid guessing. There were times when it irked her to feel that Cumhal and Brigid were always so sure of what she needed and what she was thinking. During the past few days Brigid had dropped a few nostalgic reminders of Mara's father, and of how proud he would be of his daughter's success. Obviously they were both quite worried about her relationship with the king. 'Are they out in the larder here?' she continued, moving swiftly across the kitchen. 'Don't disturb yourself, I'll get them.'

There was a small leather bucket in the larder and Mara filled it with some of Brigid's tasty sausages. Bran had gone to the beach at Fanore with the youngsters so she did not feel guilty about bestowing these on another dog. Quickly she took a couple of pork pies for herself, also. She needed food while her brain was working so actively.

✿

'Diarmuid,' she said when she arrived at Baur North to find the farmer wrestling with an overgrown hedge in the lane outside his farmyard. 'I have come to make friends with your dog.' He looked at her with a startled open-eyed gaze and she smiled at him serenely. 'You carry on cutting your hedge,' she ordered. 'Just let him out and don't take any notice if he barks.' She could see questions and objections trembling on his lips.

'Yes, I'm sure!' she said quickly as she brushed aside the thorny clippings from the hawthorn hedge, seated herself on the bank and placed a sausage at a short distance from where she sat. When Diarmuid unlatched the gate Wolf bounded out, barking fiercely. Mara ignored him and sat gazing into the distance. Wolf stopped his forward rush. He looked rather uncertain, Mara thought, watching him carefully out of the corner of her eye. His bark tailed away and then his nose began to twitch. Little by little he came nearer and then in one quick movement he snatched the sausage and then backed away with a few short defiant barks.

Quickly Mara threw another sausage from the leather bucket and this time Wolf snatched it up eagerly. The next sausage fell a little nearer to Mara, but Wolf did not hesitate to come up for it. Then Mara put the sausage on her hand and held it out, still gazing straight ahead. This time Wolf took longer to make up his mind, but when Mara felt his mouth on her hand she knew she had won. Surprisingly, for such a big, aggressive dog, he took the sausage almost delicately, his sensitive lips just touching the palm of her hand. Diarmuid let out a long breath in a muted whistle and grinned broadly.

'Put him back now, Diarmuid,' said Mara quietly. 'That's enough for today. We'll do more another day. You need to get him out and about with people,' she insisted. She had told him what to do for all of their lives and she could not resist it now. 'Let him see that people are not a threat,' she continued. 'Walk him at night for a while – that would be best. Why don't you walk him around Athgreany, where the stone circle is?' That will disperse the young lovers before too much harm is done, she thought with amusement, imagining Wolf's deep bark interrupting soft murmurings of love.

'I'll do that,' said Diarmuid obediently. 'I'll do that this very night.'

'And then take him on the same walk at daytime after you've got him used to it for a few nights,' she called after him with a smile, but already her thought had returned to the two crimes that had taken place here on this pleasant land of the Burren: the rape and the murder.

She had thought of them as completely separate. But were they? Was there a connection? What was the significance of the name that was missing from the sketch of Mullaghmore on the schoolhouse wall?

'Well,' said Diarmuid when he returned from putting the dog in the yard. 'I wouldn't believe that if I hadn't seen it, Brehon.

You're great with dogs. Look at him! He's not even barking now. There's not a person on the Burren except myself or Lorcan who would dare to come near to him the way that you did.'

His words filled her with a rush of triumph. She loved to pit her brains and her courage against overwhelming odds. This taming of Wolf was something of importance to her. He was a dog that was worth getting to know; loyal, and exclusive, not everyone's dog, but a dog whose love once given was there for life.

Then Mara remembered her real purpose in coming. She had wanted to talk to Diarmuid about his cousin.

'The dog is devoted to Lorcan, isn't he? I saw that at *Bealtaine* judgement day. I always think there can't be too much wrong with a man if a dog really loves him.'

'He's not as bad as he is painted,' said Lorcan's cousin tolerantly. 'I'm not saying that he would be above a bit of cheating or a bit of lying, but he wouldn't hurt anyone, not kill someone from the law school. Not that!'

'Oh,' said Mara, rather taken aback. 'You would imagine that to be especially wrong? To kill someone from the law school?'

'Well, it wouldn't be the right thing for him to do,' muttered Diarmuid.

She looked at him with a puzzled frown. 'What do you mean, Diarmuid? Surely no murder is right, is it?'

'Well,' said Diarmuid, turning rather red, 'I mean that Lorcan wouldn't take the risk of murdering someone belonging to you. After all, you can't rest easy now until the murderer is found, can you?'

'I see what you mean, Diarmuid,' said Mara carefully. 'But it's not just me; it is the whole community who must know the truth. Cost what it may to the individual or to the clan, the truth must be known, and the community cannot live in peace unless this is done. You know that's true, Diarmuid.' He nodded solemnly and she suppressed a smile. He was always so easily impressed by her. Still, her little lecture might induce him not to shield his cousin.

'So you were standing near Wolf's Lair before the bonfire was lit, Diarmuid. Was Lorcan near to you?' She looked at him keenly.

He shook his head reluctantly. 'No, he wasn't with me. He was climbing up on to the terrace above Wolf's Lair. I saw him there clearly when the bonfire blazed up. He was turning around to talk to the physician who was coming up behind him.'

'And the priest?' asked Mara. 'Did you see the priest?'

'I saw him just after that; he was on the fourth terrace, but he was further over. He was saying something to young Nessa. To be honest, I think he was shouting at her. He sounded in quite a fury with her. I didn't like to hear him shout at her; the poor girl has suffered enough. But her own parents were there on the terrace below so it was not for anyone else to interfere.'

'I see,' said Mara. 'Diarmuid, I was going to ask you about Oscar O'Connor. I know you gave your evidence to Hugh and Shane.'

'So I did,' he said with enjoyment. 'Just like a little pair of Brehons, they were. Clever as anything! You should have seen them cross-examining me!'

He wore the proud smile of a father and Mara thought, once again, what a shame it was that Diarmuid had never married. He had a prosperous farm here and he should have sons to help him with it.

'I read it all,' she said. 'I just wondered if you'd tell me a bit about Oscar O'Connor, his background and why he went to Galway instead of working with his father.'

'Well, the father wasn't an easy man to get on with,' said Diarmuid. 'A good, hard-working man, but he expected a lot from these lads of his and of course, Oscar, being left-handed, was a bit clumsy, like, and he was always being criticized.'

'And what about the fight with the sailor? Lorcan told me about that, is it true?'

'Yes, that's true,' said Diarmuid. 'They say that young Oscar lost his temper terribly. Someone told me that he looked half mad when he did it. I was going to tell you about that. I didn't want to mention it to Hugh and Shane, of course.' She could see him scanning her face; he was a kind man, but if it were a case between his blood relation, Lorcan, and a stranger from Corcomroe then Diarmuid would certainly want to incriminate Oscar O'Connor.

'I see,' said Mara. She got up from the bench and, keeping her face turned away, she walked over to the gate to Diarmuid's yard. She pulled another sausage out of the leather bucket and held it through the iron bars of the gate. In a moment she felt it taken from her, again with great gentleness. This time she risked a quick pat, through the iron bars, on the furry head.

'Good boy, Wolf,' she said triumphantly. 'Now, Diarmuid, I must leave you. I'll go down to where they are shearing in the valley. I might as well meet a lot of people at the same time and see what they can remember of *Bealtaine* Eve. This will save my legs.'

'God be with you, Brehon,' said Diarmuid, but she could feel his unease and he did not go back to clipping his hedge, but stayed watching her as she started to go down the road.

She stopped. There was no sense in rushing these people. Time after time she had to remind herself of this. Not everyone spoke and thought at the speed that she did everything. She stooped, picked a tiny rock rose and smelled it. It had no scent, but she guessed that Diarmuid would be quite unaware of this. She placed it carefully inside the pin of her brooch and dusted her hands before she spoke.

'Did you know that he was dead? Did you know he had died by the time you all came down the mountain that night?'

He hesitated.

'I suppose lots of people knew,' she said casually. 'I was thinking that the body could not have been missed. It would have been easy to see if you came down on the western path.'

He thought for a moment. He had the look of a man who was choosing his words carefully. 'I didn't see him myself,' he said, 'but the word went around the next day. I hadn't heard it before I went to Cahermacnaghten.'

'And who told you?' she asked.

He hesitated and then said, 'Well, Lorcan told me, he was waiting for me when I came back from my chat with you at the law school.' He smiled and added, 'I suppose I was told about it on the *Bealtaine* night, but I didn't know it at the time. It was that strange boy of Gráinne MacNamara's, young Feirdin. He came up to me and he said: "The lawyer who talks to everyone is not talking any more." "What do you mean, Feirdin?" I said to him. He's a strange lad, you know. Most of the time he makes sense, but then at other times you wouldn't know what he was talking about. Anyway, he just stared at me as if he had forgotten what he had said and he walked off, picking up stones and rubbing them against each other.'

'And Lorcan also knew that night that Colman was dead.'

Diarmuid nodded reluctantly. 'He wasn't the only one, though,' he said hastily. 'There were others whispering as we went down at daybreak so Lorcan wasn't the only one who knew. I heard the name "Colman" lots of times, but I didn't take any notice. To be honest, I thought that people had discovered that he was a blackmailer. It was only when Lorcan told me the story on Friday that I knew what Feirdin meant. Lorcan told me to say nothing for the moment, until the body was discovered.'

'Strange,' said Mara. 'Feirdin said no more, did he?'

Diarmuid shook his head. 'No,' he said. 'He didn't say another word.'

TWENTY

Heptad 47. *There are two kinds of rape: forcor, forcible rape, and sleth, where a woman was subjected to intercourse without her full consent.*

Sleth of a woman who normally frequents alehouses, without a male member of her family in attendance, will carry no penalty.

In the case of forcor, the rapist must pay the honour price of his victim's husband, father or son. He must also be responsible, if necessary, for any children that result from the rape.

In addition to the honour price, the éraic, or full body fine, must also be paid in the case of a rape of a nun or of a 'girl in plaits'.

It SEEMED AMAZING that Nessa had borne a child. She was fat, but not particularly developed or forward for her age. Pathetically, she still wore the two plaits hanging over her shoulders that signified maidenhood. Her small, round face was still babyish, though the skin was spotty. She was in the garden of her home, a little cottage near the church, and she seemed to be gardening. Or rather, she was pouring a stream of water from a leather bucket over a row of young leeks.

'You're giving them a little too much,' said Mara gently. She opened the garden gate and walked into the trim, well-tended vegetable garden. 'Look, you're washing the soil away from the roots. Here, give it to me.'

Nessa handed over the leather bucket obediently. She would probably be obedient about everything, thought Mara. Nessa's mother was extremely religious and had brought the child up with great strictness. From the time that she was a tiny child Nessa had been dragged to every possible church service; by the age of three she would have been as familiar with the smell of incense as she was with the smell of milk. Nessa would never dare to show the rebellion that Emer and her friend Aoife showed to their fathers. She would not be wild and stay out late or disappear, giggling, into the darkness with a young man. So who had made her pregnant? And why could she not tell the truth?

'Look, see, you just trickle it on,' said Mara, demonstrating the technique. 'You try now.'

Obediently Nessa took the leather bucket, but soon went back to letting a steady stream gush out. Patiently Mara took it away again. She couldn't bear to see the seedlings destroyed.

'You'll be glad of these leeks next winter when all the water-cress is gone from the streams and sorrel is gone from the ditches,' she said. 'They are getting on very well, aren't they? It's amazing, isn't it, how a tiny seed can grow into a plant so quickly.'

Nessa looked at her blankly. She seemed to be quite content

to have the Brehon walk into her garden and take over the watering from her.

'It's like ourselves,' continued Mara. 'Once we become women, once our monthly bleed starts, a man can put a seed inside us – a tiny, tiny seed – and then after nine months it becomes a baby.' I must have a word with Emer and Aoife, though I doubt either is as innocent as this poor child, she thought, while she kept her eyes fixed on the trickle of water that she was pouring carefully from the bucket.

'I liked the baby,' said Nessa unexpectedly. 'I wanted it to stay alive. I wanted to play with it.'

'Yes, I like babies, too,' said Mara softly. 'I had a little baby once, but now she is a woman and she has her own babies.'

'I didn't like the man, though,' Nessa continued. 'It hurt.'

'Yes,' said Mara soothingly. 'You were a bit too young, that's why. Wait another few years and then perhaps you'll get married and you'll have another little baby, a stronger one this time. Perhaps I'll be drawing up a marriage contract for you one of these years. Who do you think you would like to marry?'

Nessa smiled slightly. She also blushed. 'I'd like to marry Rory,' she said.

'Yes, he's very handsome, isn't he,' said Mara. 'I think if I were young again I would quite like him myself.'

'Would he hurt me?' asked Nessa.

Mara held her breath for a moment. Was she nearing the truth of what happened to Nessa? Obviously the man who had hurt her, who had raped her, was not Rory, although she – or was it her parents? – had accused him.

'I think he would try to be careful and not hurt you,' she said. 'He is a kind young man. He is good and gentle with animals.' She paused, trying to find the right words, words that would not alarm Nessa, but would elicit the truth. 'So he wasn't the one that hurt you?' she asked carelessly, still continuing to water the tiny plants. Soon she would flood them herself, and they might rot, but they would be a sacrifice to the truth.

Nessa shook her head. 'No,' she whispered with a quick look around her. 'The lawyer, Colman, told me to say that. He told my mother and my father. Colman promised that Rory would marry me if I said that and I thought I would like to be married to Rory. It would make Emer and Aoife very jealous.'

'But who was the man who hurt you, Nessa?' she asked.

'I don't know,' said Nessa simply. 'But I think it was God . . .' Her voice died away. She scuffed the wet soil with the toe of her boot.

Mara put down the leather bucket and turned around to face her.

'Don't be silly, Nessa,' she said bracingly. 'You're too old for nonsense like that. Of course it wasn't God.'

'Well, he did it to Mary, the mother of Jesus, didn't he?' said Nessa sulkily.

Oh dear, thought Mara. 'Well, that was a long time ago,' she said vaguely. It was an inadequate response, but it seemed to satisfy Nessa.

'Oh,' she said, nodding her head. She thought for a moment, her young face puzzled and concentrated.

'But what did he look like, Nessa? Was it a stranger?

'I don't know what he looked like,' said Nessa. 'He threw a cloak over my head and dragged me into a cave and then he left me there afterwards. I was crying. And then I got up and I went home.'

Mara drew in a deep breath. If I get my hands on this man I'll leave him stripped of everything he possesses. I'll drive him out of the kingdom, she thought. She could feel her stormy temper rising rapidly, but with the ability born of long training she thrust it down.

'So how do you know it wasn't Rory,' she asked softly, 'if you couldn't see?'

'It wasn't Rory,' said Nessa decidedly. 'It wasn't Roderic either. They were with Emer and Aoife. It was the night after *Samhain*. I was hiding. I was watching them kissing and . . . and all sorts of things. Then they went away.'

'So you're sure that it wasn't Rory?'

Nessa nodded. 'He smelled funny,' she said unexpectedly. 'He didn't smell like a young man . . . and his hands . . .' She stopped and shuddered slightly. 'His hands were sort of hard and dry.'

An older man? wondered Mara. The smell would not be firm evidence, and the hard, dry feel of the hands? That wouldn't necessarily rule out a young man, merely indicate a man who worked with his hands: Rory and Roderic, and, of course, the law scholars, were among the few young men on the Burren who did not work with their hands; their hands would be smooth and well tended. And yet, rape was usually a young man's crime. Then, quite suddenly, the strange face of Feirdin MacNamara came into Mara's mind. Could he have had anything to do with this crime? Ordinary girls of his age would have little to do with him. If he had been the perpetrator, then the Brehon, who had allowed him his freedom against the wishes of the *taoiseach* of his clan, would bear a heavy moral responsibility.

'And you can't think of anyone that it might have been?' she asked, watching the small face carefully. Nessa seemed very childish, but she probably wasn't as stupid as she tried to appear. She had probably found that to appear stupid was the easiest way of keeping out of trouble with her parents.

'No,' said Nessa. 'I don't want to think about it,' she whimpered.

'Well, if ever you get any suspicions, or remember something else, then you must let me know, Nessa,' said Mara, going towards the gate. 'You know, if we manage to catch the man that did this, the fine will be the twenty-three cows. That's a lot of cows. But you must be sure, so if you do think of a name, say nothing to anyone except to me. Will you do that?'

'If I had all those cows, would Rory marry me?' asked Nessa, blushing again.

'Perhaps,' said Mara. Stranger things have happened, she thought. Rory, she judged, was a fairly cynical young man. It's amazing what such young men will do for money and a house. 'Of course, the money would go to your father,' she added, 'but I'm sure that he would want you to be well settled in life.'

I could do with just one problem to solve at a time, she muttered as she went down the road. Still, this matter is probably more serious than the murder. Colman is dead and his sins are buried with him. Nothing will bring him back. But this affair of poor little Nessa needs to be settled. Rape followed by marriage was not unknown on the Burren. In fact, in some cases in the past, Mara secretly suspected that the girl had been a willing party to the alleged 'rape' in order to gain her parents' acquiescence to a marriage with the man she loved. However, Nessa's rape was a different matter; there was something deeply shocking and abhorrent about that blindfolding and violation of a girl only just past childhood.

The man who did that was a man whose mind was sick – a madman? Once again she thought of Feirdin and she frowned. She realized that part of the reason why she did not want to admit he was a likely suspect was because she did not want to be wrong. With a sigh she turned and took the road towards Baur South. She would have to go and see Feirdin and his poor mother, Gráinne.

❈

There was no sign of Feirdin when Mara arrived at the small wayside cottage where the widowed Gráinne MacNamara lived with her son. Despite the heat, Gráinne was busily engaged in weeding the stony earth of her onion patch, but as soon as she saw Mara, she hastily threw down her rake and came to the wall, blessings and greetings pouring eagerly from her smiling mouth.

'Come into the house, Brehon, come in,' she pleaded. 'I have some cowslip wine that you will like. They say that you like wine. I've never really thanked you for standing up to the MacNamara for me. I was so frightened that Feirdin would be taken away from me. That would have been the end for him. I tried to explain that to the *taoiseach*, but he wouldn't listen to me.'

She picked up the rake again and placed it carefully in the small whitewashed cabin beside her house before saying emphatically, 'Feirdin's a good boy if you know how to handle him, that's what I kept telling *himself*, but he told me that I couldn't judge what was best for my own son. I knew that Feirdin wouldn't be happy with Eoin MacNamara, but he just wouldn't listen to me . . .'

She walked towards the door and threw it wide open, hospitably. 'Come in, Brehon,' she repeated.

'No, no, Gráinne,' said Mara. 'I must get back to the law school soon. All my scholars have been to the beach at Fanore and I must be back to greet them when they arrive.' That's true, anyway, she thought, and a good excuse to avoid the cowslip wine. These homemade wines were not to her taste.

'I only called in to see how Feirdin is getting on,' she continued. 'Did he enjoy the *Bealtaine* evening?'

Gráinne's cheeks flushed. No doubt there had been some covert whispering going on. She would be very aware that suspicion would fall readily on her son.

'He did, indeed, Brehon,' she said with dignity.

'One of my lads thought that he might have been a bit nervous of the bonfire; that he went down before it was lit,' said Mara gently.

Gráinne stiffened and then nodded.

'You weren't with him at the time? You stayed down on the lower terrace?'

'Yes, I did, Brehon, but I kept him in my sight all of the time.'

'Did he have a torch with him?' asked Mara casually.

Gráinne shook her head. 'No, he doesn't like torches; they frighten him. He could see his way by the light of other people's torches. In any case, he is used to going out at night. He sees in the dark as well as any badger.'

It would be very unlikely, in that case, that Gráinne could have kept her son in sight all of the time, thought Mara. She could just picture the scene on the mountainside with the faces illuminated here and there by the sudden flare of the pitch torches. That was the only way her scholars had been able to pick out those that they knew.

'It must be very difficult for you,' she said sympathetically. 'You must never know what will upset him or not.'

Gráinne's face softened. 'That's the truth, Brehon, I never know with him. Sometimes he'll go through the worst storm with the thunder crashing overhead and the lightning flashing through the window and he'll just sit there singing a song and not even noticing it and then on another day just a rumble of thunder in the distance will set him running for the house, crying like a child.'

'What upset him about the bonfire?' asked Mara.

'Well, the young fellow that brought him down said that Feirdin had been thinking that there was a man inside the pile of wood,' explained Gráinne. 'Feirdin was frightened that someone was going to be burned.'

'Young fellow?' queried Mara. Suddenly there flashed into her mind Fachtnan's observation on that Sunday morning. What was it he had said? Something about Feirdin going down with some-one . . .

'Yes, a young fellow ... I don't know who he was,' explained Gráinne, 'but he told me that he and Feirdin had been talking about rocks and stones. He was very kind to Feirdin. He told Feirdin that he would come and see him sometime and that he would bring him a present of some stones from Corcomroe – sandstone, I think he said.'

'Oscar O'Connor!' exclaimed Mara. 'Was he a tall young man with very black hair, Gráinne?'

'That's him, Brehon,' said Gráinne. 'He was a stranger, not from the Burren, but he was a very kind, nice young fellow, all the same.'

'And do you think he'd been with Feirdin for a little while before they came down the mountain?'

'I'd say they had been together for quite a while,' said Gráinne. 'You see, Feirdin had his satchel full of all sorts of stones and to quieten him after the young fellow had gone away – he was a bit upset when he left – I asked him to show them to me. He kept picking out stones and saying, "My friend found this one" and "My friend found that one". You see,' she finished simply, 'he's never had a friend before.'

Mara felt tears prick at her eyelids. What a terrible thing it must be to have a handicapped child and to suffer with every rejection of him. She thought of her little grandson in Galway and of Sorcha's pride in his cleverness and popularity. One part of her mind hated the role that she was playing, trying to extract information from this unfortunate woman, but the other part insisted that these crimes be solved. She took a deep breath and continued steadily with her questions. 'So Feirdin stayed with you for the rest of the night, after Oscar left, did he?'

Gráinne nodded. 'Yes, he stayed until the light began to come and everyone was putting their torches out and then he wandered up the mountain again. He was quite happy once the torches were out and the bonfire had died down. I knew what he would be doing. He would be watching all the people coming down and listening to them talking. He was in a great mood when he climbed down again. He was chatting away as we walked home afterwards. He said that his friend was going to get him work carrying heavy stones. He was delighted about that, poor fellow. He would love to do some work like the other lads of his age. He's very strong. He just needs someone to understand him.'

'That would be wonderful,' agreed Mara. 'That was very kind of Oscar.'

She would talk to Oisín about Oscar O'Connor, she thought. Perhaps her son-in-law would be able to help that young man to re-establish his business in Galway, or even direct customers to the quarry at Doolin.

'And which way did Oscar go when he left you?' she asked.

'He got on his horse and he went towards the west,' said Gráinne. 'We watched him go for a while, Feirdin and myself, and then the bonfire was lit and we were watching that. The young fellow was probably out of sight by then, anyway.'

'So they both started to come down before the bonfire was lit?' questioned Mara. She had to be certain, but already she was fairly sure that two people could be crossed off her list.

Gráinne nodded. 'Oh, yes,' she said. 'It hadn't been long blazing by the time that they reached me.' She looked a little uncomfortable and then she confided, 'When Feirdin gets worried like that it's often hard to get him moving. I'd say that Oscar O'Connor had a hard job to get him down. It would take some time. It was lucky for Feirdin that he was there that night.'

'Lucky for Oscar, also,' said Mara gravely. 'What is it that the Bible says? A man's good deed shall be returned unto him tenfold.'

Twenty-One

Cáin Lánamna (the law of marriage)

There are seven forms of marriage:

1. Marriage of First Degree: the union of joint property
2. Marriage of Second Degree: the union of a woman on man's property
3. Marriage of Third Degree: the union of a man on woman's property
4. Marriage of Fourth Degree: the union of a man visiting a woman with her kin's consent
5. Marriage of Fifth Degree: the union where a woman goes away openly with a man, but without her kin's consent
6. Marriage of Sixth Degree: the union where the woman allows herself to be abducted without her kin's consent
7. Marriage of Seventh Degree: the union where a woman is secretly visited without her kin's consent

THE SUN WAS BEGINNING to move out of the south and towards the western sea by the time that Mara returned from Baur South, but the day was still very hot and she strolled along enjoying the walk. The stony lane was white with limestone dust and on either side of it the lime-loving orchids grew, massed so thickly that even the grass itself was smothered by their profusion. Every colour of orchid was here: the dark red, the pure white, the pink and the spotted purple all gathered under the hedge of May blossom. Thousands of butter-yellow cowslips studded the field beyond and a lark was singing just above her head.

Mara narrowed her eyes against the sun to try to see the little bird and then she shielded her eyes with her hand. There was someone coming on a horse and he seemed as if he were making directly for her. She stood, smiling with pleasure at the sight of him. He certainly made a fine figure of a man on his handsome bay horse.

'I was just coming to see you, Brehon,' said Ardal O'Lochlainn, 'and then I thought I saw your head above the hedge.'

'And I was just thinking about you, too, Ardal,' lied Mara with her usual easy fluency. 'I was thinking that I must come and thank you for all that you did for me on Saturday.' Hopefully he had not heard about the episode with the O'Kellys.

'It is a pleasure to serve you in any way, Brehon,' he said. 'I had business in Galway that day, so it was no trouble to me.'

And I hope your business was a pleasure to you afterwards, thought Mara wickedly. He had a glossy, well-satisfied look, his copper-coloured hair glowed in the sunlight and his blue eyes were contented and relaxed. Possibly this marriage of the fourth degree, as Brehon law named it, with the fisherman's daughter suited him well. It could be that this arrangement was a good one for many people. Marriage brought its own stresses and its own demands.

'I was going to look for your help again,' she continued, bringing herself out of her reverie. 'I just want to get the events on *Bealtaine* Eve clear in my mind. I understand that you lit the bonfire at midnight.'

'Yes,' he said. Was it her imagination or did the blue eyes become a little wary, the upright, graceful form a little tense? He dismounted from his horse with an easy swing of his long leg and stood with the bridle in his hand. 'Yes,' he said. 'It's expected of me. I didn't stay once the bonfire was lit, that's what I meant when you asked me before. I thought afterwards that I might have misunderstood your question. I apologize, Brehon. I didn't mean to mislead you.'

'No, I don't suppose that you did,' said Mara soothingly, and then, very quickly, she added, 'Which way down the mountain did you take?'

She expected him to look surprised at that question but he didn't. If anything he looked a little more wary.

'I came down on the eastern side, Brehon.'

'So nowhere near to Wolf's Lair, then?'

'No, I'm afraid not, Brehon,' he said with his usual courtesy, but the warmth had gone out of his voice.

'And did you see anyone to remember as you were coming down?' asked Mara.

He frowned. 'I'm afraid I don't remember, Brehon. I had a lot on my mind. One of my mares, one of my most valuable ones, was due to drop a foal. I wanted to get back and see to her.'

It might be true. His horses were very important to him. He bred and sold horses and much of his wealth came from this trade. He even exported many to England and to Spain. The worry about his mare would have filled his mind that night. In any case, he may not have noticed whom he passed on the way down even if he were not preoccupied. He was the sort of man who took very little interest in those around him, lacking the humanity of King Turlough Donn. Or was there another reason? Did he come down by Wolf's Lair, meet Colman and be forced to listen to what the young man had to say? She frowned slightly, thinking of that case listed in Colman's neat, small handwriting. I wonder whether Ardal had anything to do with this murder, her busy mind speculated, or was that matter too trivial?

'What a beautiful horse, she has some Arab blood in her, I'm sure,' she said aloud, patting the mare and making a pretext of feeling her legs and examining the small, neat ears, while all the time her active mind was working.

The big surprise about this killing was that no one had admitted to the crime. But if Ardal O'Lochlainn decided to silence this evil on his territory then he would not want to admit that he, the most powerful *taoiseach* of the region, second only to the king himself, had committed murder. It would undoubtedly lower him in the eyes of his followers to commit a secret murder.

Ardal did not look worried by her silence, she thought. He hadn't answered her last remark, had just smiled. In fact, his eyes were on his flock of newly sheared sheep in the field on the other side of the lane and there was a look of complacent satisfaction on his handsome face. She would not press him now, she decided. She could always talk to him again. She cast around for a neutral subject with which to end the conversation.

'The king was telling me that there is a new young king in England,' she said, moving quickly into gossip mode. 'He is only eighteen years old and he is the son of the old king, Henry VII. Henry VIII, this one will be known as. Funny the way they number their kings in England, isn't it? I knew a man once who did that with his cows. He called his first cow Buttercup and all her daughters and granddaughters were Buttercup I, Buttercup II and so on. The next one was Daisy and he did the same thing. He was a man of little imagination,' she added gaily.

He laughed politely and she was glad to see that the tension had gone from his eyes.

'I was coming to see you,' he repeated. 'I just wanted to tell you that Colman had a good wake on Saturday and a good burial on Sunday morning. Everyone was there. The bishop himself conducted the burial Mass at St Nicholas's Church.'

Can you have a good wake and a good burial when you are only nineteen? thought Mara. Aloud she said, 'That's good,' and then she waited. There would be more, she knew. Ardal O'Lochlainn would not have been coming to see her unless there was more.

'They're upset, of course, the parents.'

'Of course,' agreed Mara.

'They want justice.'

Mara nodded. The Lynch family came from a long line of merchants. The fine would be important, no matter how genuine the grief. 'I've already begun my investigation,' she said smoothly. 'When I find the guilty person, then the fine will be paid.'

'The word is,' said Ardal cautiously, 'that it will not be the full fine.'

She smiled. 'You've picked up the news quickly.'

'It's true?'

'It's true. If the murder was the result of blackmail, then the fine will be just the normal *éraic*. The victim bears some responsibility.'

'I don't think the Lynch family will be too happy about that,' warned Ardal.

Mara shrugged. It was of no consequence to her. The Lynch family could think what they liked. She had confidence in her own judgement and her knowledge of the law. The crime was committed on the kingdom of the Burren; Brehon law would prevail.

She noted with amusement that the Lynch family had not asked for the death penalty. That was the interesting thing about a lot of people that lived under English law. They tended to pick and choose between the two laws according to whichever would serve their interests best. Nothing could bring back their son, so the Lynch family had decided that a fine would be better than another death. There had been a murder case recently in Kildare, right in the heart of the territory that England still held on to, where the family had turned their back on the English judge and had brought in a Brehon from Ossary to sort out the compensation.

Ardal, she noticed, now that he had made his observation about the Lynch family, was quite relaxed in her company and unworried by her silence. He took his knife from his pouch, sharpened it vigorously on a stone and then inserted the tip of it into the loop of the bridle, dislodging some minute piece of mud. It was a plain, serviceable knife, she observed, not at all like the elaborate jewelled affair that Cian had presented to his son Hugh. This one just had a long, sharp blade and a well-moulded wooden handle. It did the job for which it was designed and made no show of wealth or status. It was like Ardal himself, she thought: handsome, well built and without pretension.

How characteristic of him it was to leave his servants and followers to enjoy the bonfire and go quietly back to Lissylisheen to care for his horses. He would not be like the MacNamara, who needed to be constantly surrounded by flatterers and subordinates. The O'Lochlainns had been kings on the Burren in the old days and Ardal retained that serene, unselfconscious air of confidence in himself.

'We'll see how it turns out,' said Mara. She smiled at Ardal, but her manner conveyed that she did not want to discuss the Lynch claim any further. He smiled back, returned his knife to his pouch and mounted his horse again.

'Well, I won't delay you any more, Brehon,' he said courteously. 'If there is anything at all I can do for you, please call on me. You have a busy time ahead of you.'

'Yes, I do,' said Mara. 'I have to talk to everyone I can find. Sooner or later someone will remember something of importance from that night.'

She looked at him closely as she said this, but his handsome face was serene and unconcerned. As he trotted away on his fine bay horse, she heard him humming a tune. She knew herself to be a shrewd observer of people and there was nothing in his manner that conveyed any uneasiness, except for that one moment of ill ease when she asked him about the lighting of the bonfire. Well, she would keep him in mind, but he didn't seem a likely culprit to her.

She would go home across the fields to Cahermacnaghten, Mara decided as she pushed her way through a hedge hung with the tiny pale pink buds of the coming field roses. The lane would be an easier route, but it led past many cottages and Mara did not want to talk to anyone for a little while. She needed time to think. The sight of Ardal's knife had made her think about Muiris, and about another man, also.

❖

The bell for vespers was ringing when Mara returned to Cahermacnaghten. Brigid had spread a meal in the garden of the Brehon's house. There were baskets of oatcakes, baskets of honey cakes, platters of golden-brown sausages, big hunks of ham, balls of goat's cheese, flagons of ale, jugs of buttermilk and dozens of hard-boiled brown eggs lying in a willow pottle, all spread out on a few trestle tables in the shade of the hazel trees.

'They're coming,' said Brigid as Mara came through the gate. 'I heard the noise of the hoofs up the mountain a while ago. I thought I'd set everything up here as the day is so hot.'

'You did the right thing,' said Mara approvingly. This outdoor supper would round off the day well for everyone. 'It sounds as if you might need some more cups,' she added. She walked down the road, shading her eyes against the western sun to catch the first glimpse of them.

They glowed with sun and fun, and laughter, and they smelled of fresh brine. They galloped down the hill, infusing the tired ponies with their own youth and energy. The crowd had swollen to double its original size; young people from all over the Burren, boys and girls, had joined in.

'Had a good day?' called Mara. Her eyes went to Hugh immediately. He looked well, she thought happily. He was covered in freckles and his small nose was pink from the sun, but his eyes were clear and shining.

'Oh, yes!' said Nuala.

'Yes, thank you, Brehon,' chorused the scholars.

'You'd better put some buttermilk on your nose, Hugh, after you have seen to your pony,' said Mara. 'Supper is ready – yes, you are all invited. Give your ponies a drink and a rub-down here in the yard and then come over to the Brehon's house.'

'I'll do some more eggs and get some more oatcakes,' said Brigid, joining her. 'What did you lot do with my poor husband?'

'Oh, the cart was too slow, he's back somewhere over there,' said Fachtnan with a careless wave in the direction of Slieve Elva. He seized a handful of grass from the roadside and started to rub down his pony.

'He told us we could go ahead once we were through the pass,' said Shane, busily pumping water from the well in the yard of the law school. 'Once we were at Gragan's Castle, he said that we could go on. He had to get down and walk up the hill, the cart was so heavy with fish and seaweed.'

'I'll rub down your pony, Aoife,' said Rory, noticing that Roderic was already rubbing down Emer's.

'Perhaps you two girls would help Brigid,' said Mara. She stood for a while watching them all and then called Rory over.

'You don't want to play chess with me, do you?' said Rory.

'You know I'm no good at the best of times, and now I'm so exhausted that you'd beat me in ten moves.' He spoke lightly but his eyes were wary and he followed her meekly down the road and over to the stone bench in her garden.

'There's a lot of talk about you and Aoife,' she said bluntly, once he was seated beside her.

He moved restlessly. 'Too many people with too little to do,' he said with a half-mocking smile on his lips.

She ignored that. 'Muiris and Áine will want a good match for their daughter,' she said.

'What about Roderic? Why don't you lecture him, also?'

'I think Roderic is serious; I think you are amusing yourself,' she said severely. 'He has his roots here. You don't. Another six months or a year and you will move on. All the clans have their own bard and none of them is old. There is no place for you here. You will get tired of this hand-to-mouth life and you will be looking for a permanent position, a seat at the board and a bed by the fire. Roderic and Emer may eventually wed – I hope so – but I am concerned for Aoife. You will ruin her reputation if you go on like this.'

He plucked an early flower from the woodbine behind the bench and shredded it savagely.

'It's that priest, that Father Conglach,' he said between his teeth. 'I suppose he is the one that has been telling you tales. We've seen him hiding by that cairn watching us. He's just a pathetic old man; you wouldn't want to believe everything that he tells you. I wouldn't have thought you were a woman to listen to gossip.'

'I listen to everything that brings me knowledge,' said Mara, eyeing him coldly. 'Don't you lecture me, young man. If you want to marry Aoife, do the right thing. Go and see Muiris and offer a bride price. If you don't want to marry her, if you can't marry her, then don't spoil her chances with anyone else.' She got

270

up from the bench and strode off. She wasn't angry, just amused; but it wouldn't do him any harm to imagine that she was.

It was only a little while later that she realized the full significance of what he had said.

❄

The supper lasted for hours. Brigid made several trips to the kitchen for more cakes, more light ale, more buttermilk. Then, when the cups and platters and baskets were all cleared away and the trestles and boards carried back into the barn, Roderic produced his horn and began to play it quietly. Rory strummed his lute; and then Fachtnan sang the song of the lover going to the fair; Hugh and Shane combined their high sweet treble voices in a springtime carol; and Emer, blushing under Roderic's adoring gaze, sang '*Eibhlín a Rúin*', 'Eileen, my love'. The O'Lochlainn boys roared out a rhythmic drummer's song to the accompaniment of their own hard hands slapping the stone bench and Brigid hitched up her *léine* and danced a sprightly jig on the clints.

'When the moon is over that ash tree, then it will be bed, everyone,' said Mara. 'We've all got work to do in the morning.' She herself felt quite sleepy after her day in the open air. For a moment she sat and allowed herself to enjoy their pleasure, but then she roused herself and walked through the scented garden, plucking a rose as she went. She stood for a moment, looking back, thinking that her garden had never looked so beautiful as it did that night. The candles burned steadily in the still air and lit up the brightly coloured *léinte* of the boys and girls. They looked like clusters of orchids in the fields, she thought, as she walked down the road to the law school with her small horn-paned lantern in her hand.

The schoolhouse smelled stuffy when she pushed the door open, but she ignored that and went straight to the wall where the map of Mullaghmore was sketched. She gazed at it steadily for

some time and added a few new names. It was all beginning to
make sense and it was all beginning to point to one person. She
didn't like her conclusions, but never in her life had she shirked
her duty or withdrawn from the truth once it was manifest. She
went to the bookshelf. Her memory was excellent but she had
been trained always to check a theory against facts. The book she
was looking for was at the back of the shelf and she had to brush
the dust off to read the words: *Bretha Déin Chécht*. She studied it
intently, then sighed and blew out the small candle inside her
lantern. She would need its light later on and the moon above the
big ash tree across the road was bright enough for her to find her
way back.

❋

'Home, everyone, and bed,' she called firmly when she returned.
She could ensure that her own scholars went to bed, but she
doubted that the others would. They seemed to have paired off
very neatly and there were entwined figures on every seat and in
every corner of the garden. Fachtnan went around lighting some
covered lanterns and then blowing out the candles and Brigid
started to usher the younger boys across to the scholars' house.
They would sleep well tonight, thought Mara. The shadow of
Colman's death had been lifted from them all. She stood and waited
while the other young people mounted their ponies and went off,
some going south down the road to Lissylisheen, some going
north to Baur and others going across the stone clints towards
Kilcorney.

'Take Nuala home, Fachtnan, will you?' she asked. 'Bran will
go with you. He'll enjoy the run now. It's probably been too hot
for him all day. Will that be all right, Nuala?'

'Oh, yes,' said Nuala, her green eyes shining with delight.

She's still very young, thought Mara, amused. She's too young
to hide the fact that she worships Fachtnan. Well, he's a nice boy

and, yes, it would be a good match in a few years' time when he is qualified and she is old enough to know her own mind. There's no reason why she should not be a physician as well as a wife and mother: the one would help with the other. The Burren badly needs a physician who can save the lives of all those young girls who now die in childbirth and those babies who are lost before they can be named and baptized.

Mara watched until they had disappeared across the clints with Bran loping effortlessly behind them. She was surprised that Malachy had not come over. He was normally so worried about Nuala that she had expected him to arrive as soon as dusk came. She was glad that he hadn't come, though. She needed some more thinking time. She crossed the garden and went to sit on the chamomile bench, breathing in deeply, inhaling the sweet apple smell of the foliage. The candles in the windows of the scholars' house were like golden spots of moving light, making the starlight seem blue by contrast. Then, one by one, the lights went out and everything became very still and very quiet. A few clouds had drifted across from the Atlantic and Mara felt a light breeze at the back of her head. The wind had turned to the west. It would probably rain again tomorrow, but this day would stay in the minds of the young people and when they were old they would look back and think that all summers were like that: golden days of sun and sea, and evenings filled with the scent of roses and the music of softly singing voices.

The moon had disappeared now, hidden behind the clouds. The garden was very dark: the deep blue and the pale blue gentian flowers had darkened and dimmed with the fading of the light, and the whole complexity and blending of colours in her lovely garden were reduced to a white glimmer of cloud-pale orchids in front of the holly hedge in the far corner.

Night simplifies everything, thought Mara; just two colours: white and black. Life is not like that, though. There is some evil and some good in every person; just the proportion varies. In actions, also, love can be the wellspring of evil.

With a sigh, she rose to her feet and lit the candle inside her little lantern. Her mind had cut through all the conflicting and confusing aspects to the death of Colman on Mullaghmore Mountain and now she had an inner certainty that she knew the truth. She had to hear it confessed, though. The truth had to be established, the fine had to be paid, and the community had to know who had done wrong. She would wait until Fachtnan returned, she decided, but she could not wait another day. She would confront the murderer this very night.

Twenty-two

Córus Béscnai

(REGULATION OF PROPER BEHAVIOUR)

There is a contract between the church and the people of the
kingdom. The people must give offerings to the church.

For the contract to be valid, the priests must be devout,
honest, properly qualified and must administer the sacraments
of baptism, communion and requiem for the dead.

ᚢᚷ

THE STONE CIRCLE WAS lit up when Mara arrived. A
candle, stuck by its own grease, had been placed on the top
of each of the thirteen stones: white light and black shadows
etched sharply on the bleached grass. They had been singing
softly; she had heard them the whole way as she crossed the flat
tableland of the High Burren and she had smiled to herself. They
did not realize how far sounds carried on a still night.

It was amazing that neither Daniel nor Muiris had come
storming down to order their daughters home. The singing had
stopped now and she could guess that they were kissing and
cuddling. At least, she hoped that it would be confined to that!

She hesitated for a moment and then moved quietly behind a small lone hawthorn tree. She hated to play the part of the unseen spy, but she had to prove something.

She waited silently, her eyes fixed on the stone cairn opposite. Could she see some movement from it? She wasn't sure, but she thought she had seen a flash, perhaps light, reflected from an eye or a brooch.

'We'd better go.' That was certainly Rory's voice. 'We'd better get you girls home. Aoife's father will probably have heard the O'Lochlainn boys clattering past and he will be looking out for her. Anyway, Her High and Mightiness has been lecturing me. I told her not to listen to gossip but she said, "Don't you lecture me, young man," and I had to say, "Yes, Brehon; no, Brehon".'

Mara grinned to herself in the darkness. That had been a fair imitation of her authoritative tones. Perhaps Rory would be better at satire than at his usual sentimental poems, she thought.

There was some more low murmuring and then Emer emerged with Roderic's arm around her waist. Even by the uncertain light of the candle, Mara could see that her cheeks were flushed very red, her lips the colour of cherries. They did love each other, these two. Perhaps everything would work out now that Turlough has promised to take Roderic on as a musician, she thought. He'll like to have a pretty girl like Emer around his court, and Daniel will surely allow the match if Turlough asks him. She continued to consider this, forgetting her real purpose for coming. After the disaster with Colman, Daniel will be worried in case Emer would be considered bad luck. And even if he doesn't think of that for himself, I could perhaps put that idea into his head.

Smiling at the thought of the few well-chosen words that she would implant into Daniel's slow brain, Mara braced herself ready to move forward, training her eyes to get used to the darkness as, one by one, they blew out the candles and placed them under the stone altar in the centre of the circle.

Mara waited until their footsteps died away and then she moved. Clutching her lantern in one hand and her tinderbox in the other, she made her way carefully towards the cairn. Although the moon still lurked behind the clouds, there was enough watery light to see the white quartz pebbles that covered the cairn, and she was in front of it before she lit the candle inside the lantern and then closed the horn-plated door. She lifted it aloft and directed its light through the broken front of the cairn. She had never looked at the cairn from so near before, and she realized that the narrow crack in the broken eastern side was indeed an entrance. So that was where Nessa had been dragged.

Mara peered in. There was a wedge-shaped chamber within; an ancient burial place, she surmised. There was another opening on the far side of the small chamber and through it she could see an open space, a sort of court with other chambers opening out from it. She squeezed through the gap, crossed into the court and stood there, holding the lantern aloft, turning it from side to side, looking into one chamber after another.

There seemed to be no living person there and for a moment Mara felt a sharp pang of irritation and disappointment. She had looked forward to confronting him, to pinning this crime on him, but it looked as if he had evaded her. She was about to turn away, when she suddenly became aware of a smell. It was not the pervading musty odour of damp earth and dry dusty bones; it was a different smell, sweeter, more cloying and more familiar. Mara realized what it was. *He smelled funny*: that was what little Nessa had said. The cairn reeked of the heavy, cloying scent of the incense that was liberally sprayed around the church every Sunday. She stepped further across the court until she reached the front of the small chamber at the end. She held her lantern aloft.

'You can come out from behind that stone, Father Conglach,' she said coldly. 'I would like a word with you.'

He emerged from behind one of the upright pillar stones,

standing at the entrance to the chamber. At even a distance of two yards the reek from the incense sickened her. It was odd, she thought, how she had never noticed this before from his priestly gown. Perhaps she had always kept her distance from him.

'You can see for yourself now what goes on here at night, Brehon,' he said loftily.

Mara had not expected him to face her so boldly. She had expected terror or contrition. One part of her mind realized that she was doing something stupid, but the other part rejoiced in solving the crime. All her life she had been courageous and determined, and so far she had been lucky. She tried to put into her bearing all the authority which had been hers as Brehon of the Burren since she was twenty-one years old.

'Yes,' said Mara firmly, 'terrible things have gone on here at night.'

He seemed disconcerted at her manner and for once words did not come to his ready tongue.

'Terrible things,' repeated Mara. She examined him carefully. She was in no doubt that he was guilty and yet his face wore the usual mask of sanctimonious distaste. Suddenly nervous, she took a couple of steps back from him. Why had she done such a stupid thing as to try to tackle this man on her own? Why had she not told someone where she was going? She knew the answer to those questions. It was arrogance, perhaps a too great estimation of her own powers. Still, she thought, I am Brehon of the Burren. I am responsible for the law in this kingdom. I will achieve what I set out to do. The thought steadied her.

'A child was violently raped here in this very chamber,' she said coldly. 'And you, you a priest, were responsible.'

'What are you saying, you wicked woman?' He thrust his face into the light of the lantern, but thankfully did not come any nearer. With an effort she prevented herself from flinching.

'Don't try to deny it; I know exactly what happened and I

know how,' she said sharply. 'You watched these two young couples night after night; don't deny that, either – I have plenty of witnesses who have seen you skulking in the shadows. You watched them, and you watched them, and you roused yourself to such a pitch that you had to have a woman.'

He howled then, and lunged towards her, pulling a knife from his pouch. Swiftly Mara moved aside, keeping one of the upright stones between him and her. She was tempted to turn and flee, but she had to get her evidence. She had to be able to swear before God and before man that this priest was guilty of that heinous crime. She had to goad him until he confessed to the rape of the child, Nessa.

'You lying bitch, you unclean woman, you filthy . . .' His face was distorted with rage, his eyes bulging from his forehead. Then, suddenly, just before he reached her, he collapsed into a sobbing heap on the ground. Behind the light of the lantern Mara felt herself tremble but remained very still, watched him narrowly.

'You should have gone out and got yourself a prostitute like any decent man,' she said coolly. 'Why violate that innocent child?'

'She was not innocent,' he screamed. 'She was a whore like the others. I saw her there. She was watching them. If she were innocent, she would have been at home in her bed.' Now the saliva was running down his chin and he panted like a man who had been running for a mile. The heavy, scented stench of the incense was in Mara's nostrils, but she watched him as she would watch a trout nibbling on the bait.

'So you just did it to teach her a lesson?' she said softly. The fish had taken the bait; now to reel him in!

'She deserved it,' he said with grim satisfaction. He wiped the saliva from his chin and tried to look pious. He seemed to be regaining his composure. He stood up and arranged his black gown with hands that trembled.

'So you took her. She thought that she knew who it was. She smelled the incense from your clothing. Poor child. She thought you were God.'

He said nothing. She tried again.

'Why did you do it?' she asked, her tone flat.

This worked. He suddenly screeched, a shrill, demented sound that raised the hairs on the back of Mara's neck.

'Because she has got the devil in her!' The words seemed to be wrenched from him. 'She has got the devil in her and I tried to get it out. I lay with her to get the devil out of her. All women have the devil in them. All women . . .'

Abruptly he stopped. He mopped the side of his mouth with a linen handkerchief from his pouch. 'And you have the devil in you,' he said slowly, his eyes suddenly narrowed. 'You are trying to destroy me . . . me, the God's anointed. You will go to the bishop and you will tell your story and you will defame me. So I must cut the evil out of you.'

Quickly he reached forward, and before Mara had a chance to move, he had snatched her left hand and slashed his knife across the vulnerable veins in the wrist.

'I've seen a man die from a wound like that,' he panted. 'He did it to himself. It was a sin against the Holy Ghost, the sin of despair: the worst sin of all. I refused to give him extreme unction although he begged me and his wife begged me. I just sat and watched him. He did not take too long to die. You will die soon, just like he did.'

Mara dropped the lantern, fighting the feeling of sickness and faintness. The candle went out instantly and they were left in the heavy darkness. She remembered the case, and the anger that came to her from the memory of the poor young wife's anguish at her husband's terrible death and lonely burial at the four crossroads lent her strength. With her right hand she fumbled in her pouch and dragged out her linen handkerchief. She knew she had to stop the bleeding as soon as possible. She wedged the soft linen against the wound on her left wrist. She felt it soak instantly, the thick material wet and sticky to her hand, but she kept pressing as hard as she could. If she sat down, she might be able to wind the hem of her *léine* around it also, but somehow she preferred to confront Father Conglach on her feet. Somehow she had to dominate him.

'The bishop would be very angry with a priest who committed the deadly sin of murder,' she said calmly. 'The Lord God gave that commandment to Moses, didn't he? Fifth: *Thou shalt not kill.* You remember that, don't you?'

She wished that she had not dropped the lantern. She would have liked to be able to see him, to look him in the eye. She would keep talking. Words were always her weapon, her means of control.

'But, of course,' she said, 'you had already tried to murder three boys from my law school. Don't deny it. You were seen passing by; Shane and Hugh saw you. You heard Enda, Moylan and Aidan down in the cave, didn't you? So you went down the passageway, took away their ladder, shut them in there and then the caves flooded. It's by the mercy of God that you don't have that sin on your soul as well.'

She cast her mind back and shuddered at the tragedy that could have occurred. This man would have had no mercy. He would not have gone back and released them. Why had he done it? There was only one explanation. He was mad; she recognized that. Had he always been mad, or was it just that the sexual frustrations, then the violent rape, and the terrible fear of its discovery had finally tipped his mind into insanity?

She heard him move and smelled him more strongly. 'Ah, but I am not going to kill you,' he said. His voice sounded faintly amused. 'I won't kill you. I won't be responsible for your death. You will die if the Lord wills it. It's in His hands now. I will leave the knife on the ground. You will be found dead, like that devil's brat, your spawn from your law school. He committed a terrible sin. He accused me of dreadful things. And then he died. He died by the knife. And now you will die, also.'

Mara said nothing. She leaned against one of the upright stones that supported the roof of the cairn. Her handkerchief could hold no more blood; it had reached saturation point and now she felt the blood drip on to the stone floor. She clenched her teeth tightly. *I must not, and I will not die*, she told herself fiercely. She had too much to live for; too much to do; too much life still to enjoy. If only he would go away, she thought, then she might be able to get out and perhaps crawl the few hundred yards to Caherconnell and get Malachy to attend to her. Was there any way she could get him to leave her? She took a slow, deep breath through her nostrils and tried to imagine that it calmed her and gave her strength.

'You had better depart now while it is dark,' she said stonily. 'If you stay you risk being seen and someone might know that you caused my death.'

He said nothing; in the fetid darkness of the burial tomb she heard his breath come in short, quick pants. He seemed to be stirring, making some kind of movement, and suddenly she was filled with a sick disgust and more fear than she had ever felt before in her life. Why had she not taken Bran with her, at least? He would have defended her against this madman. She took a deep breath. She would fight. He would not do this to her.

But at that moment Father Conglach hissed, 'The Lord bids me to take the devil out of you, too,' and launched himself at her, fumbling at her *léine*. She felt his dry, hard hands on her leg and she smelled the sour smell of his breath in her face.

Mara's father had trained her voice from a very early age. Even when she was only seven years old he used to take her to Poulna-brone and stand a hundred yards away and get her to practise projecting her voice until the surrounding hills gave back the echo of her words. Time and time again she had gone to practise, and all the years of training now came to her rescue. Her scream came out with such force that it seemed to shake the little cairn. She continued to scream, but she prayed also.

Surely there was a voice, an answer! She stopped screaming and listened. Father Conglach seemed to hear nothing. He still struggled with her clothing and she continued to resist, kicking violently; but she was sure she had heard something. A faint light seemed to fill the empty space of the entrance to the cairn. Perhaps the moon had re-emerged from the clouds, or perhaps, she hoped with desperation, a man with a lantern had approached. She screamed again. And then came a bark that rang like a bell off the limestone. Only one dog barked like that! And then there was a thud of heavy paws and a huge shape blocked the faint misty yellow light at the doorway. The smell of blood, and the smell of mould, and the smell of the man were all overwhelmed by the heart-warming smell of warm dog fur as he hurled himself on the figure beside her.

And then the priest shrieked. The dog was growling now. Growling with the ferocity of his father, the wolf, and holding on with the intensity and tenacity of his mother, the sheepdog. The priest screamed again. Mara struggled to her feet and tried to keep her balance as she shook her clothing into order.

'Call your dog off, Diarmuid,' she said. 'I don't want this man killed. I want him to stand before the community and confess to his crimes. Good boy, Wolf,' she added. She was close to tears and she bent down and hid her face for a moment in the soft warm fur and laid her cheek next to the enormous head. 'You come and see me at the law school, Wolf, and you will have all the sausages that you can eat.'

'Jesus, Mary and Joseph,' gasped Diarmuid, holding his lantern up and looking at the frothing, gibbering creature on the ground.

'The dog's bitten the priest. Look, he's bitten him on the arm. He's bleeding.'

'He's a good judge, that dog,' said Mara, filled with a desire to giggle wildly. 'He did the right thing. If you and Wolf had not come along at that moment, Diarmuid, I might be dead by now ... I hoped you were coming ... I kept thinking about Wolf ... he's a good dog, Wolf ... Tie him up, Diarmuid ... tie him up for heaven's sake ... He tried to murder me ... the man, I mean ... not the dog ... Tie up the man ... not the dog ... the dog is an honest dog; the king himself said so.' Suddenly she realized that she was sick and giddy and that an icy coldness was coming over her.

'You're bleeding! You're badly hurt,' said Diarmuid. He set his lantern on the ground and bent his head over Mara's wrist.

'Tie something over it as tightly as you can, Diarmuid,' said Mara, forcing herself to remain in command of the situation. 'He tried to murder me by slitting my wrist ... he wanted me to bleed to death so that I would not be able to accuse him of the terrible crime of the rape of the young girl, Nessa ... I'm telling you this now, Diarmuid, in case anything happens to me ... If I die, you must bear witness to my last words ... this man ... this priest violently raped that child.' She struggled to sit up, but collapsed back on to the ground. 'Diarmuid,' she gasped, 'you must take this as a sacred trust ... you must go to Thomond and tell King Turlough Donn what happened ... promise me, Diarmuid ... this man must be punished.'

A black mist seemed to be welling up before her eyes and the orange light from the lantern was shifting and spreading out into a strange haze. Her lips were cold and suddenly the pain from her wrist was unbearable. She lay quite still for a moment; it seemed tempting just to let go and slide into the cold darkness. But she couldn't do that; she had too much to do. Once again she struggled up and this time she placed her head between her knees, and a moment later a rush of hot sweat spread over her. She waited for a moment, but the icy faintness seemed to have passed. She leaned her head upright against the rough stone and tried to breathe deeply and steadily. She felt very ill and she was conscious of a strange vagueness and remoteness from her present situation. Only Diarmuid's warm hand on her cheek kept her from losing consciousness completely.

'The bastard,' muttered Diarmuid as he tore one of the loose flowing sleeves from his *léine* and bound her arm tightly. Mara took several more long, deep breaths. She touched her wrist. The blood was not seeping through yet. She allowed herself to hope that all would yet be well. Diarmuid was kneeling beside her, his hand on her wrist, his thumb firmly over the bandage.

'Mara,' he said urgently. 'Are you all right?'

She smiled slightly with cold lips. Although she always called him Diarmuid and had known him since she was a child, Diarmuid had not called her Mara for almost twenty years. She was always *Brehon* to him. There was a depth of anguish in his voice and somehow it steadied her. She tried to open her eyes and look at him.

'I'm feeling better now, Diarmuid,' she said, conscious that her voice still sounded weak and faint. 'Just tie him up while he is still unconscious. I think he has had some sort of fit.'

Diarmuid lifted his thumb and shone the light from his lantern on to her wrist. She looked down. The rough bandage was still white; no ominous red stain spread over it. The dog, Wolf, ceased his heavy panting and seemed to hold his breath, looking with interest at her wrist. Diarmuid gave a satisfied nod and went over to the unconscious man on the ground. The dog gave a low menacing growl, but then grew quiet when he could see that there was no threat to his master. Diarmuid took off his leather belt and buckled it around the priest's legs, tying them securely. Then he used the other sleeve of the *léine* to knot the arms behind the back. The priest muttered and groaned but he still appeared unconscious. Despite his harsh words, Mara noticed that Diarmuid handled him with care. The priests in the community were treated almost as gods – the news of Father Conglach's crime would be an enormous shock to everyone.

Just as well if the tale travelled around before judgement day. The people would have the time to get used to their shock and their horror at the guilt of the privileged and the sacred; and would be able to turn their minds towards justice for the weak and the unimportant, thought Mara. She waited until Diarmuid had finished trussing up the priest. From time to time she glanced down at her wrist, but the wrappings still stayed white. Her spirits began to rise.

'Go and get help, Diarmuid,' she said. 'It will only take you a few minutes to go to Caherconnell. Tell Malachy the whole story. Get him to bring some men and a cart. We will send this . . . this man back to the bishop at Kilfenora. Let the bishop look after him now. He is his responsibility.'

'Will you be all right?' asked Diarmuid. He lifted the lantern and cast a quick worried glance at her wrist. She looked also; some blood had leaked through, but not much.

'I'll be fine,' she said decisively. 'The bleeding must be quite slow now. Malachy will be able to stitch it. Tell him he'll need to bring something. Ask him to bring a piece of parchment and pen and ink, also. I'll write a note to the bishop of Kilfenora and explain everything. Tell him not to bring Nuala,' she added urgently. 'Tell him I said that Nuala was not to come.'

Diarmuid grinned at her. 'You're feeling better,' he observed mildly. 'I know you are yourself when you start giving me strings of instructions. You were always like that even when you were five years old.'

She was surprised to hear herself laugh. 'Go on, then,' she said lightly. 'Go quickly. I'll be all right.'

'I'll get you out of here, first of all,' said Diarmuid. 'You won't want to be staying here with him. Just stay still for a moment; let me carry you.'

'I'm heavier than I was when I was five years old,' said Mara, but he had picked her up in a minute and carried her outside. The night was still very black and there was a slight mist blowing in from the Atlantic. Mara tasted the salt on her lips and was suddenly filled with an overwhelming joy that she was still alive.

'Put me down, Diarmuid,' she said curtly. 'I'll just sit with my back against that stone; I'll be fine.'

'I'll leave you the lantern,' said Diarmuid.

'No, take it,' said Mara. 'I don't want you falling and breaking your leg in the darkness. I need Malachy here quickly and I need to have that priest moved off the Burren as soon as possible.'

'Come on, Wolf,' said Diarmuid. He was a man of few words, she thought, and, yes, he had always obeyed her instructions to the letter even when they were both five years old. She had absolute confidence in him.

❋

Mara half wished that he had disobeyed her instruction and had left the lantern or else had relit her own lantern. The time seemed long to her. She watched the light bobbing until he had reached the edge of the high tableland; he would have dropped down over the broken slabs there to the back of Caherconnell, she thought, her mind following his journey through the mounds of ferns unfurling into croziers of palest green. It would take him another few minutes to climb down there, and then perhaps another few minutes to rouse one of the household if they had all gone to bed. And then Malachy, never the quickest thinker, would have to collect his medical bag, give instructions to his men, the cart would have to be harnessed and taken around by the road and across the flat tableland. She strained her ears for any sound and then heard a mutter from within the cairn.

'I wish he had left Wolf,' she murmured. 'I would feel better then.' Diarmuid would not have done that because he would have feared the dog might attack her, but Mara had no fear of that happening. She knew that Wolf had accepted her. 'Dogs are less complicated than human beings; they live by their rules,' she said aloud and then smiled to herself to hear her usual clear, confident voice ringing against the limestone. Her wrist ached fiercely and she welcomed the pain; anything was better than the clouds of faintness welling up and smothering her mind. She heard a mutter from inside the cairn and hoped that Diarmuid had securely tied ... *that animal,* she allowed herself to call him in the privacy of her own mind. She strained her ears again towards the east, towards Caherconnell, and this time she heard something. There was definitely a slam of a door, and a shout. She prayed that the mist would not get worse; already it was deadening sounds. Surely she should be hearing more noises by now?

Deliberately she jerked her wounded wrist. There was a stab of pain – that would keep her senses alert. She strained her ears, turning her head slowly from side to side, but she could hear no more sounds from the Caherconnell direction. At least her faintness was not worsening. Her mind had to remain alert for the next hour or so. She had to get these two crimes, the murder and the rape, acknowledged and the price paid for them.

Diarmuid was the first to arrive. She could hear his dog panting and the noise of Diarmuid's nailed boots striking hard against the stone clints.

'Mara,' he was saying, 'Mara, is everything all right?'

'I'm fine, Diarmuid,' she said and noted with satisfaction that some of the strength had come back into her voice. Her mind was clear and alert and her wrist would heal. She felt suddenly cheerful. She would never speak of the degradation of the attempted rape to any person living in the kingdom of the Burren, she decided. There was plenty to accuse the priest of without that. She knew herself, and knew that she would find it easy to put something like that behind her; what she could not bear would be covert sympathy.

'Is Malachy coming?' she asked, with a sudden trace of anxiety. 'He's not away, is he?' She suddenly remembered how surprised she was that he had not turned up to escort Nuala home earlier in the evening.

'No, he's coming. He had to pack his medical satchel. He's coming around with the cart and the men. Look, you can just see the lights.'

'Have you noticed anything, Diarmuid?' asked Mara after a quick glance had shown her the hazy lights in the distance. 'Have you noticed anything strange?'

'No,' said Diarmuid, gazing all around him and holding up the little lantern.

'Something strange about the dog?'

'What's strange about the dog?' asked Diarmuid, shining the light on the huge reddish-brown dog sitting with a pink tongue hanging over his chin.

'He didn't bark when he came up to me,' said Mara with immense satisfaction. 'That's what's strange about him.'

Diarmuid tried to reply but his words were drowned by an explosion of barks. The cart was trundling across the stone pavements and men walked in front holding flaming pitch-pine torches. Wolf barked again and again and lunged towards them and Mara looked at him with maternal pride.

'He doesn't bark at me,' she said in the brief interval of the volley of barking and Wolf turned and wagged his tail. Diarmuid began to laugh.

'Well, I don't know,' he said. 'You are the coolest person I have ever known. You were nearly murdered by a madman and all you are interested in now is having tamed the dog. I'd better tie him up over there to one of the stones or no one will want to come near to you.'

'Are you all right, Brehon?' said Malachy, looming up out of the mist.

'I'm all right, Malachy,' she said. 'Has Diarmuid told you all?'

'Yes, he has, what a terrible business. I suppose the poor man has gone right out of his mind.'

Mara sniffed. 'I think he has had some sort of fit,' she said coolly. 'Get your men to load him into the cart, Malachy. Diarmuid has left him tied up inside the cairn. I would keep him tied up. He is guilty of two crimes. The most important is the violent rape of a child; but he has also tried to murder me.'

Malachy gave her a quick glance and put his hand out. Silently she showed him the injured wrist. He inspected the wrapping and gave a nod. Then he took her other hand and placed his finger on her pulse. Again he nodded and gave her a quick smile.

'I'm probably hard to kill,' she said light-heartedly.

He laughed. He looked well himself, she thought as she watched him carefully unwrap her bandage and mop the clotted blood from her wrist. She moved her mind away from the pain and continued to study Malachy. Perhaps it was just the dimness of the lantern's light, but the black shadows under his eyes had gone and the air of heavy depression seemed to have lifted from him. Even his skin looked brighter. Perhaps he had been sleeping in the evening and now he was rested and alert.

'I'll take you back to the house and stitch this up when I get you there,' he said when he had wrapped up her wrist again. 'Have a drink, now.' He took a small flask from his satchel.

'Brandy, I hope,' she joked.

He smiled again. 'No, water, I'm afraid, but I'll get you some brandy when we are back in Caherconnell.'

He took a pitch torch from one of his servants and strode over towards the cairn. After a minute he shouted an order and his servants came forward and then backed out, carefully carrying the priest trussed up like a pig for slaughter.

'Did you bring the pen and the parchment?' asked Mara.

'I did, indeed,' called Malachy. 'Are you able to write?'

Mara held out her right hand and Malachy came and brought her the small leaf of parchment and a well-trimmed goose quill.

'Diarmuid will hold the parchment straight for me,' she said, placing the inkhorn on the stone slab beside her. 'You go and attend to the dog's bite on the arm of the priest. I don't want anything to happen to him before he is brought, in chains, if necessary, to stand before the people of the Burren and to confess to his sin. Diarmuid,' she called. 'Come and hold this for me, like a good man.'

He came instantly. There were traces of a grin lurking under the ginger hair of his moustache.

'Yes, I know, I'm still ordering you about,' she said, laughing at the expression on his face. Funny how I have forgotten what a sense of humour he has, she thought.

'It's good to see you able to do it,' he said warmly, and there was a lifetime of affection in his voice. 'You're looking and sounding more like yourself now.'

He unrolled the parchment, flattened it on the stone slab, and held it steadily while she dipped the quill into the soot-black liquid in the inkhorn.

Mauritius,
Bishop of Kilfenora,
Kingdom of Corcomroe

She wrote carefully at the top of the leaf, and then underneath in her square italic hand she wrote:

My Lord Bishop,

It gives me much pain to report the wrongdoing of one of your priests. I am sending him back to you under armed guard. He has violently raped and made pregnant a twelve-year-old girl. He did not acknowledge his sin and did not make any amends. I got a confession from him and I am prepared to swear to it. The case will come up on the next judgement day on 10 May at Poulnabrone. I would ask that you keep this man under guard and return him for judgement on that day.

If found guilty, the fine will be the sum of forty-five séts, or twenty-two and a half ounces of silver or twenty-three milch cows.

This man also tried to murder me, but I will not ask for a fine on this count.

Mara,

Brehon of the Burren,

By appointment to King Turlough Donn O'Brien,

King of Thomond, Corcomroe and the Burren

When she had finished she returned the quill to Diarmuid and rolled up the leaf of vellum awkwardly with her right hand.

'I have no seal,' she said. 'I should have a seal with me.' I left it at the cave yesterday, she remembered. It all seemed a very long time ago.

'I have some string in my pocket,' said Diarmuid. 'That will do. I'll give it to Malachy's chief man. He won't lose it.'

'No,' she said stubbornly. 'Malachy,' she called. 'I can't send a private and important message to the bishop without tying and sealing it. We must go back to Cahermacnaghten and then I'll get a seal.'

'I suppose Cahermacnaghten will be on the way,' said Malachy calmly. 'If it's really that important to you to get a seal, then we'll go over there. I can stitch you up there as well as I can in Caherconnell. You can ride on the cart.'

'No,' said Mara, feeling a sudden sick disgust at the idea of riding next to that priest. 'No, I'll walk.'

'You can't walk,' said Malachy. 'You've just been badly injured.'

'It was my arm that was injured, not my leg,' said Mara sharply. She knew he was right, she did feel weak, but nothing would have persuaded her to sit on the cart.

'Diarmuid,' she called. 'Give me your arm, like a good man. Walk with me to Cahermacnaghten.' She set off, staggering slightly, across the clints, determined to prove her vigour by out-walking them all. Malachy tried to call out a protest but that set Wolf off barking again so his words were lost. Diarmuid caught up with her and slipped an arm around her waist, holding her right elbow with a steady, firm grasp. She leaned against him, glad of his strength and warmed by his constant affection. Wolf stopped barking and walked beside Diarmuid with an occasional turn of his large furry head towards Mara. Neither spoke. Mara was turning over in her mind the ordeal that lay ahead of her and Diarmuid was a man of few words. From behind them came the sound of the steady trundling of the cart wheels and from time to time Malachy's deep voice speaking to his men. Mara breathed deeply, sucking in great gulps of the Atlantic mist and trying to give herself energy to go on.

'Leave me here, Diarmuid,' she said when they reached the gate of the Brehon's house at Cahermacnaghten. 'Malachy will look after me now.'

TWENTY-THREE

CASE NOTES AND JUDGEMENT TEXTS FROM MARA,
BREHON OF THE BURREN, 15 MAY 1509

Judgement day: tenth day of May 1509. I judged the case
between Declan O'Lochlainn and Gabur Conglach, priest of
the parish of Kilcorney. Declan O'Lochlainn declared that his
daughter Nessa, aged twelve, had been raped by the aforesaid
priest on the day after the feast of Samhain of the previous
year.

Judgement given was that the priest, the aforesaid Gabur
Conglach, was guilty of the rape of a girl in plaits. The fine
awarded to the aforesaid Declan O'Lochlainn was forty-five
séts, or twenty-two and a half ounces of silver, or twenty-three
milch cows, to be paid within five days.

☙❧

'AND DID THE PRIEST turn up for the hearing?' asked King
Turlough Donn.

Mara leaned back in the luxuriously cushioned chair and took

294

a sip from her wine cup before answering. It was very splendid, this castle of Turlough's – or palace, as they were now calling it, after the English fashion. The stone walls were hung with painted leather and every seat had a velvet cushion. On the floor was a carpet made from velvet and the windows were hung with velvet hangings. The room was crammed with heavy oak furniture, gleaming in the light of the candles and reflecting the deep orange glow of the fire. She would make a few improvements, she thought, if she lived there. The leather was cracked, it could do with regular polishing, and the velvet hangings were dark with peat smoke. Nevertheless, it was a comfortable room, high up in the stone castle. She had felt tired after her ride to Thomond, but now she felt relaxed, lapped in the warmth of fire and affection.

'No,' she said after a minute. 'The bishop sent Fergus, the Brehon of Corcomroe, to represent him in my court. Apparently, the priest' – she still could not bring herself to call him *Father* Conglach – 'is still sunk in some sort of trance. He has not spoken and he has had several fits. The bishop has sent a new priest to Kilcorney. He seems a nice man, very scholarly, and kind to the old people of the parish.'

'Poor man . . . the bishop, I mean,' said Turlough. 'It must be a great worry for him. He's a relation of mine, you know.'

'He should go by the old ways and allow the priests to marry if they wish,' said Mara with a shrug of her shoulders. She had little sympathy with the bishop.

'And so Colman blackmailed Father Conglach? How did he know about the rape?'

'He guessed, I think,' said Mara. 'The priest thought Nessa told him, but she had no idea who had raped her, poor child. Colman was a clever boy. In any case, I think most of the young people knew that the priest had a habit of lurking around and spying on the courting couples. Rory – you remember the young bard, Rory, the handsome young fellow with the red hair? – he knew about the priest; I have no doubt that Colman knew, also. Who knows, but Colman might have been spying himself. That was probably what gave him the notion of buying Emer as his bride.' She finished with a sigh. Every time she thought of Colman she was filled with a great sense of sorrow and guilt – not guilt for his death, she was clear-minded enough to know that the murder was caused by his own greed, but guilt for his lack of morality.

'And what about the little girl, Nessa?' asked Turlough, poking the fire and then refilling both of their glasses.

'Well, she's getting on very well,' said Mara. 'I've taken her under my wing a little. Brigid is teaching her to cook and I'm teaching her to garden. She's a bit silly and giggly with the boys, but she is developing quite a mind of her own and it's good to get her away from that mother of hers. I have a horrible suspicion that her mother suspected the truth all of the time. Anyway, I've tried to put the fear of God into the parents about not rushing her into a marriage for a while. I told them to let things settle, to let people forget, and Malachy backed me up with a whole lot of long medical words. They didn't understand a word of it – neither did I, to be honest – but they said no more about marriage for her.'

Turlough nodded, his face alert and interested. He picked up the leaf of vellum again and then frowned.

'But, Mara,' he said. 'You have nothing here about the murder of Colman. Presumably this priest did it. You told me that he was being blackmailed. He could not let this scandal come out. Mauritius is a bishop who is very keen on the Roman ways; he would not even allow any of his clergy to marry. He would have unfrocked Father Conglach for this rape.'

Mara shook her head. 'The priest was guilty of the crime of violent rape of a young girl,' she said quietly. 'That was his sin, and that was his crime; the other crime cannot be laid at his door.'

She stopped for a moment, thinking of that terrible night when she was trapped in the cairn with the priest and, despite the heat of the fire, she shivered.

'Are you sure?' asked the king. He frowned in puzzlement. 'So who did it? Do you know yet? Why not Father Conglach?'

Mara smiled then. 'I would have liked to pin that crime, too, on the priest,' she admitted, 'but I could not see it happening. The priest didn't do that. He didn't have the strength to wrestle the knife from Colman. He probably didn't have the courage, either. It was a different matter blindfolding and raping a child like Nessa but no, the priest did not murder.'

'Who was it, then?' asked Turlough. 'Was it Lorcan? I always suspected him.'

'I didn't,' said Mara firmly. 'Would Lorcan have committed a secret and unlawful killing just to stop the O'Lochlainn knowing that his bull had been borrowed? I asked myself that question, but it was too trivial a matter. Ardal would have brought the case before me at Poulnabrone, of course, but everyone on the Burren would just have laughed. I can imagine the jokes! The O'Connor clan would probably have got together and paid Lorcan's fine just for the sake of the fun everyone had. No, the man who committed this crime on an open hillside within earshot of the whole kingdom would have had to be desperate; it would have had to be done because of a secret that could not be forgiven or recompensed.'

'And what about that lad from Corcomroe?' asked Turlough eagerly. He leaned forward with the look of a man hot on the chase.

Mara smiled indulgently at him. I'm always happy in his company, she thought. I'm always happy and relaxed with him. Her mind went briefly to the decision that she knew would be required of her that night and then turned back to the murder case again.

'Oscar O'Connor?' she queried.

'Yes, the stone-cutter. Was he the guilty one?'

Mara shook her head. 'No,' she said. 'It was a possibility, and I suppose that it would have been welcomed by the community. The outsider is always a welcome scapegoat. But no, it wasn't Oscar. For one thing, Gráinne MacNamara told me that Oscar had led Feirdin away from the bonfire – the boy panicked and Oscar took him down well before the fire was lit. Apparently, Oscar had been with him for some time before and had helped Feirdin to gather stones. For another thing, Diarmuid told me that he was left-handed. I guessed then that he could not have struck the fatal blow. You remember, don't you, how Malachy drew the knife out with his own right hand? We all saw then how the knife had gone in. It was a right-handed man who struck the fatal blow. I was certain of that,' she said firmly. The scene on the side of the mountain on that sunny Saturday morning would be engraved on her memory for ever, she thought, and judging by Turlough's thoughtful face, it was in his mind's eye, also.

'Strange, wasn't it, that no one saw the body that night out there on the mountainside? Think of all the people there . . .' He reached forward to pour her a generous cupful of the deep red wine. Mara swallowed a little and then put the cup down. Spanish, she thought, why doesn't he buy French, it's so much better. 'Someone must have seen him. They all had torches, didn't they? Why did no one tell you about the dead body on the mountainside?'

'I think,' she said slowly, 'that Colman was blackmailing many people. I think that probably most people on the mountain that night knew of some victim of his. I realized how unpopular he was during judgement day at Poulnabrone that afternoon, but I didn't know why. Yes, of course the body was seen by many as they came down the mountain. But no one wanted to be the one to find it, so everyone looked the other way in the fear that a neighbour, friend or relative may have been involved. That's the way things work in the Burren,' she added firmly.

'*Boirenn*, that means "the stony place" in old Gaelic,' he said with a smile. 'You breed a tough, silent race there among your mountains and your rocks.'

'I think many people recognized Hugh's knife, also,' she said, returning his smile, 'and, as a matter of courtesy to me, they decided to say nothing. As well as being tough and silent, they are a very courteous people, the people of the Burren,' she added lightly.

She said no more for a moment, just sipped her wine and looked into the fire. Then she took from her pouch a last leaf of vellum and handed it to him. 'This is the fourth case,' she said quietly. 'These are the case notes and my judgement of the matter of the secret and unlawful killing of Colman, *aigne*, from Caher-macnaghten, on Mullaghmore Mountain at *Bealtaine* Eve.'

He took it in his hand with interest. He did not read it aloud, though, as he had done before. He read it to himself, his lips moving as he read, and when he had finished, he read it through again. He looked up and the shock on his face was almost comical.

'Him! Well, he was the last person that I would have suspected. What on earth made you think of him?'

Mara considered this. 'Well, I suppose the roots of the matter were seeded in the past,' she said eventually. 'There was a death which was a secret and, I suppose, unlawful killing. But that secret and unlawful killing was done with the purest of motives and I felt no necessity to intervene.'

Turlough said nothing; he poured himself another cup of wine, but she placed her hand over her cup. She needed to keep her mind clear; she needed to explain everything to him.

'You see, this happened over a year ago,' she said carefully. 'I guessed – well, it was fairly obvious, really. But I kept quiet over it; no one was injured by this secret and unlawful killing; no one except the man himself. The man eventually struggled out of the black pit of despair and began to rebuild his life. For his sake, and for his daughter's sake, it seemed best to say nothing.'

The king remained silent. Mara tried to read his face; it was inscrutable. It was impossible to know whether he was shocked, or horrified, or disgusted, whether he felt that his Brehon had betrayed her office and his trust in her. She said nothing for a while, either. In her mind she carefully reviewed her decision taken over a year ago, and then gave a slight nod. Yes, it had been the right decision.

'I felt,' she said, choosing her words carefully, 'that no harm, but a great mercy, had been done. I felt that this man would not offend again.'

'But you were wrong, weren't you?' said Turlough, his voice flat and hard. 'The man did offend again; he killed your young assistant, Colman.'

Mara bent her head and looked into the fire. For a moment the flames blurred in front of her. She had not expected this; she had relied on his support and his understanding. Carefully she blinked the tears from her eyes and waited until they dried before looking at him. His face wore a stubborn, hurt look.

'You think I should have consulted you,' she said in a low voice.

'Yes,' he said bluntly, 'I think I should have been consulted if there was to be any bending of the law. And, I still don't understand everything.' He picked up the leaf of vellum again, studied it and put it down. 'This does not tell the whole story,' he said.

Mara gazed down at the sheet of vellum.

CASE NOTES AND JUDGEMENT TEXTS FROM MARA, BREHON OF THE BURREN, 25 MAY 1509

Judgement day: tenth day of May 1509. I judged the case between Seán Lynch, merchant, of Galway city and Malachy O'Davoren, physician, of Kilcorney in the kingdom of the Burren. Malachy O'Davoren confessed to the secret and unlawful killing of Colman Lynch, aigne, late of Cahermacnaghten in the kingdom of the Burren, son of the aforesaid Seán Lynch. The fine for this secret and unlawful killing, the éraic, together with the victim's honour price, is ninety séts. Because the victim bears some guilt as he had blackmailed the aforesaid Malachy O'Davoren, the fine is reduced to forty-five séts, or twenty-two and a half ounces of silver, or twenty-three milch cows, to be paid within five days.

'He means a lot to you, this physician, this Malachy,' said Turlough quietly.

'No,' she said, startled, 'no, it's not that. I cared for his wife and I care for his daughter very much – I care for him, but only in the way that I care for everyone on the Burren. He's a distant relation of mine, of course, we both share the name of O'Davoren, but this had no bearing on my judgement.'

'I think,' said Turlough, 'that you had better tell me the whole story.'

'You remember Mór O'Davoren, Malachy's wife?' asked Mara.

'Yes,' said Turlough readily. 'I remember her. She was a beautiful woman. She was sister to the O'Lochlainn, wasn't she? The sister of Ardal and Donogh O'Lochlainn?'

'That's right,' said Mara. 'And in a way, that was part of the problem.'

The king frowned and made a quick gesture with his hand. She continued, still speaking slowly and carefully.

'Mór O'Davoren had a malady in her breast,' said Mara, looking at him very directly. 'She had found a lump a long time previously. She told me about it, but she would not tell Malachy. Her own mother had died from a lump in the breast and Mór was convinced that she would die as her mother died. She didn't want to tell Malachy, she feared he might want to try to cut it out, and then if she died from that operation he would feel that he had taken her life. I tried to persuade her to tell, but she would not. He discovered it himself eventually, but by that time the lump was large and there were more lumps under her arm. She was in terrible pain.' Mara stopped for a moment, remembering the anguish of husband and wife and the uncomprehending terror of the child, Nuala.

'Well, she got worse and worse. There was no respite from the pain. Even the poppy juice that Malachy brewed for her had little effect other than to make her mind cloudy and confused. She could not sleep; she could not eat. She was dying slowly and painfully. I came to see her every day. One day when I came she was shrieking with pain, screaming with it. I could hear her as I crossed the fields. Nuala was in the garden crying. She had her hands over her ears, I remember. I pulled her hands down and asked where her father was. "In his still room," she sobbed. I went into the house and just as I began to open the door to the still room, Malachy came flying out. He almost knocked me down . . .'

'And . . .?'

Mara paused. Had she the right to tell the rest of the story? Could she trust this man with the secret that had lain hidden in her mind for over a year? She looked at him. His florid face was still heavy and dark with suspicion. Then suddenly she understood. He was jealous of Malachy. She had not taken his earlier question seriously. She put her hand on his.

'Turlough,' she said earnestly. 'I would rather resign my position as Brehon of the Burren, and you, of all people, know how much that means to me . . .' She stopped for a moment and then continued firmly, 'I would rather resign than bring shame and sorrow to that child, Nuala.'

'And her father?'

'He matters to me, too,' said Mara boldly, 'but not in the way that you matter to me.'

'Go on,' he said.

'No,' she said. 'I won't go on until I get your assurance that what has been a secret to me will remain a secret to you.'

He smiled then. 'I think you have gone too far now,' he said. 'I think I can guess the rest of the story.'

'You may guess,' she said, 'but it will remain just a guess. I'll say no more until you give me your word.'

He looked at her. There was a struggle on his face. His own good nature, his affection and trust in her, struggled with feelings of jealousy, consciousness of the dignity of his kingship. She waited and she watched until she saw that the struggle had been overcome.

'Go on,' he said again, leaning back in his chair. 'Tell the rest of your story. Your decision, as Brehon of the Burren, stands.'

She nodded gratefully. Her mind went back to the scene that

day at Caherconnell. She shut her eyes for a moment, hoping to make him see what she could never forget.

'Malachy had a flask in his hand. He rushed past me. I stood for a few minutes there, looking into the still room. I don't know why I was looking. I think I was just trying to gather up my strength to go and say the right thing to Nuala. I could see the table where Malachy mixes his potions. He had left everything scattered there. The mortar had some black seeds left in the bottom of it and there were even some left on the end of the pestle. There was a small pot there and it was labelled "Digitalis". I knew the seeds, though, so I hardly needed to read the label. I had helped Nuala to gather them the summer before from the foxgloves in the valley. She had told me all about them.' Mara stopped as she remembered the eleven-year-old reciting: "The seeds of the foxglove are excellent for the failing heart when given in tiny quantities. It is a medicine to be used with care as it can kill."'

'And what did you do?' asked Turlough.

'I shut and locked the door of the still room. I put the key in my pouch and I went to Nuala and took her for a long walk down the road towards Clerics' Pass, and when we got back her mother was dead.'

'And you didn't feel that it was a matter Malachy should have acknowledged at Poulnabrone?'

'I didn't,' she said decisively. 'It could be that the matter would be considered *fingal*. After all, he had killed his kin, his closest relation, his wife. I might have considered it, with his permission, if it were not Ardal O'Lochlainn's sister who was the victim. Ardal has very firm ideas, very lofty ideas, about right and wrong. It would mean little to him that his sister was released from agonized pain. He is a man who lives by the letter of the law, not by its spirit.'

'So, how did Colman know?' asked the king. 'You say the secret stayed with you. Did you write it down?'

'No,' said Mara. Her mind was still with Nuala and Malachy on that day and his question had jolted her. 'No,' she repeated. 'I never write anything private or secret down. I keep it in my head. Colman...' She stopped for a moment and reached into her satchel. 'You see, Colman made this list of cases in the judgement texts at Cahermacnaghten ... cases that he could possibly use to blackmail people. He even had the impudence to have my divorce case on his list. He lacked the courage to try anything with me, though.' She looked at him then and saw a smile pucker the corners of his mouth. He knew about her spectacular divorce; that was obvious. She grinned back at him, but then grew serious again as she thought of the human tragedies in some of those cases. She put the list back into her satchel. She would burn that leaf of vellum tomorrow, she thought.

'There was one number on that list that puzzled me for a moment, because it wasn't a judgement text; it was just a year-book, just the book that is always kept of births, marriages and deaths in the kingdom of the Burren. I looked through it for a while before I guessed. There was nothing there to form a reason for blackmail except that one death. I wondered then whether, because Malachy had been drinking so heavily, he had let something slip, or whether Colman had just guessed.'

'So that led you to challenge Malachy?' asked Turlough.

Mara said nothing. Her interview with Malachy, after the priest had been taken away, had been painful. The physician had looked so well after all those weeks of suffering the fear of betrayal and the days of guilt for Colman's death. He had taken it for granted that the priest would be blamed for the murder, also. As a physician, he had been experienced enough to know that the man had fallen into the dark pit of madness and that his word would never be believed even if he ever managed to climb out of insanity. Malachy had stitched up her wound with a smile on his lips and a ring to his voice. He had even joked about her beauty being spoiled. She had taken a small cup of brandy and had pressed some on him as well and it was only when he was ready to go that she had told him that she knew the truth about the murder of Colman on the night of *Bealtaine* Eve.

He had not begged for mercy. He had listened quietly and bowed his head, but his lips had gone white and his black eyes had appeared sunken into pits on his blanched face.

'What must I do now?' he had asked.

'You must tell the truth to the people of the Burren,' she had said steadily. 'This *duinetháide*, this secret and unlawful killing of Colman, must remain a secret no longer.'

'If it were not for Nuala, I would have told the bastard to go to hell,' Malachy had said bitterly. 'I could not bear the idea of leaving her with neither father nor mother. I am not much of a parent to her, but at least I am here with her, not lying in the graveyard at Kilcorney like her mother. I swear to you that this mattered more to me than my own life. If I were on my own, the O'Lochlainn could have had his revenge for the killing of his sister. They could have put me in a boat with no oars and pushed me out to sea and I would have lain there and given up my life.'

And it was at that moment that Mara had placed her hand in his and had said softly: 'The killing of Mór was no crime in my eyes, Malachy, and there is no reason why anyone other than you, me, and King Turlough, if you agree to that, should know about it. You will confess to the murder before the people of the kingdom and I will say that blackmail by Colman was the reason for the murder. You will pay the fine to the Lynch family and that will be the end of the matter.'

He had stared at her then and the look of despair struggling

306

with an emerging gleam of hope had reminded Mara of a sheep she had seen being rescued from a crevasse.

'What made you finally kill Colman?' she had asked with sudden curiosity. 'Presumably he had been blackmailing you for quite some time; I noticed how ill and worried you looked, but you must be a rich man; you could have paid what he asked.'

'I think it was when I saw him with Hugh's knife. I realized then that he was blackmailing a child, also.' He had stopped for a moment, recalling the feelings that had made him go so far from his training and to take a life, rather than restore a life. 'I had seen him talk with Muiris and with Lorcan and with Father Conglach – it gave him pleasure to extract silver from his victims under the eye of the whole kingdom – I guessed then that he did it for the sense of power, rather than just for the wealth it would bring him. For a moment, I thought that he might go to Nuala and tell her that I had killed her mother, that he would do it no matter how much I gave him to keep him silent. I thought I had to get rid of him so I wrestled the knife from him and stabbed him in the neck. He died instantly.'

❊

Mara was silent, reliving that moment, remembering Malachy's face and how the little mounds of peat in the fireplace of her house had suddenly collapsed into a heap of soft brown embers. The king's question jolted her from the past to the present.

'So, when did you realize first that it was Malachy?' he asked.

'I think he was always in my mind; he was always a possibility once I knew that Colman was a blackmailer, and many people had reported seeing him near Wolf's Lair around the time that the bonfire had been lit. And one small thing, but I found it significant: when he was taking the knife from the body – you remember? – well, he pretended to think that the knife belonged to

Colman. That puzzled me because I felt he must know that it was Hugh's. He himself remarked on the knife when he saw it in Hugh's hand when he went into the hazel thicket. There was no mistaking this knife. No one else on the Burren had a knife like that. Malachy himself, of course, had a knife, but unlike most of the Burren, his knife was just a small, sharp surgeon's knife. No, I guessed it was Malachy, but I had to eliminate the other possibilities from my mind.

'Of course, I should have known as soon as I had seen the wound that day on the hillside. You see, the back of the neck is one of what Brehon law calls "the twelve doors of the soul" – places in the body where death is instant after even a trivial injury. Only a physician, or a lawyer, would have known that inserting a knife there in the back of the neck would result in no spurt of blood to incriminate him, yet instant death. I should have thought of Malachy then, but I was shaken and confused, and, I suppose, filled with guilt about Colman, that I had not saved him by realizing earlier that he was blackmailing the people of the Burren.'

She reached forward and held out her silver cup. She would not discuss the other possibilities with him, she decided. Muiris's past was his own affair. She had considered him – the matter of his past was serious and might have interfered with his plans for Felim's wedding to the daughter of a *taoiseach* – but would he have used Hugh's fancy knife or would he have been more likely to use his own? She had thought of that when Ardal O'Lochlainn had produced his knife and it had struck her then that most of the people on the Burren had a far more effective knife than Hugh's close to hand, permanently living on their belt or in their pouch. The exception was Malachy. His knife would be with his other surgical tools. She remembered seeing it when Nuala had opened the medical satchel that day on the side of Mullaghmore Mountain.

'And no one at Poulnabrone questioned your decision or enquired about the blackmail?'

'No,' said Mara, surprised. 'No one ever does question my decision! Several people made a point of going up to speak to Malachy afterwards. The people of the Burren trust me.'

'You are very loved there,' said the king thoughtfully.

Mara bowed her head and looked steadily into the fire. She recognized the change in his voice and knew there was to be no more talk about the murder: now he would talk of himself and now she would have to make her decision.

'I can understand that,' went on the king. 'I love you very much also. Have you been thinking about what I offered? Would you make me a very happy man and come here to Thomond to be my wife?'

There was a lot of noise outside, thought Mara, tilting her silver cup to one side to admire the firelight sparkling in the depths of the wine. It must be getting late, why this sudden stir? She took another sip of the wine, delaying the moment for her answer. Then she put the cup down firmly on the table and turned to look at him. He was not looking at her, though. A minute before, his light green eyes had been fixed on her with the expression of a fond lover, now they were turned towards the door. The noise was getting greater. There was a neighing of horses, a clash of iron, raised voices, and then a thudding of nailed boots on the stone steps. The king was on his feet before the knock on the door came and he had flung it open.

'My lord,' said Fergal the bodyguard. 'Bad news! The O'Kellys are attacking our bridge over the Shannon.'

There was a moment's silence from the king, but no doubt in Mara's mind. This bridge was a matter of great pride to Turlough. There had been a ford there for centuries, but two years ago he and his brothers had built a magnificent wooden bridge spanning the whole wide width of the Shannon. She knew what would happen next. A decision would not be demanded of her, that night at least.

'By God, they'll pay for that,' swore the king. 'Bring me my mail-coat. Send orders for the fighting men to arm and mount. This bridge must be saved.'

Fergal was gone in a moment, his iron-tipped boots clattering down the staircase, and Turlough turned to Mara. 'I must go,' he said, pleading for her understanding. 'This bridge spans both halves of my kingdom. It was built by the O'Briens and it must be held by the O'Briens.'

Mara rose to her feet with a smile. 'Of course you must go,' she said with sincerity. She kissed him quickly on the cheek. 'Go safe and return soon,' she said in his own words.

He beamed and his arms went around her with a crushing hug, but she knew that most of his thoughts had now left her and he was already planning his action against the O'Kellys.

'You will still be here when I return?' he asked.

'Perhaps,' she said, but already he was gone, pounding down the stairs and bellowing orders.

Mara went to the window and opened the shutters. She stood with her hand on the stone mullion that divided the window into halves and looked out. The courtyard was full of men and horses and flaming torches and excited voices. She smiled. He would enjoy this, King Turlough Donn, descendant of the great Brian Boru. The clash of the clans; this was what men enjoyed. There was no necessity for it, she thought impatiently. This attack was obviously a revenge for the attack that Turlough and his clan had made on the O'Kellys last year. Already the horses were leaving the courtyard with the king at the front; his banner of three lions on a saffron background was hastily unfurled, and the trumpet sounded a battle note. She watched until they had disappeared and the last torch had paled against the light of the full moon.

I will go home now, she thought. He may not be back for a

couple of days. The moon is bright and I will cross the Shannon by the ford further north to avoid all trouble. She packed her case notes back into her satchel and then took out a clean leaf of vellum, her pen and her inkhorn.

'I have some matters to attend in your kingdom of the Burren,' she wrote. 'We will meet again soon. In the meantime, remember Mara, Brehon of the Burren, with love.'

She put the leaf of vellum on the table and slipped on her warm cloak. What's the point of all these battles? she thought as she went down the steps to collect Cumhal from the guardroom. All they needed to do, the O'Kellys and the O'Briens, was to let their Brehons get together and negotiate a peace. She knew Giolla-Patrick Maguire, Brehon to the O'Kellys. He was a quiet, sensible man. She and he could have got together and negotiated recompense and an agreement. With Brehon law everything could be solved by negotiation and reparation. Why have war when peace is so easily obtained? she asked herself with mock sorrow, but there was a lightness in her step as she wound her way down the steep spiral of the stone staircase. Now she had no difficult choices to make, no offer to accept or to decline. Safely mounted on her horse with Cumhal beside her, she heaved a sigh of relief. She would be home before daybreak.